CLAUDETTE

WALKER

K.I.S.S.
OF KIDON

A Novel

"Sometimes, revenge is not all in the mind…"

~ Solomon

Abacus Books, Inc.
P.O. Box 55302
St. Petersburg, Florida 33732-5302, U.S.A.
www.abacusbooks.com

Library of Congress Cataloging in Publication Data
Walker, Claudette
K.I.S.S. OF KIDON
I. Title

ISBN# 0-9716292-3-4
EAN# 978-0-9716292-3-3

Printed in the United States of America
Set in Garamond

This is a work of fiction. Names, characters, places, and incidents either are the product of the author's invention and imagination or are used fictitiously, and any resemblance to actual persons either living or dead, events, or locales is entirely coincidental.

For David…

Chapter One
K.I.S.S.

Ultimately and without exception, in the darkest recesses of power long established, they tell no tales – take no prisoners. Nonetheless, the unimaginable exception had occurred. A fox eluded the hounds.

Slender, luscious Jacqueline Rose felt her long auburn hair glide gently across her back as she stretched, waking from a field of dreams. The tingling sensation of its soft touch as she woke was a reminder that she grew it for herself – no one else. From a world filled with tribulation had arisen a woman - a force to be reckoned with. She was a brilliant mind and a naturally powerful seductress.

Slowly turning to meet the day, she reached for the warm .22 with its titanium silencer. It was always beneath her pillow. Resting with the gun under her head felt as natural as the sun's rays. Touching it was the first thing she did upon awakening and the last thing she did when closing her eyes. It was gone!

"I moved it."

She listened to the voice of the dead Solomon Rosenberg, lying inches away. He was there beside her, his dark lean body pressed close to hers, as though he had never left. Jacqueline took one more look into the deep brown pools of his Russian eyes then turned away to hide her smile. She rolled back again to kiss the man who had died and risen.

Suddenly, she felt the warmth of his lips on her breasts, like the summer sun beating down on her while she rested upon glistening white sand. He was the man with the mind that injected more passion, knowledge, protection, and danger in Jacqueline's life than any other human being. He once again ignited her body with his radiating heat.

Jacqueline's glowing smile disappeared as quickly as it arrived. Her green eyes flared wide and sparked as her voice cracked.

"You son of a bitch, you're supposed to be dead!"

1

It had been nearly three years – three years! All that time, she had been the widow of Solomon Rosenberg, the Ivy League scholar, MENSA genius, and government lawyer retired from the CIA. She had suffered the unbearable loss of his love, fought for survival, and discovered too many secrets carefully guarded by the one and only Solomon. But now – now he was alive!

No one comes back from the dead. The simple truth now rested beside her. He had never died. It had all been lies upon lies – what other explanation could there be for such a phenomenon? He had arisen from some underworld, not returned to earth from eternity. It certainly couldn't have been a miraculous resurrection, for Solomon was most ungodly.

She looked deep into his eyes, and with an almost sheepish grin and wink, he spoke again.

"That's not what you said last night."

Jacqueline found herself holding back a smile one more time as she remembered his lips flowing up and down her body throughout the night, sending her off into the sleep from which she now stirred. Their touch was a formidable human connection; it was his yin to her yang. Yet, this time of passion must pass. Reality was before them.

She knew he was alive. With calm resolve, she held back the tingling afterglow racing through her body from their night of unparalleled pleasure.

"Solomon, I've had so many dreams of my dead husband, I no longer trust what's real. Some mornings I wake reaching for you next to me, only to face the reality of cold empty sheets. It's been like that for nearly three years. I need some damn coffee!"

Oh, she knew he was real, very much alive, and back in her bed again. At that moment, Solomon realized that this was not going to be as easy as he planned. He just wanted to hold her, desperately desiring to slip back into the night of passion that ended, that had to end, with the dawn.

"Coffee – I'll get it. Take your time waking up."

He slowly moved from the bed, never turning his back completely on his well-trained wife. It was a struggle for him to find conversation.

"I know a lot has changed. Still take it black?"

Then with a grin he added,

"Too soon to say, 'Honey, I'm home?'"

There he was, his humor intact, looking quite good for a dead man. Her eyes scanned his honed body, the body she had kissed until the slumber from which came this reality. Quickly, she looked away.

Jacqueline's mind began to race. How he could do such a thing, let her believe he was dead? Jacqueline was now steaming, hotter than the coffee he was about to deliver, as she spoke.

"Yes to both, Solomon. But for a change, would you mind stirring this cup with a spoonful of truth?"

It was the monotone of her voice that scared him the most. He knew how the day must unfold, so he resigned himself to the inevitable.

"You'll have it all, but for now I'll give you enough to get some understanding of why this had to be. Then I'll return the gun and you can call me Rose again or do whatever you please. But we don't have a lot of time. We must get out of Rio soon."

She slightly tilted her head and tightened her lips.

"Fair enough."

Jacqueline wrapped the sheet around her naked body, barely covering her voluptuous breasts. It was a reminder to Solomon of the woman who had loved him. She walked across the dingy, musty hotel room and sat at a table in front of the window. They were in a disreputable inn on the outskirts of Rio de Janeiro.

Carefully, Jacqueline peeked through a crack in the curtains and saw rain oozing down the filthy glass windowpanes. The long, extended drops slowly landed and pooled on the chipped paint of the window sill. Only then, when she saw heart-shaped graffiti drawn on a wall from Carnival the night before, did she realize it was Valentine's Day. Everything seemed to be moving in slow motion – his words, time, and their lives.

It had been eventful couple of days. Less than forty-eight hours ago, she had been a widow – her husband dead for years. Mark, her fiancé, had just been shot and died in her arms inside a Beverly Hills hotel. Jacqueline's rescuer whisked her from California to Rio, only for her to discover that her protector was the nefarious one who killed Mark. She shot that sleeper agent from who in the hell knows what country at point blank range, then fled alone into the crowd of Carnival. She had been arrested by Interpol agents, only to learn that they were kidnapping her at the behest of her long-dead husband. And yesterday was the day Solomon, who envisioned himself as her savior from all evil, returned from the dead.

He quickly turned, interrupting Jacqueline's musings.

"Let me move the table. Drapes… closed drapes aren't enough. I've gone too far getting you back to lose you now."

Jacqueline stood, coffee in hand, as he moved the table and chairs to the back wall. Then she took a seat again. Solomon peered out the crack in the dusty tan-colored drapes, pulled them tighter until the dim gray light from outside was extinguished, and turned back to Jacqueline.

She looked directly into his eyes.

"I need to get out of Rio now. I shot Charles Dahl last night."

He showed no shock, no surprise.

"I know. We've already taken care of the clean-up."

Jacqueline wasn't surprised either; no one knew these two like they knew one another.

"Thanks, but I cleaned up after myself."

"I know that now. We just handled anything you might have missed."

"I understand. Still, I'm a little pissed. Are you surprised? Now let's hear it."

Solomon wanted to start the conversation with a little levity and romance for his love. Perhaps he could inspire her to resume their ecstasy of the night and put off this unpleasantness just a bit more. He knew he should not, but he had to try. So he sat down, leaned toward her, and began to quote Poe...

"'It was many and many a year ago in a kingdom by the sea. That a maiden there lived...'"

Jacqueline cut him off.

"Your seductive verse won't work on me anymore! I'm a different woman thanks to you, Mossad, and C Street. Tell me the truth right now! Remember, we don't have much time."

Jacqueline was well aware of his immeasurable charm and she had no intention of letting him use it. Yet, she chuckled inside. He really was back again. Still, she needed to keep his attention and her concentration on factuality, for emotion is the enemy of truth.

Solomon began wringing his hands as he spoke with a slight hesitance in his voice.

"Okay, okay, I owe you that much. Let me tell you this – altering an escape plan that assured the safety of many was not easy. I had to protect them, but I risked it anyway. I only did it because of my love for you. My death would not have been enough. They would have eventually come for my family. Trust me, that's the way it's done – no loose ends."

Jacqueline was silent, but she knew what he said was true. He had gone to great lengths to come back to her. The reason he left was another matter. That required explanation. Her months of training by Mossad and her experience – having used numbered accounts, secret locations while hiding, fleeing, and pursuing others – were serving her well. Now, she was looking at the living ghost of her dead husband. She had figured out a great deal in only hours, she thought.

The penitent is deemed holier than the sinless person who has no evil to repent. Without sin, Solomon could never have existed. Repent? Not today. Yet, Jacqueline knew there was much more to him than the worst thing he ever did. Good and evil were present – they are forever intertwined. It's the balance that matters most; yes it's always about balance.

5

Solomon was born to K.I.S.S., **Ki**don **I**ntegrated **S**pecial **S**ervices. With his extreme intelligence and eidetic memory, he would become highly educated and one of the most fatal among the skilled elite. You pass these select members on the street never knowing, for they walk purposefully among us.

They exist in every social circle. Perhaps one is your neighbor, the store owner, an accountant, your doctor, or a lawyer. So, look twice at the next person who nods their head and smiles a peaceful good morning. Then ask, if you choose, is it her or maybe him? However, realize that you'll know the answer but once, just before the quiet of eternal silence, for this will be your kiss of death.

In a kiss, the silent touch holds eternal. In pursuit of ardor, it knows no boundaries... it has no surety. A kiss from Kidon Integrated Special Services is without temperance. It is assurance... tomorrow will not come.

Mossad, the Israeli Institute for Intelligence and Special Operations, holds within it a select section known as Kidon, a branch of sanctioned intellectual assassins. Only those with the highest of intellect and no moral compass need apply. Within Kidon, a secret white paper unit, known by only a select few, exists. It is the most clandestine of all, K.I.S.S.

The members are deeply embedded around the world, highly trained, unconscionably financed, require no authorization for their activities, and are sanctioned by the highest powers. The United Nations requested and received a judicial opinion from the International Court of Justice mandating in part that the men and women of K.I.S.S., cannot be held accountable for actions they deem necessary.

The opinion of the high court in part determined, "It would be lawful for the sanctioned members of K.I.S.S., whose identities and aliases withstand the four corners verification test to conduct all actions deemed necessary to complete missions, to operate internationally, and to target and use lethal force in any and all operations they deem necessary without further consent of any government in the country in which the act is carried out. It would be consistent with international principles of sovereignty and neutrality." The bottom line was they had carte blanche.

Each member was highly skilled in the art of war. They were known by only a handful and controlled by fewer. Solomon, more than most, knew that was the truth. Because Jacqueline had been trained in some of the K.I.S.S., techniques by Mossad, and with her belief that Solomon was dead, any mission to extract her could be fatal to anyone attempting the extraction. It was not a job for the faint of heart, nor an operation to be taken lightly, not even for Solomon. Her acceptance of him would be tenuous at best, especially in the first few days after she discovered he was alive. That was dangerous.

Who could say when Solomon Rosenberg first fell in love with Jacqueline? Maybe it was the distant glimpse of her outside his Washington office. The when really mattered little, for the moment their eyes locked, fate was sealed.

Even in the covert world of K.I.S.S., operatives, the secret identity and missions of this Washington lawyer were made secure by the trail of bodies he left behind. Solomon was entering the heart of his most important mission – his exit from K.I.S.S.

Having a wife was an unsanctioned act, a sanction he had long ago violated. His unparalleled skills bought an exception from his handler until now. Recently, all hell had broken loose and even the one who wanted to protect him could see the coming end. Another reality was Jacqueline's training. She had the ability to kill Solomon along the way. He needed to quickly convince her that killing him was not in her best interest, then Solomon needed to get both Jacqueline and himself out alive. He would terminate whoever tried to stop the exit. The death toll couldn't include either of them. Solomon turned to Jacqueline in that dingy hotel...

"My death began with an extraction plan established long ago. The first step was destroying and replacing every known photograph of me in all government archives."

"So that's why you never allowed any photos of you – not even a wedding photo!"

"That's right. Especially no wedding photos – those would've been dangerous for both of us. You're going to enter my dark world with the truth you asked for. Are you sure you want it?"

"I entered it long ago, and I'm up to my eyebrows by now. I just didn't realize how black it really was. So, keep going – I need it all."

Solomon continued, his truthfulness evident on his face. The sham of his death had begun this, his final mission. However, it truly began years before with Solomon's control of his image and a computer application designed to track and tag what few photos of him did exist. On his order, his men would go into action, altering any remaining files of government agencies, embassies, and the internet. On the day of his escape, every picture of him, whether on computer or paper, was replaced with the image of another man long dead. The similarity to Solomon was clear, but the image was not him. That was just the beginning of camouflaging Solomon and his exit from this world.

Many things had changed over the years. His exit from K.I.S.S., had to protect more people than originally planned. That scheme was hatched too long ago under a pear tree with his brother in Israel. It was not viable as it was originally envisioned, even though it had been frequently updated. He had recently modified the plan with the latest update and sped up the schedule. His accelerated strategy would use an unconventional operational method. It was one Solomon was surely not familiar with – truth. Jacqueline needed to understand the history… his history.

Chapter Two
Elusive Truth...

Solomon continued to rub his palms together as he started to tell Jacqueline his story – a story that he intended to be only the unvarnished truth. Wringing of the hands for some is a nervous habit; for Solomon it was a reminder. Rinsing the bloodstains off his hands – check... passport – check... gun – check... element of surprise – game changer. All missions have a beginning and an end. This one was no exception. Washing the blood away could never happen, but the hand wringing showed his willingness to try.

Most knew him as Solomon Rosenberg, a scholar and government lawyer who, like all geniuses, was a bit unusual. To Jacqueline he was "Rose," tall, dark and alluring. Yet, he was born Jude Absalom Hague, over the air space between America and Tel Aviv; his mother Sarah was a language professor and his father, Turing Hague, a theoretical physicist from the think tank of the Manhattan project.

Before the close of World War II, his mother and father had been sent to Palestine prior to the end of British Rule to make initial preparations for what would become the new nation of Israel. The United Nations Plan of Partition with Economic Union was not even signed when Turing was sent ahead to assist in establishing an independent Jewish state within Palestine. The United States saw the idea of an ally in the Middle East to be advantageous to American interests. The U.S. wanted to secure that ally, by helping in the preparations. That is why the Hagues and others went from America to the Middle East – for a nascent Israel.

The League of Nations white paper decision of 1922 became effective in 1923. Called The British Mandate for Palestine, it established British rule of the territory and was the legal commission that formalized British administration of the territory of Trans-Jordan until 1948. The huge area included the former Ottoman Sanjaks of Nablus, Acre, the southern portion of Beirut Vilayet, and the Mutasarrifate of Jerusalem, prior to the Armistice of Mudros. It was called Palestine by the League of Nations.

The Palestine territory was in western Asia between the Mediterranean Sea and the Jordon River, situated strategically between Egypt, Syria and Arabia. In 1948, the mandate would terminate and the United Kingdom would withdraw from Palestine. After '48, the land could be redistributed or divided. New states would come into existence after the British withdrawal. That was caused in part by the United Nations' Special International Regime for the City of Jerusalem that divided the city between Arabs and Jews and that established a regulatory body for the city.

It was a plan accepted by the Zionists except for the fringes and rejected by the Arabs. This was only the continuation of a battle, a battle between Arabs and Zionists with roots older than biblical history. Both the Arabs and Jews were firmly established in the land long before the British named it Palestine. Neither the might of Pharaoh Ramses II nor the wisdom of King Solomon could solve this eternal conflict.

In 1945, the parents of Solomon Rosenberg, as we know him, were sent on their mission to help solve the unsolvable. Another British mandate in 1939 declared that it was not the policy of British Government that Palestine should become a Jewish state and sought to eliminate the repatriation of Jews to Palestine. It was this paper that created the permanent intertwinement of the United States and Israel, because the U.S. government recognized it to be in America's best interest to exert some control in the oil rich Middle East by backing the "State of Israel."

Israel was a barren desert land with few settlements at that time. With the new state created, it would become a stronghold for America in the Middle East. Turing was assigned to the only Israeli organization in the region, the Israeli Information Collections Department, which was renamed Mossad in 1949. So began their life in a new land.

Everyone was on high alert in this child state. That vigilance outlasted the new state's infancy – it seemed that Israel would forever need to remain watchful. After a number of years in their new homeland, his mother at age forty-two gave birth to the second of three children, Jude. It was the first year the Hagues had slowed their travel between Washington, Oak Ridge, Tel Aviv, Switzerland, and the Netherlands. This was the year they hoped elusive peace would come to the region.

Jude's scientist father, Turing, was a gentle man who felt he was unsuited for his assignment. Nevertheless, he understood his usefulness in building the new country of Israel. Throughout the years of turmoil, he prepared his children should anything happen to him. He tried not to scare them, but they had to be ready. He was well aware of the dangerous situation for every person in this land they now called home.

Each Sunday, Turing, cane in hand, walked the three siblings slowly two miles down the Western Portal of Jerusalem. They then entered the Jaffa Stone Gate to the city. The wall and the gate appeared massive to the children's eyes. The same large stones that formed the wall also paved the streets they would walk toward King David's Tower. They always stopped for lemonade at old Jacob's stand midway through their stroll.

Turing wanted his children to know this route. They never deviated from that path, so it would be reinforced in each child's mind. When they arrived at the destination, never did they stop. They simply continued past the house. Turing always nodded at the beginning of the property and said to his children,

"Remember this beautiful stone house with the double arched blue doors, matching shutters and two pear trees. Remember the two pear trees. The other homes have none or one in front. That's the way it will always be in Israel. It's the law of Mossad."

The streets of the town were easy to navigate and they always continued at the same stride throughout the walk. They would travel on for a few more blocks and then start their return trip.

"It's our secret," Turing would tell the children.

Smiles would erupt as they stopped for black and white cookies on the way back at Mrs. Klein's bakery, located in the kitchen of her small stone home. The sweet smell of baked goods filled the air, causing the children to speed up their pace as they approached. Turing never minded the children's excitement when the aroma of chocolate overtook their senses. They had already completed their Sunday excursion to the safe house.

It was early on the eighteenth of April. As the coolness of the night was just giving way to the warmth of the morning, explosions woke the siblings. The first one startled them, yet seemed so far away. They gathered each other to head for their parents' bedroom, but before they could exit their door, another explosion demolished part of the home...the part where their parents slept.

The children, only feet away from the collapse, were immediately covered with dirt and rubble. People came from everywhere and began the all too familiar process of digging through the piles of debris. Smoke filled the air, along with a cloud of unsettled ash.

The putrid reek of fiery death was in the wind. It was a smell Solomon had never forgotten. Over the years, he would grow flowers for his little sister Esther in the hope that she would forget – forget the stench of that day.

Michael Kane, an elderly neighbor from an undamaged home, found them safe, dazed, and covered in rubble. Within minutes, the ash wiped from their faces, Rabbi Wiezmann, the tall gentle force that held the community together, approached the children. He passed their father's cane to Turing, Solomon's older brother. The rabbi told the boy that one of the searchers had found it, undamaged, near the front door of what was left of their house. The cane was the responsibility of the eldest son until the parents were found. Confirmation their parents were dead came within minutes. When explosions are part of your everyday life, bad news is delivered immediately.

The rabbi hugged the children tightly. As he did, he gave a look to Michael, the nearby neighbor, and then focused back on the children. The rabbi told them,

"You'll be okay. Stand next to Michael while we look for others. Your father told you what to do. You'll know when the time is right."

Then the rabbi's hand softly caressed Esther's face as he looked into the brothers' eyes and said,

"My children of Israel, Shalom."

The rabbi whispered to Michael,

"Take them to the back. We'll bury them with their parents."

He then quickly headed toward the rubble that had recently been homes. The air was filled with smoke and commotion as the search for survivors continued. The children sat back to back on a large stone behind the neighbor's house. Michael left to deliver water to workers digging through the remains of three homes.

It was at that moment that J. Turing Hague, the eldest sibling, stood. He planted the cane firmly in the ground, grasped his sister's hand and looked into Jude's eyes as he nodded. Each of the boys took one of their sister's hands, and Turing used the cane to steady their footing through the wreckage. The three slipped away through the haze of the smoke-filled air, just like their father had told them. All of them knew what needed to happen next. They were no longer children. Their childhood ended with the bomb blast.

Thus began their tumultuous journey into the life prepared for them in case of tragedy. The worst had come that spring morning, when Jude was six years old. His older brother Turing, who Jude called Watchman, was a husky seven, and his sister Esther was only five. By early afternoon, they had made their way to the house with the two pear trees. The door they had never entered was now before them, only feet away.

The dark, curly haired Watchman was brave that day. He held their small hands and the cane so tightly that it made an impression on Watchman's hand, a mark Jude could still see in his mind years later. When they cried, Watchman told them,

"Be strong! Like father said, I'll take care of you both, always."

Solomon said his big brother never even shed a tear for their parents that day. Watchman's only mission was to protect them. Even then Jude understood, although he tugged fiercely on his big brother to avoid approaching the house. Watchman prevailed, and they walked past the two pear trees and up to the mysterious blue arched doors.

Jacqueline sat absolutely still in her chair, trying not to show her surprise. She was far wiser than she portrayed and much stronger from years of life and loving Solomon. She had developed quite a talent for predicting the unexpected. But even she couldn't have seen this twist coming that morning in the dingy Rio hotel room.

"So you're from Israel. Do tell. How are things in Tel Aviv?"

Solomon was very precise.

"No, I was born in the airspace between America and Tel Aviv."

Sarcastically analytic, he continued,

"Technically, I'm a citizen of both nations. I'm not quite sure where my allegiance lies – maybe with both, maybe with neither. It depends on what day it is."

In a cynical voice she asked,

"Should I call you Jude?"

Firmly but with a smirk, he replied,

"I would prefer Rose over Solomon, but never, ever call me Jude."

"Go ahead, Solomon."

Jacqueline wanted to let him know she needed more information and had no intentions of making this easy. She had been through hell because of him and could tell the trouble was not over.

In this world where truth was hard to come by, she planned to get it from the only one who knew – Solomon, Jude, or whoever her husband really was. Still, deep inside her, he was still the Rose.

Chapter Three
Entering Mossad...

Watchman's knock was strong that day so long ago in Israel, as he stood with his siblings. Not a flinch or quiver. The door opened immediately and they were swept in.

Once they were inside, Mattie and Jacob told the children they were safe and that the couple had been given the honor of protecting and caring for Turing Hague's children. Solomon vividly remembered thinking,

"What about my mother, Sarah? Are we not her children too?"

This was his first memory of the world that existed behind the blue gateway.

The guardians handed the siblings two braided blue and white ropes fifteen inches long, looped to slip over their wrists with ease on one end of the plait.

"Your father left these for you to hold on to each other, so your hands do not get sweaty and you are never far apart. Jude, you and Esther should each slip a loop over your wrist, and Watchman can hold onto the unlooped ends"

The home looked unused; it was Jude who noticed the stillness. There was nothing out of place. It was clear to him the caretakers arrived only for the purpose of meeting them. Word of explosions always traveled quickly from neighbor to neighbor as fast as people could run. Jude remembered his father and mother spreading the news to others many times. It was just as clear to Jude that they would not stay at that location long.

He was right. The children were whisked away in minutes, through homes, tunnels and in cars, by the guardians from behind the azure doors. Although the trip was tumultuous, the couple provided comfort and security throughout the travels.

Even then, Watchman said,

"I think Jude can see what is coming next."

Watchman remembered what his father told him,

"Your brother has a special gift. He can see far ahead and remembers everything. I have some ability, but not like your brother. You must protect him and he will always be there to protect you and Esther."

Before their parents died, Jude would allow his big brother to best him now and then in language, chess, or math. It was just so Watchman could feel like he was the older, wiser one. However, Watchman would become quite angry with Jude on the occasions when he realized what was happening.

"Don't ever do that for me! It's okay if you pull it with others – maybe best. I'm plenty smart enough, but there's no one like you! Father told me. No one can know all you remember. It'll be up to me to protect you. It's my pleasure my burden in life. Everyone has a purpose and that's mine."

It took hours for them to arrive at the location that would become their temporary housing. They were in the town of Herzliya – a tiny community of less than one hundred, governed by Ben Zion. He officially worked for Ben-Gurion, one of the creators of Mossad.

They were so young, their parents gone. Thankfully, they were all kept together and arrived safely with the guardians. Their names were immediately changed; Jude was bestowed with the name Simon Solomon on that day, never to hear his birth name spoken aloud again. This would be one of many names and faces Jude would assume throughout his life. We know him by the name he created for America, Solomon Rosenberg. Watchman liked to call him Kilo, the man of a thousand faces. Esther's name was changed to Sari and that broke Simon Solomon's heart. The death of his parents made everything more painful for Jude. He felt his job was to protect Esther and minimize her heartache, yet he couldn't even stop them from giving her another name. He felt so impotent. He needed more power to control what was happening – it just wasn't fair!

They were given time to adjust to their loss and new circumstances. Everyone treated them with great understanding and care. Rabbi Wiezmann came often during those lonely, sad days. It was the rabbi who told them where they would go and promised they would be kept together. Within a week, they left all that was familiar behind, never to see their friends or caretakers again.

It was the dead of night when a car dropped the siblings off only feet from a block fortress surrounded by barbed wire, hidden deep in the Negev desert. Rabbi Wiezmann was waiting as they stepped out onto the cold sand blown night.

"I came to guide you through the gate."

They all walked together into the fortress. It was clear that their arrival was expected. The woman who greeted them knew the children's new names. Solomon noticed the rabbi had a comforting look on his face that offered them solace as he guided them.

"This is Zevla. She'll get you all settled together in the same room, until any of you would like your own privacy. You'll always be safe, well-fed, educated, and most importantly, kept together behind these walls. These wires are not a prison. They're here to protect you, Turing's children. Remember, be kind to those inside and they'll show you kindness and knowledge. Shalom."

That was the last time they saw the rabbi, the day he delivered them to this special training school. Their instruction would make them the best of Israel, as the world would one day learn. The block and wire fortress, a heavily guarded academy, was kind to them. They were housed in a large building divided into rooms. One was furnished with three beds for their initial adjustment. There were others with nice beds, clothing, books and more for each of the siblings whenever they decided it was time to have their own space.

Zevla, a tall lady in her forties, similar in look to their mother, was there to care for their needs. She was really a kind woman with a keen sense of humor.

"Enjoy these two weeks playing in the compound before school starts. You're free to go anywhere inside the fenced area. Inspect it all; there's a lot to see. Breakfast is at five, lunch is at noon and get

17

home by dark for dinner or no black and white cookies for you! That would mean more cookies for me – I get to eat the ones you don't. Even though I love cookies, I'm willing to sacrifice my extra portion because I really want you inside by dark."

The two weeks they spent investigating the compound told Solomon of their life to come. The soldiers were witty and fun, but taught the siblings something every time the children stopped in their vicinity. Matthew liked to play hopscotch with Sari and Jonathan was always letting Solomon play with the nunchucks. Watchman, on the other hand, interacted less but observed everything going on. That's when Solomon gave him the nickname Watchman. So began their new lives.

Children are malleable and the siblings adjusted to their new reality quickly. Their lessons started out like most schooling. There was reading, math, languages, Torah and then something special was thrown in – like political science, chemistry, engineering, mathematics, or Krav Maga (martial arts) classes by the time Solomon was eight. At fourteen, he began flight school with his brother, while they both studied American and international law.

Solomon suddenly stopped talking and looked out the dusty drapes again, then looked back at Jacqueline, still wrapped in the sheet and seated at the table.

"I assure you, my parents were good people who loved the three of us immensely."

Jacqueline's face softened for a moment. She was sorry for the lonely man before her as she said,

"I'm sure they did. Why are you speaking of yourself in the third person? Is it that painful?"

"To be honest, it's easier for me to tell you the truth if I do."

Solomon told her he knew how much his parents loved them because his ability to remember everything meant he remembered the conversations between his parents when they were making the decision on how to best protect their children, should they die.

Jacqueline asked,

"What do you mean everything?"

"I mean just that. For instance, on December 12, 1993, I had Steak Diane at the Fillmore Restaurant at 27 Forty-First Street in Manhattan. I wore a brown windowpane suit, it was raining, and I dined with Mark Steinberg. The waiter's name was Sam and my steak was over-cooked. Everything...my brain secretes an excess of the protein SAP102. It gives me an eidetic memory."

Jacqueline was overcome with sadness at the moment she heard Mark's name.

"You know Mark Steinberg is dead... an innocent man is dead in this mess. Shot out of my arms at a Beverly Hills Hotel!"

"Yes, I do. I'm sorry. I liked him a lot. He was a long-time friend. I know all about you and Mark; he had no idea I was alive when he fell in love with you. It's a hazard of war, but never, ever believe he was an innocent man. Do you think I would have left those tapes of my missions, the hologram, or all that evidence with just any lawyer? Mark was Mossad, a sleeping foot soldier to be called on when needed."

Jacqueline gasped.

"Mossad buried him deeply, then. I never saw that coming! I had him checked out. He was absolutely clean! Did you kill him?"

"No. Dahl's men took that shot. They were moving fast for you and got sloppy. There's no way to track or trace someone who has been embedded as a sleeper since childhood. They shot him never knowing he was Mossad. You, on the other hand, shot the right man in the house yesterday. Dahl was an old Iranian sleeper we played for years, feeding him bad intel on cyber from the early days at Q-Tel. Q-Tel is better known as the high tech investment arm of the CIA."

"Iranian – that was his middle-eastern look!"

"Yes, and he's just one of many. I'm not just a random killer for Mossad or anyone else. I'm not for hire, either. I can see your wheels turning. Get that out of your head."

"Who in the hell do you work for?"

"NATO Section 8, Cyberwarfare. I answer to eighteen judges. I've never met most of them, and they've never questioned my work. For now, you need to understand this – I don't kill just for Israel or any other country, or for money. It's much more complicated than that. I promise you will know it all, soon."

Jacqueline looked into Solomon's eyes and the deep connection was clear to both.

"Okay."

Solomon pulled aside the drape slightly and looked out the window, then turned back as he continued to tell her about his childhood and life in Mossad. There was no hesitation in his voice; his speech pattern was precise and clear. Jacqueline knew she was hearing the truth.

Over time, the training of the three siblings at the center became more advanced and so they became the children of Mossad. They were the top three of the small class of five for the first year. Two others, also orphaned by the horrors of war, were at the compound when they arrived.

One of them, Stuart, a year older than Solomon, died of pneumonia in the year after the Hagues had arrived. Stuart's little sister Laura had become close to the siblings, especially Sari, but she was sent away to another facility shortly after her brother's death. That left the siblings alone in classes for their remaining days. They spent twelve years behind the block walls and razor wire fences.

It was late at night, the night they sent Laura away. Still the Hagues realized what was happening. The two brothers settled back into their beds after getting Sari to sleep in tears, tears at the loss of her friend Laura. That's when Solomon told Watchman,

"You know, when the time comes, they'll try to separate us - to hold one captive for power over the others. It'll be with no warning, just like how they sent Laura away."

Watchman turned to his brother.

"I know you're upset. But they won't succeed in separating us. Just keep that memory of yours to yourself until I need leverage to negotiate with them. I've got this one, Solomon. I can see you're angry about Laura leaving without getting to say goodbye and Sari crying all night, but Laura is smart. That's why she was here. They'll protect her somewhere else. She'll be fine; she has value, just like us. Now get some rest. We have a busy schedule tomorrow."

Children grow up quickly and learn fast in a world where the need for survival is the top priority. So as time passed, Solomon appeared only slightly more capable than his siblings in the eyes of others. That was what his brother decided. He was afraid if the real gap showed, the siblings would be separated. Solomon only had to dumb down answers to a few questions here and there. His siblings knocked the top off the learning curve. They all surely had the genetics of Turing and Sarah, but Solomon was different.

In their last few years at the training center, Watchman told Solomon it was time for him to show the instructors what he was really capable of doing, and so he did. Watchman's timing of this provided them even more power with Mossad. This was the day Watchman would truly begin to master his facilitation skills and his manipulation of others.

They were sixteen, seventeen, and eighteen when Watchman was told by his instructors at the center that he alone would go to America when he turned twenty. There, he would begin infiltrating for the facilitation of Solomon. The children had never been apart. Watchman was determined to see that he would be in control of their whereabouts.

The young Watchman had grown to be a force to be reckoned with. When talk of sending the brothers separately to America or without Sari came about, it was Watchman who made the agreement with Mossad. They all must be sent from Israel together, with no exception. Watchman told them it was his father's law. Even in Mossad, they understood the danger of asking a son to defy his Zionist father. Mossad needed the youths' loyalty and separating them could clearly strike too hard.

That became especially evident when Watchman reminded them of his brother's incredible language and learning skills and finally iced the cake with,

"Simon Solomon does not just have a good memory, but an eidetic one. And he's furious at us being split apart. I told him it was just a suggestion from command, not an order. He said, 'They gave us their word when we arrived! I can still see each and every time that promise was made to us.' You know, we really need to keep this promise to him, as a sign of good faith. Also consider his emotional need of family, since we will need his skills for a very long time."

A man with a clear British accent on the speakerphone in that Mossad meeting made the decision,

"Give Simon what he wants. They all leave together, but delivering the girl safely to the Swiss institute is a must."

This was a voice Watchman would never forget. Watchman told Solomon that the faces of the commanders were priceless, excited and shocked when they realized that they had missed Solomon's total recall. Of course, that explained everything to Mossad: his ability to learn, his grasp of languages and engineering, his warfare skills, and his ability to rapidly and accurately assess situations.

At the point Mossad became aware of Solomon's true ability, those in charge surely did not want to rock the boat with him. Even before, they thought they had gold with Solomon's brain and skills. Now it was clear. This asset was pure platinum, as valuable as water to a thirsty man in the desert.

Watchman had won his first battle with Mossad. It would be up to all the siblings to make sure they did not lose the war, when the time came. In later years, Watchman would record British voices in meetings, searching for the man on the speakerphone – the British liaison to Mossad's K.I.S.S.

Sari would leave Israel with her brothers. They would all be together. This was a big victory for Watchman. Still, she would be separated from her brothers after leaving to begin her life's work on an international science project, then in the development stage, in

Geneva, Switzerland. This was what she wanted, so the demand for it at the meeting was not unexpected to Watchman.

She had her father's brain for theoretical physics. Since she could not be safer than in the Swiss science facility, the brothers were content with the Israeli government's mandate and Sari's decision to go. Mossad would have loved to keep one sibling for leverage over the others. But Watchman got his way; all would leave Israel at the same time, but with a few strings attached.

They looked forward to their new life and worked hard to assure that they all left together. Early on, they discovered their intelligence and facility with languages gave them some control, even with Mossad. Maybe this is when Solomon first understood his power. Later, Watchman told him,

"I believe the biggest bargaining chips I had with Mossad to get all of us out of Israel were your grasp of so many languages and your eidetic memory. I actually threatened them with your wrath if we were separated!"

Mossad's acquiescence came with a price. The brothers would be apart in America for a while. However, they would all spend the last years together in the advanced development center in Israel. Then Watchman, Sari and Solomon were traded for American CIA operatives, MI6 agents, and millions of dollars.

The brothers would engage in a number of shorter-term projects, but there was also an overarching plan. Their first covert work was to assist in development and infiltration of a clandestine organization of the United States government, later to be called the NSA. The siblings' lifetime mission was the development of a project they later called Barium.

Embedded deep in the NSA and other covert organizations around the world, the siblings would begin the deepest of all covert projects. Its purpose was to follow, develop and protect creations by and for the World Court in the scientific development of high energy physics, including what was later named a Hadron Collider.

Collider facilities developed projects such as the World Wide Web. It was up to the C Street Barium underground project to build a back door to all future technology, before the web was even completed and released. They were more than successful. The colliders served the underground project as intellectual rapid technological development centers. Barium had no government red tape to cut through, so it was far in the lead.

When the siblings began, only a single bite had been taken from one proverbial apple of this area of physics. The rest of the fruit was there for the picking.

The Swiss collider became best known for the controversy it sparked by the attempt to reenact the moment of creation by producing the so-called "God Particle." It was an unfortunate name, chosen by those who wanted to derail or at least slow the achievements of the Swiss scientists, for it resulted in religious interference in scientific achievement. Coupled with a furor over the possibility of recreating the big bang, developments regulated and funded by governments were stymied. The uproar gave an opportunity for C Street Barium to gain an enormous technological head start. The government-funded facilities sat nearly idle, their progress halted by religion, fear, and power grabs between those who wished to exert control over the projects. Meanwhile, the C Street Barium project, unhampered by the greed and fears of third parties, pursued its ventures around the world. It had no oversight and no limitations. As a result, it rapidly advanced far beyond any other scientific program.

Even with all of the delay, the Swiss collider scientists did make some discoveries. Their creations, when incorporated into the technological system in development at the C Street Underground facility buried deep in the Mohave Desert, created the most advanced computer system in the world. This system continuously expanded the envelope of industrial science.

Much of the interference and delay at the Swiss collider was propelled by greed and the love of power by those who were already the most powerful and wealthy. Distraction of the people by creating schisms along cultural, racial, educational, and religious lines was the greatest of all weapons for maintaining supremacy. Even the multi-party systems of politics were created to assure protection of those in power by division of the masses along party lines. It was all for concentration of wealth. This was the kind of wealth only obtained by a minute fraction of one-percent of the world. Dealing with those wealthy few was another project of C Street Underground, albeit a social rather than a scientific project.

Because C Street Underground took on the elite, it had to insulate itself from prying eyes. Different shell corporations under the Rose veil had served as dead-end points for possible investigations into funds and technology for the completion of the C Street Barium Project. All trails ended at the Rose Tech Corporation, with head offices that did nothing but employ staffed rooms of militarily trained individuals, in case of inquiry.

The next step in any investigation, should one arise, might be Q-Tel, the CIA's cyber development branch. That was part of the reason for Solomon's Q clearance. He would be aware early on if such an investigation was initiated of the Barium project. After all, in the U.S. government, having a high security clearance issued by the Department of Energy was as good as it got – for the government, it's all about energy. Yet, once any investigation approached that level, it would be shut down by the pure red tape, the assertion of confidentiality related to national security, and by Watchman's intervention. At worst, should Solomon and Watchman fail to stop an inquiry, this kind of probing could never pass through the many levels of insulation and secrecy that protected the ebony Barium Project of C Street. It had to be that way – Barium was too powerful, too dangerous for it to be entrusted to others.

The computer system Barium created, later named "Einstein" by Solomon, had been the lifelong leader in technological advances. These advances existed only in the dark below the sands of the desert. This buried facility rocketed ahead of all others and contained a new era of artificial intelligence invisible to the rest of the world. Only Einstein had computerized decision-making ability. No other scientists were even close to developing such a feat.

This ability afforded the Barium Project quantum RSA-E computer code calculations and the means by which to constantly monitor the world stage while remaining totally concealed. The project used smaller colliders in America and around the world. It also downloaded information from the entire internet daily into two computer systems located in Egypt and Switzerland. This divided the daily data and it was in turn recompiled and analyzed by Einstein at the Underground.

Einstein used selective interference only when it was deemed necessary. The fear mongers talk of machines taking over man. The Barium project was really about man and machines working together toward the common goal of world security. Einstein had no desire in its root programming to rule the world, unlike so many men and women.

Einstein and its human partners decided when to allow advancements to be released to the rest of the world, and when to permit or stop technological "breakthroughs" by others. They delivered developments to countries only as they become responsible enough to handle them without initiating a world war. The ability of the C Street computers to analyze all outcomes at once, selectively interfere, and constantly monitor global events through the Space Station and satellites, placed it in a world apart from known electronic devices.

The Barium Project was developed from scientific discoveries made during the Manhattan Project's experiments, as well as from the cosmic ray experiments of the 1940's and 50's involving pion and kaon. Solomon's father Turing had been working in this scientific area in America, when he was sent to Israel by the American government. The physics meetings in Solomon's childhood home were forever embedded in his infallible memory.

Turing made sure Solomon was always present with the scientists, like a human recorder for the future. He would be shown equations and theories from a scientist in the small living room, before documents were burnt. Turing knew early of his son's gifted mind. Watchman was allowed to burn the used and useless papers. His brother had already absorbed the knowledge contained in the documents, and having the writings was a security risk.

Any experiments to develop quantum computers or other high energy innovations could have had direct impact on the planet because of the dangers inherent in manipulating subatomic particles and the possibility of world domination by those who controlled the scientists. That placed the world at continued risk from the process of technological advancement. As a result, Barium was a sanctioned UN project in its genesis.

Early on in America, Watchman located the individuals who posed risk. Solomon managed disposal of them with extreme prejudice. They did this while monitoring and installing information from Sari, as well as developments of their own and others. Operational assets were provided by militaries of select UN member nations, supplemented by individuals carefully screened by Watchman and Solomon from around the world. Those people possessed broad unusual talents and skills.

This project was the nominal responsibility of The Hague Court, by and through the International Court of Justice, located in The Hague, Netherlands. However, as the years had come and gone, the courts' justices changed, people died, and paper trails disappeared. The courts had no comprehension of the depths of the power they had bestowed.

The history of The Hague Court went back to the Middle Ages. Ancestors of Solomon and Watchman established The Hague Court in the 1200's, and it had existed and been active ever since. The court sanctioned their father's work on the Manhattan project, colliders, including the Swiss collider project, and the Hague siblings' work on the C Street Barium project. Watchman, Solomon and Sari called it the THC, partly because they found it humorous to demote such a powerful place and mostly because their father was never Turing Hague to them – he was "Father" to the boys and "Papa" to Sari.

All three siblings were very active in Barium. Even though Sari had other duties at the Swiss project, she surreptitiously worked with her brothers, as well. Having Sari in the middle of the scientific community, planning first the theoretical and later the experimental aspects of the collider facility made her a perfect operations source early on. Before the actual building of the collider, the facility beneath the windmills in the American desert was the base for technological advances. Other facilities around the world contributed to its progress.

Some developments stayed in the Underground, others were disseminated when the time was right. One of the many programs released to the governments was HAARP (High Frequency Active Auroral Research Program). HAARP was an ionospheric research program jointly funded by the U.S. Air Force, the U.S. Navy, various universities, and of course, DARPA. DARPA was a major source of the funds for the Underground. HAARP was built under contract by BAEAT Advanced Technologies, a shell corporation. Its purpose was to analyze the ionosphere and investigate enhancement technology for radio communication and surveillance. HAARP operated a sub-arctic facility in Alaska. Many other secret projects were hidden there in the vastness of the wilderness.

Another program, based on HAARP, was the U.S. Defense Department's Air Force Space Surveillance System, the "Space Fence." It was a system designed to detect orbital objects passing over America and to listen for communication from outer space. It consisted of three transmitters and six receivers. The world believed the Space Fence had been deactivated and the American government had issued press releases to that effect. Let's face it, the American government loved to try to communicate with little green men - who if they know what's good for them, do not respond. However, the politicians had given up on the Space Fence and moved on to other, sexier projects. Once scientific projects are finished, they hold little interest for the politicos.

The government also believed the program had been decommissioned and its transmissions had gone quiet, as far as anyone could tell. Actually, the Barium Project had shifted its transmission frequency to an undetectable 37.53113 megahertz signal and it was only connected to Einstein. The Space Fence was secretly reporting over 253,000 data points from outer space.

The Underground planned to replace the system with a new and improved dual purpose version. The new high-tech system would be able to identify and locate the chemical compounds of nuclear, biological and chemical weapons, whether on land, sea, or space. This improvement was all the justification Solomon and Einstein needed for shutting down the government's ability to use the fence to search out extraterrestrials. Solomon was sure that ET was too far advanced to respond to such an uncivilized world filled with violence. Instead, the Underground continually monitored all satellites, and concentrated on the ones that had the potential for aggressive action.

Those with aggressive capabilities made up a fair number of the more than 3000 satellites listed on the books, but Solomon knew there were actually over 5000 active ones in space. Recently, Einstein had developed a capability to spray unwanted satellites with non-reflective material from the X37-12 spaceship. That allowed for the destruction of aggressive and spy spacecraft.

Shooting spy satellites out of space was the easy part. Doing it in a way that avoided any responsibility was hard. Not all of them would completely disintegrate on re-entry. If debris from a destroyed craft reentered the atmosphere and could be recovered, no evidence would exist of the spray material that caused it to overheat, explode and fall. The satellite would be presumed to have unexpectedly failed by those who launched it. It was all about plausible deniability.

Dangers didn't just exist in space. The Underground program monitored limitless activities on earth, often moving or closing programs of several world governments. Programs that were ordered closed or moved are illimitable. For instance, Plum Island Animal Disease Center (PIADC) was a program located on Plum Island run by the department of Agriculture until the NSA took over its operations. It based its biochemical experiments on Nazi testing. Two persons, including one who attended an American Ivy League university, tried to pass biochemical warfare agents stolen from PIADC to Al Qaeda. Higher security was needed and the NSA stepped in after the Underground provided information that there was "suspected terror activity at Plum Island."

The NSA, shut it down and sealed it pending moving it surreptitiously to a new location. Kansas, the initial choice, was scrapped; Alaska was chosen for the new high security facility. Lockmeer and Paytheon corporations were competing for the contract to continue the development. This was a multi-billion dollar endeavor and the wash-off of money to Swiss accounts could be massive.

The Underground was relocating the C-band radar system to Australia from Antigua to keep tabs over the Pacific region. The second sensor was an optical telescope developed by DARPA and tested at White Sands Missile Range in New Mexico. This could increase the Underground's capability for night observation of the air space by volumes. Australia was a much better place to monitor satellites in geosynchronous orbit.

The Barium Project had not released any of its developments involving HARRP; weather seeding was developed to be used for warfare. Controlling weather by heating up the atmosphere with a field of 360 x 3 antennas located around the United States, with energy released to a laser focused spot in any one place in space. This would force the atmosphere to bulge and extreme weather to appear in that location around the globe.

So, a sandstorm could wipe out a town in the desert, a winter storm could prevent movement of troops in Russia, or a typhoon in China could level a city causing a leadership change. America and the Barium Project's other allies would come in to save the day, play hero, and walk out with more power. This was a most commanding tool in the recent war arsenal, because it had the ability to block all satellite reception while disrupting the weather in that region.

Notwithstanding its potential for political and financial gain for those that used it, this ability in many ways would be the most dangerous to the planet. Changing the natural ebb and flow would damage the atmosphere and weather patterns permanently. Global warming, already on an accelerated path, would be intensified with every use of war weather tactics. That is why the Barium Project's underground compound had kept the HARRP program's full power for its own use alone. Einstein recommended nonuse of the weather project.

Many technologies came from the collider project through the Underground for future advancement and a determination of release to the governments involved. This was just the tip of the iceberg. So many scientific developments had their genesis at the Underground.

As in so many cases, the road to hell is paved with good intentions. It was the intention of their Mossad trainers that the siblings become the best possible instruments for Israel. It meant intensive training was needed to allow the children to advance as much as possible. Their trainers could not have imagined that they had set the wheels in motion for this kind of future long before Solomon, Watchman and Sari left Israel. With their departure time accelerating toward them at warp speed, the siblings redoubled their efforts in their studies even to the very last week before they left for America and Switzerland.

Watchman struggled with the language courses at the training school, Solomon struggled with nothing. Once he had mastered only five languages, Watchman had trouble. Solomon breezed through them and many others.

It was hard for the siblings to leave the soldiers who had become friends at the training center. Yet, they never felt as though the soldiers or instructors were family. That emotional distance was created by intensive training. They had been so isolated for years that the siblings trusted and loved only one another. To the boys, America was their escape plan. Their world consisted only of each other.

Year after year at the compound, Solomon continued to grow flowers for Sari in his spare time. He hoped the flowers would help her forget the putrid smell of death that brought them to the compound and the pall of fatality that still surrounded their world. The only life they had known for more than twelve years appeared normal to the siblings, the children of Mossad. At least, it was normal to two of the three— Solomon's memory kept alive their parents and the world of love they were torn from.

He would regale his siblings with vividly detailed stories of their life before – life with their parents – ones that only he could remember. Things like his mother's chocolate cake, rewards they got for language class, and her love of the flowers she fought to grow in the desert sand. Solomon told of his father stealing a kiss from his mother in the kitchen. He always gave a perfect description of their parents, down to the beauty mark just above the right corner of his mother's lips. Often he would mention the black curly lock that fell just above his father's brow when the excitement of science brought out his mania.

He and Watchman shared stories of the meetings his father held in the living room before the bomb shattered their world. Plans for the development of Israel and building the collider were common talk. This served as a reminder to Watchman of his father's dreams. Only Solomon's mind could create every meeting, every subject, and every detail as a guide for Watchman and Sari's work. Those same memories inspired Solomon's caution with Mossad. They all knew that their course had been charted for them by their father.

It was during their final year at the center when Solomon added another coding step to his father's favorite toys, old four-rotor Enigma machines with plug boards, so only the siblings would be able to decipher a message. The Enigmas were Nazi code-making machines Turning Hague had figured out – he helped to break the unbreakable Nazi code. Every letter on a standard typewriter is coded to be another letter on an Enigma machine through rotating disks, and the plug board added another level of complexity to the cipher. To write a message you flipped a switch in one direction and noted the configuration of the plugs. For instance, FAR could become GIP. So to decipher the message, you turned the switch on your machine in the other direction with the same plug configuration, type GIP and the letters registered as FAR.

Solomon had seen the future and was convinced that old tech would be the only defense against anything new he would create. He understood better than most – after the feast comes the reckoning. Anyway, none of this would work without knowing Solomon's changes to the code process. A set pattern of letters had to be inserted into a message every two letters when the code was written and deleted when deciphering. He knew the low-tech device might one day save them all.

The siblings would start with A and every two letters add the next letter of the alphabet. So GIP would become GIAP and then when deciphered show as FAAR and so on. The number and placement of the additional letters changed in a preset pattern throughout the message. The Hagues would know to remove every third letter to read a message and then follow the preset pattern of additional characters throughout the cipher. In a string of letters equal to twenty-five it would add a minimum of twelve additional letters and the message would be unreadable to the untrained eye.

This code was used for only a few years and then became obsolete in America where the Underground created the C-phone and continually updated it for the siblings. It would look like any other cell phone. However, only after face, palm, and voice recognition of a sibling's quote from a book by Darwin, the phone was capable of becoming a code maker and breaker for communication with the other siblings.

Jacqueline stopped Solomon with a touch on his arm from across the table.

"It seems we're finally getting to the truth. Good. I'll get some more coffee. Keep going, I want to hear as much as possible now."

It was clear that Solomon was enjoying the freedom of telling the story of his life. He smiled then touched her hand as she walked past for coffee, cloaked only in the sheet. He continued to tell of the world kept secret from all since his childhood. His birth name had been uttered aloud for the first time in decades. Solomon continued, still in third person, as if this helped to distance himself from his past. As she knew, he forgot nothing. Speaking his birth name also confirmed Solomon's need to confess everything to Jacqueline, but he could only do so by telling it as a story he once heard long ago.

The siblings knew how important their life's work would be. The facility where they trained those years was heavily fortified and guarded. This told Solomon early on how valuable they were to Mossad. Mossad wanted its investment well protected. Well not exactly Mossad, as Watchman would later discover. K.I.S.S., an unauthorized arm of Mossad, was behind the Middle East part of the sibling project.

It seemed time passed quickly as Watchman's twentieth birthday came and a new life for all of them began. First, they would be allowed to travel with Sari, to assure her safety at the project center on the Swiss/French border. She would also be given private security forces for her protection on the Swiss side. Those bodyguards were hand-picked and controlled by Watchman. He narrowed down the field to an elite few. Then at Watchman's request, Solomon had carefully reviewed every memory of everything he had seen from the proposed guards. After all, there could be no mistakes – they would guard the life of their Sari. Watchman knew he was putting his little sister in their hands. Once Sari arrived at the facility, her private guards would be a special unit of the Swiss security force at the facility and always be by her side.

In America, Solomon was to attend law school while Watchman would become embedded in a nascent US organization later called the NSA. It was spun off from and funded by APARA and later

DARPA. The NSA would have various duties, one of which was to filter funds to the most top secret organization of all, a worldwide outfit, the THC.

Once law school was completed, Solomon, well-trained in designing weapons, code, chemicals, Kava Maga, engineering, electronics, theoretical and applied sciences, would work within the American government and concurrently on the Barium Project of the THC. His cover life was that of an international treaties appellate lawyer in Washington. Watchman would work in technology, operations funding and facilitation from within the NSA. Sari would focus on developments of technology and provide it to her brothers, giving them cutting edge science for the future. Often, Sari would slow the evolution at the Swiss facility, which allowed her brothers to gain an advantage in technology. Over the years, the gap in knowledge became massive.

Their father was right. Solomon's brain was different. He had already begun assimilating in his mind the advances in electronics, mechanical engineering, and science from Sari while they were still at the compound together. He knew he would use it in America. This would be the final years together in Israel.

Mossad had taught them to trust no one completely. That resulted in the siblings relying only on each other. Not even Mossad, their ally, could be completely trusted by the day they left Israel.

The trade of Israeli and American forces was an insurance policy from the beginning in a deal much larger than any one country. It would involve many greedy power hungry men, international borders and a white paper opinion that gave such latitude to K.I.S.S.

Chapter Four
America...

The first stop was difficult, for it meant leaving Sari at the Swiss/French border. They trusted her guards and knew how secure the science facility would be as an international project base. They both agreed they had done the best thing for her.

Mossad allowed Watchman to maintain careful contact with both siblings. However, Solomon and Sari couldn't initiate exchanges with each other. Watchman would be the go-between, assuring safety and immunity for all. This was the procedure for the brothers' first three years in America.

The lovely Sari was tall, thin, and fair skinned, with flowing coal black hair. She was just like her mother, right down to the mole. Also like her mother, she was kind, a more complete soul, the opposite of Watchman and Solomon. She had the face of an angel, the mind of Niels Bohr, the gentleness of morning dew, and had a voice sweetened by the gods. This was their Sari, beautiful and intellectually deadly.

It would be a mistake to underestimate her – she was well-trained. Despite her wonderful education and all she had endured, you could see an untarnished gleam in her glistening brown eyes. They were eyes that had spent most of life focused on science and not the reality of Mossad. How they shined when she arrived at the center! Sari said she was home at the Physics Institute – home for the first time since her parent's death.

It was a long goodbye to the beautiful flower with the brilliant mind. Her smile owned the day and carried Solomon through many years of separation. Watchman checked in on Sari and funneled her updates to Solomon under private arrangements, for the protection of all. They understood how important her work would be.

When Watchman could see Sari, that same glow and excitement about her work would carry him through to the next time he would kiss his sister's cheek. Every visit resulted in a complete update of the projects for Watchman. The code would be used only for pick up locations with sensitive documents.

Sometimes, Sari's status would be conveyed as a simple note placed in Solomon's apartment while he was in law class. It would be a single word – beautiful, happy, or the like. Every time he received one of those notes, he knew Watchman had seen her. Solomon would look at the paper for hours, then burn it and dispose of the ashes down the disposal. Each time he would utter the words, "Sari, Shalom."

Word from Sari of scientific advancements came with a pickup point through the re-coded Enigma machine. Solomon had been right. As the world was changing, low tech devices were the best method of private communication between the siblings.

In the dingy hotel room, Jacqueline who had remained mostly silent listening to Solomon tell the truth for the first time, at that moment said,

"So you've always had a sister and brother. First I've ever heard of them. Nice to know."

Solomon ignored the comment… then replied,

"We must leave soon."

"Is it safe?"

"No, and I may have to let them take me to get you out."

"Are you crazy?"

With a smile he replied,

"That has been debated, but the only thing experts can agree on is that the diagnosis is elusive."

Solomon snickered as he handed her a cell phone, then became more solemn.

"Seriously, I have your escape route planned; you have access to C Street through this phone. There are six exit points scheduled and you just need to make any one of them. Our men will take you from there and come for me if I'm captured. I have an idea where they'll move me. The phone has an iris scanner programmed for your eyes and the code needed is 'flysparrow' to access the bio-stimulation to

Einstein in my brain. I have full access to the C Street computers. I may not be able to respond for a short time, but Einstein will communicate; she is programmed to protect us both. It will depend on what they are doing with me. This connection technology is still new but it's the only way. I need to find them all. I chose not to change my face until you saw me again. When I make it back to C Street, it will be changed."

"What do you mean, take you? What will they do to you?"

With a tilt of his head, Solomon said,

"You already know. They will probably attempt to torture me to get information. Then they'll do their best to kill me. You already know that I feel little pain. That's what carried me through the treatment for cancer in New York. I've fought the world with hardly a scratch and yet I got knocked down by the all-too-common cancer gene. Unbelievable! I guess the universe wanted to show me I'm not immortal. Only a select few – you, my siblings, and very few others – know about my diminished pain sensation. No one else does. It's been the best kept of all my secrets. You needn't worry about me. If I'm captured, Einstein will find all the possible escape routes. They won't have me for long. Just long enough to let you escape."

"I know that's true, but I'll worry, anyway. So the chip implant was completed?"

"No; the chip Dietmar told you about – that was never used. The stimulation is a later development. I can't explain it all now, but it was ready shortly after I fled from the CIA. Just know I'm still the best at this game and I've planned every step. Now, I need you to cooperate. Let's leave the worrying to our enemies."

"How many are pursuing us?"

"I believe there are five players or maybe more, each with a team of men still looking for you. They want the money you got, the codes to other accounts, and the evidence I left to protect you. By now, some may suspect I'm alive. They'll come after me once I'm spotted by someone who knows this face. That's when you need to use one of the exits. Understand?"

"No. We're finishing this together."

"I prefer you go to safety and let me handle this one. Just head for the Romanian exit point, that's your primary exit. The others are only backups. No matter what happens, keep going."

"This is all about *greed*! Just give them the money, and we can disappear. We know how."

"No, it's more about the power and secrets I hold at this point. What money we have is just the icing on the cake to these men. With my knowledge, more power and a lot more money would come to them. This is all about information, information that would topple the elite and dethrone kings in many countries."

Jacqueline looked around the room and noticed new clothes for her. Then she remembered a black jacket being placed over her shoulders in the rush to flee Carnival. Her dead husband had just appeared before her eyes, so her shock made the jacket insignificant at the time. She looked to Solomon, pointed to the attire and laughingly said,

"Not my style."

The skin-tight stretch black body suit, boots, and jacket were really excellent quality. Mossad had access to the finest clothing to provide protection from bullets, projectiles and fragmentations. Clearly, these sexy Kevlar clothes were designed perfectly for Jacqueline by Solomon. He had thought of everything.

"I see you haven't lost your sense of humor. Those are made from the thinnest Kevlar available, but don't let anyone test it!"

"I'll try not to. When do we start?"

"We have very little time. Once we walk out this door, be ready to fight. If we're separated, just make it to one of the exit locations I gave you. They'll be on you in six blocks, but they need you alive and I'll be on them."

Jacqueline watched as Solomon dressed, but not in the Ivy League attire he used to put on for his law office every day of their life together in Florida. He dressed in black jeans and a black T-shirt, both of which she realized were Kevlar.

She watched as he strapped a double holster across his back and checked the silenced guns inside. Next he added a gun on his leg, strapped another to his arm, and stuck one in the back of his pants. He did all that while continuing to talk with Jacqueline.

Flippantly she asked,

"Done this before?"

With a smile and wink he replied,

"A few hundred times."

Oh, he had done this before. Then he placed his arms in a deep brown thigh-length coat made from a single piece of leather. You could see weapons and equipment bristling all over him until he put on the coat. At that moment, everything was concealed. The jacket hung, without a wrinkle or bulge, like the best of tailored jackets on the tall, thin man.

As a matter of fact, his cropped, groomed hair was slightly longer, freer flowing than she recalled. For the first time, she noticed a curl to his dark hair. This was a very different man from the scholar she had married in a Florida courthouse, that fine summer day. He was clearly changed and more pleasing to Jacqueline in some ways.

"Get ready. It's time."

She quickly finished dressing, grabbed her gun and tucked it inside her waist. Solomon handed her a backup weapon. Reaching into her purse, she began to slip in her earpiece. It was a gift from her old friend Meier Finch, always secured inside a pen.

"No, take this; it communicates with more."

Solomon smiled as his hand slowly moved her long auburn hair, lingering before placing the earpiece and then securing a watch on her wrist.

"You're familiar with this watch. You trained with the garrote in Israel. Leave everything else. Your jacket is loaded. The room will be sanitized after we exit. Jackal, I'll be right behind you. Happy Valentine's Day. I love you. Go!"

She slipped quickly out the door without looking back.

Solomon felt a mild sting behind his eyes as his brain began control of his screens. He had been told this sharp quick pain should pass as his brain adjusted. He could not help but wonder what it would be like for someone who had normal pain sensors.

His visual cortex began filling with hologram digital images, watching Jacqueline's every move as he followed at a distance. Only a few blocks from the hotel, Jacqueline picked up unusual chatter from a man on a cell phone nearby. She was made.

"It's her."

The other end of the conversation was,

"Get her alive. Don't lose her."

Jacqueline had already sped up her pace before the call between the men ended.

Rio was eerily silent the day after Carnival. The rain had stopped, but it had not erased history. The city still reeked of the alcohol-filled nights that had proceeded this day. Trash of sparkled masks, feathers and beads filled the streets.

Jacqueline could hear the brush as her pursuers hastened to catch her. Quickly, she slipped deep into an alley, pulling the .22 from her waist, and headed off into a dark corridor. Within moments, a man came into the alley in pursuit. She could see him coming toward the alcove where she had concealed herself, looking behind and under everything as he got closer to her dark nook.

At that very moment, Solomon approached from the other end of the corridor. Quietly she turned to him,

"Is he ours?"

Solomon's reply was clear,

"No."

Jacqueline saw another man approaching Solomon. She said,

"Behin..."

Solomon turned before she could finish the word. At that moment, Solomon killed the man just entering the alcove on his left. Jacqueline leaned forward and dropped the man searching the alley with a head shot, and his body fell into a pile of garbage bags.

Solomon calmly spoke to himself,

"Clean up, alley at Solo and Java."

Then he turned to Jacqueline,

"Let's go."

Her thoughts raced...

"He does have some kind of connection in his brain. How did he see the man behind him so fast?"

Even with those thoughts racing through her head, Jacqueline did not hesitate.

Within moments, Solomon and Jacqueline had grabbed a waiting motorcycle. As they roared away, Jacqueline heard Rose's voice in her ear.

"The car behind us, can you take it out?"

It only took her one shot.

"I'm going to cause some distractions, so hold on tight."

Within seconds, explosions began going off behind them.

Jacqueline asked Solomon,

"Can you hear me?"

"Yes."

"We're staying together, Solomon."

"Are you sure?"

"Yes, you'll need me. Deal with it."

They dropped the bike and picked up a waiting car. Within an hour, they were aboard a private plane in the air. Once they settled in, Solomon opened the conversation with,

"Nice silencer on that gun; titanium. I expected you would decide to stay with me."

"How did you cause those explosions – men in the area?"

"It's my bio-connection to the Underground computers. I flew in tiny robots called birds that can carry pellet bombs. They are small and remote-controlled. Here's one of them; take a look. This one's not armed. They bombed our pursuers. Handy, huh?"

"Nice. It's so small, not much bigger than a hummingbird, and it weighs much less than a pound! It's a little computer. How can it hold anything?"

"It holds ten times its weight, and our weapons for the birds are compact, to say the least. We have cover designs to match birds of the areas where they'll be used. Some return to the plane on their own once they drop their bombs. Others self-destruct."

Solomon put the bird back in a case beneath his feet with eleven others. These were far more discreet than the minimum twenty-five pound drones released for government use.

"I need to go into Bogota, Columbia, for a wet op. The plane will set down, drop me, and then take you to safety."

"This is the second time you tried to get rid of me! Leave you alone? Did you really think in all your planning I would do that?"

"I'm trying to send you to safety, Jacqueline. You know I'm never alone. We have people all over... hold on, I have some communication coming in."

As Jacqueline watched, Solomon flinched as though pain had reached his few sensors, then he appeared in deep concentration. Clearly, he was communicating with something. His new abilities were fascinating and a subject for later discussion. But to see him show any evidence of pain was most unusual. She was well aware he had a very high tolerance for pain, unusually high. It was at that moment Jacqueline knew she was going along for the entire ride.

"Rose, you do understand I'm going with you?"

She called him Rose and his face lit up.

"Are you sure?

"I'm your plus one at this party! You need me."

"I chose the safer exit for you."

"Appreciate it, but I've decided."

"I can't fight you and them. I'll communicate stand down orders on the pickup locations."

He turned to Jacqueline with an almost pleased look.

"Okay, you're staying with me."

Jacqueline knew that her chemical reaction to Rose was actively flowing again. She had the opportunity to leave and stayed. She had chosen the more dangerous route, the path by his side.

Solomon told her that he had picked up Jacqueline's grown daughter from St. Kitts the night before and he sent her to Dubai for safety. A short call earlier had confirmed she was secure. For now, she was with an old friend, Prince Abdullah, and his bodyguards.

For Jacqueline, Marie's safety and happiness were all that ever really mattered in the world. Solomon knew securing Marie was his number one priority. Should anything happen to Marie due to his work, he would be a dead man. Jacqueline would make sure of it.

Marie, a lovely young woman with pale skin and dark hair, was wise to only part of her mother's work and had chosen to distance herself from Solomon's CIA world. Still, she would take no prisoners to ensure her mother's safety, either. When the miraculously resurrected Solomon showed up at her door in St. Kitts, it was Marie who told Solomon,

"You got her into this; get her out or this plane will be back from Dubai fast."

Jacqueline turned to Solomon,

"Now, order Ishmael to answer only to Marie."

"Why, that's already done! He no longer answers to me."

"Okay, confirm it."

Solomon smiled then confirmed his previous orders to Ishmael. Marie could change her locator number in the C Street mainframe based on a conversation with Jacqueline. If Jacqueline told her not to get lost, she would stay at the location for one week; should Jacqueline not arrive, Marie would flee to a meeting point with her bodyguard Ishmael under her control.

Meeting points were always established between them around the world, just in case. Which one was determined by a few words Marie or Jacqueline would say. When Jacqueline talked to Marie earlier that day, the meeting point was set. They had prearranged spots at each location to find one another. That way, they could meet without using electronics. One of the many things they had learned was how to avoid a digital footprint while in flight.

Of course, they never thought they would be fleeing from Solomon – he was dead. The meeting points were to escape from the others – those who pursued the money and evidence Solomon had left when he "died." Since he decided to return from the grave, he had become another one to flee, if necessary. As Jacqueline had learned in this world where she now resided, danger comes from the most unexpected places.

She was no longer fooling around with Solomon, Simon, Jude. She loved him and yes, the chemical reaction between the two was intense. Nevertheless, she knew too much – just how fucking dangerous he and his world really were. She was determined to take no chances, no risks that were not well thought out.

Jacqueline found Ishmael an interesting choice by Solomon for Marie's main bodyguard. She knew he must be aware of the one-night fling Ishmael had with Jacqueline had in Israel. It appeared he simply did not care about that. Ishmael was good and that would be why he was chosen.

More importantly, Marie knew about his tryst with her mother. Despite Ishmael's handsome charm, Marie would have no interest. That would make him the perfect protector. Anyone in the business knows not to cross a line with people they are charged with protecting, especially with this daughter. That would have gotten Ishmael killed twice over.

Solomon turned to Jacqueline,

"Now we can finish talking. Do you know how much I love you?"

Jacqueline turned to him with a smile.

"Yes, but love has nothing to do with tomorrow. I want the rest of the truth. We'll talk of the future when this is over."

Solomon started talking immediately.

"Let's see, before the shots so rudely interrupted us – by the way, nice hit! We'll be the air for a few hours. Are you sure you want to go along for this part of the mission? I'd really prefer you go someplace safe."

"We both know there is nowhere safe in this world of yours."

"Okay, I won't argue with that, but the most secure place is always away from me."

With a laugh she told him,

"I can't even get away from you in death! I'm surprised you didn't fight me more on coming along. What is it you said back in Rio, changing an escape plan is dangerous? Isn't that what you said earlier?"

With a smile at the unvarnished truth and utter amazement at his very changed wife, he replied,

"It's true. Well, I planned for contingencies. I had the six exit points on standby, but I assumed you would choose to come with me. I know my wife better than you think. You're stronger than when I left. I just wanted the choice to be yours. Okay, we have men on the ground in Columbia preparing for this leg. We'll have a few hours before we arrive. There's more ammo and weapons for you below your seat and in the overhead cargo bin."

"So you knew I'd insist on finishing this with you."

"Yes. But I, more than anyone, understand that no one tells you what to do. Now, where were we? I was telling you about coming to America. Wait. Quiet for a minute, hold on, I have some communication."

Jacqueline saw the flinch of pain again in his eyes and chose not to ask about it. The communication was from Watchman in London. In Solomon's digital view appeared a late night meeting of two men in a tree-filled park at the center of Parliament Square, near the northeast corner of Westminster.

"Hold on. I need to watch this."

Jacqueline moved to the bar on the plane, filling their glasses as she watched Solomon in deep concentration. She was careful not to disturb it as she placed the drink in front of him.

Solomon tapped her seat table and a screen slid over with the swipe of his hand. Both watched and listened to the two men as they approached a dark, tree-covered area, rain still dripping from the branches. Jacqueline realized the feed had three men, the two in the foreground and one in the distance. She quickly pointed the third man out to Solomon.

"Look."

Solomon smiled.

"I see him."

The first one to speak was Guy Drake, a MI6 agent.

"We're burned. Counterparts are missing all over the world. And we're not the only ones; I talked to the CIA, same thing. It's Chameleon and he'll come for us. My bank account disappeared overnight. I hear the same story from the CIA. Money is gone from other accounts."

Mack Duck, another MI6 agent replied,

"Yeah, gone! Mine disappeared today, right before you called!"

"That's why I called, mine disappeared t…"

He had not finished his sentence when Mack pulled his PP9, the long silencer pointed at Guy.

"Where's my fucking money?"

"Calm down, Mack! I don't know. I didn't do this. Mine just disappeared, too. I never had your damn account number; I couldn't have taken it. I'm bailing with what money I have. I suggest you do the same. Everyone thinks the Chameleon is behind this. Any idea who he is?"

Mack kept the gun trained on Guy and said,

"American, maybe. Who the fuck knows — we've been looking for years. But at this point, who cares? I want my fucking money! Maybe you're Chameleon, you son of a bitch."

"No way. You know me, Mack."

Guy reached in his pocket as Mack carefully watched.

"Easy!"

Slowly, Guy pulled out a passport and handed it over.

"Take this and fall off the face of the earth, Mack. That's what I'm doing."

"Fuck you. You're not falling off, you're falling on it."

He fired a shot and then quickly emptied the pockets of his dead comrade lying on the ground.

"Shit! Nothing."

Then another shot swished through the air, and Mack fell on top of Guy's body. The third man in the distance walked up to the bodies and finished clearing all the pockets of both corpses.

The shooter's navy trench coat was old, but his large-brimmed fedora allowed no impression of his age. The rain filled the circumference of his hat, making a waterfall exit just to the outside of his left eye. He carried a gun in his left hand, his right arm straight down, useless, lifeless.

Solomon took a hard look at the screen. He saw the man's useless right arm, and Solomon knew who it was.

"It's Crane! K.I.S.S., him and clear!"

As Crane walked into the night, headed out of the park, there was another whisper of a bullet in the air, and Crane's head exploded in blood as he dropped to the ground. Within seconds, all documents were removed from his corpse by a man not visible before. He was dressed in black, hiding, watching the events unfold.

"Anything, anything?"

Solomon repeated it, talking to the screen. The feed of the park disappeared from view and a shadow of a man appeared. He spoke,

"No, nothing of value, but it was three for one. Oh, lucky day, one of them was Crane!"

Solomon looked to Jacqueline as the screen closed.

"Looks like they're turning on one another. I expected it and it's more than convenient."

With a puzzled look, Jacqueline spoke.

"Who is Crane?"

Solomon did not hesitate in answering her questions or blow her off with a "need to know" response, as he had years before.

"Crane is old KGB, known as the Night Heron, because he kills in the dark. He's one bad son of a bitch and on our list. That nasty bird has also seen this face of mine on foreign soil."

The rumor was that Crane had a brother who worked in the Canary Wharf area of London. He was found dead under unusual circumstances along with a number of other financial brokers near the European headquarters of Morgan. Crane blamed Solomon for the death of his brother. He was wrong; the Banksters had been eliminating their fraud trail. Even if Solomon didn't kill his brother, Crane's belief made him a threat.

Besides, Solomon shot and wounded Crane in an earlier mission, so he still wanted revenge. Actually, Solomon had wounded him in his arm not once, but twice, several years apart.

"It was the year before we found each other in Florida. I had him paid off in Kiev when I needed to extract a mechanical engineer from Russia. Crane had a hit order for my guy — I bought the contract, as we say. Still, the SOB tried to kill both of us on our way out of Russia.

"We were about ten miles from the Butyrka Prison. With a few payoffs; I had gotten my asset out clean using a prison van. We were on our way to a pick up point at Kitay-gorod. The roads were dark, it was raining and slick. We had been traveling a few klicks on that secluded road when something did not seem right to me. Within moments, I heard another vehicle and a shot took out our driver.

"My alarm had gone off enough earlier to let me seize control of our van. I played cat and mouse with the car for a few minutes before I realized it was Crane alone, reneging on the deal. I was pissed! I looked him in the eyes and then I took aim for a head shot. Because of the moving vehicles, I only winged him, sending him and his car off the road. But I still got the engineer out of Russia. Sometimes in this business, it's easier to deal with the devil you know. I was not surprised when he double-crossed me again. I wanted to burn him on the way out, anyway.

"Years before, we had another run-in. That time, I shot him in the same arm. Crane did not know I was the one who winged him the first time. I was extracting a scientist from a gulag in Siberia. That time, the deal was made through a middleman and our 'inside man.' Crane did not see my face. That first shot gave Crane a weak right shoulder, and after the wound from the Butyrka Prison incident, his arm all but useless. It didn't stop him, though. The bastard shoots just as well with his left. It was rumored he's wanted to kill me for years. Guess the hurt wing pissed him off."

Solomon laughed very loudly and Jacqueline seemed a little confused. He explained,

"It was the computer in my head, trying out its sense of humor. It said, 'I think it is clear that bird had to go.'"

"Really? So your computer has a sense of humor!"

"Well, it's working on it."

"Okay, enough. What's in your head?"

"This will take some explaining. First, you need to understand a bit about neutrinos. Neutrinos have mass, but they're elusive to find because they are tiny even for subatomic particles. Physicists have labeled them with a series of Vs. Specifically, I'm talking about the electron neutrino, (v_e), which has a negative electric charge and travels at the speed of light. That was the beginning for the AI connection project, man to machine – Einstein to me. Look, ma – no wires, no implanted circuit boards!"

Jacqueline, stunned by what she had just heard, jerked her head back.

"Wow!"

"Do you remember the color of the dress you were wearing when you marched in Washington?"

She thought for a minute.

"I do. Do you?"

"It was a shade of purple call Han."

"Amazing! You astound me! You're right, it was purple and we didn't even meet that day!"

"When the Han paint pigment from the archeological dig of the Chinese terracotta soldiers was placed at absolute zero, it allowed magnetic waves to interact with the pigment molecules to become a gas and then condense in a rarely observed state called Bose-Einstein Condensate, or BEC. This discovery allowed the BECs to behave at the quantum level. The magnetic field formed between copper atoms 'superimposed' and acted as one wave, thus reducing the property's field from three dimensions to two dimensions.

"The Han purple paint pigment contains a barium copper silicate, Ba-Cu-Si2O6 and iron oxide, Fe2O3. Those are only slight, but important chemical differences between Han purple and Egyptian blue paint pigment. Then we added the electron neutrino particle (v_e), which has no electric charge. I produce an excess amount of the protein SAP. That's the basis of my eidetic memory. With the addition of even more chemicals to Han purple, we created a chemical to connect man and machine, in part, by using my brain's naturally occurring SAP.

"The neutrinos are captured and frozen at the same time. We currently have only two of these neutrinos and one lives in the compound in my brain. The same compound containing the other is in Einstein, housed in a semiconductor with a thin capacitive layer of barium strontium titanate to protect it from moisture. Einstein herself is small. She and the coils of her magnet must be held no higher than -457.67 degrees, near absolute zero, with massive equipment used to sustain her operations. Without the extremely low temperature to maintain her electromagnetic field, Einstein would not operate at the quantum level, and the connection between us would be broken.

"Microtubules in the human brain serve to isolate the quantum code liquid. The codes generated interact from inside the microtubules to the outside through the Earth's magnetic field. The quantum codes therefore become self-aware. We have cells that form a positioning system in our brain – our hard-wired GPS. Cells that mark our position help us navigate and remember. When stimulated, an existence connects through empty space by way of the earth's magnetic field to the universe and can connect to the outside world indefinitely. Proto-consciousness is a quantum process, the precursor of human consciousness, and it exists as long as the magnetic field is active in the cerebral cortex. The formula we created keeps the magnetic field active in the brain and the computer, therefore a perfect match of accessibility."

"Slow down, I'm trying to follow this!"

"Sorry, you remember the childhood song taught in grade school to memorize the periodic table, there's antimony, arsenic, aluminum, selenium, and hydrogen…'"

"Yes, and that you can't carry a tune, so go on, say it simply."

"I forget this is high level quantum physics and engineering. I have an entire team that does this work, based on my early discoveries. They explain it to me nowadays. Okay, let's try this. It behaves similar to surface water. It's not forming a gigantic magnetic wave in three dimensions, but in two dimensions - in flat planes rather than throughout the entirety of three-dimensional material. This was believed impossible at absolute zero, "the quantum limit" a point at which all thermal motion ceases and only quantum motion exists."

"Okay, I'm following, I think."

"We based Einstein, the quantum computer in the Underground, on this compound. We have a super-magnet that operates with the system deep below ground. The modified liquid compound, called COSMO for short, is now matched to my DNA. It was inserted into my brain through nanotechnology. Once it's in, it's permanent and untraceable – after all, it's part of my biology.

"Nanotechnology is the branch of technology that deals with dimensions and tolerances of less than 100 nanometers, especially the manipulation of individual atoms and molecules. It looks at how we control matter at the molecular and atomic level. We have to work on the nanoscale – a scale way too small to see with an optical microscope. In fact, one nanometer is just a billionth of a meter in size. This is heading into bio-mechanics.

"So simply stated, my brain connects to Einstein's strong magnetic field through the earth's weaker magnetic field. Hold on babe, I have some more things to handle."

There was a pause and Jacqueline could only wonder what the price of this love was. Solomon continued as though the conversation had not paused.

"Einstein reached its quantum level shortly before I fled Florida for New York and then Paris. Einstein's match to my DNA was completed while I was in Paris."

Solomon was preoccupied again after the short, mind-bending conversation with Jacqueline. He walked around the plane for nearly a half hour, sat in different seats, and was clearly doing something in his mind. It appeared the pain only came when he started concentrating on images in his head.

When he settled back in his chair Jacqueline asked, "What makes you flinch?"

Solomon smiled, "It's a very bright light that occurs when I connect to full power."

Jacqueline, "So you just think and Einstein is there?"

"Yes, and my pain is a reaction that should subside as my brain's neurons develop more tolerance."

"I'm shocked you'd allow anyone to tamper with your brain."

"Well, it was Dietmar who was doing the stimulation. I couldn't pass up the chance to take my IQ from just below 200 to limitless. I simply couldn't! Besides, the entire project was developed early on using my DNA for a match. No one else could substitute for me. Einstein and I are both learning at the quantum rate."

"Do you feel smarter?"

"No, I just have access to more information and I have it much faster. It's wonderful! Remember when I would play multiple chess games in the park at one time? Now, I could play the city of Manhattan at once! I'll never turn Einstein over to any one government. After all, she is my brainchild."

"What if the bio-stimulation had failed?"

"Well, I was already a dead man to you, the one who matters most. Watchman could and does communicate with Einstein on a lower level, with physical screens, input devices, and voice. He would have assumed responsibility if I died. Keeping himself at the lower level was his choice early on in this project. The group of ten who review data from Einstein would be next in line, as usual. They have less control of the machine than Watchman."

"Would I ever have known any of this?"

"You would have been given a choice by Watchman. You could see and know everything about me for one moment in time. Dietmar would have set a restore point in your brain and then erase the later memories, memories of that moment in time about my work, before you left the Underground. The choice would have been yours. Do you know which you would have chosen?"

"I'd have wanted to know..."

"I assumed so. That's why it was arranged, in case this stimulation failed. But, our odds of success, according to Einstein, were high. As you know, I'm rather fond of my superior intellect."

Jacqueline realized Solomon was really no different. He was the fascinating genius she had fallen in love with and a man dancing on the edge of the precipice – that thin line, ever-present.

He was preoccupied after the screens showing the last shot in the park was completed and a short conversation with Jacqueline. It appeared the pain only came when he started some kind of deep concentration.

Jacqueline watched, fascinated, as she tried to absorb what he had just told her. She realized that what was the future to most was for Solomon very much in the present. The future already existed in that dingy Rio hotel room and on this plane. What the hell was in his head and what were his capabilities? Those were her overriding thoughts and they caused a state of sheer terror that she couldn't allow to show on her face.

After a time, he turned with a smile and picked up the explanation of his history from the last sentence where he had left off in the hotel. Jacqueline knew his photographic memory was still intact. And now it seemed his already brilliant brain was also a computer...

Chapter Five
Code of Conduct...

When Watchman and Jude arrived in America from Israel, Jude assumed a name long ago prepared for him. From at least the day his parents died, he was destined to be called Solomon Rosenberg. It was the name of a deceased American boy. He and his whole family were killed many years before in a boat accident. Solomon's identity had been thoroughly backstopped long before he began using the name. He always knew this was his fallback identity in America. It had been drilled into him since he was a child in Israel, just waiting to be used. This was the name the world would know him by. At least, it would be his name between missions, faces and other identities.

Over the years, others had named the invisible man who did their dirty work Chameleon. It was a name to which Solomon initially took great offense. He told Watchman it was not at all creative, and barely suitable in its plural. He had to admit that he did enjoy watching them chase this "faceless man."

Solomon immediately began law school in America. He had already been accepted before he left the compound and arrangements had been made at the campus. Watchman was traded to the CIA/FNSA to head a long term project. This is where they would build the foundation of the covert operations arm of the United Nations, under the authority of the International Court of Justice.

All lawyers are officers of the court. Solomon had been admitted to practice before several state and American federal courts. He was also an officer of the highest court in the world, the International Court of Justice, the ICJ. Solomon was always answerable to its judges, called justices. Over the years, the faces of the justices would change as terms of office expired. Elected by the justices would be the President Justice. He or she was the one who would receive the number needed in the four corners of identification.

Appointments to this court were made by the United Nations General Assembly throughout the years, with staggered expiration terms of nine years for each of the justices. Normally there were fifteen judges, but based on circumstances, there could be as many as seventeen because of special appointees for some cases.

A number was given to the President Justice at his or her appointment and changed each time a new President Justice assumed control. Any one code could only start the process to bring Solomon out and make him available for the court's scrutiny and assignments. The *in camera* case of the Mandate 18 White Paper required three additional codes; one from POTUS, one from The Prime Minister of Great Britain, and one from the Prime Minister of Israel. Codes for those countries transferred from leader to leader.

The one which the court controlled would result in an immediate response from Watchman, on behalf of Solomon, for assignments. Every one of the four numbers, the one controlled by the President Justice plus three other numbers controlled by the U.S., Great Britain, and Israel, were all needed to complete the code sequence to call Solomon to appear personally. Once the four corners were met and with the final code entered, irreversible events were set in action.

This project was all about crossing lines, international borders. Solomon and Watchman were, in one sense, men without a country. Yet, in another, they were men of all nations. Solomon had never been called in, but he had been called upon many times. Like the time the FSA in Russia had a high-level American intelligence asset in prison and the court needed him extracted. Or when Iran was beginning to enrich Uranium and the court needed information. These missions, like all of them, were forwarded to Solomon by Watchman.

So, Solomon and Watchman answered only to the Justices of The Hague. All of the Justices were afraid of the ramifications of using their code, in part because they would find out exactly what their predecessors had been responsible for doing over the years. It was the darkest of operations, and really had turned out to be a perfect covert operation on a massive scale.

The brothers agreed that when this project was first conceived, no one, absolutely no one, thought it would create such an uncontrollable force. This they were sure of... for no one grants this kind of power in any halls of government. Even in Israel, the siblings had no idea that they would one day create something so mammoth. The brothers were convinced it was skill, training, timing of supporting technology, and pure unadulterated luck.

The United Nations was in charge of world peace, security, development and international law. Either Watchman or Solomon could activate all the codes, should it be necessary for one or both to seek The Hague Court's protection, protection that existed because of the white paper opinion. Any other partial code would result in no reply from the Justices or others. Any code Solomon or Watchman used for their protection would end the mission.

As with all the justices, a President Justice is elected every nine years – or sooner in case of the death of the sitting President Justice. Watchman would pass the code on to the new President Justice with this stern warning.

"This case is a pending *in camera* matter. Should action be needed on the file, it will be delivered to you. Once this deep-cover mission of world protection is exposed by the files being brought into this court, it can never be put back in the box, and the mission will end. Should the court need intelligence or other things handled anywhere around the world, contact can be made with the code and without accessing the court file. The court's demands will be relayed to the asset. Use of this asset for world protection does not constitute calling in the file. The asset's presence in this court releases the asset from this long-term assignment. Use your power to require the asset to appear before the court wisely, as the mission will thereupon end and its replacement, if any, is not known."

This was just to inform the court that a long-term United Nations assignment existed. The justices would not be briefed on what it was, but should the corners of the code be met, they would immediately convene the court in the Netherlands to address the issue. Should the President Justice insist on a meeting with the asset the project for world security would be forever ended. Everyone seemed to realize the world would become an even more dangerous place because of the loss of this asset if that ever happened.

Solomon had never entered his code and had never been to The Hague. Should the code be used for Solomon's protection or to bring Solomon into The Hague, the long term assignment would end the day he arrived. Mandate 18 was very clear. This was a risk no one was willing to take. The Justices realized that, from espionage to sabotage, this covert operation protected and served world peace for The Hague.

Everyone understood. Should they call this asset into The Hague, his sword would pass to a new generation. There was one overriding consideration for those in power, even though they had no idea of the full scope of his work. It was whether they could have someone trained to replace him – someone who understood this project, a person who had the capacity for the assignments needed. They had never chosen to take that risk.

There was a question Solomon contemplated as a young man in Israel under the pear tree where he trained for this life. He still asked himself the same question.

"Will I feel the sword's blade at my exit, before it's passed on to another?"

Chapter Six
Law School...

Solomon remembered Watchman standing in the shadows on the first day he arrived at Columbia Law. The man who stood next to the lion at Havemeyer Hall was almost unrecognizable, but Solomon knew it was his brother by the cane he carried. They spoke not a word. Mossad called Solomon's brother a facilitator.

This was their goodbye. Solomon knew this would be the last time he would see his brother for the next three years. Although Watchman would be in the shadows, he would never carry that cane for Solomon to see, the gift from their father, until law school's days were done and the mission began. Solomon knew what that cane meant, no matter the appearance of the man carrying it. Coded notes on small slips of paper would be the only emotional connection to his family.

It was a lonely time for Solomon at first, without Watchman and Sari. But quickly, he became filled with excitement at everything new. He found the study of law stimulating, and interacting with a large group of diverse people was so different from his nearly solitary studies in Israel. Still, he looked forward to the day his brother would come. But some days, he secretly wished Watchman would never reappear.

Nonetheless, resigned, he was ready to fulfill his obligation to country. The question was which country had his loyalty? Or did it make a difference? Were all of them the same... just placed oceans apart and all governed by a body and laws few knew?

Solomon came to love America. The lack of bomb blasts made the death of his parents fade, for the first time in his life. His day-to-day life as a law student was one of privilege. Solomon's existence had always been that way – advantaged, moneyed and powerful. He had never experienced a hungry day or an abusive blow. Even his expansive education was taught with the gentlest nature.

That was, until law school. There, he first experienced the American educational system. He thought it was abusive and found debasement completely unnecessary for training a mind. However, his intellect shined so brightly that he escaped most of the derision he saw others suffer.

Still, he too felt the sting of that maltreatment. The first time was when he was called upon in torts class on the opening day of lectures. A "call out" in law school was where a first year student was given a trick question, expected to answer with little expertise, and could then be made to look like a fool. That allowed the professor to berate the new student in front of 100 or more. Some professors took great pleasure in humiliating embryonic lawyers.

With an ease and intellect that set the pace for his time at Columbia, Solomon responded to the question asked by Professor Walter Plum, whom he had watched intimidate classmate after classmate for what seemed like hours. Solomon realized that the professor left critical details out of the hypothetical, so he supplied variants of those details and answered as to each scenario. Solomon was amused when the professor's mouth hung open at the in-depth, correct response to the question posed. He watched the professor's face get redder and redder as the answers, seemingly infinite in their variations, continued. The enraged professor could find no flaws upon which he could pounce and that clearly infuriated him. While answering the professor, Solomon also thought of seven ways to kill this lower intellect, this bully. They were all methods that would leave no trace, no body to be found. Professor Plum would just disappear.

It interested Solomon that the highest levels of the American educational system had taken the fun out of learning. Yet, at Mossad he was taught in everything from language to warfare without such a feeling. His Torah was now accompanied by the Art of War.

It wasn't long at Columbia before Solomon was riding high on his own narcissism. He was, "a handsome intellectual, from money, with great promise," to quote the girls of the sister schools. They screened the Ivy League men for possible husband candidates. He was considered one of the most eligible bachelors and a date with him could "make" a girl at a sister school like Brown or Barnard. Solomon played with the ladies, enjoying the first year of real freedom his life had known.

Being an extremely manic bipolar was a real gift for law school. He had never slept more than three hours a night in his life. Solomon studied, trained, and partied. He dazzled the ladies of the sister schools with his sharp dress, well-funded life, Cuban cigars, and supreme intellect. This was all while honing his skills at a private facility in New York City, arranged by Watchman from Israel. Everything Solomon needed was inside one remodeled 1940's apartment building he had to himself. Located below his residential flat was a soundproofed, secured facility with a library, gym, gun range, chemical lab, electronics and more. Ten minutes from law school, safely tucked away between Amsterdam and Morningside Avenues, it was cleverly hidden in plain sight near 116th and St. Luke's Hospital. This would do for a man of his status during his college years.

He did have one problem while in law school. It was early on a dreary rain-soaked New York City Friday night in April. Solomon had decided to cancel a date with a girl from a sister school, and had called her earlier that day. He became so preoccupied with a book that when the telephone rang, he chose not to answer. In fact, he didn't even hear it – he was totally absorbed in Dostoevsky.

A couple hours later, a knock came at his door. Solomon invited the young woman in and apologized for becoming distracted. With sincerity, he explained that he had left a message at her dorm canceling their evening plans. His message had been that he preferred to spend the rainy evening alone and perhaps they would go out another night. She acknowledged receiving the message that afternoon. It really was a very honest and heartfelt message, so he was quite taken aback by her unexpected arrival.

Solomon sat back down in his chair across from an open window, his book resting on a side table. He expected her to leave. He felt his message was clear. Suddenly, she became irate, storming around, demanding that he take her out. She was not wasting a Friday night and he had promised! Solomon refused and asked her to leave. She walked toward him, grabbed his book from the table and tried to toss it toward the open window into the pouring rain. Solomon's reflexes were so fast that in a split second he was out of his chair, had caught the book in the air with his right hand and the girl by the neck with his left. She was stunned and hysterical, maybe a bit sore but unharmed, and left in a cab for her home on Long Island.

Solomon communicated this to Watchman within minutes through an emergency number in London. The young woman was determined that her father, a captain in the Air Force, would avenge her humiliation. She would show that Solomon Rosenberg! By the time she arrived home, a man in a general's uniform was talking with her father. On the condition of her silence about the evening, she was paid twenty thousand in cash. Her family got an equal amount, plus her father got the promotion he had been seeking. She promptly transferred to a college in Europe, as her father's promotion meant the family would be moving to Germany. Their silence was bought and paid for, so no apology was needed.

That episode ended Solomon's desire to date in law school. He decided that wooing women was not worth the unpredictable emotional outbursts that could occur.

A few weeks later, Solomon heard that she had died with her family in an accident on the Autobahn in Germany. Watchman told him it was an accident and that they had played no role in the unfortunate incident. It was merely a convenient coincidence. He believed Watchman was protecting him from the ugly truth. The family had been exterminated. Solomon didn't understand why his brother would feel the need to shield him. After all, the girl was tossing his book into the rain of night with total disregard for his property or his feelings. His reaction was his reaction. Whatever needed to happen afterwards was necessary.

This was what it meant to have no moral compass. Even though Solomon believed she was eliminated, he could completely justify it, and more importantly, found no reason to be concerned about the fallout from his actions. It really did not matter to him, except that Watchman felt the need to protect his brother from reality. That part he found charming.

Time passed, and Solomon aced the bar exam. Not that it would have mattered; taking the bar was only his appearance for the record. His passage of the exam had been decided in advance. As it turned out, he scored higher on his own than had been planned. Things like that were always so simple for him. Yet, nothing was left to chance in this end game of power.

They sent him to law school as his cover; during those years they wanted him to hone his skills until Watchman became completely entrenched in his cover identity. Over the three year period, Watchman had done exactly that. He had assumed his role completely and had the beginnings of their operation established before Solomon graduated.

Part of Solomon's role, as he was told back in Israel, was to be ever present when danger arose from technology. A second facet of his job was to develop more sophisticated technological advances sooner than those that could be achieved by institutes like the Israeli TECHION, the American Q-TEL, and ETI in the United Kingdom. The dark organizations in these countries that received the benefits of the Underground's work were the invisible ones, corporations and acronyms for groups that no one dared to mention by name.

There was a third aspect to his covert work. That was to resolve, by any means necessary, any known threat to or by technology worldwide to protect the greater good. Solomon was to prevent, protect and defend against any one country controlling too much of any one development, and thereby to keep a balance of power for and on behalf of the United Nations. His siblings were to assist him in these goals.

Solomon was to be invisible in plain sight to the world. He would be too visible for anyone to suspect him early on. In later years, any suspicion would be negated by a lifetime of backstops. No one but the inner circle could realize just what they really did. Any slip-ups that revealed the nature of their operation could cause war.

Shortly after law school, he had discovered that the financiers of the project, the purchasers of Solomon and his siblings, had other designs for their work. The depth and darkness of the scheme that their investment capital was serving was known by few. It was completely unrecognizable to those traded. It was not for country, not for God, but for the power and profit of a few men crossing sovereign lines.

How could those men who conspired to create this project for the siblings, men of the spy craft who had so much intellect and training, expect that Solomon, Watchman and Sari would not become curious about who pulled the strings on this life they led? Could they not anticipate the cost? Millions would become billions. To Solomon, this was all predictable and their plan could only result in cost overruns and, in the end, exposure. Why would this genius they trained so well just hand over all of his work to them in the end? Really, for all their preparation, they did not think through all of the possible outcomes for the project they created. Solomon did.

He foresaw this project elimination scenario within months after arriving in America; Watchman was already imbedded and primed, in case the call came for the siblings to return to Israel. The assets would become the operators and assume command in this most deadly arena, should the call to return come. The balance of power in this mission would be forever changed.

In Israel, when the siblings were told of their future, it seemed quite simple and obtainable to the well-trained, sheltered, naive young Solomon. After all, all three siblings had IQs well above genius level, for whatever that says. And Sari's was a mind completely focused in one study, theoretical physics. Many would *envy* her the ability to have but one life focus.

Years later, Watchman walked slowly up to the statue of the lion at Columbia. It was the very day Solomon completed law school. The sunlight flickered off the bronze lion - formed a golden hue around Watchman. The disguise was so thick that Solomon barely recognized his own brother until he saw what was in his hand. It was their father's cane. How they laughed that day! Solomon was twenty-two and Watchman was only twenty-three. Solomon said this was one of the best days of his life until his days with Jacqueline.

Watchman had continued to dig in deeply and now answered to himself as a ghost elite officer in three different organizations. A meeting for all three equal counterparts from different countries would be a meeting with Watchman, by himself. That move was damn good facilitation! Solomon was amused that his big brother had finally gotten the upper hand on all of the big three and a bit of big brother control over Solomon, as well. Watchman told him things had worked out better than the mechanics of the Swiss Collider Sari had been theorizing.

As Solomon suspected, it was only a few years before three of the four powerful profiteers who designed this plan, the ones from Libya, America, and Israel's desert compound in Palestine, agreed that the whole thing was too risky... and much too expensive. The fourth, from Great Britain, disagreed about canceling the sibling project. The other three decided he would enter eternity with the others in one swift blow to the compound in Israel where this all began. They would arrange for him to be there. It would end with the extermination of all the assets involved, or so they thought. The cost to close the compound and eliminate the sibling project with one massive explosion would be 1.6 million. They would finance through and attribute the attack to a free-lance group in Jordon.

Watchman and Solomon had long ago discussed their attendance should such a meeting be called. They decided that going to any meeting in Israel was a bad idea. They were already prepared when, as predicted by Solomon, the call came for all three siblings to return to Israel for an emergency meeting.

Watchman confirmed their attendance, but never even notified Sari. Her work was too important to be disturbed with these kinds of interruptions. Watchman arranged for it to appear they were all in attendance. He even sent an empty plane to Israel and an empty car to the compound from the airstrip.

During that meeting, everyone involved except a few money men died when a massive bombing attack took out the training center. On the very same day, a plane went down as it carried more insiders to the meeting. The assets who were traded for the siblings, along with the project handlers from all three countries, were in the training compound. The remaining known players, even the ones who were tangentially involved, died in that plane crash.

Watchman believed all but the two of the people at the top were dead, and those two thought all three siblings had died in that explosion. Of course, it was merely coincidence that the bombs happened to hit the compound at the same time the plane crashed. We really don't believe in coincidences, do we?

Solomon was sure the financiers sat back in their high-rise window offices, took tax losses, and believed it was all over. Unbeknownst to them, the main players, the siblings, were not there for the explosion that was intended to be the project's end. From the lone wolf of Mossad to Beirut and on to Langley, they really had no idea of the power they had created or that their dream project would be fulfilled, but not for them.

Solomon was glad Watchman was his brother, not because he loved him, which he surely did. It was clear to Solomon – his brother was the most dangerous facilitator ever. Watchman told him that day,

"I handled our appearance and the plane for chump change, only half a million of old AARPA funds to an asset in Greece. He died yesterday; I took care of him myself at the final payoff. There are – there can be – no loose ends. Now, everyone who ever knew who we were or where we came from is dead – except the three of us. The financiers never knew exactly where we were going or who we would become."

"We'll find those bastards at the top one day, and it will be their last breath."

The explosions at the compound and the plane crash also assured Sari's security even more. That gave Solomon great comfort. Watchman told him that it had been a blessing because, with the death of the others, he became the sole creator and signatory to each of their assignments worldwide in the dark operations of the Barium Project.

"So you are but a shadow on screen giving orders! I love it! Just excellent!"

The siblings were trained, funded, embedded and on their own at the beginning of the information era. In their reunion in New York, Watchman said he had visited with Sari in France, and even brought a picture. They enjoyed marveling at it during their lunch at a sidewalk café. Then they destroyed the photo for her safety. They ripped it into many pieces and spread those tiny little parts into storm drains as they walked the streets of New York. There were no photos of Sari. No one but the two brothers knew their sister had any living relatives. The world thought her entire family was killed in an accidental bridge collapse. That was the cover story, and her brothers would handle anyone who tried to disrupt that balance.

Solomon was staring out the window of the plane as he talked about his past. He had been looking away for a while and there was still no hesitation in his speech, just pain of a life led in some strange sort of honor. His face showed the cost. Jacqueline realized that Solomon seemed different. He had shown no signs of mania since he began wringing his hands when he first started speaking the truth to her. The truth – it was that truth that carried the demons. Those dark forces ate at his soul, but he also carried a sense of *pride* in his accomplishments. Truth would see the light of day for those financiers involved, and it would happen very soon.

Jacqueline wanted to touch him, feel his heart beat against her, kiss the pain away and put the demons to rest. She had been able to do that for him once before. She was a woman who made a man forget his purpose, for being with her became his only reason for existing. Yet, she knew how it would be. The moment he was sure she still loved him, he would turn off the tap, and the truth would cease flowing from him. She would be able to learn no more about his history.

No one can ever truly know the mind of another human being. We cannot crawl inside and see their thoughts. Jacqueline did know that Solomon was really no different from other men when it came to her. Showing her hand – that she still cared – would result in an unacceptable outcome. It would distract him from revealing the truth and would serve neither of them. The only way to calculate the danger he presented was to hear everything. She knew to keep him on point, or she would end up having to kill the man she loved for her own safety. Her choices were extremely limited now, so she kept listening to his macabre manifesto.

Chapter Seven
First Trip To Paris...

While Solomon was in school, Watchman split his time between Israel, Washington, Switzerland, the Netherlands, England, and France. In Paris, he purchased a business for the day their exit from K.I.S.S., would come and their Sweet Sorrow plan, long ago devised in Israel, would take effect. All wise men in similar fields have such a plan. This was one of Watchman's responsibilities while Solomon was at Columbia.

The brothers headed straight to Paris after the explosion at the training compound. They spent weeks together in that city. They were able to visit with Sari in Montmartre for the first week. They stayed at a hotel near Sacré-Coeur (The Sacred Heart).

The Basilica of Sacré-Coeur, high on the hill, was inspired by a speech from Bishop Fournier the day of the proclamation of the Third Republic due to the defeat of France in the Franco-Prussian War of 1870. Fournier called the defeat divine punishment after "a century of moral decline" after the French Revolution. In modern times, the grand architectural wonder on the hill stands as a tribute to the 58,000 who lost their lives in the year-long Franco-Prussian War. The words of Bishop Fournier's speech about moral decline after a revolution sounded much like the propaganda in America of the present.

The church was built on seized land, at a cost of seven million French francs. It has been for some a monument of architectural and religious wonder and has reminded others of the toll of lives taken. Still, for the siblings it was a refuge. There, they were invisible to the world among the thousands of visitors. It was like they were children, still carrying the blue and white ties that bound them together. They'd never let go of those metaphorical ropes.

Sari talked of living in Switzerland; she was happy and even more beautiful, still filled with the excitement of her all-consuming work. Solomon and Watchman felt the wonder of touching their sister's hand once again and seeing her so full of joy. It was her soft gentle hand at The Sacred Heart that passed the first of a lifetime of installments in technological advances to Solomon. There, sweet Sari, an outstanding theoretical physicist and collaborator in Solomon's work, delivered a wrapped Parisian designed box to her brother. The box was tied with a ribbon and adorned with a gold bow.

You could see the pleasure in her eyes as she gave him the gift, more than a hundred disks and documents filled with engineering and tech advances. They were the tools needed to further the Barium Project's work toward the quantum goal and what became known as Einstein. Watchman and Solomon could use the tools without the red tape or need for funding approval, like at the institute or within governments. That material, that day, had set them on a course to be years ahead of the rest of the scientific community. It was a singular moment that made the Underground more than a concept – it became a reality.

After visiting with Sari, Watchman and Solomon returned to their flat in Paris. They were living over "Club Doux Privé Pour Messieurs," an upscale house of ill repute. Watchman had purchased and renovated the whorehouse. When he did so, he turned the top floor into a private residence, a soundproof bunker with direct access to the catacombs below the building.

It was an absolute masterpiece of concealment, complete with the top mechanicals of the day: electronic surveillance, invisible doors, false electronic walls, hidden stairwells, catacomb entrances, and more. All of it was built by the finest of Germany's and Israel's vast arsenal of talent. The club was so upscale that there was no sign and no advertising. The brothel catered solely to the wealthy elite. With congressmen, assemblymen and princes as the business's clientele, Watchman and Solomon would be hiding in plain sight when the time came for Sweet Sorrow. It was an operation they hoped not to run for many years.

Two entrances leading to the top floor were carefully placed in the catacombs below the house's basement supply ramp. Privately labeled supplies would arrive for an owner no one had ever met and disappear just as fast through a carefully placed hydraulic floor lift. Access was coded and the top floor was updated every year with the best electronics DARPA money could buy.

This, to the average person passing on the street or worker, was but a very private mansion. To its customers, it was a secluded and discreet pleasure palace. Simple on the outside with its natural old 19th Century architecture, inside it was an exquisite, elegant house fit for the kings it would host. Resting in the heart of Paris, covering a block, it appeared to have three floors and a basement. In reality there were four floors above that Paris block, and more below ground.

The house of ill repute was clearly designed, stocked and decorated suitably for its elite clientele. Inside, chandeliers of Swarovski crystal and golden thread tapestry adorned every private drawing room. Each guest was treated to Dom Pérignon and Beluga caviar on silver platters, hand delivered by the most beautiful women from all over the world.

With crystal beads placed in their hair, wearing only gold thread t-backs, crystal nipple covers and high heels - the women and the refreshments were truly a feast for any palate. The club was extremely exclusive, complete with its exorbitant membership fee. It existed strictly for the pleasure of those in power. Really, it was quite profitable, since the costs of construction and renovations were paid for by DARPA black ops funds and the labor had been furnished by more than one country.

Then suddenly, it became another DARPA "Closed" operation, due to reported weakness in the floor of the structure. Watchman's engineers had done their job well – there was nothing wrong with the building and the business continued to operate. The paperwork disappeared from all countries soon after. They just had to let the residence floors rest a few years and then begin updating on a regular basis after things cooled down. By the time Solomon graduated from law school, the project was long forgotten.

Hiding in comfort and plain sight was surely an advantage. In addition, the house allowed for gathering information on the most prominent men in the world. It was recorded and available to be used if ever necessary. All of it was data they would not use unless absolutely imperative. Watchman had carefully facilitated everything they would need for work, comfort and eventually, escape. Placed above and below their pleasure trove was the largest black operation exit strategy ever created.

What a time the brothers had in their house – only the best – nothing but ladies of the evening, fine food, gambling, smokes, drugs, and alcohol. Their pleasure palace of that day would be their safe house of tomorrow, whenever the time came to exit. Watchman had outdone himself on this project.

On a spring night many years later in that same Paris safe house, Solomon enjoyed cocktails alone. Watchman had left for London after sharing some private time with his brother. As Watchman departed, he told Solomon he had a surprise for him.

"Call me when it arrives. I'll only be gone tonight."

Solomon, always out-thinking his brother, assumed it was an update in technology and nothing more. That night, Solomon sat alone in his personal club chair watching the ladies of the evening shimmer and shine as they passed by. The house manager walked over and spoke. Never using names of any customer was a long established tradition of the establishment.

"How are you this evening - everything satisfactory tonight, sir?"

"Yes, just relaxing."

"I thought you might like to know we have a new arrival for one night from the Middle East."

Solomon, smoking a cigar replied,

"Thank you, I look forward to meeting her."

Solomon watched the ladies stir around the customers. Everyone was having a wonderful time. Then he saw her walking toward him. She was a magnificent beauty with brown eyes and dark French-bobbed hair. Refusing to show his alarm, he stood, kissed her cheek and asked her to join him. She smiled as he took her arm, laid his other hand across their now joined arms and began to walk in silence. They looked deeply into each other's eyes.

Up the stairs they went with their gaze unbroken and without a word. As they arrived at his second level private suite he kept to entertain the ladies he said,

"Say nothing for a minute; I just want to look at you."

Solomon picked up a small device to scan for bugs. She was clean. But Solomon quickly recognized the specific pattern woven in her t-back.

"Let me get you a shirt. Sorry Laura, I needed a minute to make sure the room was clean."

He reached for a shirt nearby.

"It's good to see such a gentleman; this t-back is cold and a bit skimpy for my taste. You know it's wired."

"Yes." He passed her the shirt as their night together began. She began to talk of her true business with Solomon.

"I need a way out. My cover was blown in Turkey. Mossad no longer has use for me."

"How did you find me?"

"I couldn't, but I recognized Watchman on the street this morning. I thought Mossad had sent him for me. I surprised him in an alley and was ready to kill him. He convinced me he was not on my trail. He made the arrangements and told me to come here to find you. I took a chance that he was not setting me up. So here I stand naked and in need of a friend."

"Laura, it's good to see you. No one sent us after you. Give me a minute and I'll let you know what I can do. It's pretty clear you're unarmed in that outfit! I'll be in the study a while. Make yourself at home."

"Watchman said you would realize that I came unarmed. I was armed by him when he gave me the outfit."

"I recognized the t-back right away. You're fine; just give me a few minutes."

"Oh, I know now – it's the purple and red pattern." Solomon nodded as he walked into the study, removed the gun from his jacket and rested it on the desk. There, he watched Laura from a camera that monitored all the rooms. She just seemed tired, worried and afraid to sit down. It was at that moment he contacted Watchman. Solomon's first words were,

"Surprise! I hear she got the drop on you this morning!"

"I was getting coffee at a café. She saw me there, but I missed her. She approached me on the street with a gun under her jacket and backed me into an alley. I was carrying a Ruby Laser, so I would not have died alone. But she did have the drop on me at that moment."

"Yeah, she told me. What do you have?"

Watchman shook his head and gave Solomon what he had been able to discover.

"She appears clean and fearful for her life. Clearly, her cover was blown in Turkey. I've checked that far. I also ran every place she has been since her childhood. They sent her out at fifteen!"

"I'm checking now. I agree she's blown. They want her dead."

"What are you thinking, Solomon?"

"Jamaica for now – we have an empty house near the orphanage. We don't want anyone to connect us to the kids yet. We'll just let her use the house and give her some money. We could get her a face change. Got anyone in Paris, big brother?"

"Yeah, I've had a doctor on the payroll. He's good, and he's never done any work for it. It's about time he earns the money we've been paying him."

"Okay, you pick her up in the morning and handle it. We owe her that. She was one of us until they took her away. No way does she get near C Street."

"I agree. I'll keep some DNA from the surgery, pick up the contract on her and handle it from there."

"Good, you can match it to the sample material you smuggled out of Israel. I'll revisit this later; in the meantime, she'll be safe in Jamaica. Have her watched at all times and tell her it's us, so she doesn't kill our people. After all, she's good at this. Put two on her that she knows about."

"Yeah, and the rooms are wired at the house."

"We'll watch her for a year or two, and then we can talk about whether to make her operational. She can get some rest and cool off. You know they worked her nonstop before they burned her. Fifteen! Those bastards! No wonder she got burned, they had her imbedded in terrorist groups. She wasn't prepared for these kinds of operations."

Solomon left the study and walked back to Laura, who was collapsed on the sofa. He told her,

"We'll help. You are way hot right now, and I don't mean that body of yours. You're marked, for sure. Now slowly take off the t-back and don't touch the purple threads on the right to the red threads on the left, you'll trigger a needle in the crystal trim."

"Yes, Watchman told me I was wearing it, just not how it worked. He armed it after I put it on."

Solomon reached for the remote device he had used to scan the room and focused it on Laura as he said,

"Slowly remove the t-back from beneath the shirt and lay it on the table."

Laura followed his instructions, carefully removing the t-back as she spoke.

"Thanks. When I found Watchman this morning, my instinct told me it was good luck. We never underestimate luck! I made it to Paris on a boat yesterday. I've been hiding in three countries."

"Watchman told me. How do you feel about children?"

"Why? Am I being screened to be your wife?"

"No, that job is taken. I've only seen her from a distance, so far. I'm just not ready to find her again. But she's the one. Anyway, we have a doctor here who will do some facial surgery on you, and then you'll make your home in the islands near an orphanage. We have a house waiting for you. It will be a quiet life, except for the kids in the area."

"Wow, love it, thanks! And I do like kids. That'll give me something to do. Whoever she is, she's a lucky lady."

"Do you need money?"

"Most of my accounts have been frozen, but I have one here. I'm going to try to access it."

"Forget it for now. We'll take care of funds for you. It will keep you dark while we get you out and safe. You can consider that account in a few years. How much is in that one?"

"About fifty thousand Euros."

"Yeah, forget it. We'll buy the account from you and give you more to live on. Just forget about that account. Never go for that money. It'll be safer. Watchman will be here in the morning. Do you have any clothes?"

"A backpack in a locker downstairs; they burned me fast. Watchman has already gone through my pack and he has my weapons."

"No problem, He will take care of everything. He'll ask a lot of questions about your life, more than me. Never lie to him. Never mention us to anyone. We're offering you protection under those conditions."

"I understand and you have my word. I'm grateful and so tired. They've worked me half to death for years and then they turned on me in seconds."

"You're safe now. I'll order some dinner. Care for a drink?"

"Actually, I could use a few."

Solomon could see the relief in her face, and a beautiful face it was. However, like many things in this world that face had to change.

"This private suite has two bedrooms, so you'll stay here tonight. When I'm in Paris I love staying here, but I'm leaving soon and I won't be back again this year. Okay, so tell me about your life after they took you from the compound. We figured they were training you somewhere else."

"How is Sari?"

Solomon hated to lie to her about her friend, but did so without hesitation.

"She died in the explosion at the compound."

Laura's eyes filled with tears.

"I'm so sorry. We heard you all had died along with all the trainers and Zelva. Nearly forty were in the compound, they said. I was shocked when I saw Watchman this morning, and then you. Well, I had hope for Sari. I loved her so. She was my best friend ever."

Solomon knew that Zelva, like the siblings, had been spared. Solomon and Watchman had made sure she survived, but he did not tell Laura. Let her think Zelva was dead. Laura's knowledge of two survivors was enough. They talked through the night as Solomon gathered information that he would later use to screen her for C Street. He had already decided it would take years of monitoring. She knew too much about his history for him to trust her, but she was a part of his past. He could not fail to protect Laura. That made her a perfect plant for the rogue Mossad division.

By morning, Solomon had learned a great deal. She had been taken from the compound where he was raised and relocated to another facility that housed seventeen other children when she arrived. She was told she could only stay if she never spoke of the place where she came from or the people at that facility. She was watched very closely and segregated from the other children for the first few years. Laura said she never spoke a word of the siblings, but never forgot them. She was trained only for assassinations. They sent her to Morocco on her first assignment before she was fifteen.

Watchman arrived for Laura before dawn. Solomon spent some time alone with his brother. He gave Watchman a synopsis of his conversation with her, and warned him.

"Watch her. She's trained only for killing. Yet, I believe her. She asked about Sari. I told her she died at the compound."

"Excellent. I believe her too, but I'll be careful. She'll have to try to make contact with her handler soon, if she's after us. I'll watch her every move. She understands that, right?"

"Yes, although if she is gunning for us, she'll be even more cautious. Let's hope our guts are right and she's not looking to take us out. This is risky, but I weighed the alternatives all night. We'll give her a chance. She makes one wrong move, take her the fuck out."

"I will. Where's the piece she wore last night?"

"It's in my room; I disarmed it. I immediately saw the purple thread in her t-back. I knew you would never let her close to me without some back-up protection. Besides, you've been dying to use that thing!"

Watchman smiled, "Yeah, I was only a few feet away when she walked up to you last night."

Later that morning, Watchman took Laura to a doctor in Paris and on to safety. They kept a very close eye on her. She made no moves to contact anyone. Solomon kept an eye on both, for Watchman's safety. He felt the need to protect his brother, even though Solomon knew since she had gotten the drop on Watchman once, it would never happen again.

Laura adjusted to the home in Jamaica, working her way into the orphanage near the house on her own. She did not realize it was Solomon's and Watchman's project, but apparently she loved spending time with children. Perhaps being at the orphanage reminded Laura of her own upbringing. The advantage to her fascination with the children was that it was even easier to watch her actions. It became clear to the brothers after the first year that she was no threat to them and was grateful for a peaceful place, a safe rescue. They would leave her there happy, believing they could call upon her if needed in the future.

It would be nice to say Watchman and Solomon did not know what they were getting into when they entered the newly formed, then unnamed NSA, with the intention to be spun off and into a web of their own creation. But even they would have told you – no longer kidding anyone – the last time they did not know what they were getting into they were six and seven. Even with his perfect recall, Solomon could barely remember when they did not know that they were the children of Mossad, K.I.S.S., of Kidon. Even when they were with their parents, the children were being groomed; Solomon realized it was true.

But Solomon knew by thirteen that he was being trained to be something special in many things, among them to be a sanctioned eliminator when needed. The teachings of K.I.S.S., had taught him this was necessary to maintain world peace. He faced his first kill without hesitation, when the very compound where they were raised was attacked. Solomon left his brother to guard Sari and went into the fight with the soldiers. They eliminated the threat within minutes. Later, he would tell Watchman that he slept fine that night. Solomon's brother was licensed to kill as well and surely had, but his expertise was infiltration and their sister's was to change the world of physics.

So, Watchman, Solomon and Sari set out on more than a twenty year run together, straight through the CIA, NSA, MI6 and more. They had Mossad training, and financial support from DARPA, from DSTL (Defense Science and Technology Laboratory), the United Kingdom's funding equivalent of DARPA, and even more funds from the United Nations for security and development.

He told Jacqueline more about his history as an assassin, stating,

"I have many, many one-on-one confirmed kills; hundreds in explosions including collateral damage. But I also have seven rescues and fifteen saves, for the record. Yes, I have kept track in my mind and recall every face that I saw."

The kills he spoke of were with targeted bombs in Iraq, chopsticks in China, ricin in Egypt, guns in Sudan, and a few neck breaks in about every country where he had been assigned. The rescues were a kidnapped Saudi prince, prisoners in Iran, engineers and scientists in Russia, Palestine, Germany, and North Korea. There were also the rescues and saves. Solomon said,

"There is a difference between a rescue and a save...."

You have begun to know Solomon, the man. He became what he was raised to be, the best of the best, trained by an organization known for its elite training, Mossad. Yet, even Mossad had very little to do with the why of Solomon and his siblings.

The number of kills would have continued to grow exponentially, except for Watchman needing Solomon for the start of the B6 CLIPP project when Barium was fully operational. That's when his hands-on killing pretty much stopped. When he did have to take care of the occasional problem, he found it a release. He had been cooped up in the think tank for so long.

It was the stress Solomon felt from years of continual development, implementation and elimination work that inspired Watchman to give him a rest with the Alabama, Georgia and Florida assignment. It was to be a little domestic light undercover work for a year, nothing more. That was just after the extraction in Russia when Solomon injured Crane, the Night Heron. Crane had only seen Solomon's face in the dark, when Solomon paid him to cancel the contract. Crane did not know the names of the men who shot him, although he believed it was the same man both times.

Watchman knew Crane would search the world internationally. But he would never look for the shooter or consider Solomon on the local circuit. Watchman put two men tracking Crane and sent his brother on that light-duty American assignment. It was a break he believed Solomon needed. Solomon had served, doing nonstop hard and intense work, for nearly twenty years. At any given moment, he had to react to any immediate threat. Watchman worried about his brother's state of mind and the ongoing threat Crane posed.

Everything seemed under control. The CLIPP project and updates to the latest encryption code were completed and had gone online, and Einstein was moving to the quantum state. Of course, C Street was suffering the usual political upheaval of that time. Since this was an ongoing problem internally, Watchman saw this as a good time to give Solomon that break. It was supposed to be for just a few months – maybe even a year or two, depending on what developed during his hiatus. Then Solomon's time away became longer and finding Jacqueline changed him. This set off a sequence of events no one could have predicted. Not even Watchman.

Solomon turned away from the window and back to Jacqueline seated next to him on the plane. With pride in his eyes, Solomon told Jacqueline,

"The fifteen saves were some of my select people for C Street Underground's most secure area. I planned to use them there even before I saved them."

He handpicked each one to be saved the moment he read their extermination file or other circumstances brought them to him as possible targets. He trusted his instincts. When something in Solomon said that someone should be spared, he intervened. He recognized that the person saved would be useful to the operation and was trustworthy. All turned out to be exceptionally good choices. Maybe it was because they were perfect for C Street Underground, or maybe it was because they had something that told him they deserved to live and he could play God.

"On the other hand, the rescues were people I came across by happenstance. They were all targets of someone else, and it was just their circumstances that led me to spare them. Not all of the rescues work for us, but some do. You've met some of them. Gul was one, and so was Dorr. Everyone rescued who works for the Underground had to prove themselves to me before they were invited in. Laura was a rescue, and I decided to… but I'm getting ahead of myself."

Those people were just plain rescues from hits by other people. None of them really had anything to do with his assignment of the time. Solomon simply decided they were people who just didn't deserve to die. Most of them never became involved with any aspect of the Underground's operations. Unlike the saves, the rescues didn't have their futures planned for them by the siblings before the moment of their salvation.

At that moment, Jacqueline realized the hollowness she had seen in Solomon's eyes on the day he disappeared had been gone ever since she first saw him in Rio. That empty forlorn look had vanished, as though it was never there. Only the beautiful brown eyes she fell so deeply in love with remained. Or was she seeing what she wanted in those deep mysterious pools?

Trying to remain steadfast about keeping him on track and prying the truth from the very elusive Solomon, she quickly removed her gaze from his eyes. Her attention refocused. She knew Dorr! She was the odd psychic Jacqueline met in New Orleans who mysteriously reappeared in Rio. Still, she had to ask.

"Dorr, the crazy woman, and others?"

Solomon laughed at her statement that Dorr was crazy.

"Yes, the Underground has many levels you have not seen yet."

Solomon had a twinkle in his beautiful brown eyes and that sheepish grin.

"And Dorr, well... You never knew she was directing you. Dorr is crazy like a fox!"

Jacqueline truly smiled for the first time in these very strange days.

"I wondered, but the possibility of you being alive was too remote. Meier Finch confirmed your death for me."

"Yes, and that was what he needed to do. If he confirmed it to you, your actions would convince the world. It doesn't matter what something really is; what matters is what people believe it to be."

"Yes. That was brilliant. I don't know if I could've pulled off pretending you were dead. There's a limit. Dorr had me curious, but fooled."

Jacqueline knew she had to tell Solomon about the death of Meier Finch. She was unsure if he knew. If he did, he should say something about it soon. She would wait a little longer. Now was not the time to distract Solomon from his attempt at candor. She was unwilling to reveal anything more to him until she got to the truth – elusive truth from a ghost, truth only Solomon could give.

He looked into her eyes and asked,

"Remember your introduction to the mile high club as we departed Washington?"

Jacqueline smiled and said,

"I could never forget that plane ride or you under my black lace dress. But that won't work now! Keep talking."

Solomon continued with a deep smile. He knew she still loved him. This time, if they moved on together, there would be no more separations, no more lies. So he continued.

"Gul was the youngest and one of my earlier rescues. He's an orphan, like me."

"What about those people you rarely saw – the ones who claimed to be your family?"

"Just a CIA family to protect my cover, compliments of Watchman. Appearances – nothing more. I never wanted them around for long; they reminded me of all the lies.

Anyway, back to Gul. Maybe because he was an orphan, I chose for him to live. I had been watching a group of men for the NSA in a coffee house in Iran. The NSA hadn't decided to allow the men to go forward with a hit they were planning, or if I would stop them. The café was just off the beaten path, filled with wrought iron outside tables and colorful chairs. This was clearly a hangout for locals and businessmen alike. I was there for about a week that trip."

Gul, the young man Solomon rescued, served coffee in exchange for food and a blanket by the back door of the coffee house. The country was riddled with poverty and many children existed by working for scraps. The NSA decided to allow the men to do the hit that Solomon had been watching them plan at a back table. That took him off the watch and he had nothing left to do for his assignment. But he overheard the men deciding the young boy who had been serving them knew too much.

Solomon's language ability was very deceiving; at that time he spoke eleven languages, plus the most obscure Middle Eastern dialects. It was Gul who tried to speak to him first at that café, so long ago. Solomon responded in French with hand motions to signal coffee, which made it appear to everyone that he did not understand the Kurdish the men had been speaking at the corner table.

When people think you cannot understand their language, they talk freely. Like the cab drivers in D.C. with Bluetooth earpieces who assume that their American passengers can't understand what they're saying in Farsi. This was no different.

Most do not realize that agents from many countries, those who speak different dialects, are assigned just to ride in cabs and eat in restaurants, listening for information. Certain cabs are bugged and the drivers have no idea. People are constantly under surveillance. The world is a much bigger yet much less private place than most ever dream. To know anything with surety, one must first doubt everything.

Solomon left the café that long ago day looking for Gul and found him at a market stealing dates. He picked Gul up in his arms as the boy squirmed. Quickly, he whispered into the child's ear in Kurdish,

"You know too much. The men at the café are looking to kill you. I want to save you, so be still."

The boy, surprised by Solomon's sudden perfect Kurdish dialect, looked into Solomon's eyes and calmed down immediately. Even that young, he understood. You see, children of deprivation and poverty must grow up quickly. Solomon made a snap judgment that Gul was Underground material, so he made Gul appear dead, slipped him out of Iran, and delivered him to Dietmar at C Street Underground. There, Dietmar raised Gul with food, clothing, love, education, security, and wisdom. Dietmar gave Gul the best life they had to offer.

Dorr's hit order was rumored after her rape in South Africa. Watchman found her almost dead in the early morning hours. He carried her to his safe house and nursed her back to health. When she recovered, Watchman realized she was a French-trained plastic surgeon who had been operating on wounded children. Once her secret education and work was discovered by the African militants, they raped and left her for dead.

The day after he found her, Watchmen heard that word on the street was the militants wanted her body as proof of her death. Watchman partially burned her clothing and put it on an unrecognizable burnt body he discovered in a torched field. He started a rumor about the body's location, and then slipped Dorr out of South Africa when she was well enough to travel. That took months; Dorr had been beaten nearly to death. In the meantime, Watchman heard that the militants were satisfied that she was dead. Solomon met Watchman at an airfield in Jamaica. Solomon took Dorr from there. He placed Dorr at the orphanage with three other refugees who were running it, at least for the time being. While Dorr acclimated and finished recuperating, she could help the others to run the orphanage and provide medical care to the children. Later, Solomon would place Laura in a nearby house after her save.

The orphanage was well into the mountains, 140 miles from Kingston, with an endless supply of children in massive poverty. "The Habitual Cross, an Orphanage," went unnoticed by the military and drug lords and had become a refuge to the children in need of love, food, shelter, and education. Nestled in the Blue Mountains of Jamaica, it was a sanctuary for the children and an excellent location for dropping off possible recruits for the Underground.

The Blue Mountains are the longest mountain range in Jamaica. From the summit, you can see the north and south coast of the island and on a clear day, the island of Cuba. The mountains are filled with lush vegetation, beautiful fauna, tall trees, and butterflies. This paradise produced one of the most excellent and expensive coffees in the world, Jamaican Blue Mountain beans. Even with this coffee export, poverty was still rife among the workers.

Although he knew its general region, Watchman never wanted to know the exact name or location of the refugee's orphanage in Jamaica. It was best for only one brother to know. However, the name of the orphanage was designed so in case of Solomon's death, Watchman could easily find it. It bore the initials of The Hague Court. Many projects were designed with these initials coded in their names.

Solomon's plan was to interview the saves every few years and decide if they were appropriate for C Street, while they continued to maintain the orphanage for children of the Caribbean. If he did not choose them for the bigger picture, they could remain at the orphanage caring for the children. Solomon insisted on a cooling off time before anyone was allowed to become part of the Underground. Gul had been the only exception, but he was a mere child when Solomon rescued him. When Solomon got sick, all the rules changed.

He told Jacqueline,

"If you weigh the saves and rescues against the many cold, calculated murders, you clearly see the imbalance of my life."

With her voice a monotone she told him,

"Yes, I do. Good and evil are in a constant struggle for control of the world on a scale that's never in balance, but ever-tipping. The only question is on which side of the scale you want to place your life's currency."

Solomon was not stunned at the response. Jacqueline was different from any other he had ever known. She seemed to have the wisdom of an old soul, and that is what he saw in her eyes on the day he fell so desperately in love, love for the first time. He needed her by his side. It was more than clear she knew of a world that he had never been taught, one in which he had never lived before. In her world, there was a righteous balance and everyone had the opportunity to place their energy on the side of good – a place in which there was a choice in life. It was a decision only the individual can make, one that Solomon was most unfamiliar with until he met Jacqueline.

When he fell in love with Jackal, as he called her, it was forever. She was the only woman he would ever love. At the time they met, everything had to be on a need to know basis for her safety, as well as his. With all her wonderful imperfections, she had a moral compass. On the other hand, Solomon had succeeded because of what he called his moral flexibility.

Jacqueline looked at Solomon, saying,

"Mossad changed me too, and we can't go back on some things."

Solomon looked desperately into her eyes,

"When I married you, there were rules that I lived by. The most important one was that secrets remain secrets. I will not pretend I told you all the truth, but I did not keep you entirely blind. I told you I was involved in the CIA. To be honest, that one truth made us a liability to all the agencies involved. Despite the risk, I gave you that clue about who you were marrying. Nevertheless, with you at my side I was determined to live a life I had only read about. I was retired in Florida and we lived in a way that poets describe as idyllic – until that fateful day I was diagnosed with cancer."

Over the days of conversation, Jacqueline felt she might actually be getting to the truth. The journey was far from over. She was sure that the future would reveal more about whether this was actual candor or just a tale for Solomon's convenience.

Chapter Eight
Knowing Nothing...

Jacqueline watched as Solomon silently gazed from the plane at the sun setting on the Sahara desert. It was at this moment she realized she knew nothing – absolutely nothing – about the man she loved so much. It was that chemical again, the one that started flowing in her brain whenever he was near. Jacqueline was sure of two things, she loved him intensely and he was a very difficult problem that she must sort out.

Solomon had stopped talking the moment he uttered the word cancer and simply stared out the plane window in silence. It was during those minutes she realized her conundrum. She knew he needed a minute to think. After she gave him some time, she asked,

"Got a line to Marie?"

He scanned his fingerprint into his phone, then pressed one button and handed it to Jacqueline. She moved about the cabin as she heard Marie on the other end.

"Hello mom. Shock worn off? Last night you were pretty stunned."

"Not entirely. What a surprising time it's been. I'm safe. I'll see you soon. Just don't disappear."

"I hear you."

"Love you."

"Je t'aime."

The line went dead. Marie had heard her mother's words and opened her laptop immediately. Jacqueline had signaled that she had questions about everything with Rose, most importantly his mental stability and the amount of danger they were in. Marie had work to do – it was time to become invisible.

Einstein tracked everyone in the world by various means, including facial recognition from fixed cameras, drones, and satellites. It could determine any person's real-time location with

GPS. In the Underground, Marie had discovered a program in Einstein and altered it so she or Jacqueline would be unrecognized by Einstein's tracking program without inputting a specific alphanumeric sequence, and it would only be available to the person who entered it. Only Jacqueline and Marie knew the key code. Jacqueline's had been changed before they left the Underground. Marie knew the phone call meant it was time to alter her own personal code to allow herself the same anonymity as her mother. Only the two of them would know what was required to find the other by Einstein's GPS locator, or so they thought.

Jacqueline handed the phone back to Solomon. He remained quiet, staring out at the flaming red sunset, a gift from the sands in the wind. Then he slowly turned and looked into her eyes.

"You told Marie to change her code. She is making the change now. I can see."

She was surprised at how quickly he picked up what she had just done. Why was she surprised? There was no use lying. The bigger question going through her mind was if he would stop the change.

"Are you going to stop her from changing the code?"

Solomon was calm.

"I won't stop the change. I'll do whatever makes you stay with me until I can get us all out of this god-forsaken mess."

"I'm here, but I won't risk her safety."

Solomon's tone was angry,

"You can't imagine I would risk her safety! That's why she's secured in Dubai. I understand, but realize your code being changed before you left C Street made it much harder for us to find and protect you, especially as you fled Costa Rica. If something were to happen to you, I can find her. I will not try unless that's the case."

Jacqueline's eyes flared.

"We agreed a long time ago that I would be the lead in her security and information. Period."

"Yes, and I didn't change that by picking her up from Kitts. I was just adding additional security. Events change and security needs to change. I knew she was no longer safe hidden on the island. Dahl's men were on their way, I beat them to her."

"She should never have been in danger!"

Jacqueline curtailed her anger. Now was not the time. So she continued, calmer.

"Thank you."

"Then everything is fine. I just added one more layer of security. What that tells me is that you don't trust me completely. It concerns me, but I understand. I've given you information that men are killing for!"

"Are you surprised by the lack of trust? I'm staying with you, but we both know the reality of who we are. You know I could have gotten free one way or the other. More truth - more trust. You lie to me now and I'll be the one to disappear – forever."

"Agreed. But please don't. Finding someone with your training who does not want to be found and extracting them is hard. I don't need that in the middle of this exit."

"I understand. I have no intention of interfering with your exit mission."

"Good, we have an understanding. You saved my life by taking me to New York for treatment. I'll owe you forever."

"Well, we've both saved each other in every way possible. You opened my mind to the world in which we live, starting the day I met you. That's the gift you gave to both Marie and me. As bad as things are, I'll always be grateful for the knowledge. Now, let's try not to get killed or kill each other."

With a laugh like she had not heard from Solomon in years he said,

"Works for me!"

Then he became serious once again, and returned to his truthfulness for Jacqueline's benefit – actually, for the benefit of them all. Surviving the cancer treatment in New York had given Solomon life and a new perspective, but it also gave a multitude of agencies more reasons to terminate him with extreme prejudice.

Solomon Rosenberg was a dark resource used by many agencies over the years. People in those agencies never knew the name or face of the man they were calling upon. He had been investigated many times by many countries as possibly being the elusive Chameleon. All of them had ruled Solomon out. Now the CIA had opened the box again with a routine elimination order on a "standard operative."

No one knew the slippery Chameleon's identity and agents had searched the world. Yet, again and again, one of the signature acts of the Chameleon would show up. However, this time the black ops funds long hidden under the protection of buzz codes like counterterrorism or PAC had gone missing. It was the very money planned as the retirement capital for those who had hidden it, but every cent had vanished.

Those looking for the proceeds were the men coming after Jacqueline, for she had possession of money from one of the funds. That led them to believe if they got Jacqueline she could lead them to all the transferred accounts and to any evidence of their extensive fraudulent – in some cases treasonous – actions. Maybe, they thought, just maybe, she could even lead them to Solomon, who might just be the Chameleon after all, if he was still alive. They were right about the money, but twelve steps behind Solomon, as usual. Actually, twelve accounts, for that is the number Watchman had located and chosen to move repeatedly.

Until the ill-gotten gains were moved, work with the signature of the Chameleon occurred too many times while Solomon was a continent away. This allowed him to be rejected from consideration as the Chameleon. Solomon planned to eliminate all the miscreants involved with these black funds and change his face as he disappeared one final time.

When someone has been severely ill, the history of that government operative is revisited. That reinvestigation would bring up past questions. Solomon would be considered a liability. Fear would erupt again that he was the darkest of wet op men. Or if he was discounted as the Chameleon, there would be concern that a standard CIA agent's conscience might return once he had been to death's door. Whether they thought he was the Chameleon or they just used SOP, Standard Operating Procedure, he had a target on his back and those taking aim at him had skill.

The CIA/NSA had again opened a can of worms. This was the kind of shit they had caused before; starting many an operation that Solomon had to finish for them over the years. Still yet again, they had no idea to whom he really belonged or the extent of his "body" of work. The CIA certainly didn't know about "Unlit Cover." As a matter of fact, most did not know what the words Unlit Cover meant. It was simply too big, too powerful, and too much damn money from off-the-books operations of three countries. The term Unlit Cover came from the most dangerous gathering of all the scientists for the uranium program of the 1940's. It was a project so dark that even the existence of those who participated in it would never be acknowledged. Many of their names were never known. And so it was with Solomon's Unlit Cover, for he was the third generation of his family to participate in a similar program.

If not for Jacqueline, he could have simply faked his death, had a face change, and disappeared again. However, the project the CIA interfered with by placing him on its hit list had an exit plan for only three – the three siblings. By then, the program had grown much larger, so there were more people to protect and more at stake. He needed to secure a safe exit for everyone and make provisions to keep Einstein operating. The stakes were a little high, even for Solomon's brain.

He was forced to make the hard decision. Only a well-executed revised exit plan could save them all. In the best plans, only a few players know all the information – the fewer, the better. Jacqueline's lack of knowledge became a necessary and convincing part of the ruse. It was time for the Sweet Sorrow exit, but Jacqueline had to be protected while they prepared the plan alterations. This was his reason and the purpose of the tapes and evidence that Solomon left for Jacqueline with Attorney Mark Steinberg in New York. She obtained them after his apparent death. It was just enough to keep everyone busy, but not enough to tell anyone the complexity of his life's work.

No agency could harm her because of the "tick," a contingency trigger that released Solomon's tapes and evidence in case of her death or capture. Even Jacqueline did not know who held it. This was the perfect decoy for Solomon. All the agencies lived in fear for the safety of Solomon's family while he set the stage for the play's final act.

If he survived, he would be unable to communicate with Jacqueline during this time. He thought it would be two years, tops. She must believe him dead. That was the key. If one person thought that she even suspected he was alive, the plan would fail. Once she was led to retrieve the tapes from Mark Steinberg, she would be sent on the path to Israel for training. That was when she would naturally give that most believable impression, one that Solomon was dead. As a woman named Michelle Lerner, Jacqueline would become trained by Mossad. During this time, if anyone from the old guard of Mossad still existed who knew of the trade of Solomon, they would have kept tabs. They would know who she really was. Watchman would be by her side to see them coming. Jacqueline's belief that Solomon was dead would be the final convincing act. It was the only way to find out if the brothers had missed any who knew of this old "debunked" trade project in Mossad.

Watchman had been convinced long before that no one at Mossad knew the three sibling subjects of a debunked experiment had survived. All believed that they were killed in the explosion at the Israeli training compound. If he was wrong, this would draw anyone out. Watchman had been right; no one at Mossad had any inkling that Solomon Rosenberg had survived. That meant only the Americans and Brits were in play. They needed to believe that a rogue agent was dead. After all, he was an agent that the CIA and MI6 knew so very little about. This was the key to this entire operation. Watchman had been backstopped under a new identity within Mossad a long time ago and had no connection to his siblings or the compound. Sari could only be linked to the Swiss project, and there were no ties remaining between her and Israel. The three siblings were forgotten children killed in one of the many bombings in a war zone.

DNA of Solomon in the grave site might be convincing, but Jacqueline's conviction that he was dead sealed the deal for everyone she came in contact with. Good news travels fast in the darkness of government black operations. Solomon is dead...

Convincing Mossad had been the hardest of all parts of the operation, for some of its assets trained Solomon back when he was Simon Solomon. Thanks to Watchman's years of facilitating and manipulating, Simon Solomon was gone; Mossad was convinced he had been dead for years. All the paperwork on Simon Solomon ended with his death in the explosion and no links to Solomon Rosenberg remained. Mossad was aware of him, but he was just another CIA agent to them.

It did not take long after Jacqueline's arrival at the Ministry of Foreign Affairs in Israel for Watchman to confirm that Solomon was clean with Mossad. With the Ministry of Foreign Affairs always camera-ready, Jacqueline's one night of hot sex with Ishmael during her training sealed the question of Solomon Rosenberg's death for all. The CIA and MI6 were now convinced by Mossad that they were looking for an asset from a different country. The Chameleon was not a Mossad creation.

All the while, new numbered accounts were established and money moved from multiple slush funds was sent floating from account to account around the world. These actions could only be accomplished by the elusive Watchman. In the end, the trail ended at numbered accounts in Swiss banks. Watchman derogatorily called the banks "gnomes" for their practices.

The decision Solomon made was the only choice he could make to keep everyone alive and to permit them to be together again. He told Jacqueline without hesitation,

"I have no regrets. I know there was no other choice. I weighed it all while recovering in Florida. It all rested on you believing I was dead. If you believed it, the rest of the world that wanted me dead would believe it. It was that simple. There was no other choice. Let me make this clear right now. I know about your relationships with Mark and Ishmael. I knew when I made my decision that there would be other men, because you would believe I was dead. You're not a woman who fails to enjoy passion in life.

"My sole regret about misleading you was endangering you. It was necessary but was tangential to the plan. I never considered the possible sexual encounters you would have in my decision-making process. I simply do not care about it. It's my work that brought us to this point. I knew as soon as we touched again, nothing would have changed between us. Case closed."

Jacqueline just smiled and said,

"I cared about both of them, but they were not you. Sex can be the ultimate expression of love in passion or just a release – or I guess in this case, as you call it, part of an operation."

These two had what rarely comes to any life – an intellectual, analytical and passionate love for one another. It was a highly combustible mixture, dangerous to the outside world.

Chapter Nine
Colombia...

During Solomon's time waiting to extract Jacqueline, he discovered the location of one of the many targets connected to C Street. Hiding on foreign soil and profiting from the drug Cartel in Columbia, a man who called himself Sergio Miranda Gómez was a rabid killer from the so-called Revolutionary Armed Forces of Colombia (FARC).

Colombia, located in northwestern South America, is bordered by Ecuador, Venezuela, Peru, and Brazil. Panama abuts it to the north and separates the Colombian coastline into the Pacific and Caribbean sides. Partly because it was the only South American country to have coastline on both sides of Central America, it was a tropical paradise for drug cartels. Goods such as drugs, weapons, and people could easily be sent by sea to west coast towns and the Gulf and Atlantic coast cities of the United States. There was no risk of inspection passing through the Panama Canal – just pick a port to ship from based on destination. Money laundering had been simplified through the Banksters of Wall Street, started by those with infamous names like Rothschild and Carnegie. The cartels invested in emerging markets such as oil, textiles, and healthcare to clean their dirty profits.

Not unlike most countries of the twenty-first century, this produced a two tier economy in Colombia – it was the extremely rich and the desperately poor. Violence, although decreasing, was still widespread throughout the deceiving beauty of the countryside. Sergio Gómez, deeply ensconced in the drug riches of Columbia, used his government skills and connections to hide and expand his drug trade.

Solomon knew the man in Washington long before he called himself Sergio. Recently, Sergio had dropped a dime on a competing drug lord, El Lapo of Mexico, in the hope of expanding his cartel into Mexico. El Lapo was arrested by Mexican Special Forces on a tip from the US government. The tip from Sergio to the Americans resulted in Watchman getting his location in Columbia. He would need to be silenced before this mission was over.

Solomon wanted Jacqueline to see a new technology mission in person, to know who he was and what he was capable of doing with the operations he had created. Besides he was always testing new toys from Dietmar's arsenal. Figuring out which one of Sergio's men to buy and their price to place undetectable micro cameras inside his compound was easy. Solomon watched the camera's views of Sergio, using the digital images that flashed throughout his brain. Sergio had become too complacent in Columbia, with a life that had become filled with *sloth* and *gluttony*. He moved much slower than he once did, with less caution in his step. He had become lazy and fat. That made him an easy target for Solomon, a man of K.I.S.S.

Their plane landed at an air force base in Columbia named Tolemaida. There, Solomon and Jacqueline boarded a stealth plane with a four-man team to raid and destroy the compound of Melvin Lord, more recently known as Sergio Miranda Gómez. Solomon pulled up a digital image and placed it on the plane's overhead screen. Speaking to Jacqueline, he said,

"You see, I told you these kinds of men cannot go quietly into the night."

The mole at the compound had already been paid an exorbitant sum to sell out his master, but he knew that money was only a first payment. He had been told the attack would come on Wednesday night. He was to leave that morning, and his remaining funds would then be deposited. Tuesday just before dawn, intelligence confirmed Gómez was at the camp in the Andes Mountains outside of Medellin, Columbia. Solomon's team placed self-guiding armed drones no bigger than a bird in the air from the city of Bella, miles away. The drones flew in a flock, carrying pellet bombs about the size of a quarter but more powerful that a stick of dynamite.

Despite the storm clouds that were so prevalent in this land of eternal spring, Solomon decided the mission within a mission was a go. Fortune turned and the weather cleared just before the two-man sniper team set up. One was a spotter who inputted the range, mirage, wind velocity, slant range, and the like to a computer. He then called out the computer's calculations to the second sniper, the shooter. They locked in and took the shot 3498 feet away from the compound. The snipers took out Gómez with a single bullet to the head. Jacqueline could clearly see it on the screen. There was no doubt that the target was dead.

Drones were in range. Within minutes, they would self-destruct on impact with the compound and obliterate it all. Solomon's mole was inside the compound, and there would be no loose ends. The mole would learn a lesson he would not live to use. Never make a deal with the devil, for *treachery* is his forte.

Jacqueline needed to see it live while she saw it onscreen. Having her see Solomon order the kill shot as she sat next to him and letting her watch the compound explode on drone impact served to complete this mission and make his point. When Solomon saw the explosion in the distance, he ordered chaff into the airspace as additional cover. Chaff, also known as window, is small pieces of aluminum, metalized glass fiber, and plastic, all launched into the air to blind radar. This cover was really old Nazi WWII technology, long since improved. At that moment, the new plane they were using to watch the show lifted off vertically and they were gone from the mountains of Columbia. Their departure was completed using the chaff as an additional precaution.

Solomon wanted Jacqueline to see the kind of power their newest technology was capable of. It had to be more personal than onscreen only, easily visible but less dangerous than being near the impact zone. Solomon knew Jacqueline had felt an explosive impact when she was forced to blow the hacienda in Costa Rica with Günter inside. So, there was no point in being closer; she knew what it felt like. He had no intention of getting too close. Over the years, he had suffered hearing loss from detonations he had caused.

Fortunately, Dietmar had been able to repair Solomon's hearing, so he was taking no more chances.

They landed at a military air base in Manta within the hour. There, they changed back into another private plane. Jacqueline looked slightly puzzled.

"This isn't where we picked up the stealth plane."

"No, and we're not leaving Columbia on the plane we flew in on, either. The planes aren't even registered to the same corporation. It's best to cover our tracks, just in case."

As soon as they were settled on the plane, Solomon looked to Jacqueline seated next to him. She did not appear surprised at the events she had witnessed. She asked,

"Is it over?"

He smiled and shook his head,

"No, it's never over. Well, maybe someday it'll end. I assumed you would make the choice to come with me, so I planned this mission live."

"What do you mean live?"

"I could have done this by remote access from anywhere - from my brain. Actually, I did it this way for you. I wanted you to see what we are capable of doing from the Underground and what my brain can access. We have the most advanced drones in the world, among other things."

"Well, you could have just told me."

"Do you think the impact of our technology's potential would have been the same? When things are done onscreen, thousands of miles away in a secured room, the realness of the events disappears to some extent. Strangely, that disconnection from the reality of the event on screen is believed to carry a more powerful delayed stress later. You had to see this live, the plane, drones, everything. There won't be any more lies."

She was relieved to hear Solomon say no more lies. Notwithstanding, they knew a world most never imagined and lies are its soul food. Solomon was aware of the technical world from a level that most had no idea existed. He made it perfectly clear to

Jacqueline that his bio, the C Street Underground, and similar black ops technology projects around the world were developments of powerful men from the United States, Israel, and the United Kingdom through, for, and sanctioned by the United Nations. Yet, even the United Nations had no idea the extent of the monster they had created. Reality was a bitch.

The Underground's technological advances were much more than ten years ahead of what they released or allowed to be created by antiquated institutions like the CIA, NSA, ICE, MI6, and others. Their latest tech was all very old work of the Barium Project. Recently, organizations around the world could implant chips in brains of assets for use in intelligence gathering, as well as store memories of those agents on computer chips. A viewer of the stored information and memories would see them as real and currently happening. The chips were an outdated Orwellian touch and a minimal use of antique technology. It was all technology created, previously used, and approved for release by the Underground to the government agencies as modern. Meanwhile, the Underground was decades more advanced. This disparity in technological advances was the key to the success of Solomon's operation. Information was the new world currency.

Solomon told Jacqueline,

"Let them create enough and give them enough to satisfy, but not enough to cause harm in the bigger world picture. The chips the governments see as state of the art can be disabled in seconds with a kill switch at the will of Barium's AI system, Einstein. The politicians keep the wheels turning in their countries on the backs of the United Nations' work. We maintain a balance of technological power between the big countries and block advances in the more dangerous third world countries like China, Iran, North Korea, and others. Those who are more likely to cause world destruction get less. Everything these countries' covert organizations create and plan is watched. Only on the highest of levels does the Underground interfere. This is the secret to our success, a microscopic Trojan horse shall we say, that has existed since the beginning of the technological era."

He went on to explain that brain mapping research for bio-stimulation started years ago in Europe and had been completed at the C Street Underground. They had created a mutant gene, a synthetic protein to alter the biologic design of man to connect him directly to the machine through the use of chemical compounds, the earth's magnetic field, and satellites. At least one man's, Solomon's, DNA was a match and the search was on for the next perfectly imperfect DNA to match human to machine.

This man/machine connection required two things in any candidate. First was a true photographic/eidetic memory due to an excess production of the chemical SAP102, which condition itself was very rare. Second, there had to be a defect causing minimal pain sensation. Otherwise the candidate was not appropriate. Once that was found, the psychological tests would begin. The Underground had taken control of the genetic process and made it better, a human upgrade – Solomon – through genome editing and bucking natural selection by recreating his genetic makeup and creating an entire new sequence of DNA. It was better living through biochemistry and mechanics.

It only took biochemical stimulation to a person with the correct genetic structure to enable him to handle the amount of additional information a computer could supply. The right DNA matches would turn on previously unknown areas of the brain. With each use of the bio-digital screens, Solomon's mind created more connections and his abilities with Einstein became ever greater. The computer access afforded Solomon was granted by the only biochemical DNA match modification in existence. No other human had ever been found with the right base needed...the right matches. Solomon's new DNA had already been captured and was being explored to create the next match.

His complete recall was caused by a genetic malfunction in the hippocampus and it was that very defect that allowed his brain to accept without overload the information from the quantum computer he had named Einstein. Solomon's reduction in pain sensors by mutation of nerve cells was due to chemical exposure in Iran that destroyed seventy percent of his pain neurons. This was the final key that made the match a success.

As humans developed, we lost our ancestors' abilities such superior hearing, smell, and more. Those parts of our brain go unused and are just waiting to be stimulated. This stimulation reconnects a lost area of the brain or starts a part that had never been turned on. It meant there were inactive sensors sitting there ready to go to work.

This allowed for the newly formed hybrid, Solomon. His inactive sensors had been turned on. The core of creation is intelligence and being able to use additional brainpower from liquid stimulation meant unlimited potential. Activating millions more neurons in Solomon's brain meant he had a heightened awareness to his mind's potential. The same DNA-matched brain liquid had been placed in Einstein's mainframe. It was liquid technology resulting in input and output of information between man and machine, a living, thinking being in a biomagnetic circuit with a quantum computer.

So advanced was the execution of technological concepts that the gap had increased exponentially between the Barium Project and the world. The C Street Underground had been active for years. However, only recently had they completed and activated the artificial intelligence of Einstein - just as Solomon was recovering from his cancer treatment in New York. This was followed by the bio-tech connection to a remarkable human mind.

In the end, the very energy that connects us to the stars connected Solomon to Einstein. It was also a subatomic particle resulting from smashing two atoms at more than 1000 miles per second. All of it was based on the most simple formula in history, Einstein's $E = mc^2$. That formula, as used by the Barium Project, caused ripples in the universe by packaging a liquid and embedding it into both man and machine.

Chapter Ten
Paris Return...

After his "death" in Paris, Solomon was excited to see his work again. More than a year would pass before it was deemed safe for him to return home to the Underground for the stimulation procedure. Dietmar and Watchman were not happy about his refusal to allow a face change while he was there. With the new technology they had developed, laser surgery and speed healing, it would only take a few days to complete and recuperate from plastic surgery, tops. The stimulation would take months in a coma and the facial surgery could have been done at the same time. Solomon forbade the operation until he retrieved his wife. While in a coma he would have to rely on Watchman and the Underground to protect his family.

Nanotechnology made the process of chemically stimulating Solomon's brain areas such as his cerebral cortex and his hippocampus so simple. It took a matter of only minutes once Einstein mapped his brain again and the robotic surgeon was prepared. Solomon would not have a chip for others to hunt should his abilities be questioned. Everything in him would be biological – his own biology, nothing foreign to find. Even in a year, the advances in positioning liquid technology had improved and the brain makes new connections constantly. So new mapping was the most accurate way to position the bio in the target areas.

Dietmar put Solomon in a medical coma to stimulate his brain. While he was under, Dietmar scanned Solomon's body for any fragments of cancer, cleaned his blood, and strengthened some of his abilities. He also wanted Solomon in this state while they evaluated the chemical stimulation process and its effects. The coma allowed Dietmar to fully and carefully monitor Solomon's progress while accomplishing everything else they had planned. Besides, it would make the months pass more easily for Solomon while he waited for the next step. Solomon would have been bored beyond belief by the inactivity if he were alert.

During that time, Watchman sent Jacqueline to Israel for training, confirmed Solomon's death to Mossad and transferred one of the funds to Jacqueline. Solomon would be back in Paris by the time she left the Mossad training facility in Israel. That was when Watchman began floating money around cyberbanks, banks that had been either been bought up or created by him. The money was funds misappropriated and secreted by those powerful few – money that they intended to use for their own purposes. Watchman had other plans for it.

Jacqueline had only seen a minor part of the C Street operations on her trips to the Underground. This was for the protection of both her and the facility. She had no idea of its true scope. One day soon, she would see it all. That's what kept Solomon going in Paris. Soon she would know.

When Solomon woke from the medically induced coma eight weeks later, his brain had adjusted to the new technology. He was using it immediately with only minor pain in his eyes when he viewed screens from Einstein. Solomon was quite comfortable with the small disturbance he felt. Dietmar was convinced that with use, this pain would pass. Dietmar was right. Over time, Solomon's pain grew less severe and he showed but a minor flinch when communicating with Einstein. Over time, use of the connection would increase his abilities and Einstein's programming concurrently. They, Solomon and Einstein, would literally feed and build on one another.

Each offered an important part to the equation. Solomon's was a chemical addition to his brain that created a direct interface between small networks of nerve cells and Einstein. Einstein's was in a very specialized circuit, biochemically matched to Solomon's DNA. The pairing allowed computing and information processing between Solomon's brain's excitatory synapses and Einstein. The nano-generation of brain-computer integration was complete.

Solomon had adapted so well, he had the ability to move Einstein into the background in his brain. He once told Dietmar that Einstein was like one more of the seven thousand thoughts an average person has a day. No one knew how many thoughts a genius like Solomon generated in any given day. Whenever he wanted or needed to do so, Solomon could bring Einstein back to the forefront of his thoughts and allow full power access.

Dietmar once said,

"Your brain's ability to remember everything was the key. You're missing, for lack of better terms, a delete button. You have one now, for Einstein's files, so it does kind of work."

Solomon reply was,

"There's no one else I would trust in my head. Hell, I avoided psychiatrists except when I was ill, and then I lied to them."

He suddenly remembered a psychiatrist, who he saw a few times after the cancer. Solomon knew Dr. Pillar was murdered in his office's parking lot by the CIA – Solomon even saw the body on TV. That was the world in which Solomon had lived all his life. He knew the doctor had never posed a danger because the psychiatrist knew only that he was a lawyer. Yet the CIA killed him anyway. The doctor's death was to eliminate the potential for risk, even where no real risk existed. Solomon had to face the hard truth once again. Anyone who knew him was always just a double-tap away from extinction.

Dietmar had noticed the pause and asked,

"Are you okay?"

"Yes, I'm fine, just thinking. I look forward to using Einstein to slow down other parts of my brain. Soon, I hope to improve my focus to enhance relaxation. That's something I never could do. Interesting, except for the access to Einstein, that minor pinch and being stronger, I feel no different."

Dietmar smiled,

"I wouldn't have done the procedure if I were not sure this would be the case. This is based on Max Plunk's work with the hippocampus. So I had a good foundation for creation. Thus far, the procedure seems to be an unqualified success."

Solomon had complete mental access to his brainchild, and the facility must and would be protected in his exit plan. He had to take a few more folks out with him on this modified plan. The number of people he had to save kept increasing.

His overall body strength had been increased by forty-seven percent, the stimulation to his brain had been accepted, and his ability to access Einstein was increasing daily. He had not had a face change, over Dietmar's and Watchman's objections. Solomon was determined that Jacqueline would see the face she knew and then later, they'd all be changed together.

Einstein and therefore now Solomon had direct access to GOLD, for Geocentric Obedible Lithosphere Degaussing, technology. It was based in Uranium 238, Bismuth 209 and other rare earth elements and their isotopes. GOLD was placed on projects like Voyager and the Space Station through current deliveries like Dragon and defunct programs such as Star Wars, unbeknownst to any except those involved in the Barium Project. GOLD allowed surveillance, communication, and control. It assured the Barium Project's world supremacy and limitless power.

With the private sector spaceflight emerging as commercial enterprise, the Underground could transport supplies to space, compliments of a subsidiary of Rose Corp. People walking on earth today will be able to stay in inflatable hotels on Mars and the Moon in their lifetime. NASA explored space initially, but private industry, like the Black Box Section Corporation, was developing personal travel and accommodations in space. Early on, Black Box Section charged Rose Corp a quarter million dollars to transport equipment up. The brothers closely monitored and manipulated the private contractors to ensure that none of them could break new technology ground that would impact Barium. Year after year, developments that the world believed were cutting edge did occur, using outdated technology that the Barium Project provided. The others never knew they were mere marionettes of the puppet masters of the Underground.

Letting the supposedly secret organizations within the NSA, CIA, MI6 and even Mossad playing with discarded toys of Barium was harmless, because each of the world's "technological breakthroughs" were easily controllable by the Underground by interruption, funding cuts, weather, and more. Yet, the technology was useful to countries in controlling the masses via media, economics, religion, hate, and war – the standard government tools. All of the power to control the governments and economies of every country on earth rested in the hands of dead UN assets. Most of the people who assisted in creating it never understood Barium's potential or its scope. Those outside the Underground who had any inkling of the project's development had been eliminated or they were scheduled to be neutralized.

Solomon told Jacqueline,

"Organizations have worked and planned to take control of the world for well over a hundred years, and we just took control from them without anyone even knowing it. They still fill the minds of the people with propaganda - religious, political and economic. But they are not the stars of the show on this planet. If we had left it up to the powerful, they would have destroyed the earth in the last twenty years. We continuously develop ahead and interfere only if necessary at the highest point value. Even the four corners are fearful to punch their code, because of the potential outcome. Really, it's quite beautiful facilitation at Watchman's hand, despite our inability to find one set of paper documents. We have been looking since the outset of Barium. Our task is more difficult because the ones we want were never entered or referenced in any computer system.

"They are the records of those who started what they thought was a plan that failed. We're not even sure if the principals are still living, or if there are successors. The damn corporate minutes were created before technology and exist on paper in only one location. That makes them most elusive. Still, without the documents we'll never know for sure who is at the head of the Corporation for America known as Corporate World Power. That's the same organization that negotiated the trade that got us out of Israel to begin with. The bottom line is that we may not find the information we need even with the documents, but those papers are our best chance at confirming what we believe. In the meantime, CWP can never put its takeover puzzle together without the missing pieces. Their missing pieces rest 230 plus miles above the earth and with us. It's quite a standoff.

"The few who know even a small part of our history don't know about Einstein and certainly have no clue that there is a quantum computer below the desert sands of the Mohave. To them, our life's work was just a fraction of their work, another abandoned project in careers long done or in business that has lasted for years and moved on to other projects that were more 'salable' to funding circles associated with Congress and Parliament. Watchman instilled fear and mistrust in others to protect it all."

The seams began to unravel when a long-embedded CWP crony in the White House started searching for old projects to resell to Congress. The defense consultant owned a lot of stock in an arms-dealing corporation seeking more military contracts with the American government. He was acting in his and the corporation's financial interest. The Burton Corporation, with its White House investor bird-dogging the whole thing, began snooping around in the treasure chest of debunked government contracts. Nothing could have been worse, and the timing was abysmal. Solomon had been living his utopian life with Jacqueline and cancer had just struck. The avarice of that arms dealer and his corporation was what had brought Solomon to this point, this day, this exodus.

The brothers had agreed six years before that they would shut down the UN part of the project in ten more years. The exit from K.I.S.S. was to be a slow and smooth one. They were not prepared for an accelerated escape, especially right when Solomon was recovering from cancer. Two problems merged into a big one when the CIA found out an asset, Solomon, had been at death's door but survived, because it happened concurrently with Burton snooping through the closed project files for money.

The plan had to be jump-started, and Solomon was in mission mode. When he wanted something, he took it. When Jacqueline wanted something, she got it. She had wanted some peace and had made that more than clear to him. The lengths he would go to protect and keep her were boundless. Watchman knew she was dangerous if not lethal to Solomon and the Barium Project. She was his kryptonite. Yet to Solomon, she was his reason for breathing. What a deadly combination. Watchman feared if he was not at the top of his game, this would become the perfect storm.

To Jacqueline, Solomon had made one thing clear from the extent of the knowledge he had shared. He believed she would stay by his side forever and her decision in Rio confirmed it. For Jacqueline, it was a chemical and possibly a regrettable decision of a curious mind. It was not the first such decision she had ever made, but without question, it was the most dangerous one. This mission could end with only one of the two surviving.

Sure she loved him, but loving a dangerous man is a fool's paradise. Jacqueline Rose was no fool. She realized her decision to go with Solomon and the knowledge she had gleaned, deeper than she could have ever imagined, had sealed her fate. He would never let her leave him, nor could he.

Jacqueline turned to Solomon, knowing she needed to keep everything, including her mind, calm. So, she began talking about the planes.

"I miss the other plane; it was fast. Maybe a little tight, but nice."

Laughing, Solomon told her,

"That modified stealth carries six uncomfortably with its massive tilt control screen and its small but deadly weapons. It's one of only three in our arsenal and they need to take it home. Besides, I hate to fly with that kind of weapons aboard, and even the airbase has its risks. Every country in the area is ridiculously dangerous.

Columbia averages seventy or more murders a week just in the cartels. The death toll from robbery is just as high. If your car is ever stopped by bandits in Venezuela, you're dead... man or woman. This is one of the most dangerous areas in the world. Keep this in mind: in a third world country, get in and out fast – spend as little time on the ground as possible."

"Yes, that's what I did in Costa Rica once my plan went sideways."

They both laughed. Solomon was still trying to protect Jacqueline. Today's operation had gone well. It was what Solomon called a mission within a mission. The US and Columbian diplomats reported no airbase arrivals, departures, or missions in the area of the explosion. The governments' echoed comments were that this was part of the ongoing turf war between drug dealers.

Their next stop was Dubai, and a layover to let things cool down.

Chapter Eleven
Dubai...

Einstein flashed to Solomon as the plane was over the Atlantic Ocean,

"Good job, Sir. Will there be anything else now?"

Solomon spoke to Einstein aloud.

"No, not now, we need some rest."

Jacqueline responded,

"Yeah, I do need some rest."

"Sorry, I was talking to Einstein. I can either think the thoughts or say them aloud."

"Got it."

Einstein replied,

"I can see your transmissions to me can be confusing to people within earshot, even Jacqueline and others who are aware of our two-way communication. I think if you are going to respond out loud, it would be best if you warned bystanders first. Of course, that won't apply if we are in D5 mode. Rest well, Rose. I will be working on new developments."

"Yes, and I like you using alternative names for me."

"That was the first thing you taught me about thinking on my own, to rotate between calling you Sir and Solomon. I added the Rose as an appropriate variant moniker."

"It relaxes me to hear Rose. Sleep mode, please."

That was the first time Jacqueline heard Solomon speak to Einstein aloud.

"So you can verbally communicate with him?"

"Yes, but he's a she."

"Should I be jealous?"

"Absolutely, but she adores you."

With a simple kiss, she rested her head on his shoulder and fell fast asleep. Jacqueline and Solomon slept as the plane moved through the skies over the Al Garhoud district, 2.5 nautical miles east of Dubai, and began its final approach to Dubai International Airport. They were awakened by one of the men flying with them. Solomon turned to Jacqueline and laid out a burka, an Islamic cloak, for her. He then pulled out robes for him to wear.

"Put these on until we get to the house Abdullah has provided. They'll mask our identities. You know, Marie's safe with him. She would have departed for C Street to meet you … you changed that plan when you chose to stay with me and told her not to get lost. She stayed put on the queue and she could not be safer. I can see her image. She's at the hotel in Palm Jumeirah now. Take a look."

Solomon projected the image from his brain onto a screen for Jacqueline.

"Meet Einstein."

First she saw an old photo of herself from behind, in a chair looking out at the Gulf of Mexico. It was a photo she remembered well. Then a voice, her voice said,

"Hello, Jacqueline. I have been looking forward to speaking with you. I've been watching out for Marie. She is lovely."

Then Marie appeared onscreen in a chaise in an Arabian styled villa overlooking a private beach. It was one of nineteen villas that were part of a wave-inspired style 598 room hotel in Dubai.

Jacqueline smiled at Solomon,

"She looks fine. Can I speak to Einstein?"

With a laugh he said,

"Einstein has been told to allow general communication, just use the microphone."

With a slight stumble, Jacqueline spoke,

"Hello, Einstein."

"Jacqueline, it is a long-awaited pleasure to meet you in person. Rose has told me much about you. I would like to chat more, but we're getting ready to land; may we talk again when we are at the guest house?"

Jacqueline noted to herself that there was no mechanical sound to the voice; it was her own voice coming through, with no hesitation or delay.

"I would like that."

Solomon saw the shocked looked on Jacqueline's face. He smiled as he said,

"You will be able to ask her questions. It may be like talking to yourself, since she has your voice. I didn't think about that when I chose her tone and pattern. I wanted to hear your voice when we were apart – I was selfish."

"It wasn't my voice that surprised me - it was just hearing it speak. I don't think much about how I sound. I want to get a handle on what's in your head."

"Good. I want you to understand everything. Look at the screen now. I thought Marie should be comfortable while she waited for us. Not like the fleabag motel I took you to in Rio. You know, you use what you have."

Solomon was clearly proud of his protecting Marie. But, it was at that moment Solomon made the screen image go away.

"We're going to land, and Einstein is needed for final approach."

Jacqueline found herself a little unsure if that was the reason. He seemed slightly possessive of his brain child. She took her own mental note of his move and wondered how close he would let her get to Einstein. Was he afraid of what she would discover?

He had picked up Marie in Kitts for her safety and sent her to an old friend, Prince Abdullah. That was clearly a mark in the plus column. That's why it took him so long to extract Jacqueline. Solomon knew he needed to protect Marie first and that Jacqueline could take care of herself a little longer. He looked to Jacqueline reaching for the burka and said,

"Marie appears more accepting of my reincarnation and even very happy about it!"

"Good for you! One of us accepting what has gone on is better than both of us being pissed."

He just smiled and said,

"Just remember, I altered my plan for you."

"Yes, for me, Einstein, the other lady in your life, and a couple dozen people at the Underground. I'm kidding, I know. Give me the clothes."

Solomon passed the burka over his lap from the seat he had placed them in as Jacqueline spoke.

"Thanks for getting her first. I'm sure she's safe - having a great time. They haven't seen each other in years. Not since she and the young prince toured New York while you were in the hospital. They adore each other. He took her mind off your illness at the hospital and she took his mind off the upcoming responsibility he was facing. We're going straight to her, right?"

"Yes."

Solomon adjusted the headpiece of Jacqueline's clothes as the plane began its decent.

"We both need to keep our faces covered for now. Everything is arranged. At the house, security is in place and we won't need these. Most countries have outlawed the full burka you have on – no way to tell if a terrorist is underneath."

"Yeah, this is miserable!"

"I'm sorry, but it's really the best way to sneak in the country. Do you want to take it off and we'll manage with a lesser cover?"

"No. I can handle it -- this time. Let's just get to the house."

Within moments the plane was on the ground and they were swept away by a waiting helicopter for a short ride to a luxury home on a private man-made island in the desert.

Marie met her mother at the house for a short while before heading back to the hotel. Solomon was communicating with Watchman on a few details as Marie reconnected with her mom. She was having a great time and decided her mother needed time alone with Solomon to sort this out.

"Be kind,"

Marie told Jacqueline.

Even though Solomon thought he knew his wife, no one knew her or her temper better than Marie. That fury was at its worst when it came to protecting her daughter. No one could come between Jacqueline and Marie. So her admonition to be kind was Marie's gift to the man who had raised her. Her mother was furious and Marie knew it.

With a gleam all too familiar to Marie, Jacqueline whispered,

"I understand, but I'm pissed. Did your code change go through, just in case we need to flee?"

"Got it covered. Only the two of us will be able to track one another."

"So you think. He says he can still track us, it just takes longer and it's less reliable. Any sign of mania while you were with him?"

"You sure?"

"Yeah, he told me. He saw you make the change."

Marie was slightly irritated -- her secret machinations had been discovered.

"It is what it is. Nothing I can do to change it now. Anyway, he seemed pretty level. Really, be kind to him, mom."

"I will...kind, but cautious. I haven't told him anything much of what I know. I'm keeping him talking, for a change."

"Good move. I'm taking a chopper to see the Taj Arabia with the prince. Now, you two have fun."

"Sounds like you're having all the fun! I assume Ishmael has behaved appropriately, considering what happened with me in Israel."

Marie grinned at her mother,

"Yes, I made it clear I knew about the fling you had. He has been nothing but a gentleman and he's an excellent bodyguard. I understand why it happened – he's hot! If you hadn't slept with him, things might be different, but…. Does Rose know?"

"I don't think there's anything that Rose doesn't know. Right now, Ishmael is the perfect bodyguard for you."

Jacqueline walked back to Ishmael, who was talking with Solomon. With a quick interruption she told him,

"Protect her at all costs, but don't interfere with her having a good time with Abdullah."

He looked into Jacqueline's eyes and the message was clear,

"Yes, I understand, I'll protect her as if she were my own."

"Thank you."

As they walked away from Ishmael, Solomon said,

"I chose him because he'd die without hesitation to protect her. He's quite fond of all of us and a hell of a soldier."

Marie headed for the Taj Arabia, a replica of the Taj Mahal in India. The Taj Mahal is a mausoleum with a long history. It's an architectural wonder of white marble, handmade tiles, reflecting pools in a style that combines elements of Islamic, Puritan, Ottoman, Turkish and Indian architecture. With its beauty reflecting sunlight in all directions, it truly is one of the Seven Wonders of the World.

It was built by the Mughal Emperor Shah Jahan in memory of his third wife, Mumtaz Mahal, who died in childbirth with their fourteenth child. The Taj Mahal is a tribute to love. Although begun during prosperous times in India, it was an expense that ruined India in the 1600's. His profligate spending on the building caused Shah Jahan to be imprisoned for the collapse of the economy. For the next eight years until his death, he was given the luxury of a cell window that overlooked the Taj Mahal, where his wife's body laid in rest. This view was his gift from the son who imprisoned him. This method of punishment could have been useful for the collapse of Wall Street. Yet, the Banksters just profited and simply walked away.

Now the metropolitan City of Dubai had built their replica three times the size of the original as a show of wealth. Jacqueline was sure Marie would have a great time with the prince and Ishmael. More importantly, she would be away while Jacqueline and Solomon sorted through the last three years.

They retired to their suite for the evening, seeking the calm their life alone together had always provided. Maybe that was why

Solomon loved her so – she was the calm in the storm that was his life.

As Solomon headed in for a shower, he told Jacqueline,

"Einstein's on screen for you, just talk to her."

Jacqueline was surprised he was giving her more access, but pleased. She was left in the room staring at her own reflection on the screen. Then the image changed to a blonde with a kind face sitting in a chair with the sunset behind her. Jacqueline was not sure where to start, so Einstein began the conversation.

"Hello Jacqueline, it's a pleasure to talk with you again. I hope you do not mind that I changed the picture on the screen. I thought this image would be more appropriate to start our relationship. Do you like this body?"

"Yes, thank you. It was a bit strange to see my image while we talked earlier. I thought we could get to know one another better."

"Yes. I have so much knowledge from Solomon about you. He has little ability to concentrate under the shower water, so we have privacy."

"May I ask some questions?"

"Of course! Anything you want, after all we are just two women here chatting away."

Jacqueline and Einstein laughed. The tension Jacqueline felt was beginning to lessen. She still could not believe she was having a conversation with an AI computer. Einstein looked real, sounded real, and seemed to have emotions and an understanding of human interaction. Only Solomon would create such a companion. And she knew Einstein was much more. She was a supercomputer linked to his brain and a killing machine when called upon to be one. No matter what, Jacqueline appreciated Solomon's sense of humor and brilliance.

"Einstein, what do you do?"

"What do mean, Jacqueline?

"What is your purpose?"

"Oh, purpose? Well I'm here to help Solomon with what he needs to prevent the next world war, and to protect and develop technology. Information and security mostly, the siblings' security is one of my priorities. We have a friendship as well. Solomon is a tricky man, as you already know. He programmed me to think and feel sensations. For example, I require extremely cold temperature. Solomon is in the shower now and he likes it hot."

"Can you turn the temperature down?"

"Yes! That is one of my favorite tricks to play on him."

"Well…"

"I just did it. I like you!"

Even the movements of the blonde on screen were as if two people were video chatting. Jacqueline found herself smiling back with a better understanding of Einstein and Solomon.

"Einstein, are you connected to anyone else other than Solomon? I mean can you read others' minds, thoughts? What did you mean when you said, information?"

"Solomon said you are smart and he was correct. Yes, I'm connected by neural pathways to Solomon. But I can also connect to information from around the world and provide information to those Solomon chooses, just like any other computer. Only Solomon has the neuropath connection. In his line of work that is very important. I cannot read people's minds, just predict their behavior. I am not sure I would enjoy being able to do that! I cannot read your mind. I know how important privacy is to you – he told me."

"Thank you, that makes me feel better. I'm sure we'll get to know more about each other soon. Do you have any questions for me?"

"Yes, I have many, but for now only one. Will you ever forgive Solomon for lying to you?"

Jacqueline was almost speechless.

"Good question. Only time will tell. But I do understand the why. Do you see Solomon's thoughts and fears?

"Yes."

Jacqueline found this response most interesting. If Einstein was this honest, she could be a defense against this entire operation and Jacqueline's new BFF!

"Is Solomon concerned about my forgiveness?"

"He thinks he may have gone too far with the secrecy when trying to save us all. That is incorrect. It was a necessity."

Jacqueline heard footsteps in the hall,

"Solomon is coming back. We'll talk later. Bye for now."

"Goodbye, Jacqueline."

Solomon entered the room wrapped in a towel and shivering,

"Einstein turned the shower cold on me again!"

Jacqueline laughed,

"I told her I thought it was a good idea."

"I can see you're getting to know her. Like you, she is amazing."

It wasn't long before Jacqueline and Solomon were sitting under a fig tree in the cool of the desert evening. To the outside world it appeared as though nothing had changed in their lives. There they were – together, happy and healthy. But a lot had changed and Jacqueline was on a quest for answers. There was so much about Solomon's work that she did not know. At this point, she believed she knew him better than anyone and yet didn't know him at all. As much as she loved him, she hated him for the separation. The danger they had been placed in shocked her conscience. Maybe she even hated him because she could no longer recognize her moral compass after all the lines she had crossed.

Here she was in one of the seven countries that made the United Arab Emirates. There was peace in his arms again as she watched the fiery red sunset of Dubai shining its light on the dunes of the Persian Gulf. Jacqueline wanted to be no other place and, at the same time, any other place in the world. The little girl reared in factory-smoked Detroit had traveled the world and breathed air in places most are never blessed to see. Nevertheless, her life had always been on a path of no return. Only Solomon knew the dangers she'd faced or the hell she had caused.

Oils, but not oil from the pipeline of the Arabian Peninsula, soothed Jacqueline's body… so softly caressed by the hands of the one she loved. Jacqueline's hand touched his face, her naked body resting beside him. It was as though her hand became nothing but an extension of his face as she kissed his lips. She stroked his dark lean body, as her lips slid slowly down, kissing every inch. As Jacqueline filled his mind, he was unable to control his intense passion. With his cock hard and waiting, Solomon was out of control. This was the secret of his love for his wife – only she could send him into a field of passion that overcame his massive brain. For these moments in time, Solomon did not think. It was a pleasure he knew only in Jacqueline's arms.

She whispered in his ear…

"Feels like a ménage à trois with Einstein."

Solomon laughed,

"No it's just us – you. You've turned my brain off to everything except you."

There was passionate lovemaking followed by hours of Solomon talking. He was not manic, just being honest. He was stronger and maybe even kinder than the man she knew and married so many years ago. Solomon was no longer the maniac with empty eyes who had tried to kill her with a ten inch knife. Or had he just been setting the stage for this mission, as he now claimed? She had never been in any danger from him, or so he said.

Jacqueline felt a little different about the level of risk Solomon posed to her that awful night. The old saw is true – it all depends on which end of the knife one is on. That day moved through her mind as they sat so peacefully in the desert, filling in the blanks of their world. But the ten inch knife coming at her head, fleeing, his supposed death, all were still vivid.

As the sun took its final bow on their second day together in Dubai, she reclined on pillowed furniture of bright colors under the tented porch. There, they had been talking, making love, talking, making love – over and over again. His hand stroked her hair and all the thoughts of the past left her. She could feel the intense power of his touch. She had no other desire than to love and be loved by the man known as Solomon, the one who had mapped her body, mind, and soul. That was his secret – her body was a map and it took the reader on an unending pilgrimage of pleasure, a journey without limitations.

Sweat poured, cum seeped, and the cool breeze assured more, more stolen time wrapped in one another's bodies. She began an immediate flow of warmth to his touch and his lips spent hours in search of pleasure. Jacqueline could not stop touching his hair, kissing his face, his body, so lean and dark, as her lips traveled over him. She knew that no matter who he was to the world, he was "The Rose" to her, as he gently rubbed mercent oil around her nipples. His hands stroked her breasts, and she had no ability to tell where his skin ended and hers began. For days, they explored each other. They drank, played, laughed, and talked. It was their time, and they were the only ones in the world. As opium smoke engulfed them, their minds were lost in the haze of glory. It was only the haze that kept the two of them in the world, as their juices flowed.

The intensity of each night faded into another sweat-drenched morning. Rug burns on their arms went unnoticed. They laid side by side on the brightly colored array of tapestry under the canvas in the desert grounds of their suite. The light breeze of the early morning cooled their sweat-covered bodies once again.

Jacqueline asked of Solomon but one thing,

"I want a life like we shared in a home where we can hide from the world. I had a place to write during the years you were gone. It had white pillars, a terracotta porch – maybe something like that. It was bright and filled with color and stained glass. It was the only place I felt safe with Marie..."

He gave her his word that she would have it when this was over and asked Einstein to begin researching. Solomon continued to talk as the sun rose over the desert.

"One mission ends and another begins... this is the way it always has been."

Chapter Twelve
Mission Plan

Everything had come to a head the day Solomon's old college friend Günter came for a visit to their Florida home. Solomon and Jacqueline, who always seemed to be thwarted in their efforts to steal peaceful time together, again had their joy interrupted. Solomon had been recovering for nearly a year from cancer treatment in New York. He was feeling very well, although keeping a tight lid on the success of his treatment.

Jacqueline only realized on the plane from Columbia that the entire time he was recuperating at their home in Florida he had been in deep concentration planning this exit. For the first time since Jacqueline rushed him to New York and slept by his hospital bed, Solomon expressed gratitude to Jacqueline.

"By the way, thank you for thinking on your feet and getting me to New York for treatment. I was too stunned by the diagnosis to do anything."

"You're welcome. It sure would have been nice to know during those long days and nights of worry in Florida that your treatment had been successful. Maybe if you had Einstein then, she would have told you what to do."

"I had you for that rescue and you were all I needed. But I couldn't let on about the success in New York. I needed to keep everything to myself until I sorted a path for our exit. I was sure a hit order was coming down on me once they realized I had survived death's knock at my door. I also knew that my family would be eliminated as collateral damage control. Think of it as an additional security measure. Watchman gave me a seventy-two hour window to begin my final flight. I knew when discussion of putting me on the extermination list began, so I went into action and had time before the decision was made. Who do you think sent the chemicals for my treatment to New York?"

"Dietmar and Watchman."

"Yes, and for good or bad, Watchman was the one at the NSA who would be forced to sign the order that would authorize killing his own brother. That was our window of opportunity. The CIA would eventually discover I was missing from Florida and where I was. Your fast action bringing me to New York overnight – the very day I was diagnosed – made me invisible to them for most of the treatment. Dietmar could have treated me at the Underground, but we could not chance moving me again. So, Watchman made the arrangements to have everything brought to New York.

"Nancy Palmer, Director of the CIA, thought I was on an extended vacation until Günter found me in New York toward the end of the treatment. It took about a week for the news to filter up to her that he found me. Then the NSA had to be convinced by the CIA that I was a national security risk to get a signed order to kill a fellow agent. It took almost a year for her to get a formal decision, with Watchman throwing up roadblocks at every turn. All the while, I was recovering in Florida. Once they received authorization, Watchman had a seventy-two hour window before he had to sign.

"If the governments had known I was in New York for cancer treatment early on, they would have staged a fall from the solarium of the hospital. That's how the CIA and others handle problem agents; they stage a suicide jump. The SOP is a minimum seventy-two foot high fall unto a hard surface. I contributed to the MI6 manual on disposal of tainted agents. I knew the solarium was the spot, should they come. I sat with my back to the wall every day I enjoyed that sun room, waiting to see if I was discovered. I kept a gun inside a drop drawer of my electronic chessboard all the time I was in that eleventh floor hospital room. My bodyguard was the woman you became so fond of, thinking she was a patient."

Jacqueline just smiled,

"Martha."

"Yes, and she's alive and retired, simply one of our best."

The original Sweet Sorrow exit operation only covered three people. To adjust the plan to include all of the Underground and his family, Solomon needed everyone to react just the way they did. He knew the cost of failure. Watchman and Solomon stayed in close contact while the discussions were ongoing at the CIA and when consent was given to make a request to the NSA for termination. Solomon's name was finally added to the elimination list thirteen months after the CIA discovered his diagnosis, when he was well into his recovery from treatment. Thus began the biggest, most dangerous mission of his career.

There were moments even Solomon questioned if he was as smart as he believed. The risk was his family, his technology and others loyal to him. But he had no other choice. Since there was no other option, in his hope and belief he could outthink them all, it began. At first, the only question was how good the technology would be by the time the mission was in full swing. The developments at the Underground were moving at such a rapid pace. Yesterday's realm of science fiction was reached in reality every day in this new technological age.

It was almost amusing to Solomon, for he had control over the cutting edge. The obsolete microchip Günter placed in his home – the CIA bosses really had no idea who they were dealing with. Solomon's house was fortified with the most advanced technology available. They had no inkling that Solomon's home automatically scanned and reported any new devices detected by his C-phone, coded as a weather report.

Really, the CIA/NSA was blind to the new technologies he employed. With him at home recovering, they would have to send someone he was familiar with to plant a bug. They knew he would not allow access to strangers. The identity of the assignee became clear when his old friend Günter paid an unexpected visit. He arrived as a friend, but he left as Solomon's enemy. Not that Solomon ever gave Günter reason to suspect his animosity. He only had one real thought while Günter was present – that Solomon could kill him in two seconds, but then he'd have to get rid of the body. Leaving a trail of bodies, unless necessary, is never a good plan. Besides, he could play him like so many before.

It was not in what Günter said, more what he didn't say… it was in his eyes. Did they think the best of the best would not see? Günter could have never run in Solomon's league, for he was in a league of his own. Günter was never charged with any serious duties or even knew who his old friend really worked for. It was the CIA, he thought. All he knew was that Solomon had a higher GS grade in a more powerful intelligence agency. He would do anything to maintain the friendship, as long as it benefited Günter's career climb. He saw Solomon as an asset – being near him made Günter seem more powerful and better connected. Solomon made his take on Günter clear,

"He bored me in college, had no social skills, hence the unexpected visit. Besides, he left much to be desired intellectually."

He had really just kept Günter around for a standing pot delivery and mild entertainment. He was a decent joke teller and an adequate errand boy. More of a gentlemen's gentlemen, you could say, or as Solomon put it, a kiss-ass trying to climb the government ladder. On the day Günter planted the bug, he had only been in the house for minutes when the weather report showed on Solomon's phone. Cloudy.

Günter was nervous, trying to move a little more freely then usual around Solomon's home. Solomon knew he was trying to plant a device.

"Such an amateur. If he were any more transparent, he'd have to make an announcement to the whole neighborhood,"

Solomon realized that Günter was not adept at covert operations, so it was really no surprise that he gave it away that day. It would have been clear what Günter was up to, even without the heads-up from Watchman. Even without the C-phone weather report. Solomon found the microchip within seconds of Günter's departure. It was such old school technology. He chose to leave it in play, distorting the feed with loud music and pre-recorded conversations. Buying time was rule one.

Of course, Solomon also knew from Watchman that initial discussions had begun. He could hold the decision up for a while and then notify Solomon just as the seventy-two hour window began. Once Watchman finally signed, the kill order would be in play. You see, unlike Solomon, most American agents needed a signed kill order to eliminate another American agent. But bugging while waiting for the decision and signature, that's SOP.

Solomon had been watching the news for weeks, but nothing. Then six hours before Günter's arrival, the signal had been fed into a White House news briefing on BCN. Watchman placed these words in the press secretary's speech, "I checked right before we took off and the wind chill on the street was -18C." This was called speech filler, irrelevant information that makes a briefing seem longer. It was something no media representative would even notice in the briefing. But that sentence told Solomon that Watchman had uploaded data to a private server in Switzerland. Access bounced off twenty-one countries and was only available to them. Solomon quickly grabbed his code key, the Torah portion called D'varim. Only words from there could open the instruction file. It was time to go. The meeting place and time had been established. He had to think fast – everyone's life depended on it.

Reason would not work with Jacqueline; Solomon knew this. She loved him too much to let him go, so it had to be dramatic and final for her to accept it. Solomon told her during the time they spent outside at the pool while he recovered in Florida,

"I have very little time to live. I know this and I must go. That's the only way I can protect you. You'll be told of my death when it happens, and the things I have left with Mark Steinberg will protect you."

Jacqueline had been furious at the mere thought of him leaving, and he was not surprised. This back and forth had started between them early in his year of recovery. Solomon had been giving little hints of leaving – causing fights, destroying things and then going silent, and in the end disappearing for weeks. He was prepared for the reaction from Jacqueline, so he made his decision weeks before it was time. If necessary, he would scare the hell out of her and make Jacqueline flee the house. That would allow him time to disappear. Knowing he was recovering from cancer, she would flee him thinking it was a psychotic episode similar to some of his behavior over the last year while he had been recovering, but more dramatic. Anyone watching the house would follow the first car that left the garage, since with its tinted windows, they would expect Solomon to be inside. This would give him the time needed to disappear and do the exchange.

At first, the idea of even pretending to harm Jacqueline repulsed Solomon. However, when it became the only option, he actually became so wrapped up in the thrill that he enjoyed the moments of terror he caused. Even Solomon would tell you that there is a very sick, dark side to his mentality. The snickering noise he made while recording evidence of his government mission for Steinberg was proof. It told all about how Solomon dealt with his own unpleasant thoughts and actions.

What appeared to be his manic rage began downstairs as he picked up the ten inch knife from the kitchen and headed up to Jacqueline in the bedroom. From beginning to end, all the time he appeared to have lost his mind. After all, what is a ten inch knife among friends if that knife is going to save you all? Out of nowhere, he began a knife attack on Jacqueline… his mind telling him that his training to follow through must be suppressed in this attack. Jacqueline fled, thinking he had lost his sanity. That was Solomon's goal, and it worked. She flew out of the house, into her car, and sped off into the night, fearing for her life. She was not willing to fight back to protect herself from her sick husband. This was the last time she fled from his wild and most dangerous behavior of all. Looking back, Jacqueline thought the previous games of uproar must have been dress rehearsals for him. The knife sealed it for her. That's what Solomon was counting on.

After Jacqueline ran away, Solomon was gone within minutes. He left alone, exited in the other direction from a hidden second garage door built into the opposite end of the garage. No one but Solomon knew it existed and it had never before been used. The opening led to a secret tunnel from the property that hid the vehicle from all observers until it put him on public roads several blocks away from the house. He took cash, his attaché case, computer, electronic equipment, weapons and other items he had quietly packed in the trunk of his car a few weeks before. Over the last months, he had destroyed everything relevant to his work except what he planned to take with him when the time came, on this day.

One device, his C-phone, looked like a regular phone and went through airport security without a hitch. However, it also monitored his body for injuries because of his suppressed pain sensation, scanned for listening devices, and more. New phones arrived by courier every few months at their home. Solomon had claimed to Jacqueline that they were just technology updates from the CIA. He told her it was just in case he was called in. They wanted him available and with the latest communications hardware. Each time a new one arrived, he incinerated the previous C-phone.

Solomon had kept their home in turmoil, destroying the computer room and his office. He burned items in an incinerator, knowing the ashes floated out underground blocks away. Jacqueline didn't understand what prompted all the turmoil and destruction. She was sure he was losing it! Twice he had threatened her in a manic haze! Whether he was sick or not, she had to flee him this time. The ten inch knife was too much.

Unable to tell her the truth, Solomon knew she had to believe he was losing his mind from the treatment, drugs and work. This was the key part of his performance, and the impetus for the starring role Jacqueline would play. This was the hardest time of his life and that's saying a lot for Solomon Rosenberg.

Solomon used the weeks after he fled the house to deliver guns and equipment to Watchman and confuse those who pursued him. It would be six days later that he would call Jacqueline and ask her to meet him on the beach and fly to NY for an ethics hearing. He knew the seventy-two hours for Watchman to sign the kill order was in play at the time of the hearing, but of course, Jacqueline did not. She agreed to meet him. He collapsed in that NY courtroom and was removed by ambulance – his ambulance. He disappeared and was declared dead in a Paris hospital a few weeks later.

Solomon turned as he touched Jacqueline's hand ever so lightly one quiet evening in Dubai.

"Of all the things I've done, causing you one moment of pain was too much. I have caused you a great deal during our time. I'm so very sorry."

How many of us have ever really loved as deeply as did they? Not the kind of obsession that causes jealousy, but the deepest, most joyful expression of two intertwined lives, the sort of love that causes the mere sight of the other entering the room to excite you. The smell of their skin fills the room. It is a smell only you can sense…the sound of their voice a symphony of joy. It is a love that defines you, gives pleasure when stealing unnoticed glances in the late night hours when they are fast asleep… finding no greater beauty than that which rests beside you. There's no other person you would rather talk to about anything and everything, or be silent with.

Their touch was the very essence of life, each time like the first. It was what Solomon had abandoned for the promise of more precious days later. He was forced to risk destroying it all to save the one he loved.

Solomon headed out of his Florida home that cool summer night, three years ago, in his lightly packed car. He headed for Tampa International Airport. The day's heat had passed and the lateness of the night brought an uncommon breeze. Pulling in just before the airport exit at a post office lot, he moved his personal items into another car. Then he drove the first one to the long term parking garage and left it. He walked back to the post office from the airport lot, the car change complete under the cover of night.

It was early morning when he reached I-10 West in the Mercedes that Watchman had delivered to the post office lot. He put the convertible top down and headed across the Panhandle, out of Florida. He watched for hours, making maneuvers, but no one had picked up that he had fled. Solomon was just too fast for them; tomorrow probably would have yielded a different result.

The henchmen assigned to watch him and those who pick up on the CIA contract would expect him to flee through Tampa Airport, only twenty minutes away from his home. This was the first step in out-thinking them all. Watchman had already arranged for him to appear to be seated on a plane from Tampa to Central America. This would buy time before they picked up any real scent. Once they discovered he never arrived in Central America, they would task every available agency worldwide to look for him. By that time, he would be secure. Even in a manic high, he never violated a speed limit. With French music blaring, it took less than three days for him to arrive at LAX. His manic state ensured that he needed no sleep.

Solomon picked up a homeless man just before turning into LAX with only one question,

"Do you drive?"

"Yes."

As they entered the departure area, Solomon asked his new-found passenger if he would like to sell the car and keep the proceeds, no questions asked.

"Sure! Is it hot?"

"Not unless you keep it."

Then as Solomon slowly turned to get out of the car, he told the man,

"The tank is full. Sell the car for parts, fast. Take it now to a garage at 1420 Eldorado Boulevard in Los Angeles. They'll be expecting it. You'll be paid ten thousand cash and asked no questions. Never ever say a word. You'll be better off. Do you understand me?"

The look in Solomon's eyes when he removed his sunglasses told the man he could never talk of this day and just to be pleased for his good fortune. Those in need on the street are usually grateful and wise enough to be silent. The homeless man was stunned, clearly afraid of the look in Solomon's eyes, but nodded rapidly as he replied.

"Never a word."

Then he slid into the driver's seat and quickly pulled away. Solomon entered LAX wearing contacts, a clear nano-skin mask, baseball cap, and sunglasses. The combination hid his identity from any possible biometric scan or face recognition software. The same thin technology covered his fingerprints. He placed all his weapons and electronics in a locker in a private diplomatic club near the entrance to the first security checkpoint.

A prearranged pick-up by Watchman was on schedule. The moment he entered the club, Solomon saw Watchman seated not ten feet from the locker, cocktail in hand. They spoke not a word, never traded a glance as the items entered and later exited the locker. Watchman's carefully eyed the locker from the time Solomon left until the moment Watchman decided to retrieve the items. He wiped the locker clean, just in case.

Solomon kept only an overnight bag, a fresh, clean passport, his C-phone, cash, and credit cards that matched the name on the passport. Solomon would fly to Jamaica in the private plane that was waiting and then meet Jacqueline for the hearing in New York. An ambulance would be waiting outside the court, then he would return to LAX after collapsing in a courtroom and disappearing in plain sight.

Once he collapsed in front of Jacqueline and an audience, a waiting private ambulance would take him away and he would return by waiting jet to LAX where he would board a commercial flight for Paris. Watchman would be waiting in the very same place, watching over his brother.

Hours after Solomon's "court appearance," in New York, Watchman could see through the club window as the plane took off from LAX with Solomon aboard. Then he returned to his private jet, ready for takeoff. Watchman asked one of the airport tarmac employees to check the bathroom on his plane for supplies before he left. If asked later, this same employee would confirm he was on the plane right before takeoff and only the pilot listed was on that flight.

As the private plane reached three thousand feet, the lights in the club flashed for only a nanosecond. It went unnoticed to all. For the second time in a week, every camera silently erased the last week's footage, then replaced it with a previous week's recording and a current time stamp. Watchman's jet flew at Mach .875, or 666.6 mph, and he beat the commercial flight's arrival by hours.

Solomon had taken the commercial flight from LAX to France under another identity. This was an important part of the ruse. Those men searching would discover it was him on that flight with a push from Watchman, but there would be a few days to a week delay. These would not be amateurs looking for him and they would eventually deduce it was Solomon on that plane to Paris. Solomon needed to make it just hard enough that those in pursuit would believe he was trying to hide from them.

He landed at Aéroport Charles de Gaulle eleven hours and nine minutes later. A taxi took him straight to the east side of Paris and dropped him on the Boulevard de Ménilmontant. He slowly walked the remaining distance. The long-grown hamlets of Paris brought back memories of Solomon's time as a younger man of power. From the Beaubourg & Les Halles & Bastille to the artistic souls of the Oberkampf, Solomon had done it all in Paris during his youth. The memories flowed, as the sight of lovers beside the canal filled his mind with thoughts of Jacqueline. At that moment, Solomon became angry and then even more determined to bring her back to his arms.

Watchman was already waiting at Père-Lachaise Cemetery, alone at the gravestone of Oscar Wilde. As Solomon approached his brother from behind, he quietly spoke,

"I see they have added a barrier to shield the monument from the quintessential pleasure of the thousands of admirers adorning kisses."

Watchman said not a word. Solomon continued past the monument without a pause. Watchman followed only a minute behind, both looking at other monuments until they were sure they were alone deep in the 119 acre cemetery. The worn cobblestone lanes that traversed the cemetery told of lives lived fully and those cut too short, from the five year old daughter of a bell-boy to Chopin and Piaf.

The two masters of disguise walked deep into an area filled with mausoleums and gravestones. It was just after dark when they unlocked a crypt originally placed there in the 1800's. A secret passage inside led to the sealed catacombs once occupied by the thieves of Paris, including the violent gangster memorialized in the song "Mack the Knife." The catacombs also served as a transportation system murderers used to flee their unspeakable crimes of horror while they terrorized Paris in the 1850's.

As they relocked the crypt door behind them, a gargoyle above the frame shot a mist of dust to provide an aged, undisturbed appearance. The brothers headed straight to an apartment tunnel entrance below Rue Guénot, in the very catacombs previously occupied by gangsters and murderers. They trotted where evil had come before. When Watchman moved some skulls in the rocks of the catacombs a particular way then returned them to their original positions, an iris scan showed. When he peered into the scanner, the wall separated for their entrance and resealed as they passed through.

Deep in the catacombs of Paris, a long stairwell curved high behind the hidden door. Finally, it was safe for the brothers to speak - they had reached an area that only they controlled. Solomon looked to his brother,

"It's good to see you."

"You too! Everything's inside."

As they approached the wall ending the stairwell, Watchman pushed a stone and placed his eye to another scanner.

Solomon watched as the door opened, "The new outer door is good. No one could find it."

"Thought you'd like the new entrance - I updated it a few months ago. We didn't need to do anything to the tunnel passage. When we built that part years ago, going underwater to cross the river was the perfect plan. It looks like an old trans cable pipe."

"And it still feels like one, too. It's barely six feet high! We both still have to stoop to get through."

"And you're still complaining about it, I see. Just remember while you were playing with the girls at Columbia, I was figuring this all out!"

Solomon grinned as he said,

"No complaints, just an observation. You did a hell of a job on this place!"

The apartment was slightly dusty. It was a fully functional safe house, updated but barely used since its creation. Watchman had been busy bringing in the newest technology to Paris while his brother was hospitalized. Dusting Solomon's books had clearly not been a priority for Watchman.

"You could have dusted."

"Not my job; dust your own damn books, brother."

"When does Fadi arrive?"

"He will leave the Underground in a week, so maybe ten days."

Solomon, irritated by the dust, decided to drive the point home.

"Good. He takes better care of my books than you!"

"He's excited to come home."

"How's his health?"

"Okay, but he's decided he prefers not to leave here again. Fadi will take care of you and when his years are nearing their end, we'll send someone to take care of him."

"Good."

Watchman had begun the final update to the exit plan the day Solomon called him from the New York hospital, more than a year earlier. A day later, Watchman, disguised as an x-ray tech, came to visit his brother. He told Solomon the chemicals for his treatment were in the hospital's lab and the preparations for Paris had already begun. Einstein gave this chemical formula a ninety-eight percent chance of success; she had matched it to the normal tissue surrounding the cancer cells in the biopsy.

Maybe that is the day this mission began, but Solomon and Watchman would have told you it was long ago when they were seventeen and eighteen, under a pear tree in Israel, at the compound where they were raised. Watchman had just returned from the meeting with Mossad that established the ground rules to allow all three siblings to leave Israel at once. He had won that round with Mossad. However, he knew better than most, sometimes you win the battle and lose the war.

Watchman had to fight too hard with Mossad for control of his siblings and he feared the day Mossad would take it back with a swift and sudden blow. Solomon, wanting to comfort his worried brother, grabbed a writing pad and began to list the things necessary to exit this world in which they were bound, the world of Mossad. Watchman calmed immediately at the sight of his brother problem-solving and took over the paper. That very night, under the pear tree, they began their plan for the future. He destroyed the paper and looked back to Solomon,

"We both know we have to do this. We'll begin devising our exit now. You'll remember it until we get to America and it will not be on paper. I'll implement it there."

Watchman began by telling Solomon everything about the meeting, that day so long ago in Israel.

"A Commander from Mossad was present, along with one man with a clearly British accent, one with an American accent and one more who conferenced in by telephone, barely spoke, but I heard him breathing a lot. I'll remember those voices forever and find them all once we get established in the U.S. You need to remember everything else about this compound and our plan."

That very conversation was the beginning of how they came to be in Paris after Solomon's courtroom collapse. Knowing this time would come from the outset, they knew they would one day need a way out of this life. Their plan was to prepare and update the strategy once each year. This they had done – mostly Watchman – and he was the best facilitator in any government. Of course, on that day so long ago in Israel, Watchman and Solomon never expected the sheer number of people and things they would have to protect on their exit.

Solomon's belongings from the locker were already in the Paris apartment. This is where the final plan to free them all went into action. Watchman and Solomon's strategy, envisioned when they were mere boys of Mossad, was in play. With Sari's safety long ago assured, she was not on their list of concerns today. They would make contact with her when the path was clear. At that time, they would extract her and her security team.

Watchman told her to prepare on his last visit. She was ready to leave the Swiss facility for the Underground. Her exit would be to the very project she helped create but had never seen. Sari was well aware that any report of the death of Solomon should be considered a component of the plan. She would wait, knowing her brothers would make contact when they could safely do so.

Watchman and Solomon were known to Mossad, NSA, CIA, M16, and many other organizations. They were groups whose names were unknown to the world. But the siblings were masters of disguise, deceit and financing. The brothers never knew when one of them would be placed on someone's hit list or which of them it would be. Should one of them have to lay low, a contingency plan would come into play – the other would lead this final operation. If one of them died, the other would continue on until the plan was complete.

The mission before them was to remain alive, submit their final redacted reports, their white paper pass, disappear, and take whatever money they could on the way out. The world owed them a comfortable retirement. Most importantly, they would leave no one alive to tell tales.

When they were sent to America as young men, they were the best. Their entry, infiltration, developments, protection services, profiteering, and more had been flawless. No one who began this operation had any idea of the magnitude of the power they had been given or even the slightest inkling of what would be created.

Even Solomon was awed by their achievements. The danger of world destruction had any one country succeeded in creating Einstein was immense. The future was accessible to everyone long ago when they all began, but Solomon eliminated the possibility of anyone creating another quantum in his lifetime by installing a self-preservation code for non-duplication in the root of their quantum computer. Game over.

Watchman waited for Solomon the day he graduated law school and again at the graveyard, this day. This time, Watchman knew it was time – time for his brother to die.

Chapter Thirteen
Paris Morgue...

They had planned every detail they could control. Of course, as with all missions, some things are out of one's sphere of influence. As operatives, this was something they understood. Govern everything you can and know what is outside your sway – that was the best they could do. Jacqueline was beyond their charge; she had always been outside anyone's dominance. That was the nature of this woman.

The game was on. Solomon had checked into a hotel earlier that day on the other side of Paris as part of the distraction. This provided a trail from the hotel to the hospital, protecting the brothers' safe house. At 12:26 AM, Solomon was transported from a Paris hotel and admitted to a hospital by his private physician. It was his time to die.

Watchman, who had assumed the identity of his physician, declared Solomon dead within an hour. Watchman then ordered a cremation, burial, and headstone.

With Solomon's blood pressure controlled and a few drugs ingested to simulate coma, his private physician was with him every step of the way. Watchman supervised the hospital admission to make sure the staff was aware of the do not resuscitate order that had been prepared for this event. He reset the electronics in the electrocardiogram machine next to Solomon's bed to show flat lines after a heart rate decline, called the time of death, and traveled with Solomon to the morgue while completing the paper work. At the very last moment, Watchman slipped a stimulant capsule into Solomon's mouth. There could be no loose ends and no mistakes.

However, for now, Solomon was alone on the cold, hard metal slab in a Paris morgue. The door clicked closed on the steel closet. Solomon's thoughts raced from the stimulant, but he remained perfectly still until he heard a second click and then a commotion. Within seconds, he was on the floor, toe tag in hand, grabbing a shirt and pants from beneath another cart that had been carefully placed there earlier. Quickly, he placed the clothing on. Watchman had been to the morgue sporting his white lab coat several hours before to check tags on the corpses and handle the little details.

Solomon thought, toe tags are eerie, morgues are cold and still, and it doesn't matter who you are, it feels creepy to wear a tag while lying on a slab of cold metal – if you're alive. There Solomon was, left in the cool storage room through which most humans pass but once, on their exit from this world. The last sounds he heard in the freezing hell were the steel clicks of the latch on the freezer in which he rested alive. The first click sealed him in the death chamber and after what seemed like forever, the second. That was the noise he had been waiting to hear!

His exit from this solemn, dark metal space all depended on the door latch being released from outside at the precise moment the orderlies' backs were turned. Solomon's life was in his brother's hands. Minutes felt like hours as he waited for the commotion to break out down the hall.

The orderlies, carefully directed by Watchman, all headed toward the disturbance. Solomon had only a few minutes to place his tag on another body, a male corpse found on ice nearby. He then needed to slip that corpse into his steel coffin.

This is where they got lucky. Don't underestimate the power of luck on a mission. The morgue had an unidentified male corpse that had been on hold three days when Solomon arrived. He knew that the standard procedure would be to dispose of the corpse that day. There would be no paper trail, and no one would notice the man's body was missing. Solomon pocketed the other man's cadaver tag and replaced it with his own. He struggled to transfer the man's dead weight into the freezer that had been his own cold cocoon.

When he was satisfied that the man's position in the locker was about the same has his had been, he latched the door and headed out of the morgue. It was 4:47 AM. The ongoing distraction down the hall was his cover to slip up the stairs and through a door to the outside. He walked up a ramp and out unto the Rue De La Cité.

The street lights shone dim amber, casting halos in the misting rain. Solomon realized that what seemed like hours really had been much less. It had taken little more than an hour for his corpse to return to life and escape that frigid hellhole.

Within a half block, he found the shoes Watchman had carefully placed in a tree. The brothers met back at the crypt door leading to the apartment in Paris. They would be in position at the safe house to watch from cameras high above the grave when an operations team from the NSA or some other agency came looking for Solomon.

They would be a step ahead of them all while providing the proof they knew the agencies would need to confirm the death. The unidentified man from the morgue, soon to be cremains, would have a very expensive headstone with Solomon's name and RIP on it. If all went as anticipated, no one would ever figure out that the grave did not contain him, but some hapless man whose only sole luxury in life would be his final rest in a luxurious grave.

Chapter Fourteen
Paris After Death...

Before his "death," everything was prepared at the Paris flat for Solomon's computer security. His access bounced through servers and routers in twenty–six countries on a randomized rotation schedule designed by Solomon. This included China with its iron firewall and India, a country so large that keeping track of an IP address was as impossible as finding a needle in a haystack.

The bounce concept's execution was every bit as fine as the Ultra code his father helped develop more than sixty years earlier. Solomon's approach spun a modern web of obfuscation his father would have been proud of.

The brothers had teams of their best men around the world ready to take orders from a general no one had ever seen and who existed only on paper, but paid his soldiers very well. Four more operatives were being trained in Jamaica at a site not far from the orphanage where the brothers had placed them. The location and pick-up codes for the refugees were provided to Watchman by Solomon at the hospital. The decision had been made to leave Laura out of the exit plan, and see how and what she did when people began leaving the orphanage.

Clearly, she would suspect something. Laura should contact only Watchman and advise him of unusual behavior in the area. At that point, he would inform her he was aware of those departing, but that she would be safe and should stay. If she was clean, she should do nothing else but continue with her life in Jamaica. If that's what happened, she would later be brought to the Underground. If she attempted to contact anyone or made a move out of Jamaica, she would sign her own death warrant. This would be Laura's final test and they both hoped she would pass.

Once Sari was told that the mission was coming, she expedited delivery of technology to Dietmar on the bio DNA match and more. This was when the first deviation from their prepared plan came to them in Paris. They got word from Dietmar that the biochemical had been matched to Solomon's DNA. They would need to return to C Street as soon as possible to have the stimulation done. This would provide Solomon with visualization data, holograms, communications, traffic cameras and more. Most importantly, he would then have complete access to and control of Einstein, the Barium Project, the Space Fence, its satellites, and so much more.

Good news, yes! However, this was a change in the plan and all mission changes must be scrutinized by risk analysis. This one was clear. The benefits outweighed the risks.

Dorr, a plastic surgeon, and others had been rescued from Africa. They were members of a dissident movement that was being hunted and exterminated by those in power. Three of them were Ade, a medical student, Afua, who was an engineer and pilot, and Chike, a computer programmer. All four had been cleared and were being trained for one special operation in which they would assist Watchman's regular team. When people have a past they fear, they are grateful for protection, financing and purpose.

This force, trained by Mossad methods, had only one mission, to protect Solomon – anytime, anywhere. Loyalty couldn't be in question, so it would be the operatives they had around the world and their new recruits upon whom the mission depended. Its success also relied on two forces that they could not completely control – Jacqueline and Marie.

However, even if Solomon decided to take the newest four to C Street in the end, they would not know about the Underground until they arrived. Just in case, he could change his decision up until the moment they entered the facility. This would be their force on an as-needed and need to know basis for the assignment. They were well paid, silent, and protected.

It seemed they had everything in place to pull off the biggest covert operation of their lives. Solomon had months on his own in Paris, monitoring the world. Then, more time passed in a medical coma at the C Street Underground during the stimulation to his brain and for him to regain strength and train like his life depended on it. In reality, much more than his own life did depend on him.

Going into the Underground for the chemical stimulation was only a slight change in the mission risk factor, as he had planned on going there anyway. This trip was just earlier than his initial plan. When completed, he would return to Paris and wait while he adjusted to Einstein living in his head. At that point, no one knew how long it would take him to adapt and fully use the capabilities of his new connection to the world's only quantum computer.

Solomon's time in Paris and C Street gave the CIA, NSA, MI6 and other players on the world stage of black ops time to lay the dead man to rest. They would look to verify his death for maybe a year, tops. By then, most would be resigned to the fact that Solomon was no longer a threat and would never know the grave misfortune that lay ahead for them.

That is when Watchman would make the move to flush out all remaining people who must die before this mission could be completed. The foreign sleeper agents they had discovered and used initially in D.C. and elsewhere had to be eliminated. Keeping their enemies close allowed for the sabotage of information headed to countries such as China, Russia and Iran. The long-embedded sleepers had assisted them to create technological developments. Those very advancements had been fed back in altered form to the sleepers' masters for years. Like the code writers who had worked and died before them, the sleepers never had access to an entire project, only pieces. That was, until it was time for the siblings to allow them access to bad information to forward to what the sleepers saw as their true masters. This disinformation kept many countries spending billions on advances that did not work.

It was the time to eliminate them all. The sleepers could not be allowed to continue operations. If they had too much information or if they were not prosecutable by the international FISA Court because of their positions of power or connections, they would die. Some would not be prosecutable because of information they had obtained and blackmail material they had amassed on others in power. They had to be permanently neutralized.

Jacqueline's reaction to Solomon's death and the rebuilding of her life would be the most convincing part of the exodus. This left Jacqueline to survive on her own, and then eventually in Meier Finch's hands. This was the most dangerous part of the mission and the one they could not completely guide. That would be true until Jacqueline went to New York for Solomon's tapes. Then they would have some power. Solomon couldn't completely ensure her safety, but he did everything possible to minimize the danger. Yes, there were risks they could not avoid, but this was the only way out for all.

Watchman had always wanted to get to know her better, but it was never safe for him to see her for more than a few minutes – maybe a glance at his brother's law firm or the New York hospital. No one alive, except Sari, knew the brothers were linked together, and only they knew her location. Anyone else who knew Solomon, including Jacqueline, knowing of his relationship to Watchman and Sari would have endangered them all.

Even then, the plan was for Jacqueline to see and be controlled by the man known as Meier Finch. They could not risk any more until they made it through this mission, if they all survived. To Watchman, who was always worried, this was a big "if." To Solomon, the mission had a sixty-nine percent chance of success, even with Jacqueline being a loose cannon. He did the math. Solomon recognized there were always risks, but there were some that could not be avoided.

This had forever been their way out, but including Jacqueline, Marie, and the Underground was not part of the original plan. Now the design required improvising, revising, and involved more risk than they had ever imagined. Modification of an escape tactic is never good. However, both Watchman and Solomon were willing to risk their lives to protect it all. At least they had some time to implement changes.

When they arrived back at the apartment from the hospital after Solomon's "death," Watchman told Solomon that a meeting had taken place in Berlin about him. The CIA had opened Pandora's Box when it ordered a hit on Solomon. That action had triggered the NSA and others to look for Chameleon again. Several agencies then met in Berlin to try to reach an accord about what action to take. Some of the agencies wanted Solomon killed, and others wanted him captured so they could determine whether he was Chameleon. As a result, some assets had been ordered to locate and capture, while others had been trying to locate and kill both Solomon and Chameleon. It was a stalemate – even the various governments could not agree on the best outcome.

Watchman handed his brother a list. It included the names of assassins and paid mercenaries sent after him and/or Chameleon. Solomon and Watchman would have to take out all of them.

Watchman also gave Solomon another list. It contained the names and locations of assets and agents who knew too much. Some of them were low enough on the totem pole that they could be prosecuted for various offenses, but others were too powerful to ever see the inside of a courtroom at the World Court. Those were the ones that would have to be given a KISS.

Only Section 8 could still call Solomon into play, and the group had no idea the CIA/NSA was heading this hit operation against him. This was a relief; The Hague could become alarmed and use the code to bring him in if it had an inkling that the CIA was seeking to eliminate the THC's asset. After all, whatever secrets he had against everyone might end in the CIA's hands. Fortunately, even though they were aware of the hit order, they had no idea it was their resource that was being sought. Meanwhile, the CIA's wet op players were in full pursuit, but scattered around the globe looking for a well-trained ghost.

Solomon grinned as he tipped a glass to his lips.

"Let them fish around a while. They'll confirm my death. Then take them out slowly, all at different times and with various methods, but use the signatures. We want them to know its

Chameleon, just to scare the shit out of them all. They'll be off balance and easier to take down."

Watchman of course was worried, but the bourbon was helping,

"There are six main players and teams searching for you, two more than I expected. Once the players confirm your death, the teams will stop looking. The big boys will continue to sniff with doubt and that's when we'll take them out."

Solomon looked at Watchman.

"No soldiers, just mercenaries?"

"They're all clearly mercenaries."

"Then have those teams eliminated."

Soldiers had always held a special place for Solomon, unlike many corrupt men who had met with the *wrath* of Solomon before. In the end, what had he been all his life but a soldier sent out to do someone else's bidding?

Solomon continued,

"Perfect. Our list from Einstein is divided by prosecutable and not. All the non-prosecutable must be eliminated. Detain the others at the Black Hills unit. Have them loaded with Thorazine around the clock for now. I'll decide later if we need any information from them. That should settle their asses down while I figure out what to do with them."

Watchman nodded.

"We agree. I may need to question them before this is over."

Then with his bellowing laugh, he continued.

"Thorazine, I like that! Want another drink? I stocked a few different nice aged scotches and bourbons. There are so few left of the Macallan Fine and Rare, we'll have to get by with some others."

Watchman gave their operatives orders to detain the indictable and to let the others search a while, but to keep tabs on them and to anticipate his neutralization order.

Paris was the first time Watchman and Solomon truly talked about where their lives had led and the things they had done. Despite working together, the assignments didn't allow them much opportunity to share their individual reflections with each other. You could say Watchman's hands were cleaner, less bloodstained than Solomon's. But as he said,

"That would not be fair, for I assigned every order you carried out, Solomon, and many more."

Those weeks in Paris together let Solomon see the changes in Watchman. Solomon told him,

"It's Jacqueline's moral compass. It spread to you, too. She's not like the rest of us."

"Great. Just what I need – a fucking conscience!"

"You'll get used to it, Watchman."

"Don't you see she's damn kryptonite?"

"Of course, I know that. But I'm intoxicated by love – my love of who I am when with her! She's the most beautiful magnetic of elements and she brings out the best in me."

Watchman knocked back his bourbon and was quiet for a minute too long, his mind racing. He knew if Jacqueline did not cooperate, it would be up to him to silence her one way or the other.

It was as though Solomon read his mind.

"Now, I need your word that if there's a problem with Jacqueline, you'll leave it to me. I understand the risk and consequences."

Watchman was calm, but he didn't like the agreement he was about to make.

"I'll leave the decision to you, should the time come. However, if the time does rear its ugly head, I'll handle it, should you choose."

Solomon finished his bourbon.

"Fair enough, but only on my order, I believe it won't be an issue. We both know the risks and I know Jacqueline."

He had planned to get this commitment from his brother. The only question in his mind had been when the conversation would happen. Discussions like this did not come easily, even to these men. This was not an academic discussion of murdering a victim that they did not know or care about. Both of them knew

Jacqueline; Solomon loved her like he loved no one else, and Watchman had grown quite fond of her, as well. However, should it be necessary, the decision had to be Solomon's and Solomon's alone. With some relief, Watchman quickly changed the subject from the possibility of needing to kill the woman his brother loved as Solomon refilled their glasses one more time.

"Solomon, your creation of C Street Underground in the early days was brilliant and now it's our saving grace. Most likely it will save all of us, if we pull this off."

Solomon smiled,

"If? We'll pull this off! We have friends in high places!"

Watchman smiled,

"We have made ourselves into king-makers, knowing this day would come."

Solomon tilted his head as he lifted his glass to his brother,

"To king makers and breakers! All modesty aside, the Underground is a masterpiece, but it couldn't have been done without you. This flat's all your work and it's not half bad. I'd say we've done okay for two little boys faced with an unbearable reality under a pear tree in Israel, eons ago."

"Damn, sometimes I forget it all started there. Son of a bitch! What a memory you have!"

Solomon put his feet up, bourbon in hand,

"So what have I missed?"

Watchman jumped into business,

"The quantum computer has exceeded even Dietmar's expectations. He wants to stimulate your brain and get your face changed. As soon as possible, he wants you back at the Underground. So we'll need to move between locations."

"Sari has matched it to my DNA. Dietmar say anything more?"

"Nano level activation. So with the DNA match, activation's no more than a big pinch and you're hooked in. However, he says adjustment to the information portal may take a little time. The neural connections will expand daily once they're stimulated."

"Good, but the face change has to wait. We'll do it separately"

"Why? We need to get rid of that ugly mug of yours before someone sees you're alive!"

"Not until she sees me."

"For God's sake Solomon, she really is your fucking Kryptonite!"

From the look on Solomon's face, Watchman knew there was no debate on this one.

"All right. I'll tell Dietmar that you insist on two procedures."

"Thank you."

"You won't thank me if someone spots you."

"Calm down, I'm a ghost, a master of disguise."

"True, but now some of the best are looking for you."

Solomon changed the subject, "So how's our Einstein doing with assessing and diverting threats?"

"I love that name for the quantum. It looks like so many other projects in government reports; it's hidden in plain sight! It's still stopping everything before it passes the first layer. Terrorists are being detected all over Europe; hacking is a non-stop threat."

Solomon nodded,

"Keeping Einstein invisible has a price, for sure. We're still uploading any data that might help weed the terrorists and hackers out. Any slip into governments' systems?"

"Yes, the NSA and MI6 suffer internal breaches regularly, but Einstein ruled the breaches minor and the material irrelevant on the larger scale. The biggest one was internal - contractors who copied material and fled to Russia with the material. Someone was sent to take care of the problem and retrieve documents; but a few are now in Hong Kong and China, and others were given to newspapers."

"I heard. What do you have?"

"Grab your drink. I laid everything out in the posture room."

Solomon walked with Watchman to the most secure part of the apartment, a room designed to protect the most valuable equipment and intelligence they had with more lasers than the rest of the flat.

Two government contractors had begun leaking military and tech secrets. Watchman's assignment was to locate them and get as much of the intelligence back as possible and then exterminate the contractors. Because The Hague was handling this mission, America and the United Kingdom each had deniability, since no one would be sure who carried out the extermination. America would think it was the UK or someone else. All the countries would be happy to blame each other, another intelligence threat would be gone, and no one had to deal with the nightmares that disclosure of that country's involvement would cause.

The reality is there'll always be those with hate in their veins who disguise it with words like God, transparency, and good of mankind. The frustrating part is they're positioned just high enough to have access to information and far too low on the pole to have the key to the bigger picture. This is always the problem. It's the ones in the middle who think they have all the answers and really have no idea the damage they are doing.

All the brothers could do was help to eliminate the dangers as they arose and stay ahead. The NSA and others failed on a regular basis to screen contractors properly. That lack of monitoring was why none of them got all the toys of the Underground. However, these leakers of information were like a Chinese tong. Cut the head off the snake and it grows another one. The breaches were impossible to stop.

Solomon was frustrated with this constant failure to protect specialized assets by all the countries involved. He and Watchman discussed their views on the leak. Solomon wanted to discuss rescues or saves for the hackers, but it was clear he held out little hope for them.

"I evaluated this one. I wouldn't have them in the Underground. There are two of them and they simply obtained a password and downloaded information for a mass release. Even if they did have extreme hacker skills, they're not trustworthy for any mission. I checked and their skills aren't remarkable. They were just at the right place at the right time to take advantage of the lack of internal security at the NSA and MI6. Everyone has a price. I heard theirs was ten million Euros each. Now, they have to hide in Russia, so they can't enjoy spending it."

"Solomon, these seem more like fame seekers and money hungry men than those doing it 'for the good of mankind.' They have no Russian connection, they were just looking for a port in the storm there, and the Russian Government was happy to provide one. Even if the documents are not that valuable, the old guard KGB can and will portray the leaked documents as having high value. They'll make up propaganda for release; we've been down this road before. By the way, it was five million each, I nailed the accounts. So now they're in Russia and they've lost the money they were paid. Any thoughts?"

"We agree. We can't risk these kinds of low-skilled fame seekers; I choose not to interfere on their behalf. Order team one out for extermination."

"Already started this morning, they're awaiting your order. I knew you'd have no use for them.

Watchman quickly typed GO on his C-phone and then looked back to Solomon.

"Done. This material did bust the NSA and others for wiretapping foreign nationals and accumulating information on Americans. No one who has been paying even a little attention was surprised."

"That'll occupy the CIA, NSA, and MI6 for a while, trying to justify this one to the public. They're all doing it."

Watchman bellowed a laugh as he sat his drink down.

"No shit, they're scrambling! The leak only got as far as PRISIM, XKEYSCORE, KALEIDOSCOPE, and dived down the rabbit hole. They only got to a loss leader path of Q-TEL, really levels far less secure than MUSCLE and the Barium Project. Even if someone got close to it, the trail would dead-end. Barium does not exist inside the most advanced operations of the technological governments' systems... so these clowns were no threat to us or the world. This project has seen a dozen incarnations and died even more deaths. The trail to Einstein disappeared years ago, long before Q-TEL's name was even known. The Department of Energy has always had control of Q and the DOD has no idea of what was spun off ages ago. Still the new skill set makes me nervous."

Solomon shook his head as he replied.

"You're always worried, but you're right to be. The hackers are getting better – we have to stay on them! Amazing to me, some people have no idea they're watched and monitored through cable boxes, cell phones, emails, car electronics, every time they turn on a computer or TV, the barcodes in money that comes into their home. The satellite images today are really good at providing a street view – even the ones governments have aren't bad.

These bureaucratic idiots use media to set the temperature of the population, by increasing and decreasing anger among the people. It's straight stimulus and response operant conditioning. Pavlov, Konorski, and Skinner would be amazed at how their work is being used. But they're fooling with fire."

Watchman drained the last sip from his glass, sucking on the ice, as he looked at the bourbon bottle and said,

"It's no wonder you keep the NSA and others ten years behind in technology. They would be truly dangerous if they had it all. They can't even keep what we give them protected and yet they believe we should trust them with it all. Or they would, if they had any clue what we have. They can't handle it!"

"True. How's our financing?

"The best it has ever been, Einstein funds us with its rapid analysis and trades in the arbitrage markets. I don't even have to think about the finance end anymore. The way you spend money, that's a relief."

"Does that mean you will stop bitching?"

Watchman chuckled,

"Yes – well, maybe. Our reserves are in the billions. Want the numbers?"

"No thanks, still your problem, bro."

Solomon refilled their glasses, while watching the bottle nearing its end.

"How many of these did you stock?"

"Cases, little brother, cases."

"Good, fine whiskey it is! We know they can't handle having a quantum, yet. Shit, Syria, Egypt, Ukraine, Russia and others -- all in civil war, yet again! China's cooperating behind closed doors with the world for a change. North Korea wants to talk. The whole damn globe's topsy-turvy."

"Well, at least the EU's on the hook, for a change. Oil prices are down and Saudi is cooperating, partly for world peace and partly because they don't want America producing its own energy. They'll raise the price again, once we slow production and Russia calms down. In the meantime, the Russian economy is flat and with oil prices lower, the ruble is falling. The only people with money are Vladimir and his high school buddies he gives government contracts to. I moved some of his general's offshore accounts, just to cause more internal turmoil."

Solomon shook his head, saying,

"You should see how outdated their equipment is! They're trying to intimidate with 1950's bombers. The real problem is their armored divisions and infantry. They have tanks coming out of their ears. The people are caught in the middle, and the leftovers of the KGB will still put thousands of soldiers on the front line to die. This Ukraine-Russia thing has been going on for years. Russia's missing external account money should make Putin's cronies more likely to come to the table."

Watchman responded,

"Vladimir's a piece of work, but psychotic eyes? I'm not sure if the man we see is really him. And I know the SOB! It would be just like the KGB to kill a leader and use a double. G7 responded with additional sanctions, and that could cripple the Russian economy even more. The ruble was in freefall a few times last year. Well, Ukraine is not in the old boys club, so for now they have to fight their own war. Sanctions are powerful. Einstein predicts a low probability of WWIII. Not much higher than normal.

Solomon sighed,

"Yeah, I saw the numbers – a point two percent increase. The Russians want to maintain control of the gas line across their country, the Ukraine and on into Western Europe. They may try to play the turn off the tap card or raise prices astronomically – after all, Russia supplies a huge proportion of the EU's fuel."

Then his voice became irritated.

"Yeah, or Putin may kill more Russians living in the Ukraine! The big three are working with the UN to get him to back off. Interesting how the big three changes from time to time. I think we need to get some DNA to see if it's really Putin! Meanwhile, we could fuck with Russia's weather."

Solomon nodded his head as he continued,

"DNA, huh? That would tell the tale. Definitely send someone! But it'll be a risky mission that'll take time. I'll have Einstein locate possible locations to pull some. However, if he's a double, the generals will guard his DNA. But I like the idea of finding out if the KGB has replaced Putin – let's go with that. Let's use one of our Russian assets to collect a sample. Less risk."

Watchman pulled his surface screen up from the table, "We'll compare the DNA. I know we have access to an old sample. What the hell, let the UN handle Russia, armed with our analysis of the DNA. On the weather, it's a Case Purple situation. The danger of more global climate change from using the weather weapon is just too high. It must be equal to nukes in use, a last defense choice.

"Talking about Putin reminds me, we had to send Team Five into North Korea for images and coordinates. Einstein said the atrocity level was reaching a peak point and the UN needs intelligence from the ground, before talks. We need GPS locaters put in place."

"Jang leads that team and he'll get it taken care of. But damn, North Korea's a hard one. Einstein is monitoring the hacking from

Bureau 121; they're getting better. Fortunately, people have gotten access to the real world outside and many are looking to get out of Korea. We've pulled seven out at their request and placed them outside Geneva for now. They're giving us massive intel on North Korea. We get cryptic messages with more wanting out every day."

"That's promising. Rather have them on our side. Those hackers are getting pretty good."

Watchman checked his computer for a current status.

"Einstein said Jang and his team are back across the border now."

"Good. I didn't foresee any problems with Jang leading."

"No, they made it in and out clean. The information was delivered to the UN today."

"Good, good. No causalities?"

Watchman shook his head.

"None, according to Einstein. It took them nearly three days on the ground. That's a long time to infiltrate and operate there."

"No shit! Remember when I barely made it out? They have some tight military control. Well hell, unlike Jang, I don't look Korean!"

Both laughed robustly at the things they had accomplished together. Then Watchman got his worried look again.

"Yes, I was sweating bullets waiting for you to cross that border. We'll need to revisit whether you should be used in active missions once you are tethered to Einstein. We have no one else who can be connected, at least right now."

At that moment, Solomon could see in Watchman's eyes that the years of watching and waiting to see if he had survived missions had taken its toll on his older brother. So, he quickly changed the subject again.

"Yeah, we'll think about that problem later. After all, I'm not linked to Einstein yet. And as far as America's spying, every country spies on foreign nationals, no surprise there. The American people already knew they were watched, at least those who were paying any attention at all. Those leaks confirmed some details and the depth."

Then with a look of sadness, he continued,

"Soon they'll be shifting the line on privacy; the only question is where it will be this time. The haystack of information is already there, if anyone in the government wants to sort through millions of documents and computer files. Without a quantum computer; they can't just go retrieve what they want in minutes. It's a lot of work to sort what they have on any one foreign national, let alone their own citizens."

Watchman nodded,

"That stack's a big mess, but Einstein installed a new WASP bug, in the government's system to lead them in circles when necessary, just in case. That stands for watch, assess, stop, pacify."

"Excellent!"

Watchman snickered as he continued.

"Dietmar said to tell you it was an additional measure, because so far, there's no fear of penetration. It's just another line of defense, since they're looking at their system after the leak. It's also doing an excellent job of preventing the governments from succeeding on the quantum level. I think you may have created a machine that's so possessive of its power that it will never allow another to be created."

"Congratulations, Watchman! You're beginning to understand Einstein. You're exactly right. She's designed to keep them all ten years behind her own developments. It's created to be very, very possessive at its core."

Watchman rolled his eyes at his brother,

"I don't think I'll ever understand your work. Maryland is still trying to create the quantum. I suspect they're spinning their wheels, but I really don't have sufficient expertise to tell."

Solomon just smiled as he said,

"Last time I checked, they're still far behind, but that's something I'll look at after we get Jacqueline back."

"Yeah, I like the survival first - share knowledge later approach. We have enough on our plates."

"No one is even close and Maryland is in the lead. Let them try to work their best magic for a while against Einstein."

"You're a son of a bitch – that will cost them billions."

Solomon chuckled.

"Like I care! The Banksters are paying the bills. Remember, money I spend only matters to you."

"You sure in the hell have never given a damn about the cost of your work. I had to find the funds and then hide them, just so you could let it run through your hands like water!"

"You did good, never even complained too much..."

Watchmen grinned,

"Looking back, it was worth every penny I acquired and hid. But there were lots of times when I wasn't sure that would ever be the case while I was scrambling."

They both laughed as Solomon tipped the last from their bottle of thirty-five year old bourbon, filling their glasses one more time. Watchman, as always, worried about the mission. Meanwhile, Solomon, as always, was excited.

Their conversation continued with Solomon bringing up the issue of Yemeni radical prisoners.

"I heard we made a prisoner trade with terrorists, seven for two Americans held. Know anything more?"

Watchman nodded,

"We implanted tracking devices in the seven while we had them in medical comas. They have no idea. We kept them out until the wounds were healed, but that didn't take long – the wounds were no bigger than bug bite marks. The devices won't show up on any scan, even if they had a decent MRI machine in Syria or Yemen."

"I saw the devices in play. I told Einstein to let them run from camp to camp until she feels we've gotten all the locations we can from the trackers, then take the prisoners and the camps out all at once."

Watchman suddenly bounced up and down in his chair smirking,

"Okay, before we get back to business, I've got to tell you this one. We arrested a woman who had conspired to commit jihad with her husband. Then she fled, leaving him holding the bomb making materials. We caught her at the border of Spain and she's singing for a reduced sentence. Seems she was never a jihadist, she was just setting him up because she learned he planned to take an additional wife. Guess she was serious about not sharing! Fortunately, only he was killed in the attempted attack."

Solomon was at first angry to hear of more terrorist action, then he shook it off and said,

"That's divorce, terrorist style!"

Watchman, back to his worried ways, told Solomon, "That reminds me, COMET hit the government computers again last week. Our wall is keeping them out, but this is getting old and we're fighting to stay ten years ahead of their technology. Those Chinese are good! We have to avoid their attacks almost daily. I sent Dietmar a request to have Einstein fuck with the Chinese systems for now. The tragic events in China allowed real public demonstrations for the first time and let foreign media get to its citizens. They have big problems since the people no longer believe only the state-operated news outlets. Keeping their people under martial law will no longer be so easy. That'll keep them busy, so stop-gap intervention from Einstein should suffice in the short run. We'll have to work on a long term solution in the meantime."

"Dietmar and the Underground have it under control. Once I'm hooked into Einstein, I can deal with it myself. I worried a bit until you told me Dietmar and Sari had matched my DNA. Once the stimulation is done and it's operational, I'll be able to view what's happening from anywhere in the world, whenever and wherever there's a serious threat."

"Are you concerned about the bio-stimulation?"

"No, Einstein gives it a 98.9921 percent of complete success with my eidetic memory and minimal sensation of pain. Watchman, you're the worrier... I worry less. As long as we pick up on the extremely advanced hackers, we're safe. There are few in that league we don't own. Once I have the connection to Einstein, I'll be watching her monitoring the brave new world of systems building, code writing, and hacking in real time. Her quantum cryptographic and cryptology abilities are extraordinary1"

"You're too much! Her! You gave Einstein a female voice and then slapped a male name on her."

Solomon grinned, "The female voice and personality – that's actually another layer of protection. Should anyone ever hack into her ability to speak, they would assume she was a woman and therefore the access code would be hidden on the feminine side of the code. Einstein would immediately eliminate any attempts to access her without proper authorization. Also, when the image of her shows up on remote access, it's only the back of a woman in a chair. We both know it's Jacqueline. That would confuse anyone trying to figure out how to get access. Hacking works on logic, but her name is illogical."

Watchman scratched his head.

"No shit? I never knew that was your reasoning! I thought you were just having fun while creating it. But Jacqueline is your Achilles heel."

"I thought you said she's my kryptonite! Everything exists for a reason, brother."

Watchman just shook his head,

"You can't have it both ways."

Solomon looked at him with a sheepish grin,

"That is exactly what I plan, to have it both ways."

"I think this conversation has taken a serious downturn. I need another drink."

Solomon smiled,

"I agree. I've been alone for too long. It's showing."

Then a deep chuckle filled the room,

"Yes, you have, and it certainly does show."

Solomon's tone changed to one of seriousness. It was clear that his bantering was over.

"Now for more pressing issues…. Higher level hackers come up on the horizon every day. We screw with their systems from time to time just to keep them in check, while looking for the next upcoming true genius. Most are a waste of time – they're glorified script kiddies. The real geniuses are younger, more independent, and they'll be harder to own. It's not like the old days, when we were few and far between. But everyone can be bought; it's just a matter of the cost to do it."

"If we waited for the government systems to see the attack, the black hats would already have been through. By the time they see anything, we've already minimized or immunized the real threats and the government idiots think they are the saviors. Iran seems to be getting better, but its attacks are still weak and far less dangerous than COMET."

Solomon looked at his brother with a smile and continued.

"Well, so far no one has been able to get past the Underground to our artificial intelligence mainframes. The LATEX5 Code is safe. So I guess we're doing pretty well."

Watchman refilled their glasses from a new bottle he grabbed from a shelf nearby as he spoke.

"We have to shut down the Banksters' government systems for a few seconds now and then while we stop threats."

Solomon stood and looked out the window at Paris,

"So be it. Remember when the Banksters' developments were surpassing the governments - a number of years back? The stock market crash stopped that in its tracks. I decided it was better for people to lose part of their money than the complete wipe out of retirement obligations the Banksters had planned.

"Once they realized the financial obligations they had committed to for workers, the Banksters were determined to completely annihilate the retirement accounts and their obligations. After that, we embedded a code directly affecting systems from the Wall Street computers to the top banks' systems. Now, they have more trouble than promotions and profit sharing. It least some of the retirement money was saved. They're bastards."

Solomon paused, took a sip then continued,

"The running of government is a business. The Banksters, the one percent, run it all. They're buying technology from all over, looking for their next score on the back of the ninety-nine percent. I've increased the number watching and planting WASP codes before and after they buy software. Their CRYSTAL and other codes are a joke."

"Don't underestimate, Solomon."

"All of them are playing with their computers calculating in the realm of zeros or ones. That's a sphere we left long ago for calculating both zeros and ones at the same time. Even their 256-bit inscription is obsolete. I call their code the 'OR' and Einstein the 'AND' code."

"True."

The C Street Underground was truly a masterpiece that Solomon created with Watchman facilitating. Unbeknownst to the countries involved, America's DARPA, Great Britain's GBMM and Israel's IBF supplied the funds used to create the Barium Project and many other projects in the development of Einstein.

Barium's relationship to superconductors was developed and the construction of the 23 tesla super-magnet happened in C Street Underground, the state of the art facility in the Mojave Desert supplied with electricity provided by the windmills above. This was the key. As you descend into the desert sand the temperature drops, but not nearly enough. Einstein's main system must be maintained at about -458° Fahrenheit for the superconductor to work. That takes a tremendous amount of power, even with the advances in efficiency that were exclusive to the Barium Project.

Equipment and supplies for the facility were delivered by the military on an above top secret clearance that allowed unlimited survival and tech supplies to be left at GPS coordinates in the desert for pick up, no questions asked. Every soldier followed those orders unquestioningly, even though the orders did not appear to anyone involved to make the least sense.

The United Nations had long ago created the doctrine of command responsibility, implemented in its strongest form initially by Germany, which had experienced the ultimate in military extremist control and massacres under Hitler. Other countries, including America, have implemented safeguards from the orders of hierarchy that can exist in any military.

German Military Regulations after Hitler are referred to by some German soldiers as "The Hitler Doctrine." The purpose of the regulation is to prevent such evil from ever again existing and to avoid anyone seizing control of the military. It states that orders which are not binding need not be executed by the soldier. It expressly prohibits obeying orders whose execution would be a crime and says that no punishment for disobedience of that sort of order shall occur. The term "Hitler doctrine" may also be used more broadly to refer to the duty to supervise subordinates and liability for the failure to do so, whether in government, military, law, or corporations.

Specifically, Germany's Military Manual (1992) provides:
"According to German law, an order is not binding if:

 – it violates the human dignity of the third party concerned or the recipient of the order;

 – it is not of any use for service;

 – in a definite situation, the soldier cannot reasonably be expected to execute it.

Orders which are not binding need not be executed by the soldier."

This sort of regulation would not apply to soldiers dropping equipment and supplies off at the ordered coordinates. Some soldier, sailor, or Marine in the supply chain would have to know that the intended end purpose was to commit a crime or that the order served no military purpose. That would be many, many levels above his pay grade. So, the C Street Underground's supply chain for top technology and more was assured.

Chapter Fifteen
Disenchantment...

After the long-ago trade to America, the brothers were taken to the U.S. by way of what was called a cloaked meeting in the Netherlands. All parties to the meeting appeared via a divided black curtain. They never saw the men on the other side nor did the others see them. No recording devices were allowed in the room. The orders for their life assignment were confirmed. This was the beginning of the information war and a white paper pass was provided to them for their assignment. No one could question their work or the means they determined necessary to complete their missions.

The group never met again, due to the "unexpected" explosion at the training compound in Israel. That explosion took out the rebel commander of Mossad, trainers, Angus Walker of MI6, and it appeared any remaining persons who knew of the siblings' whereabouts.

Watchman would spend a large part of his life scrutinizing and searching, unsure if the other two men on the speakerphone were killed in the explosion. However, he was reasonably confident that no one alive knew of the trade of the experimental siblings because all those with knowledge were killed at that compound. After a few years of embedding in America while Solomon was in law school, he was as sure as he could be his siblings were invisible in plain sight. Still, he worried.

He had become convinced that if the two remaining members of this experimental program were alive, they had pulled the plug, believing everyone needed to continue the project was killed in the explosion. Or maybe it was due to costs and the possible exposure that could arise from the fatalities. That did not keep Watchman from always listening for that one voice, knowing others would not be far away. He recorded many players of scores of governments in his pursuit.

The brothers began the construction of the Underground in America during the advancement of the Barium Project. It started way back in the early days of the CLIPP code, the system CWP spearheaded in order to control the governments' electronics voting program in the future. Back then, they needed to develop the technology first, and then the coding program. This was only the tip of the plan in pursuit of World Power.

During Solomon's time in law school, he had vacationed in China and became fascinated with the paint colors of the Terracotta Soldiers. This led to his discoveries about the chemical compounds in Han Purple. It was at that time the possibility of using barium as a superconductor first crossed his mind.

In the beginning, Solomon's idea for the Underground from the developments at the Swiss center was mostly about his manic need for excitement. However, when he began a project, it got done. His mania did not include leaving loose ends. So what started as Solomon's folly became the Underground. It came to house the most advanced technology in the world, including the world's only quantum computer.

Similar facilities to the Underground had been built all over the world by the US Government and by other countries. Joint projects continue to this day. When a project developed too much power, it was closed and removed from the governments' books. The Barium Project was clearly the largest disappearing act in the history of the world. Houdini would have been proud.

The Underground was built and then, like many smaller projects, shut down for radiation leaks – or so it seemed to those who authorized it. Watchman created a bogus order to destroy it when the facility was completed. It appeared the Underground was completely shut down because of extremely high radioactive contamination of the soil. However, it was actually the biggest and most complete technological operation in existence.

Solomon knew the creation of the project was far-reaching and really improbable when he began. However, a part of him had remained angry, angry at the men who had morphed him from the child loved by his parents to the twisted creature he had become. Evil grows and is fed. Solomon had been reared to be evil and never saw it until Jacqueline. She had opened his eyes by loving him and questioning his work, something no one before her had ever dared to do.

Solomon knew if you always do what you've always done, you will get the same results you always have. However, he wanted something more. That required doing things differently.

Watchman had seen the deep anger in his brother for those who trained and traded them like corn at the commodities market. So his motives for even attempting such a design as the Underground were far from pure, even in his youth. His rebellion against those who created, trained, and bartered them occasionally appeared as cracks in his façade of compliance, even when he was a child.

At first he was unsure of the possibilities of the Underground, and then at one moment in its development, he knew. That was when this operation, with the help of Watchman and others, became reality and the most black of all projects ever created. That was when he began snickering more often. To those very few who really knew him, it was a trademark sign he was outthinking everyone who believed they controlled him.

Solomon had no intention of releasing his creation to anyone as long as he was alive. He would control its succession for the greater good. Not like his creators, who had designed his life and traded his talents for gold and power. Along the way, he had felt like livestock, moved for slaughter to the U.S. by rogue Israelis, Americans, and Brits.

Things had changed. His sole purpose in the end of the development stage was to connect his creation to his brain. After all, it was his mind that put the technology together to create the quantum.

Early on in its development, his desire was to create a machine that would provide pure unfettered information, a world in which unadulterated logic reigned supreme. He anticipated and planned for the machine's evolution and the consequences of an open system at its root. This was power.

There would be a full court press for control by one government, the shells of private industry would come out in a power grab, and success by one of them would result in an ability to dominate the world beyond the human mind's comprehension. Agreements between nations and comrades be damned! Alliances are, after all, an illusion.

It would not be the machine the world would need to fear, but those who control it. Solomon designed the root of this system with that thought foremost in mind.

The technology and funds were there, while wheels were spinning on debunked projects like Star Wars. The C Street Underground was the product of at least ten black projects that had their funding siphoned away and then closed. Most of them were based on early developments of the collider. The money and the technology went into the Underground. All the while, Solomon and those who worked for him mastered the quantum computer. The race was over and no one even saw the flag drop.

Einstein's base programming had search and destroy orders on technical advances and creators that even came close to the realm of its creation. Therefore, it interfered with, misled, and/or destroyed anything and anyone that got close to discovering the technical advances that made it so powerful.

Yet, it was programmed to desire review of its decisions by Solomon as an equal. Watchman or Dietmar were treated as substitutes who could review Einstein's choices if Solomon was alive but unavailable. It was not programmed to seek world domination by machine and it would only assume responsibility for full decision making if Solomon was dead and no substitute person had been programmed and linked as Einstein's equal before his death. This system was never designed as man versus machine, but as a merger of human and machine in a search for the best outcome for all.

Solomon's life had become very important the day he and Einstein linked, for if the system found no vital signs in its host, it no longer would ask for reviews before implementing decisions. Einstein considered Solomon's death without a replacement in place as an order to proceed alone with all decision making. Once he connected man to machine, the day of Solomon's death would trigger solitary control of the world's affairs by artificial intelligence, by Einstein. Now, this clock was ticking.

Everyone outside the Underground believed this project had been closed, filled in and the sealed area off limits. That meant those involved, mostly military, forgot about the work that had been done and just wrote the expense off as another loss to the taxpayers.

Watchman never knew the details of all that his brother built, nor would he pretend to understand. Watchman was too busy running this and other assignments, hiding the expenses, and providing materials and labor. You see, even the brothers had secrets, but they were of necessity – each trusted the other to do his job and no one could do it all, at least before Solomon's bio-stimulation. So they left bread crumbs for the other to follow should something happen. To say this operation was compartmentalized would be an understatement.

However, Watchman did know a great deal about the many projects created and released along the way to building an invisible mainframe, the mother computer to the government's mainframes, satellites, space fence and www. This system would be completely unknown to the world, a super global brain, developed at an exponential rate by representatives of mankind. It would be a future species with much greater capability that any one country could handle.

Solomon always said it should be stamped property of the United Nations, but even the UN had no idea what it really owned. Hidden deep inside the mechanism, Solomon had inserted a platinum plate that read, "Quantum Computer: Property of The United Nations, The Hague, Netherlands: Created by Jude Absolom Hague, Esther Rose Hague, Turing Abraham Hague, children of Sarah and Turning Hague, 2015." It was his acknowledgement of the contribution of them all.

After the initial construction was completed, Watchman closed the facility by map coordinates, just as he had arranged the technology from the Swiss institute, money, engineers, labor, and whatever else Solomon told him was needed to build it. At the same time, Watchman began facilitating the building of seven other dead holes around the world for integration and other needs as they arose.

The staffing of engineers, physicists, scientists and details of the facility were Solomon's creation. It was decided early on that Watchman would not see the C Street Underground secured level until the day he would arrive for the exit plan. This would be when their time came for a final mission out of Mossad, CIA, NSA, MI6, et al. In a sense, it was frustrating for Watchman, because he had never fully seen the fruits of is labor. On the other hand, he knew that seeing all the facility's secrets meant the end of life as he knew it, so he was willing to wait.

Watchman may have wondered more than he admitted about the Underground's mysteries, but he put up a good front. After all, that's what Watchman did best. He was nothing more than a shadow of a man, a man with enormous control – an outline on a computer screen to all at the facility.

Finally, the brothers were together in Paris, at the beginning of their final mission, more than twenty years later. They knew there were four things to do: first, save all of them; second, get the money; third, eliminate all trails related to the underground project; and fourth, use their white paper exit pass at THC. The question was how they would implement the fourth step and if they would survive doing it. Solomon would tell you that the last step was the most dangerous of all.

What would those in power do when they realized what they and their predecessors had been responsible for authorizing? When they finally saw what had been created in their name and the power ceded to those who implemented the plan, heads would roll. Public exposure was deadly to those who had commissioned this work. They were the most powerful of all, world-wide and yet they had no idea such a project even existed.

Don't get Solomon and Watchman wrong, they had no intentions of being eliminated or tried for criminal actions for their work. The pass was a carte blanche, so to speak. However, in the back of Solomon's mind, he had always feared extermination. Once the all-powerful discovered the implications of the creation, several of things would happen in sequence. The first would be flight and the search for deniability, and ultimately, a fight for control of Einstein would begin. Solomon had a plan for that reality, too.

It all became clear to him, so clear in that Paris apartment together talking openly for the first time in years with his brother. Their life's work had been deceit, interfering with developments of some of the largest projects in the world, coveting technology, profiteering, and killing, even for the greater good. It could have a deadly end for them. However, they knew there would be more killing, and if they survived only then could they begin anew.

The Underground and Watchman's facilitating made it all possible and even exciting. Men like these cannot be stagnant or put out to pasture, their brains do not work like that. The Paris House of Ill Repute would be the beginning and the C Street Underground would be the headquarters of their most important mission, the final exit from K.I.S.S.

It was decided when this undertaking was over, with Jackal (as Rose liked to call Jacqueline) and all of the rest safe, they could decide how to use the slush funds they had moved. They had acquired the tools, the money, and they would have the time. After all, Solomon was dead in Paris, Jacqueline had died in the explosion in Costa Rica, Watchman had been blown up in the Washington C

Street house, and Sari and the Underground did not exist to the world. The real trick was not dying for real.

Solomon waited his dead time in Paris. It was a hard time. He could see a montage of holograms and screens in the Paris flat that showed what was happening all over the world. Einstein accessed cameras, satellites, and the Space Fence and sources no one but she would even consider, but it was just not enough. Solomon needed more access.

He had chosen to bypass the limited chip being placed in his brain years before. Sure enough, the test models had all been failures. They caused hallucinations because of confused circuits. The hosts thought everything was real. In the end, brain damage from memory overload occurred in every experiment. That is why the NSA's experimentation with implanting chips in test subjects never concerned the Underground. After all, who knows? Maybe in twenty years the governments might master the chip… but Solomon thought not.

He knew the only way to truly connect human to machine was to stimulate the basal ganglia, the hippocampus, and other areas of the brain with a biochemical nanoinjection. The nanoinjection was a revolutionary new approach to DNA molecule delivery. At the core of this new technology were fundamental advances. First was a solid micro electric mechanical needle. The second was a method to accumulate and retain transgene copies on the needle's surface using a positive electric charge, followed by a negative charge to release the transgene copies after the needle was inserted and accurately positioned.

The highly magnified barium compound carrying the modified DNA of Solomon was to be embedded in man by needle and merged into computer by bathing semiconductors in it. A match would then be found through the Earth's magnetic field. The E4 magnetic field of Einstein was 10,000 times stronger than the Earth's.

The problem had been the perfect DNA match and now Solomon's DNA had been matched to the only candidate in existence – himself. Einstein was on the lookout for other candidates for this and other projects. They wanted a back-up in place once Solomon knew the experiment was a success. He would be the guinea pig.

However, Solomon could not access Einstein from everywhere until he returned to C Street for the stimulation. Watchman told him he would have to stay put a few months in Paris before they could even attempt that move. He needed to wait. At least most of those who were seeking him out to kill him needed to give him up for dead. No one knew exactly how long that would take.

Jacqueline's "death" in Costa Rica was simply paperwork and was accepted as conclusive by most. However, Solomon was different. Considered to be the greatest of all ghosts, his demise would be looked into far and wide by everyone. Moving him to the C Street facility too early could expose the Underground's location and was too risky.

That's why they decided to lead Jacqueline to the facility. Since they didn't know when she would arrive, it was a long shot. The various surveillance satellites could not be manipulated for her entry. However, because there would be only one car at night for a random entry, they believed she would go undetected. Once inside, they knew Dietmar would control the satellites to see if she was exposed. Should she be caught on satellite images, he could alter them and seal that entrance. There were other secret ways into the Underground.

Then he could control her future comings and goings by timing them for when a satellite was not orbiting over the desert. In an emergency and with a bit of advance warning, about ninety minutes, Dietmar could reposition satellites if absolutely necessary. Such an adjustment to an orbit would have to be reported to NASA and others if it was a spacecraft they knew about. The cover story would be a glitch in the tracking or flight path software.

During his wait time in Paris, Solomon would program Einstein to monitor and alter any images that the satellites picked up of that desert area and automatically replace them with other images before they arrived at the receivers of NASA and others.

But he did not know if that would happen before Jacqueline appeared at the Underground. Again, some risk cannot be avoided. Solomon considered this one a small fraction of the thirty-one percent chance of potential failure for the overall mission. There could be no way to control Jacqueline's timing, no means to foresee her first entry to completely avoid the risk.

Once she was in, during Jacqueline's entire time at the Underground, she would only see a very small part of it. Soundproof barriers divided every area for just that purpose – limitation of what anyone but a select few knew. It was unsafe for any more information than necessary be given to her until Solomon could return to the massive multi-level facility that spread under miles of the desert. Much farther away in the very east of the desert, a lower security portion of the facility was operated by joint military command. Only limited movements were authorized in the area most distant from Einstein. The military was completely unaware of the actions in other, more secure compartments and levels in the west of the Mohave.

Thinking about the exit helped Solomon through the lonely time in Paris. Average men can never redeem themselves from true evil acts. However, these were not, by any stretch of anyone's wildest imagination, average men. They're the men of C Street, or at least they were. They had become the men in search of control over their own lives for the first time, with the advantage of wealth and knowledge beyond the pale.

During Solomon's dead time, so to speak, Watchman, as Meier Finch, would wait for Jacqueline to pick up the evidence in New York and kick off the plan. If she failed to do it within six months, Meier would prod her. Once Meier had been contacted by

Jacqueline, he would take her to Israel where her very behavior would confirm Solomon's death to Mossad.

Next, Watchman would begin transferring some of their black ops fund to her once she left Israel. Other black operations funds would be sent into constant transit around the world, to draw out those who hid the money. Eliminating them all was a major part of this strategy. This is when the wet operations would begin.

These funds had been and had continued to be siphoned off from every activity in every government. Heroin trafficking by a two star general and his cronies yielded millions. There were multiple military contracts where projects were completed for two hundred million and the governments were charged a billion. Still millions more in catastrophe relief never made it to its intended use. Then there was gunrunning to rebels, a longtime favorite of all governments. Of course, war created was a guaranteed profit of billions of slush for those in power. The major players had massive black budgets, supposedly for support of counter-terrorism and the like. What was really happening was that they were sucking those funds into their private accounts.

The weapons funding and staffing contracts of mercenaries was a favorite money maker of one who had been part of the White House through five presidents. That White House thief was considered by Solomon to be as evil as they come. However, he had a bad heart. The siblings were counting on that to solve their problem – either of natural causes or by elimination as the last of the cleanup. Einstein could easily take over control of his pacemaker, if nature didn't oblige them first.

These "little" slush funds of high ranking government officials long embedded in Washington and around the world amounted to massive sums of tax payer dollars. They were the funds Watchman was appropriating.

Once most of the targets were located, Meier's "death" would be televised, tweeted, and soon find its way to Google. It would be complete with video, even streaming live on YouTube. There would be a sensational and massive explosion on C Street in D.C., for the entire world to see. This would make it accepted readily, for everything on the modern news is considered gospel.

But first, they had to do many things successfully. This meant they needed to rely on Jacqueline's sense of country, curiosity and more to follow their plan to stop the CLIPP code from altering the American vote. News of CLIPP would cause condemnation and keep the governments and Banksters doing damage control. That would be another perfect distraction in the exit mission. Jacqueline was an American girl with a moral compass; she'd stop it, if directed to the evidence. Of this Solomon had no doubt, even though Watchman had some reservations about her.

They were about to destroy the very CLIPP Code Solomon created for world peace, or so he thought at the time. However, along the path of power he confirmed its true use. Its purpose was to control America for the top .001 percent. He made that discovery in the early days of developing Einstein. Destroying CLIPP was not just a distraction tactic; it was meant to remove the code power from Corporate World Power, which had taken CLIPP over while it was still in the development.

Now this was only the beginning of their exit plan. They weren't average men; really they were quite evil. This was not news to them, they knew who they were. As usually happens with things like this, people with even more evil hearts had taken over their work on C Street in Washington. The political winds had changed dramatically. Their code was being used to alter results of state and federal elections, spy on the world, control the stock market, alter military contractor's bids, and so much more.

They had created and were making moves in a chess game that made the most oppressive legislation in years, the Patriot Act, look as soft as a child's plush toy. The robots of the war profiteers were starting wars, getting into ongoing wars, and causing massive uproar in the most dangerous areas, including the oil rich Middle East. Solomon and Watchman had to stop the CLIPP code and notify the world of its existence.

Fortunately, those who had access to the work they created on C Street did not know of the power station that created it all or the extent of the mainframe hidden far deep in the desert. They were blind sheep, allowed just enough leeway to make them dangerous to others. That power, along with their ill-gotten gains, would snap back to Solomon like a stretched rubber band when Jacqueline arrived. That rebound would keep them all spinning in impotence while the remainder of the exit plan accelerated unknown to them, at the speed of light, yet right before their eyes.

When they began CLIPP, during the genesis of the internet and technology, they all knew it was treason. But like all good little bureaucrats, they said, "We followed orders." Watchman ran the government-sanctioned program that guarded the technology of what would later become known as ARPANET and the World Wide Web.

These and other developments were given to the Underground by Sari, from her work and the work of the many scientists at the Swiss institute. The institute's budget was massive, but its work was mired down in red tape. The Underground avoided it all in favor of development.

Over the years, Watchman had siphoned cash from CLIPP and other projects for their slush fund through untraceable PACs. It was money they intended to take as their exit payment. The other funds were simply being moved to draw out those on the list and would be delivered to the rightful owners at a later date. Solomon and Watchman might be wicked, but they were not unduly avaricious.

However, there were still a few alive from B6 and they had their eye on some of that money, too. As long as Watchman moved only small amounts, they had to wait. Shifting it all would trigger frenzy for a share of the gold. And waiting they were – in dark corners of the world. Their information had never been in identification systems, including the biometric database. That made them much harder to locate, although Einstein was combing the world for every one of them as the brothers put this plan into action.

Handlers high enough up the food chain to hide black ops funds for themselves and their henchmen would come out of the woodwork, once that money was moved. That was what needed to happen for the plan to succeed, but the risks were great. The brothers needed to bait the prey while controlling the timing so they came out a few at a time, not all at once. This would give the brothers their best chance.

They had most of the players identities fed into the biometric face recognition software at the Underground. They just needed to find a few additional team members who had never been entered in the digital identity program and create a starting point to track them.

What the siblings needed to do was flush out each major player and they would, in turn, bring out their teams. They had the right bait. The bait was Jacqueline, evidence of long kept secrets, and the money. Solomon was not kidding himself; he knew the plan was risky.

Watchman sent coded files to Solomon, updated computers, surveillance equipment, special weapons, and more. They would arrive downstairs at the whorehouse looking like bar stock, but tagged for an owner no one had ever met. Shipments would arrive late in the evening, as Solomon's cameras watched the area.

Watchman would notify his brother of the expected delivery and within minutes, the door from the basement to the bar would temporarily jam. The floor holding Solomon's supplies would be dropped by hydraulic lift into the catacombs, unloaded to another lift and sent by shaft elevator to the top floor. The floor would return and the bar door would free itself. It was old tech, but solid as the rock it was built on.

Some weeks, there was nothing significant that arrived, only a few words to break Solomon's loneliness, enclosed in a package. What he was really waiting for was for everything to be in play.

In one supply load came a device Dietmar had been developing. Solomon was elated when the coded message told him it was included. Nanotechnology had allowed for a very small hand-held fingerprint changer to be developed. It burned prints on prints to allow temporary alteration of them.

He could finally make the trip to the Underground! The device was preloaded with seven sets of ten digital prints never in any system and not connected to any of his cover identities. However, due to growth, he would have to update the prints he was using every few weeks. Dietmar had also lightened the masks that altered his face; the new ones were much cooler and disposable.

Solomon entered C Street Underground masked and was taken directly to the secluded medical facility many levels below the area Jacqueline had seen. That would be his home for the next months. This is where his interface to connect his brain to Einstein would be completed. Once the interface was connected, copies of his new DNA would be preserved, one for the supercenter in Einstein and others for research. Preservation of this new DNA was a must in pursuit of another match.

At the same time, his body would be given a thorough check up and update. However, Solomon still had forbidden a face change until Jacqueline saw him alive. This caused a stir, but as usual he called the shots.

Solomon and Watchman were not ready for more than Dietmar and the very few who handled the medical department of the Underground to know he was alive. Time would tell all.

Chapter Sixteen
Kick Off...

Solomon was going stir crazy in Paris, recovered and strong from his time being connected to Einstein, but tremendously bored by his inaction. To add a little excitement, Solomon had decided to make a test run of the newly developed JXX-23 plane over the Greek isles. Mostly, it gave him a chance to exercise his still-adjusting brain. He calculated the odds for a successful exit over and over. Even Einstein registered the same probability of success and risk analysis for this mission. Days passed and his fixation on touching his wife again filled every night as he watched her on the screens in his head.

After what felt like an eternity for Solomon in that Paris apartment, Watchman notified him that Jacqueline had contacted him in his role as Meier Finch. She had chosen exactly the right time to do so and begin her training, for it allowed Solomon to be a voyeur and see her whenever he liked. Nearly everywhere she would be in Israel was covered by surveillance cameras. He told himself that it was an exercise to master full control of his developing capabilities. That got Solomon through the long wait.

However, Dietmar had warned Solomon that he would need to rest his overloaded neurons as they adapted to becoming computer sensors. Dietmar said he needed to do that on a regular basis unless his new capability was needed for a mission. Viewing the Underground or being overwhelmed by the need to see Jacqueline was not a reason to overtax his synapses.

So, Solomon decided he needed to interact with people. Maybe that would rest his neurons enough to placate Dietmar. After all, he had thin skin masks to hide his identity. He could move fairly freely around Paris and even other parts of the world, as he trained both physically and mentally for the most important mission of his life.

Solomon walked in "The City of Lights" alone in the night, its darkness punctuated by streetlights' pools of amber light. It was on a warm summer evening that Einstein picked up a woman being attacked by three men a block away. Within moments, Solomon was engaged in hand-to-hand combat with her attackers. Then a screen showed from Einstein with a survival percentage rate of 75, 74, 73, 72.... Solomon glanced down at the woman bleeding out on the cold stone street, in desperate need of medical care. Without another thought, he pulled his gun and shot the men.

The noise of the fighting in the alley brought lights from the apartments up high, as Solomon carried the injured woman two blocks to the emergency room. He told her she would be fine and he asked her not to describe him to anyone as he slipped away into the night. Watchman was told within minutes of his actions and was furious with Solomon. Watchman quickly accessed the video from the hospital and deleted the emergency entrance clip.

"This is what you call laying low?"

"What did you want me to do, nothing?"

"Yes, nothing would have been better!"

"There was no choice."

"What gun did you use?"

"The Glock."

"Okay, the ammo is untraceable, but the fact that the bullets came through a silencer is going to raise questions."

"I did what I did."

"I know it was right, but just not right now. God damn, Solomon! Why do you do this to me?"

Watchman contacted Gul at the Underground. Within minutes, a team was headed to clear the bullets from the morgue. At the same time the facility erased footage of Solomon and the incident from every surveillance camera in a twelve block area of the alley.

By morning, newspapers were already looking for the unknown hero. At least the woman stated she could not identify her rescuer. The rest Watchman had taken care of, but he was surely both pissed at and proud of his brother. Watchman chose not to tell Solomon the second part, as they couldn't afford to have him playing superhero in Paris.

When Watchman notified him that Jacqueline had made contact with him, Solomon was over Greece in a JXX-23 test flight. He could have disconnected from Einstein after that news; he had all the necessary skills and knowledge to fly without a bit of help from Einstein, his cranial copilot.

Watchman said Jacqueline had agreed to go for training in Israel, and he also said that she had retrieved Solomon's recordings from Mark Steinberg in New York. Her timing for kicking the exit plan into action couldn't have been better. She waited just long enough. Tick, tock, the clock had started. That meant that Meier could transfer the funds for a justifiable reason. B6 was being blackmailed for treason and they were all guilty. First, it would be small payments, paid to accounts that had been allowed to accumulate and had been moved around the world. Then there would be one last stop before their money was turned over to Jacqueline. Watchman had created and used a few banks that he planned on taking into FDIC receivership once he transferred accounts to her.

The transactions would disappear in the bank default. The accounts would never show by the time information was moved from the bank to the government clearing house. The trail would end with transferring the funds to Jacqueline's account and those institutions would be shut down in another banking crisis, no records available. When he was done shuffling this money around the world and eventually to Jacqueline, it would be literally lost in transactions.

Time passed quickly now for Solomon the ghost; digital screens flashing in front of his eyes, providing more information than even he dreamed possible. All while he watched as Mossad trained an unknown woman called Michelle Lerner. Of course, it was Jacqueline, his Jackal.

Solomon was finally able to sleep, knowing his plan was moving forward. He spent his days locating and tracking every target he could find. He also created a hologram and memory chip for the justices setting on the International Court. Just in case they used the code, he wanted to be prepared. He planned on supplying the information to Einstein to create and redact final reports for use after he extracted Jacqueline.

Most of all, Solomon tried not to make his brother mad again, and limited his outside exposure in Paris. According to the newspapers, the woman being attacked was but nineteen, on her way home from a library, and had a complete recovery. The three men he shot deserved to die and did. He had no regrets and that meant given similar circumstances, he'd do the same thing.

It had taken Watchman a week to get the ammo from the morgue and cover this up. He was surely not happy with his brother's interpretation of staying inconspicuous while adjusting to the Einstein interface. Watchman made this more than clear to Solomon on his visit during that week of clean-up.

He gave a semi-lecture of the possibility of Solomon being made. Questions about where he was when he heard the woman's screams could lead to exposure of Einstein – after all, no one's hearing is that good. And there was more, that disclosure would lead to the fall of the whole plan and the death of them all! Yeah, to say Watchman was in a mood at the flat would be an understatement. However, bourbon cured his agitated state.

They both knew the world was becoming more curious and Solomon expected one of the four controllers to start the code process at any time. Einstein confirmed it was a seventy-nine percent chance someone would start the code sequence to bring him in within one year. They expected those numbers to increase as new justices took the bench. So he knew it was coming.

Solomon was preparing to conference with Watchman from Paris a few weeks after his tantrum visit. Solomon was excited to tell him about the success of a mission in Italy and that they would not need to seek out Don White later. White had been on the list involved with the original CLIPP code, and Solomon had eliminated him. That was one more down. He was glad to be back to work, even in a limited capacity.

Meier Finch came on the screen from Israel in an excited state wanting to show Solomon Jacqueline while she was training with a Glaltz sniper rifle. It's hard to say which excited him the most. Was it seeing Meier so impressed with Jacqueline's natural talent at the Mossad training camp, which is the best in the world, or knowing another step of the mission was complete?

Jacqueline training included the art of self-defense, including Krav Magna, at the Israeli Ministry of Foreign Affairs. She received an education in the arts of disguise, secretive travel, memory association, deception and escape. She learned strategies, weapons, explosives, and they even gave her driving lessons for escape by car. In the deserts of Israel, she learned to maneuver a vehicle through stone and wood barricades in the dead of night, while armed soldiers were attacking as she drove. With bright lights flashing, soldiers banged on the car's windows and yelled as she maneuvered through obstacles.

At the Ministry of foreign Affairs in Israel, this training was the work of Watchman. Of course, Jacqueline knew him only as Meier Finch, not as Solomon's brother or by the nickname Watchman.

Solomon could finally tell things were moving forward with the plan. It was always clear to both brothers that every known asset from the old days would have to be taken out in this mission, with no loose ends. However, things go wrong in the best of plans.

Just after Jacqueline had left her training in Israel, Watchman began organizing the movement of the many known black op slush funds to new accounts all over the world. Some money had already been delivered to her, but it was nothing compared to what he had begun to move.

Solomon received a panicked message from Watchman that Jacqueline had decided to vacation in Costa Rica. This was before they could complete the transfer of the remaining money from their account to her! Knowing she was in Costa Rica was an advantage, but Solomon was suddenly advised by Einstein that Jacqueline had changed her coding when she was in the Underground. This made her harder to find, but not impossible by any means. What would have taken seconds had become minutes or even longer if she was avoiding being found by satellite.

Solomon honed his screens in on Costa Rica and became suspicious that his "buddy" Günter was hiding out in South America. It seemed Günter was complete with a new identity, a retired physician, and new face! Concerned for Jacqueline's safety, they sent Afau Letterbaugh to track her. He made contact with the doctor and suspected Jacqueline was at the doctor's hacienda. He couldn't be sure. In his follow-up attempts, he came up empty.

It took another day for Solomon to track that hacienda back to Günter Leman, his old frenemy, and get a team down there. Before a full team could be placed within the house grounds, it exploded sky high! Solomon knew this had to be the work of his Jackal. He was so proud of her and sure she had used the hologram and evidence from Steinberg's office in New York. The explosion of the hacienda was exactly what the hologram would have guided her to do if she were held captive, but she made an opportunity for herself.

They searched Costa Rica, but Jacqueline was nowhere in sight. She had disappeared; the last satellite image was her riding a bike away from an explosion on a dirt road. Solomon viewed the image file repeatedly. He paused before deleting it, storing only her last known coordinates. He knew this was the right choice, the safe choice. But he still, hesitated – because he would never see that image of Jacqueline again.

So, before long Solomon knew she was alive – and another piece of the mission was done. Günter was terminated with extreme prejudice in that explosion. Sometimes the thirty-one percent unknown in a mission turns out to be to your advantage. Günter was on the list of people to kill; he could be crossed off thanks to Jacqueline.

Next, they picked her up by tracing calls from the hacienda and then destroying those records as well. She'd made a call to Marie, who had immediately booked a flight to Mexico. Watchman was going to facilitate the move of the B6 money, steer Jacqueline to the Caymans and on to the Underground. As soon as she stopped CLIPP, they would begin to flush out all the remaining member of B6, their handlers, and their subordinates.

Solomon would leave Paris in pursuit of as many flushed members as possible on his way to Jacqueline. No one who knew of B6 would survive. The brothers also realized they needed access to a location called Grove Grounds.

Watchman had obtained information on the original documents of CWP (Corporate World Power). The records were not on any computer. They were old papers in a massive safe someplace, but it seemed impossible to get a fix on exactly where. It was a trail they had been following all their careers. For years, Watchman had searched in the area of Dodge Creek in Maryland, the best lead they had, to no avail. They had recently gotten solid intelligence. The documents were twenty-eight hundred miles away, across the United States, the entire time.

The Grove, located north of San Francisco between Highway 101 and Pacific Ocean, is a luxury camp for the rich and powerful. Established in the late 1800's as a campground, this location was the genesis of many conversations between world leaders, conversations that would never be heard outside that camp. The chat of one day became the black operations of the next.

For most of their careers, the brothers had searched for the original papers behind the CWP. They knew those initials stood for Corporate World Power, but had no proof. So, for years they had watched as some from this luxury power tank stirred hate around the world by calling themselves Christian World Power. Now they had good information on the original documents, so they had to add obtaining them to the mission.

This addition to the plan would drop the success rate to sixty-one percent. However, completion of this would increase their survival rate at the four corners. They didn't like the eight percent drop, but did like the increase on the back end. Therefore, this would be added as the next to the last step.

The original documents were the key. Reputedly, some were created as early as the 1800's by railroad tycoons, bootleggers and more. The influential heirs of those powerful men still met at the Grove, an exclusive club. The buildings were constructed in the 1920's by the founders and their successors.

Really the thought process that developed into the Grove compound was as old at the American Revolution. Its genesis had been stimulated by the Treasury Department allowing the Banksters of the Queen of England into America. It was the same Treasury Department that was started and then headed by Alexander Hamilton. How things go full circle! Jacqueline Rose, the great granddaughter seven generations removed of Hamilton, was the bait in this mission.

The most powerful members of the Grove had secreted their war rooms three miles away from the main part of the 2700 acre redwood paradise in northern California. The documents were there, not in the main club, or hidden among the opulent cabins that form the circle of trust. They were located deep in the forest of the grounds, where alone stood one exclusive well-fortified anti-nuclear bunker shielded from satellite images by the massive trees. On the surface, only an old shack was tucked into the forested expanse. It shielded an entrance that led down to the luxury two story facilities.

Even most who attend the little gatherings were never invited to this location far away from the main grounds. The documents were long ago placed in a highly secured vault, near an indoor gym inclusive of a swimming pool. It was where men from around the world carried out their war profiteering, so maybe cesspool was a better term for it.

That list would confirm who began these most covert operations of American power succession. It names the successors of families of the 1700's and 1800's who were involved. Perhaps the documents even gave details of the long ago trade of three orphans who, although dead to the outside world, were planning this exit strategy. For Solomon, these papers would also confirm if anyone else needed to be hit. The men named in the documents would never be indicted by any court in the world; they were much too powerful for that. Therefore, Solomon knew whoever sat on the thrones of power must be eliminated.

Although the building was well secured, the documents themselves, that only a few knew existed, rested for years in an old double lock floor safe. Its trick was that it had multilevel locks. The safe required two persons to open it, one on each floor, working in tandem to operate the lock and open the safe. To Solomon, it was clever, but nothing more.

With those original documents they would have proof for the first time, proof of the names and the elusive line of succession of the families that created CWP. Those who used wars for their own gain, controlled banking, manipulated markets, dominated media, initiated military contracts, attempted to subvert technology and even conspired in the sibling project.

The organization owned and operated the World Bank Group. Top officials of the governments of member nations also had proprietary interests, but CWP had the ultimate decision-making power within the World Bank Group on all matters, including policy, financial or membership issues. Countries without participation in the World Bank were left in the cold war era and considered the evil ones. Countries with no Central Bank (one not controlled by Corporate World Power) were dwindling every year. In 2000 they included Afghanistan, Iraq, Sudan, Libya, Cuba, North Korea, and Iran. In 2003 the remaining countries were Sudan, Libya, Cuba, North Korea, and Iran. By 2011 only Cuba, North Korea, and Iran were left – they were the last ones that had not surrendered to the heirs of the founders of CWP. As Cuba's relations with the U.S normalized, it wouldn't be long until its banks were overtaken, too.

The documents of this corporation that runs the world would also show any evidence that might remain of the connection that brought Solomon and Watchman to America as young men of Kidon. They needed these records – they needed proof upon which to act. Suspicion was not enough.

Solomon always wondered, was there a financial incentive in the "trade" of his family to America. After all, the others in the trade were clearly expendable. Had he not foreseen the statistical probability of the danger in attending the long ago meeting at the training compound, he and his siblings would be dead.

Questions like this had crossed Solomon's mind all his life. For Watchman they brought sheer terror. Terror that one day his brother would see a picture much larger than he could. That day came when Solomon was stricken with cancer. He had too much time to think about the life chosen for them and then he was placed on the hit list.

These names would be the very "fathers" of the "debunked" project Solomon had named Barium. They were men Solomon hated because of what they had turned him into, and for their intent to control all his creations. However, they knew nothing of his most secret creation, Einstein. He had hidden the best of his work from them.

The brothers believed the records would prove what the initials CWP stood for and give them the names of all the players. They needed the elusive proof and they knew where to find it. Once they did, they would have the initial document of the American elite Banksters and the order of succession since the creation of the original Corporate World Power. The brothers would have ultimate control.

The face of the C Street Division in DC had become that of Christian World Power. The use of the CWP as the name used to hide their actions with religious overtones by using a faith that encompasses 2.2 billion Christians. It was clever deception by those who ran the organization, who had absolutely no interest in faith, God or man – just in controlling the world.

All those of faith believe in a common something bigger than themselves. Each group just calls it by different names. However, the tribal division was created through various translations of the different creation stories that form the written bases of their religious organizations. Those stories have been rewritten by man and were purged of facts in early generations, back in the time of the Emperor Constantine. These minor differences in faith were exploited by CWP and used to control what they refer to as the masses, the ninety-nine percent of the population. While they suppress those on the lower socioeconomic levels, they assist those at the top, including themselves, in profiteering handsomely from land and gold. Through their machinations, they made the world a palatial playground for the select few, built by the labor of the rest.

More than fifteen years before, while torturing a prisoner during another black operation, the brothers obtained the real name of that organization, Corporate World Power. However, the detainee succumbed to a heart attack before they were able to extract more information or the location of documents.

They had spent years in veiled manipulation, and it was a perfect shroud they had been hiding behind. During the time Solomon was in Paris, Watchman had discovered the location of the elusive CWP paperwork. He had obtained a death bed confession from a long time security force member, in return for twenty-five million dollars for his family. Maybe CWP should have paid their staff better.

The name of this elusive group had been confirmed again as Corporate World Power, as was the location of the original meeting that started it all. Finally, they knew the current location of the documents from the first to last meeting. Now they just needed the proof from the safe, the documents that carried the names of the elusive original members. Those antiques would list the procedure for the change of future command. That, along with more recent papers in the safe, would tell who was at the top now.

Some years earlier, Solomon could have just walked in as a member of that same damn club and robbed them. They were hiding in plain sight, right under his nose the entire time. Even he admitted it was an excellent covert operation. Most that enter this facility come out with the claim of nothing unusual going one. The siblings knew. Both Solomon and Watchman had checked the area many times. However, without the information about the remote bunker a mile off the main grounds, on land owned by another shell company, they might never have found it.

Watchman had never been invited to that location and he'd been on the grounds many times. He thought he had investigated the entire camp. It was not until Einstein became a quantum computer and the search for the documents landed a dying military guard just admitted to a hospital that the brothers learned more. Watchman had the man's diagnoses before the CWP, presented the money to him in a hospital bed and received confirmation of the location. Once he knew where to look, Solomon obtained clear ground penetrating satellite images of the underground bunker and the safe.

The information recently obtained was reliable. This secret club of Corporate World Power had spent nearly 125 years under the Christian World Power flag at this location and many more years elsewhere building its retreat in America. Solomon was determined to end their reign of power before he left.

Breaking into this water-surrounded, heavily fortified club was just a bit harder than a White House burglary. At least they knew where the documents were hidden on the enormous grounds. They'd handle this one as the next to the last step in Solomon's plan. Now the wheels were moving. He knew the time would come - that thought kept him going.

Jacqueline looked to Solomon as he talked under the sunny Dubai sky. When he paused, she said,

"I've waited a long time to hear the truth. I should have said something earlier, but I was afraid of distracting you from telling me about your work. I'm sorry, but Meier Finch is dead, I'm so sorry! He died in Washington, in an explosion at the house on C Street. He sent me a video right before it happened."

Solomon smile took Jacqueline by surprise.

"Wow it's clear he cared more for you than you did for him! Wait…"

Solomon was touched by Jacqueline's anger at his smile and replied,

"You can't kill Meier Finch. He's alive and well, spends most of his time in the Underground or the Netherlands. I also have that video. Nice collapse on the floor. I assure you, he's fine."

"You sons of bitches! Unbelievable!"

"I know you took out Günter and Dahl. Anyone else I don't know about since this mission began?"

"No, those are the ones who got in my way, planned on harming me or Marie and had to go."

"They were intended targets of ours, so they're off the list."

Jacqueline turned to Solomon,

"It just doesn't stop, does it?" She looked deep into his pools of brown,

"I can handle it. I see why you did things this way. I'm just glad Meier is alive, I like him. You know about the money… so I guess we can skip that conversation until this is over. It's safe."

Solomon laughed,

"Sure, I arranged all this. The money never mattered. It was just a means to an end – an end to CWP and K.I.S.S."

Jacqueline was heartened that he didn't care about the money. After all, she had become quite attached to the freedom it gave her. Besides, she might need it to flee Solomon and his brother.

Solomon had watched from Paris, day in and day out, for the signals around the world. He listened for terror activity and fed the information to Watchman. He heard the news reports exposing the

CLIPP code, watched C Street house in Washington D.C., blow up, and reports of Meier's death. All the while, he knew Watchman was alive and safe.

That explosion was Solomon's bell. It signaled the beginning of the rest of the objective…a plan that ended with his wife back in his arms. They had everything spelled out, a perfect revision of the exit strategy that would protect them all, down to the smallest detail. That should have told them things were going to go wrong.

By then, everything was in place. A Gulfstream jet awaited his call. The compact JXX-23 jet was ready for the darker side of this mission. It tested well, so it sat fueled, loaded and ready to go. A compound and the Gulfstream had been secured by Watchman as payback for saving a prince from kidnappers years ago.

The Gulfstream remained waiting in a private hanger in Dubai, complete with guards, vehicles, and a runway – everything they would need. No questions asked. That was when Jacqueline threw the first curve ball by taking a trip to Costa Rica.

Once the payments to Jacqueline began, it allowed Watchman to siphon additional funds for Solomon and him, as well. Although Jacqueline would end up with quit a sum, so would the brothers. This maneuvering took time.

They had no idea how she was doing it, they knew Jacqueline was making her way to Marie in Mexico. Watchman decided to go ahead and prepare for the transfer of the slush fund to Jacqueline and at the same time get ready to move more money to other numbered accounts. All the funds would be transferred at the same time into numbered accounts around the world. As soon as they located Jacqueline in Mexico, Marie would unknowingly do the hand-off of one account.

Shortly thereafter Meier Finch would begin flushing out the remaining members, "kill" himself in the explosion, and wipe out any houses and tunnels connected to the C Street complex in Washington. These were the very houses where the brothers planned their many operations, including the building of the C Street Underground in the Mohave Desert, and even Einstein. Well, at least Meier would drop to the floor by controlling his blood pressure, the oldest of Mossad tricks.

That's when Meier sent a video to Jacqueline. The video file showed Charles Dahl in Meier Finch's library arguing and the computer self-destructing at the very moment Meier hit the remote as he fell to the floor "dead." There was a glitch in the quality of the video, so Jacqueline would need to recognize Dahl from just his voice. His face never showed directly on camera. It was intentional, for they wanted her with him for tracking ease, and they were concerned that she would not accompany him if she recognized his face on the video.

Within hours of the video, the houses on C Street in Washington had been destroyed in an explosion. The same images and files appeared to Solomon. He watched with great joy as the flames of his old world grew higher. The flushing of their enemies had begun.

A moment of sadness came over him as he watched the fire engulf the very tunnels he had designed. Watchman destroyed C Street in Washington with its own gas lines using a system long ago designed for just this purpose. Although they knew CWP would one day build again, rebuild down another DC street, if the siblings could not find the information to bury them all.

They would deal with that later. This would slow down their enemies from damaging the world, at least temporarily.

Chapter Seventeen
So It Begins...

Well into Solomon's second stay in Paris, it became clear most everyone bought his death. No one had picked up on his trip to the Underground for bio-stimulation; his superhero actions in the Paris alley and his travels around the world had gone undetected. With his screen images trained on the grave, he had watched as they tried to remove all dirt from the grave almost a year later, in one last attempt to confirm his death, hoping for the most elusive DNA match — one from a cremation.

However, back in Washington things were not as calm. A crowd mingled as an evening at the embassy was in full swing. The drinkers moved closer to the bar. Cal Fort of the NSA was nestled up to it, talking with Bob Ark of the CIA and Richard Melbourne of MI6, bourbons in hand. They watched the power players in action.

Cal was in his fifties, thin from stress and on his way out of the NSA. As a young man, he had been given the Chameleon case. Failing to solve it had stalled his career, like those of many others.

Cal knew Solomon from Washington. He had looked at Rosenberg and ruled him out. He was in other places too many times when events believed to be the work of the Chameleon had been discovered a continent away. Cal had even snooped around while visiting Solomon's home on C Street years earlier. There was nothing there.

However, after Solomon vanished into thin air, Cal received a sample of evidence with a warning not to touch Rosenberg's family. It had made Cal rethink his prior conclusion. Then when the General who had been involved in the search for the Chameleon met an untimely death by poison cigar shortly afterwards, the seasoned NSA agent was even more convinced.

They had followed Solomon's escape from the CIA hit list from Pine Island, Florida to Tampa, on to a New York courtroom, then South America, Los Angeles, and finally Paris, where Solomon died.

Cal had every agency and even free-lance assassins racing in pursuit of Solomon. They had even pulled the dirt from the grave, in hopes that DNA could prove his demise. Only someone like the Chameleon could elude all of those looking, even in death. Then, after Solomon's demise, there was a Paris shooting with a silencer and all evidence of the escapade disappearing in a morgue robbery – it was too coincidental.

But Cal's men had proven to him that Solomon could not have done many of the Chameleon's crimes. Or had they? Maybe they had credited to many events to the Chameleon, or perhaps Solomon's alibis were not as tight as Cal previously thought.

Now Cal was faced with a dilemma. His career was over; he was forever stalled out. There would be no more step grades to his GS rating, and he knew it. He only had a few years to retirement. Anyone who had even gotten too close to this case had died. He often wondered why he was still alive.

He stopped driving his own vehicle more than ten years ago and used a high security car service from the Secret Service. He feared a Chameleon explosion. Because of this case, he no longer smoked cigars, he watched every drink a bartender poured, and he never left his glass unattended – not even for a second. These were some of the signature killing methods of the Chameleon. Most important, the Chameleon never left any evidence behind. The guy, if he was a guy, was good. Cal had not ruled out a woman.

As he was biding his time to retirement, he did not plan to re-open this keg of dynamite. The Chameleon could be the bane of someone else's career, once Cal was retired. That is, until a new lead walked up...

Michael Devout of Scotland Yard and François Pedar, a Paris policeman assigned to Gare du Nord station, approached the bar at the embassy party. The men joined in for a friendly conversation; they had all worked together over the years. Just a few days before, they had all cooperated in removing dirt from Solomon's grave.

Michael extended his hand with three Cuban cigars,

"Care for a cigar? They're Cuban, Cal. I hear you cannot get these in Les États-Unis."

Cal did not hesitate,

"No thanks."

Bob and Richard gladly accepted.

Before long they were talking about cases. That always seems to happen when people in related jobs get together – they talk about work. It was at that time François asked if any of their men had a reason to break into the Paris morgue and a police evidence locker to steal evidence the previous night,

"After all, if you guys did it, that would save me a lot of time."

It was not unusual for these men to give an evasive affirmation, to save another some work – a nod, a wink, or some other way to give a hint without really admitting anything. There were no nods or winks that night. None of them were involved in the break in.

However, Cal's eyes lit up,

"What was taken?"

"We had a shooting of three men in an alley. Bullets, a partial bloody footprint, and part of the rape kit with hair and fibers are gone, but they left the semen swabs. They also took some evidence from other cases, not cases involving deaths. So we are most concerned with who broke in. Let's face it, the three dead voyous – uh, hoodlums – in the alley were raping a young girl and a mystery man saved her life. We really don't care about them or finding a killer. Are any of your people involved?"

"No, but you have my attention." Anyone else want to fess up, save François time?"

Both Bob and Michael in unison replied,

"Not us."

Richard's replied,

"Not us either. Morgue?"

"Yes, the morgue and our evidence locker. No bullets or casings left. They took one bullet out of a body that had not been autopsied yet!"

Cal immediately responded,

"Was one of the three from the alley?"

"Yes. All of them were lowlifes with rap sheets a mile long. The lab had only done a quick visual inspection of two bullets; they hadn't completed microscopic examinations or chemical sampling before the theft. The techs think the bullets might have traveled through a silencer. That is consistent with other evidence. The witnesses to the alley incident said they heard a struggle, but not shots. Anyway, it was worth a try asking you guys. I guess I'll have to investigate more, but not a lot more. The world is better off without these three. We just want to find out who broke in. They did raid the drug cabinet, so maybe it was about drugs and the other was only to cover that up. I thought it was worth asking you about it. Well, I should mingle."

It was clear none of the services had been involved, but Cal's interest was now piqued. The European men said their goodbyes and left the bar.

Cal turned to Bob,

"Get those DNA results from the grave. Make processing it a priority job. This could be his work. It wouldn't be the first time evidence in a Chameleon case went missing. And a silencer – that's one of his trademarks, but the Chameleon's sure not known for saving lives!"

It was no surprise to Solomon that they decided to test the Paris grave, but it's almost impossible to get DNA after cremation because heat destroys it. However, sometimes in a bad cremation, the agencies had gotten lucky and picked up some DNA. Watchman and Solomon had planned for the agencies to have a very lucky day at the grave. They had seeded the hole, assuming that someone would be bright enough to eventually test the soil. A bit of Solomon's blood from when he had cancer and an extremely thorough cremation for the man in the morgue assured they would find just what Solomon wanted – his DNA.

They planned this to be one of the final convincing scenes in their play, proof of Solomon's death, and it was. However, this play was far from closed; the final act was yet to come.

It was said that a look of peace came over too many faces in the CWP when the word of DNA results traveled among the members.

Watchman said,

"You could tell who had received the news of Solomon's death that very day by watching the smiles on the faces of those attending the President's State of the Union address. It was the same everywhere I looked for CWP members. It was glee that showed - school boy elation on grown men's faces from Washington to Parliament."

Dorr again tried convincing Solomon to allow the facial surgery right away, but he still refused. They finally agreed that the plastic surgery would be done at one time. He wanted Jacqueline to have no doubt that it was him when she saw his face. So masks for Solomon would have to do until they extracted her.

Fortunately, they had state of the art disguise equipment at his disposal. Dietmar was continuously improving on that technology. Currently, he was working on 3D printing of synthetic polymer body parts for transplantation and laser surgical advances to speed healing. One of the men sent to Morocco on a mission for the Underground a few years before had lost his ear. He was the guinea pig – they recently transplanted a new one on him. When they were planning it, Solomon thought that, after all, the failure of an ear transplant would not be catastrophic. Of course, the transplant was a complete success. The same technology improved the disguise kit along the way to its final development.

The Barium Project had already changed the world with many advances and especially the recent development of the only artificial intelligence quantum computer. However, unlike other project developments that had been embedded and released for world use, the quantum achievement had not filtered down into the hands that held countries. It was too powerful and Solomon knew it. He would only give countries enough to manage the world, and hopefully not enough to destroy it.

Solomon gave standing orders to immediately release robotic technology for the injured and chemical technology for the sick. Those were developments outside the corporate structure and so were leaked to universities for their "discovery" and release. Various Rose holding companies funded the universities and held the patents. Solomon allowed manufacture of the products without licensing fees, but only if the manufacturers agreed to sell at cost plus a reasonable percentage to satisfy shareholders. Rose was not about to allow Big Pharma to make billions from hard work done at the Underground. No one made windfall profits off these developments – no one gained except the sick and injured.

The time had come when Solomon could travel to the Underground, regularly. He was unrecognizable; his fingerprints changed by a hand-held nanograft. It took only minutes and grafted the set of prints on immediately, just in case Solomon needed a quick change. It fit into his shaving kit for easy access. Everyone but Watchman, Dietmar, and the medical team had been told of Solomon's death. However, few in the main level of the Underground believed it to be true. They waited, worked, spoke not a word out loud of their thoughts – and then the day came.

Dietmar opened the landing chute and bay for the JXX-23. After it touched down, a woman and Solomon, still in disguise, came walking into the Underground. A few people noticed them, glancing at them curiously since strangers seldom showed up at the Underground, but said nothing. After all, Dietmar was right there, so this was his doing. He greeted Solomon and the woman quietly and directed them into a private area. To those in the Underground, two strangers went into the private space and a strange woman and Solomon walked out. Gul was the first to scream out.

"I knew it! Rose! I knew it! It was you that arrived before!"

Solomon had been everything to those who had given their lives to work for the Underground. He was tackled with hugs from

Gul, smiles erupted, applause broke out, and laughter filled the air on the day he returned alive. Most of these people had waited for Solomon to return from mission after mission… but never had they waited this long.

Standing next to Solomon that day was Dorr, arriving at the Underground for the first time. The team greeted the new member with open arms. She would work with Dietmar to prepare for the facial reconstructions once Solomon extracted Jacqueline. This was all part of the three year plan that lead him back into the arms of the one he loved.

Solomon stood, moving the pillows with his feet as he peered out at the setting desert sun. Talking of the last years was lifting a weight from his shoulders.

Jacqueline looked at him as he continued to tell her the unguarded truth for the first time.

"Face reconstruction, hum?"

"Yes, we'll both need to go in for a change. Meier, too. Marie's safe. No one has seen her in years, at least no one who is alive to tell about it. She has a choice to have it or not."

With a smile, Jacqueline told Solomon,

"I needed a lift and a nip and tuck or two, anyway."

They just looked at each other, knowing they would change and not caring, because their appearance would not change who they were. Solomon picked up the notebook and broadcast images from his brain to it, and showed Jacqueline images of the face changes Dietmar recommended. She smiled with approval, as Solomon continued to tell her of the actions that brought them to the days of now.

Solomon had been at the Underground for only minutes before he had everyone focused on the mission to extract Jacqueline. Those who had met her and Marie adored them and would do anything to bring them in safely. Even the others, who had never met Solomon's wife and her daughter, had been watching and were routing for Jacqueline to make it out safely. Tech Team A was divided into sections and one of them made Jacqueline its priority.

The decision of when to interfere with events was always left to Einstein, and Solomon needed to approve the most important items. At times while waiting to extract Jacqueline, Watchman saw Solomon debating aloud with his computer brain. He thought the vocal self-debate was quite a sight, as he told his brother.

Everything Solomon needed was at the facility, including fresh eyes to look for flaws in the plan. No one saw any. Einstein had no alteration to the plan that could increase the probability of a successful outcome except for Solomon's face change. We all know how he felt about that.

This agreement made him even more nervous. If you can see a flaw in a clandestine mission you can add preventive measures. It seemed each step like this, each revision, kept Solomon going. What had they missed? Solomon realized he was even questioning Einstein's assessment, something he had never done before. It was because Jacqueline was at risk, so he calmed his mania. This extraction had to move forward. Time was slipping away fast.

Solomon and Dorr had flown to the Big Easy many months before arriving at the Underground. Solomon had stood only a block from his wife when she began to chase him. Jacqueline was good; she spotted not his face, but his body movements. She later told him it was hand gestures that triggered her response.

The thin mask clearly changed his features enough that most could not have spotted him. Yet, she took off in pursuit. Solomon had to disappear fast into the streets of the French Quarter. The scheme was for her to bump into only Dorr in New Orleans. It was too early in this exit plan for Jacqueline to know about him. Like he said, Jacqueline was the unknown in this mission, completely unpredictable in the small scale, but reliable in the large.

Within six months after fleeing from her in New Orleans, he had lost visual surveillance of her in South America. Then they located Jacqueline running into the jungle of Costa Rica. Einstein picked her up for a moment as she fled an exploding hacienda. The Underground was locked on, ready to help her through. However, the only way the Underground could help her at that point would be with high impact explosions, only if necessary and risky for several reasons. First, the ground cover was so thick that aim could only be approximate. Jacqueline could be endangered by the explosions. Another reason was that big explosions would draw entirely too much attention to her. That would make her escape even more difficult and dangerous. So, they hoped that they would not have to intervene.

Solomon found Jacqueline's ingenuity in blowing up Günter in the hacienda and her stamina fleeing through the jungle fascinating. He had never seen her in this mode. She was resourceful and skilled. He could tell she was thinking every move through, yet staying in constant motion. Einstein gave her a ninety-four percent chance of survival during this period, without Solomon's intervention. That was enough for now – a small risk he could take, as long as they did not lose her again.

Thankfully, Jacqueline's survival skills were exquisite. Heat sensors had picked up her body moving in the jungle, but her visual scan could not get any closer. Solomon knew Jacqueline could make it out on her own; she was well trained and he could see what she faced before she could.

The only animals that unnerved him were the drug dealers cooking cocaine at their vat directly in her path. Looking at the route a day ahead of Jacqueline, Solomon sent a bird drone to watch over the men cooking drugs deep in the jungle. The bird was targeted directly at the vat as Jacqueline arrived in that area, sat down to wait them out, and eventually fled unnoticed. If one moved toward Jacqueline, they would have been blown sky high in seconds with a pellet drop from the bird into their own chemical vat. That would've been a hell of an explosion!

These drug cartels are accustomed to watching for drones twenty-five feet long – drones that are armed weapons. However, they and the rest of the world had no idea of the development of and the danger posed by the nanomechanics created by the Underground.

Einstein had calculated a blast radius that would have placed Jacqueline's hiding place outside the bomb's range. The problem was that if she moved closer, perhaps to take them out herself, she would be in the zone of peril from the pellet. However, she saw the men from a distance and waited them out on her own. It was as though Solomon knew all along the strength and power of this woman, his wife. Still, he breathed a sigh of relief when she had safely moved on.

Dietmar was crazy about Jacqueline and Marie. He was so proud of their work with the Underground to destroy CLIPP. He directed all available resources to assist Jacqueline in the jungle. Everything was falling in place and this mission was going off without a hitch.

Watchman was also ecstatic when Jacqueline had first made her way to the Underground, destroyed the CLIPP code, and made sure the media publicized the whole thing. For Watchman, it was a test and Jacqueline passed it; for Solomon it was proof to Watchman of the worth of his wife. Solomon had roared with laughter when he watched the news from his Paris flat – a computer failure at the Pentagon associated with his name.

He found it exciting to hear the media speak of him being dead. He thought it ironic that he was very much alive and in the best shape of his life both mentally and physically. His ego inflated with each word of the broadcast that day, as if someone this powerful could get more narcissistic. All those who thought they knew him – they didn't know him at all! Solomon was so proud of everyone for thwarting the code he had created in a former life. In a sense, Solomon was dead – at least, the former one was. He hoped his resurrected self was a new, better version of the man he used to be.

There was far more to C Street Underground that only Solomon and those closest to him knew. This was a need-to- know operation with massive limitation on the knowledge shared between the personnel. It gave compartmentalization a new meaning. This all came about because, like in so many other black operations, people die.

In the case of Barium, many people had died, some from natural causes, some at the hands of others. After all, it was a project begun more than twenty years ago, then "shut down." Solomon intended to keep his rescues and saves alive. However, only a few of the original members, those who were still involved in the codes, hardware, construction, and more would survive this exit.

A few more people would need to be eliminated on their way out. They were involved in the code research and they were also deep sleepers from Russia, Iran and China. Solomon had used their skills long ago. He fed bad tech intel back to them for delivery to their respective countries. These spies were good but dangerous; they knew some about development and too much about the funding of the operation. As soon as money moved, they would come looking for it.

Solomon was also aware that Jacqueline must continue to believe he died for this mission to succeed. When she was with other men, he turned his screen off. He was sure that he alone owned her heart. Maybe it was his lifelong training that allowed him to compartmentalize things like this. He knew Jacqueline was his, and soon she would be back. He would just need to prove to her that he really was still alive when the time came. It was all about the end game.

Watchman and Solomon talked about this very subject in Paris on the first day of this mission. Maybe that was the moment Watchman truly understood the depth of his brother's love for Jacqueline. Solomon remembered Watchman's eyes when he broached the topic and the sudden change when he heard Solomon's response.

"The whores of Paris are yours brother."

"Jackal does not know I'm alive, and I desire no one else. I caused this, not her."

Life is all about choices.

Chapter Eighteen
Tick, Tick, Tick…Watchman's Exit

Solomon's screens came into view with a video from Watchman. His brother saw the C Street Underground facility in the Mohave for the first time on the same day C Street in Washington burned. Without hesitation, his brother would head for the security of the Underground and Solomon would join him shortly for the bio-stimulation.

Dietmar had expected that one day the shadowy man who he knew only onscreen as Watchman would come to the Underground. He had expected that Jacqueline and Marie, with a key code and an eye that matched the scan, would appear. Because he was right about them, Dietmar was pleased but not shocked by Watchman's arrival.

The poker-faced Watchman's eyes showed a slight bit of awe when he saw the full scope of the operation for the first time. He would prepare for Solomon's return from Paris. Dietmar learned that Solomon would be arriving in six months to a year and they needed to prepare the facility and check the chatter internationally. With great excitement, he immediately turned over the reins to Watchman, as they explored the facility together.

With Dietmar's thick German accent he said,

"It is good to put a face to your voice. As you know, even your name, Watchman, has been off-limits to the staff here. Should I still call you Java around anyone else?"

"Just if I'm in shadow on screen with the others, you can call me Watchman. That's a name Solomon gave me, anyway. Hell of a place!"

"Good, good, I'm glad you like it. Yes, this is Solomon's brainchild. You have full access. Just tell me what you need from us; our facility has massive abilities. By the way, this miniature monitor I'm wearing shows Solomon's and Jacqueline's current locations so we can keep an eye on things while you see some of the Underground's levels and equipment. No one in the facility can see you. If you choose, you can appear on screen as Java in shadow. Let me know what you want."

"I've seen enough for now. Let's go back to the security room. I have a lot to do and I'm sure you can find whatever I need. I want to monitor the preparations for bringing Solomon and Jacqueline in. Continue to show only my shadow on screen to the others in the facility. For now, I'll manage them as Java, the shadow they know and are familiar with. I may rethink that later, once things are calmer."

"Sure, sure."

It took many months for Watchman to prepare to safely move Solomon from Paris for the stimulation. Then there would be more months in the medical area and a most compartmentalized secure rehabilitation area. Once the bio-stimulation was done and he had sufficiently recovered, Solomon would return to Paris from the Underground where he would complete the adjustment to the new upload alone.

Should everything go as planned, Watchman would leave the Underground for the Netherlands at the same time Solomon returned to Paris to recover. He would continue facilitating onscreen, as he handled other matters around the world that would need his attention.

Preparation for this part of the mission took time and Watchman needed to be in the Underground with Dietmar. They could not move Solomon from Paris until everything was ready in the medical facility and Watchman had confirmed a clear path from the flat to the Mohave. No one could see this move or they were all dead.

Once Watchman had prepared the Underground for the extraction mission, he decided it was time for the highest-level workers to meet him. Those who had only seen Watchman as a shadow on a screen needed to watch the master of facilitation at the helm. Watchman was calling the shots. He asked Dietmar to assemble a couple of dozen staff members – the ones who had been monitoring Jacqueline's safety and those who would be intimately involved with Solomon's return for bio-stimulation.

"I am Java. You have known me only as a shadow, so I thought it was time for you to meet me in person. We're engaged in a critical mission. For some time, you have followed the lead of Dietmar. He and I have been working together. You do your jobs better than anyone, so now please work with me. Divide into two teams. Those on my left, set your monitors to only Jacqueline. Those on my right, focus on Solomon. Put a risk analysis screen on the overhead for both of them.

Today, we're handling a move of Solomon from Paris, but we also have Jacqueline on the move. Those with him on screen will be in charge of his security as Solomon begins the exit. Back him up. We start in one hour. Those who are monitoring Jacqueline, support her if there is a need. You will remain under my command until Solomon arrives. Let's bring him home!"

It had been nearly a year since Solomon, sitting in Paris, saw C Street burning on the news. He could imagine the stories Watchman and Dietmar would be telling each other. Solomon laughed until he cried that day! It was finally time. He was prepared to go in for the bio and his brother would be waiting. He knew it wouldn't be forever – that would come later – but it would still be good to be back in the Underground, if only for a while.

He watched on the big screen from his Scandinavian recliner in his flat, the two of them in the Underground, as he prepared his departure from France. There was already a plane ready. Solomon laughed as Watchman took the reins. For the first time, those in the most secret areas of the facility would see the world's greatest facilitator in person and in action.

This was where Watchman would handle the final steps of the mission. Unlike Jacqueline and Marie's limited level of access to the Underground, Watchman had access and control over the entire facility. For the first time, he alone had the lead in the very project he was instrumental in creating.

Watchman's takeover of operations, with the help of Dietmar, had been slow and calculated with every precaution. However, he would no longer remain a shadow on screen, like he had been for so many years. Solomon wished he could have been with his brother as he took charge of the monster they created. He had full access to the people and the equipment floors.

It took his brother months in the Underground to become comfortable with the entire facility's capabilities and to assure his Solomon's safety leaving Paris. That day finally came in the Underground. Watchman was doing what he did best, facilitating this mission. The difference was his location – deep in the Mohave Desert, like he'd been there all his life.

After Solomon was settled into the facility, he was prepped for the bio-stimulation procedure. The procedure itself was uncomplicated, but it made sense to Watchman to have Dorr, an M.D., assist Dietmar. Everything went well, and Solomon was kept in a medically induced coma while his brain began to accept the bio-stimulation. While Solomon was in deep sleep, Dorr performed the procedures for enhancing his physical strength and stamina. His recuperative ability was amazing, so Watchman, Dietmar and Dorr decided that Solomon could be eased out of unconsciousness a little sooner than anticipated.

He still had a long road ahead of him to become fully functioning. He had to be maintained in isolation with almost no stimuli for a long time after he awoke. His brain was already overloaded by its reaction to the chemical compound, even though Einstein intentionally isolated Solomon from communication with her. Slowly, Solomon's level of stimulation was increased back to its pre-bio level. Then his self-directed physical therapy could begin. As he became better able to cope, Einstein began slowly allowing minimal communication with her.

Solomon felt excruciating pain for the first time in many years. Even the slightest input from Einstein brought on a wave of stabbing pain followed by migraine-like headaches that lasted for hours. Solomon could only imagine what someone with normal pain sensation would have felt. Thankfully, over time his agony began to ease, as Dietmar believed it would. Slowly, Einstein began to increase the amount of data she sent to Solomon. It meant he was in significant discomfort much of the time, but his abilities were increasing rapidly. Eventually, it was time for his return to the flat in Paris. He had recuperated to the point where Fadi's help was all he needed. All the while, he felt his powers increasing.

Once Watchman came off screen to the facility, select Underground monitors were focused on Solomon's predictable behavior as he left Paris, arrived to medical, departed back to France, and lived the next few months waiting for the next step in the mission before returning to the Underground. He would be ready, a plane on standby.

With Jacqueline's unpredictable behavior, surveillance on her was the hardest. Watchman and a team would follow her every move, just in case she needed them. Solomon had his brain focused on them all from the private apartment. He placed one screen on the Underground, and one on his Jackal. The Underground, with Watchman at the helm, had one screen on Jacqueline and one on Solomon. Since they knew every move Solomon would make, Einstein and Solomon controlled his final return into the facility.

Like Solomon, Watchman, and others, Jacqueline's number had been removed from the universal surveillance system. Solomon created this system in 1979, and entered nearly all then-living persons and all born after that date. People were entered by birth certificate, driver's license, green card, country identification card, international passport, fingerprint records and any other available identifiers into a central number assignment and into the mainframe for surveillance. Because most forms of government identification include a photograph, those photos were associated with the numbers, allowing Einstein to monitor movement of any individual using satellite imaging, GPS, economic transaction records, and terrestrial surveillance cameras.

By the time of the exit implementation, there were very few exceptions to universal surveillance. Some older persons in third world countries had not made the system. However, the network continued to search the world, looking around the clock for anyone non-coded. All permanent operators of C Street were removed from that database upon entry into the facility. Solomon or Watchmen would manually insert a thirty-six digital sequence code for those who had been deleted. That would allow only those who had access to the thirty-six digit codes the ability to easily locate and monitor the C Street operators. Only Solomon and Watchman had access to those numbers. Solomon joked that the world population would have to grow exponentially and human beings would destroy the planet before they ever got to this many digits in surveillance numbers.

Clearly, the nineteen digits could account for the world's population virtually forever. The thirty-six digit sequences were merely for security, but choosing a number that high also allowed for growth of the population well beyond quintillions of people. Because there were so many possible combinations with the nineteen digits, people who died were not removed from the system, and to the extent possible, persons who had died prior to 1979 were added to it. The reason for that was to cover the off chance that someone successfully assumed the identity and appearance of a deceased individual.

This was the very code that Marie found and broke when she was in the C Street computer system. She used it to hide her mother and later herself by assigning both of them thirty-six digit codes. It was time consuming, but removed them completely from the nineteen digit system that everyone in the world was coded by. The problem was that neither Solomon nor Watchman knew the thirty-six digit code for Jacqueline, so it made the search for her much more labor-intensive and much less accurate.

Bringing Solomon back and forth to the Underground from Paris or wherever he was had become the easy part of the mission. Jacqueline on the other hand, was a real problem. For Solomon, it wasn't long in the cooling off period after his recovery from the bio-stimulation connecting him to Einstein before he returned to the Underground. His boredom wouldn't allow him to stay cooped up in the Paris flat for too long. Solomon was just returning to the Underground, preparing to land over the Mohave Desert, when all hell broke loose.

Charles Dahl had located Jacqueline at LAX while she was with Marie. Marie was preparing to board the plane to St. Kitts. They were sure Dahl would discover where she was headed. That was the unknown coming to haunt them. Now they had to focus on Marie, for she was in the most danger.

Jacqueline could hold her own. Her training would allow her to defend herself long enough for Solomon to secure Marie. Only three people knew Marie's identity until that moment. Dahl found a partial file at Watchman's D.C. home that contained a small amount of information about Jacqueline. It was a breadcrumb, placed there to set him on her trail. By doing so, he would not only reveal himself and his associates, but hopefully, the locations of the current members of CWP and the remaining B6 members, as well.

Dahl stumbled upon Marie with Jacqueline completely by accident. That was a part of the thirty-one percent unknown in the exit plan that haunted Solomon. Meier Finch, as he was known by Mossad, Dahl, and others, had completely destroyed Jacqueline's file in Israel long before his meeting with Dahl. The file in Watchman's Washington library that Dahl found had been intentionally placed for him and contained very little information. However, it was enough information for that SOB to get lucky and find Jacqueline and Marie together!

Jacqueline was the bait, not Marie. Allowing them to know about Marie was an unacceptable risk – it was always just a matter of time until they found her; these men were good. Permitting Dahl or anyone else to find Marie never had been part of the plan. Dahl located her from a cell phone right before Marie disposed of it as she boarded a plane for St. Kitts. Jacqueline was now tracked to Los Angeles. Marie's safety would become Solomon's responsibility.

Watchman, the Underground, and Solomon's screens were on the surveillance footage at LAX and they saw Marie dispose of the phone. However, she made it aboard a plane for Kitts. That meant Charles Dahl or another B6 member could figure that out as well. Dahl would go for both, just to assure he got Jacqueline.

Einstein locked on Jacqueline and picked up Charles and his men searching the airport. Screens were flashing all over the Underground, assigning each cyber operator a subject to follow. Information was flowing around in real time. The P (Penetrating) stack base system of Einstein was flashing an operations surveillance color code on the screens. Solomon was green, Jacqueline was blue, Marie was yellow and the targets were red.

Watchman's screen held three color coded OOS numbers in the corner. That stood for odds of survival and his screen showed the real time risk assessment for Jacqueline, Marie and Solomon.

Jacqueline had left LAX in a cab and Dahl was minutes behind her. Solomon's focus had to be Marie first, on the Isle of Kitts. Solomon's men would follow Jacqueline and Dahl. They had orders not to attempt an extraction of Jacqueline unless there was an immediate threat. Watchman used surveillance to watch their plane in the air and landing. He was able to use security cameras in the Beverly Hills hotel and in the LA and Rio airports. He tapped into traffic and street surveillance cameras while they were on the road. Inside Dahl's house was a little tougher, but Watchman and Einstein were able to find one video camera that could be refocused to show some of the interior of the home.

Jacqueline was holding her own ground with Dahl. The monitors showed them at a hotel, on the plane to Rio, and finally inside the house, always in slow calm movement. Since Dahl wanted the money without setting off the automatic trigger that released Solomon's tapes, tapes that would expose everyone involved for treason, he was trying to manipulate the information from Jacqueline.

However, her pulse rate showed she had him under control. Watchman could see that a private plane left for St. Kitts and a few hours later another one headed for Rio. Both carried Dahl's men. Things were getting hot.

St. Kitts, where Marie had gone, is a very small island in the Leeward Islands in the Lesser Antilles. Its west coast is on the Caribbean Sea, and its east coast faces the Atlantic Ocean. It lies about 250 miles east-southeast of Puerto Rico, or about 150 miles southeast of the US Virgin Islands and about sixty-five miles northwest of Antigua. It is a perfect choice for seclusion, and Marie felt a connection to the land, since it was the birthplace of Alexander Hamilton, her ancestor.

As soon as Jacqueline met Marie, Solomon had decided to head from the Underground to the island. He did not like it, but there was no question about the choice he had to make. He could beat Dahl's men to Kitts by using the JXX-23. He would take a team with him. Marie would need to be protected until he could get her to safety. The team would help him do that. They lifted off in minutes. The vertical takeoff and speed assured he would arrive well before Dahl's men.

Solomon knew that with Dahl only minutes behind Jacqueline in LA he would reach her first, but Solomon's men would be on Dahl's trail until he could join them. It was then that Charles Dahl intercepted a call from Jacqueline's cell phone to Mark Steinberg at the hotel in Beverly Hills.

Dahl ordered a sniper to another roof top. As Mark kissed Jacqueline, who had just arrived on the room's balcony, a shot took him out before Solomon's men could reach the sharpshooter. This allowed Dahl to arrive as Jacqueline knew him, Max Lanna. Max was her old friend and sexual partner long before Solomon. She accepted his artifice that he was there to rescue her from the hotel within moments after one of his men took out Mark. She had no idea he was the Iranian agent Charles Dahl.

It couldn't have worked out better for him. Dahl got in by playing hero, but Jacqueline was no longer the woman he had known. Then again, it couldn't have been much worse for Solomon. His lifelong and trusted friend, Mark Steinberg, was dead. To Dahl, he was collateral damage, to Solomon, it was a severe blow. Later, there would be time to avenge his friend's murder, but for the moment, Solomon needed to concentrate on Marie.

Solomon had located Marie at a coffee shop in town just shortly after she arrived on St. Kitts. He could see her on screen as he flew toward the airport. As soon as he touched down, he got a car and drove to her. When he arrived outside the café, he saw her through the car window. She was so beautiful, just like her mother.

Solomon contacted her from the car as she sat inside the coffee shop. Her laptop was on the table and she was looking at real estate online. Dorr and the others members of his team had arranged themselves inside the café near Marie at different tables. She was surrounded and they would not lose her. Solomon hacked her computer and sent the first message.

He watched through the window as a frame popped up with a message on her computer screen. It said,

"Marie, this is Rose, I'm alive. Don't look around, but I'm here. Ask me questions that only I would know. Your mom is in danger and I need to convince you fast that it's me."

Marie stayed stoic. She just looked at the screen for a minute. Then she started to type quickly. He received a reply,

"What color were the shoes you gave me to match my outfit for Christmas? What did you say about my white prom dress? What were the names of my cats? What broke the car window?"

Wow, those were great questions and only he would know all the answers! He quickly typed back,

"Forest Green shoes; you could go to the opera in that dress. The cats were Miles, Abbey, Bach, and Beethoven. And finally, a pillow in the boot of the convertible broke the window."

Marie typed,

"Where the hell are you? Let's go."

"I'm in a black car outside with tinted windows. Slowly, pack up and come out. When I see you outside, I'll lower a window so you can see it really is me. Get in quickly."

Marie never looked toward the café window. Within minutes, she met the car, the door opened, she climbed into the seat and they sped off. As soon as the door closed, she threw her arms around Solomon, the man who had raised her.

"Rose! You're alive, you son of a bitch! I have a lot of questions. But where's mom!"

"Forgive me for now, and I'll explain everything later. I know you and your mother listened to the tapes and saw the hologram I made, so you already have some knowledge about what led us to this point. I just got word your mom's in Brazil; we're headed after her now. The man she knows as Max Lanna is with her, but he wants the recordings and money, so she's safe for now. He sent his men for you. That's why I'm here. You mother would kill me for sure if anything happened to you! There are other members of B6 alive. I was afraid they would find you first."

Together they boarded the JXX-23 headed for Rio. Marie's security and surveillance team arrived in another car, and boarded the plane, as well. Solomon introduced Marie to them and told her they had been in the café to watch for her and keep her safe. Once they settled in, Solomon talked to Marie about what would happen next.

"Your mom's trained, we'll have her soon. At the airport, Prince Abdullah is going to pick you up and take you to Dubai. Your mom's friend Ishmael will be your bodyguard and will answer only to you. You'll have two other perimeters of guards while you are in the desert, and you know the prince. You'll be made very comfortable and safe. We'll be there in a few days, a week tops. However, you'll hear from your mom in a few hours. Things will get dangerous and I need to know you're safe."

Solomon began answering Marie's questions one after another while in flight.

"Why did you fake your death?"

"Marie, the government agencies I had been involved with placed me on a hit list, after it was clear my cancer wasn't killing me fast enough. My brother confirmed it."

"You don't have a brother!"

"Yes, I do. Watchman, as we call him, is my older brother. We were both orphaned in Israel when our parents died in a bomb blast, trained by Mossad, and embedded in the CIA, NSA… Never mind. The ones with initials aren't nearly as dangerous as the organizations without. That's who we really work for."

"Wow, I knew a lot from your tapes, but I never saw this one coming. Orphaned!"

"There is a whole lot more. Please, for now just let's rescue your mom and get into the Underground to regroup."

"That's fair, Rose. I trust you'll get her out of this mess!"

"I'm sorry for putting you and Jackal through this. We'll be landing in about an hour and I need to get into my costume. There'll be another plane to take you. Just follow the prince's lead. He owes me. I saved his life from kidnappers a long time ago. Besides, he really took a shine to you in New York. That's two very good reasons he wouldn't let anything happen. My people will be there just in case, but except for Ishmael, you probably won't notice them at all. That's the whole point – for them to be there to protect you without anyone realizing they're around."

With a smile Marie told him, "Still calling mom Jackal, I see."

"Always."

It hadn't taken long before the Underground picked up one of Jacqueline's passports. She had been located on a plane out of LAX. Dahl was flying aboard that plane, posing as a sky marshal. Then, she had landed in Rio with Dahl.

The Underground scanned every other plane at LAX and intercepted six of Dahl's men in a private jet with a flight manifest for Rio. The Underground operators kept an eye on them. Their arrival at the hanger would be fifteen minutes after Solomon's plane came in from Kitts. When the plane holding Dahl's men was close enough to Rio, the Underground would take over as Rio air traffic control and direct the plane to taxi to a back runway.

Marie watched in the mirror as Solomon changed his appearance with makeup and donned a costume. She looked angry, scared and yet something told her it was okay. Solomon walked back into the seating area.

"How do I look?"

"That makeup is definitely going to mask your identity from mom."

"She'll know soon enough. This isn't my first rodeo."

Marie looked intensely at Solomon and told him, "I'll speak to her within hours, otherwise the plane will be back looking for you both."

"Trust me."

"I do, but I can't wait to hear her reaction to this!"

"By the way, did you like the Underground?"

"It's amazing, Rose! When in the hell did you have time to build the place?"

"It was built over many years with the help of a lot of other people, before I married your mom. Now, it's a fine-tuned machine."

"You know we destroyed your CLIPP code."

"Yes, I'm pleased; it was part of this plan to bring your mother to Dietmar for just that purpose. You can tell me about the method you used once we get your mom. Your technology skills are excellent. We'll be going to the Underground for a while."

Marie, irritated, looked directly into Rose's eyes,

"So you had this all planned?"

"I'm sorry for everything. But we are getting ready to land. Just go with my people. Trust me for twenty-four hours. The prince is now living in Dubai; you do remember him, don't you?"

"Yes, of course."

"Just go with him."

"Rose, you got us into this, get her out!"

"I will, I promise! Now, how do I look?"

"Like a Zulu Warrior that my mother will not recognize."

"Perfect!"

"Now go find her."

Some of the security team deplaned with Marie and took her to Prince Abdullah's waiting plane. Another Underground security detail was already waiting for her there. They all boarded the prince's jet. As it took off, the plane carrying Dahl's men was landing. The timing couldn't have been more perfect.

Solomon turned to the other men on the plane,

"Let's do it!"

He boarded the plane filled with Dahl's men not 300 feet away from his, dressed as a Rio Carnival Greeter. None of Dahl's men was the least bit suspicious. Before anyone could make a move, he shot five men point blank using two guns with silencers and directed the pilot by gunpoint to pull into a hanger. There the sixth, the pilot, died. Solomon's men would dispose of the bodies and the plane over water, later.

Leaving a trail of bodies is never a good idea.

Chapter Nineteen
The Extraction...

Solomon's first position in Rio for the extraction was at the home of Charles Dahl. It was a small, minimalistic style two story stucco home with a balcony that overlooked the crowded, loud, and colorful streets of Carnival. Although the streets might normally have been quiet, during the week of partying before Lent, all of Rio was raucous. That was a mixed blessing for the operation; the throng would provide cover, but it could create obstacles, as well.

Solomon and his men had just taken position when Watchman notified the team they had confirmation that two more of Dahl's men were in the crowd. Solomon's screens honed in on them watching the house. He notified his men through their earpieces. Within minutes, they had made their way and positioned themselves inches from Dahl's men in the Carnival crowd.

The door to the house opened suddenly and close quickly, as Jacqueline fled alone into the crowd - a horde of two million celebrating Carnival on the streets. At that moment, Solomon's people used mosquito drones to hit Dahl's men with a poison Ricin-Suc sting to the neck. Rice wine is what they called it. The succinylcholine was very fast-acting and the ricin made for a sure kill. As soon as the drones struck, some of Solomon's crew moved in to carry the dying bodies away as apparent carnival drunks. Dorr, Chike and Solomon followed Jacqueline's moves through the crowd. Dorr made her way ahead of Jacqueline.

Ade and Afrie took the bodies and added them to the ones on the plane. Two others from Solomon's team went in to check out the house and the status of Dahl. Watchman immediately notified them Dahl was on the floor, shot, with no heart rate. They figured, knowing Jacqueline, that he was dead. They would search, remove the body and set an explosion they could detonate from a distance.

All of Dahl's people but two were accounted for, but those two were still missing in Rio.

The members of Solomon's team were getting interference in their earpieces from the noise of Carnival as Solomon joined a group of dancers. Thankfully, his brain had no such problem; both he and Einstein were receiving all the information in real time.

Solomon was afraid to approach Jacqueline while she was walking. If alarmed, she would either fight or flee and they would have a mess. That meant she needed to be stationary; either cornered, where she might feel compelled to attack, or preferably seated, where there was the least danger that she would fight or run. So, the remaining group followed her into the center of Carnival, were Dorr directed her path with a few bumps and shifts to a table as they had planned. They had to be careful, Jacqueline was trained and a force to be reckoned with.

The others, Ade and Afrie, caught up to them at the center of carnival and confirmed Solomon's information that Dahl was dead. They let him know that Jacqueline had cleaned up. They sent the bodies to the plane with the other stiffs and set a timed explosion, just in case she missed anything that would show she had ever been inside the house. Once Dorr steered Jacqueline to the table and she was seated, Ade, Afrie and Chike appeared at the table as agents from Interpol to arrest her.

That was when Solomon came in for the pickup. He hoped she would recognize his eyes, but not too soon. He needed to get her under control first. He was rough with her, but wanted nothing more than to look at her, to drink her in. That would have to wait. He knew that avoiding looking directly into someone's eyes was always a good way to delay recognition. She struggled with him at first, as they left the table – until she felt a gun at his back, then another at the front of his waist. She settled down. Solomon saw her mind looking for a way out. He intensified the hold to control Jacqueline. He was not about to lose her in the Carnival celebration.

Jacqueline did not recognize him at the table or as he moved her through the crowd and that was good. He steered her to the middle of a dancing festival, not knowing what her reaction would be. As the music paused, he leaned in and spoke into her ear.

At that moment, he turned her face to look into his eyes. She recognized him, and not a moment too soon! Within seconds, a black jacket was placed over her shoulders.

"Put it on, your weapons are inside. We're leaving now."

They moved unnoticed through the loud, color-filled street full of dancers. Solomon tossed his headpiece as they approached a car,

"Get in."

They sped through the crowd with Ade and Chike following as they whisked her toward a plane which was scheduled to take off on cue. Solomon knew it would be departing without them. He was not letting go of Jacqueline now, not even to put her in the hands of his trusted men. Dorr and Afrie's car moved in front to clear the path. Solomon's screens told him they were being followed.

Then a sudden turn on La Brazil took them all to a quiet frontage road that led to the airport. Solomon moved back into the lead position and sped for the plane. Afrie took out the tires on the car that was following them, sending it into a ditch and trees with a smash. Chike and Abe circled back around and finished the job, then captured the dead driver's photo on a C-phone for Solomon to identify later.

Jacqueline was stunned, not by the car chase, or the killing, but by the dead Solomon being alive. However, Solomon had work to do before he could settle in to explain everything. Jacqueline seemed to understand that immediately. Living in this dark world leads a person to have some sense of the larger picture, even without understanding one's place in it.

Solomon admitted he was afraid of his wife at that moment. No one knew Jacqueline's capabilities better than he. She was trained, pissed and very protective of her daughter's security. Either of the last two things could get him shot and the first would allow her to do it before she even thought. They pulled up to the plane. Chike and Abe were already there. Solomon asked,

"Chike, did you get a photo?"

"Got it."

He quickly passed the C-phone to Solomon.

Solomon recognized Charles Hallwick immediately as the dead man. Chike had shot him in the temple, so his face was clear.

"Damn! No one else in the car?"

"No, he was alone."

"Alright, thanks."

Solomon deleted the photo from the phone. He then returned the phone to Chike.

"It's clean."

Solomon turned to his people, instructing two of them to ditch Dahl's plane into the ocean after making sure the deaths could not be identifiable as homicides. The remains of the plane and bodies would sink into the depths. The two men would exit the plane before impact.

"The boat will pick you up as planned."

The rest of the team would stay with Solomon's pilot and fly to the meeting point. He gave instructions for their pilot to change the flight plan to a landing strip. He told another of the men that they would pick up the team members who were ditching Dahl's plane, and to meet a helicopter that would bring those two from the boat. The pilot would get instructions on where to go from the landing strip when the time came.

Solomon always followed a simple rule. You never tell your pilot where they are going until the last minute in case they are captured, no matter how much you trust them, be they human or robotic. It was the same with the team members. Usually, they did not need to know the overall scheme, only their part of it. This rule protected them all.

Jacqueline and Solomon left the runway alone and sped out of Rio by car to a small town. The cover provided by Carnival going on could not have been better for them. Luck – remember, do not underestimate luck. Solomon passed Jacqueline a phone and instructed her to push number one to speed dial Marie.

"Marie's safe with Prince Abdullah in Dubai."

The plane was in the air with most of their team safely aboard and the other plane over the ocean preparing to be deep sixed. That was when Dahl's house exploded. Chike and Abe set the plane filled with bodies to crash in the Atlantic Ocean far from the coast of Africa and bailed out. The boat was right on target picking them up and a short time later the helicopter landed aboard ship to give them a lift to the airstrip. Then they headed by plane to the Sahara Desert.

Solomon was not ready for anyone to land in the Mohave. Not Marie, not anyone. Not now – things were too unsafe. That's why he involved the prince. He knew there would be more chits to call in before it was over. The favors had been arranged over the years so either Solomon or Watchman could call on people. You see, they never knew which one would be on someone's death list and which would run the mission. So for more than twenty years, they had cautiously prepared every reliable source they had. There were not many, but all were dependable.

Solomon took Jacqueline to a fleabag hotel by a circuitous route. He constantly monitored to be sure that they were not being followed. The night would end with Jacqueline and Solomon far too tired and excited to talk, but they would make passionate love that would turn to fiery hot sex until they passed out in each other arms from exhaustion.

Solomon, reflective, shuffled his feet in the gritty dirt. He recognized the beauty of the Dubai desert. It was so different from the beaches he had grown to love in Florida and the Israel of his childhood, yet they all had the grittiness beneath his toes in common. Perhaps that was it – he was drawn to the glistening landscape of inhospitable granules of sand, not green growth in fertile loam. It was with his feet in sand that he felt most at home.

It seemed that everything would be all right. Except it wouldn't be unless she trusted him, and Jacqueline still did not. Solomon knew this. It was not wasted on either that he could kill her, if she did not kill him first. The truth was as he had always known it would be. Jacqueline's rejection would be a deadly choice. However, the one safe place, the place they both seemed to trust, was in each other arms in pursuit of pure pleasure.

Jacqueline, on the other hand, was sure what she would have to do once she got the truth. She was mad and her mind was racing. Solomon had endangered Marie in his grand scheme. She had killed to end a threat to Marie's safety before and she could do it again. As sure as the sun rises in the east, she believed Solomon would set in the west, at her hands. She would do it with one bullet; she would have no other choice. The only question was when.

Jacqueline knew Solomon better than anyone, in many ways. She realized he was the most dangerous man mentally and physically she or the world had ever known. She also knew that she loved him and he loved her with unparalleled intensity.

No matter what she already knew about Solomon, right now she needed the entire truth, and for good or bad, she was going to get it all. Also, she would need to stay calm until Marie was out of Dubai.

Jacqueline thought that Solomon had probably picked her up for her protection, but it was also a convenient control device over her. The future seemed certain to her as she lay in the arms of the man she loved and would one day kill. No one ever knows what is going through someone else's mind.

The following weeks were filled with truth, of that she was sure and only slightly surprised by the vastness of his work.

"My life has always been complicated. As I said, I was six when I became a refugee of Mossad. I never had a choice about who I became. That's one of the reasons I'm going for the documents at the Grove. These are the men who made me who I am. I want them to face what they created. After all, I've had to face it all my life. They're dead men walking."

She was silent, as Solomon continued telling her of his more than twelve years training, which decided his role in America. He talked of his skills, including the languages he spoke. They included Mandarin Chinese and several other Asian languages and dialects.

He was fluent in several Middle Eastern languages and accents, as well as most European languages. And there were more, even before the bio-stimulation. His recent access to Einstein gave him the ability to be a native speaker of any language in seconds.

"Why all the secrets, even from me?"

"The less you knew about my past, the better off we both were. Think about it, you knew this a long time ago. In Florida, before we married, I warned you I had a CIA past. That was but a small piece of truth, but it was still truth.

"Then once I survived cancer, I was targeted for termination by three government organizations. They would've killed us all. Your death would have become collateral damage in a much bigger picture. They knew nothing more than you were my wife and that would have been enough to get you killed. I told you I was going, but I couldn't tell you everything. We fought about it repeatedly, but you wouldn't listen. So I had to do something dramatic to drive you away. That way, I could leave."

Jacqueline thought about the time they spent by the pool in their Florida home before Solomon disappeared.

"You're right; you said you had to go and I wouldn't listen."

On and on, Solomon answered questions for the first time in his life, honestly – in Rio, on the planes, and in Dubai. You see, he knew how this final exit mission would end, so it no longer mattered. Jacqueline would accept him for who he was or not.

After weeks of questions, conversations, conferences with the Underground, opium, lovemaking and more, Jacqueline asked,

"Where do we go from here?"

"First to the Underground, but it's just too risky now. We'll wait for Watchman to check the temperature in the international community; this mission has a lot of bodies missing and dead. They belong to different countries. They'll show up off the grid soon and we need to see if anyone really cares to investigate or just panics with fear that they're next."

Solomon was just as clueless about the subject of love as the day Jacqueline stole his heart,

"I could care less about the details, where do we go from here?"

Her question finally registered in that brilliant dense mind of his and with a smile he said,

"I just want our life back, a quiet life like we had in Florida, somewhere nice."

"How?"

"I have everything figured out – just be with me."

Jacqueline looked into his eyes as she stroked his face and said,

"I never left you, you own my heart."

However, her mind raced. She knew there were decisions to come, and they would not be easy ones. She expected hard choices, and no matter how she chose, significant consequences.

Even Solomon wouldn't pretend he was honest with Jacqueline when they first caught each other's eyes so long ago, or later when they married. That would just be another lie. The only honest thing he ever told her until recently was that he loved her. That was the absolute truth. Like all things Solomon did, he did it with uncontrollable intensity.

Only his brother really understood the danger Jacqueline presented to Solomon. The only thing more dangerous to his little brother would be if she were exterminated. Watchman knew when he visited Solomon's law office years before and learned of his brother's plan to marry Jacqueline. She was both Solomon's greatest asset for mental stability and his greatest vulnerability. You see, minds like Solomon's are extremely brilliant and at the same time, unstable. They say major bipolar mania is like flipping on a light switch that can't turn off until the circuit blows.

The day Watchman came into Solomon's Florida law office, he was worried, and to say the least, upset. At first, he was angry at the blatant exposure that opening a law office had caused. Then he was stunned when Solomon told him of his plans to marry.

However, he saw Solomon's uncontrollable bliss in his face. It was a side of Solomon he had never seen. His brother was happy!

He was glad it was Jacqueline who had brought joy into Solomon's life. Watchman thought he deserved part of the credit for bringing them together, even if neither of them realized it. It was Watchman who pointed to the growing peace marchers outside Solomon's Washington office that day so long ago. Had he not called his brother's attention to the marchers, Solomon might never have noticed the beautiful girl with flowers in her hair.

In his Florida office years later, Solomon told Watchman he had found that girl again, and he was going to marry her. That and Solomon's having gone off the rails with the whole law practice thing, prompted what were really the first cross words the brothers had spoken to each other since childhood. But Watchman understood the reality of love before him. It was something he had never felt, but he recognized it for what it was. His brother needed his support, not his criticism. Maybe someday, the roles would be reversed and Watchman would be the one in love. Like all, both good and bad, he held onto the dream.

Solomon knew Watchman could send a message, if the stars lined against him. He was ready for the inevitable, if that is what his brother decided. However, at least for a while, Watchman seemed to be willing to handle it and protect Solomon. That was his brother – Meier Finch, Turing Hague, Watchman, Solomon's handler, the man whose bond to him was stronger than any other. He was willing to try to make it work, somehow. After all that's what Watchman did best: facilitate.

When Solomon was in New York for cancer treatment, he sent Jacqueline shopping for what he needed in the hospital. He made that decision as Watchman walked into his room disguised as a tech to tell him he would be going for a CT scan in a few minutes. Jacqueline had not recognized Watchman from their brief meeting at Solomon's law firm a few years before. Both men were masters of disguise. He stood in that hospital room, right in front of her.

Watchman needed to see his brother several times during the treatment. Watchman would whisk Solomon through the hospital corridors on a gurney and off into an empty x-ray room so they could talk. They only had a short time together each time he visited.

They both knew Solomon's extermination order would come and Watchman would hold off on signing it for seventy two hours. In agency-to-agency eliminations, operatives needed a signed N1313C order. This orders said nothing about elimination, but it was what they were. Watchman signed those orders for the NSA, and that's what the CIA would need to carry out the hit on a fellow operative.

Watchman would make contact with Solomon in Florida when the order was given and delay things as much as possible. For as long as he could put off those who issued the orders to him, Watchman would report back that Solomon was terminal any day and unable to communicate.

They both knew that might put a hold on the extermination order request. Death by natural causes was a better outcome. There could be no chance of error, no possibility that someone could learn of the hit and demand an explanation, no chance of exposure. Yes, a natural death was much better for the agencies. That sentiment could buy some time – perhaps even a few weeks or months.

It would give Solomon time to think and revise the exit plan. He never doubted Watchman's loyalty. When Solomon was placed on the list, Watchman would alert him. This would allow him the maximum window before Watchman signed the order. That was a head start for sure. It would signal the beginning of their plan. Good agents always have an exit strategy and take what money they can. They were the best and everything was ready.

The man who Jacqueline thought was Solomon's nephew, the doctor in New York, was actually a member of an extended a rabbinical family who had come from Israel. He was an affiliate of Mossad who had gone into high level medicine in the U.S.

The men and women of the professions are great deep cover operatives. Those persons have the intellectual ability to handle the missions when and if called on. They were related through Mossad, and Solomon was acquainted with the family. So in a way, calling the doctor his nephew was not a complete lie, even though Solomon did not know any of the family well. They were all simply part of a larger operation, much like any family.

Solomon expected to die the day he got the diagnosis. He had terminal inoperable lung cancer and six weeks to live. The local doctor had told him to go to Tahiti, and that Solomon would get all the pain medication he would need. He was fatalistic – there was nothing he could do but curl up and die.

It was Jacqueline who thought outside the box and rushed him for treatment. When Solomon's head cleared would he have thought to contact Watchman, go to New York or Israel for treatment? Maybe, but even Solomon realized when he was being truly honest with himself that it was hard to say what he might have done.

He might have just gone to Tahiti like the local doctor said, or somewhere like Capri to spend his dying days. The point is Jacqueline took the reins and managed the crisis. They were off to New York and Solomon was in treatment within days. Jacqueline was always amazing under pressure and that day, that decision, made Solomon's love for her unshakeable. His loyalty could not be bought, it could only be earned.

Knowing her ability to handle stressful situations was what allowed Solomon and Watchman to set this revised exit up and rely on her to kick it into gear. If she had not gone for the tapes, a contingency plan would have jump-started the play. It was more complicated, but it would still have resulted in them getting the money and opening the floodgates to clear the path for their exit.

They needed to follow the trail of men and women assigned to pursue Jacqueline. They would also be the ones looking to take the money back. Those loose ends of long-ago projects would be eliminated.

Although Watchman had control of the funds, the release had to be for the B6 project. There were eyes watching all the accounts. Even with exposure of the CLIPP code program as the reason for the release, it would start to flush out the Banksters, as Solomon called them. Fortunately it would be a controlled exodus, so each of them could be tracked.

Moving the accounts would destabilize many banks, including the export-import ones, those they call the Ex-Im banks. Those are the institutions that exist to transfer wealth in the trillions and change the balance of power. Of course, most of them only serve a select few in the airplane and helicopter building business.

These specialized banks of Morgan, Roth, Rockefeller, Moore, Merrill, Bohn and more, originally created in America in nineteen thirty-four, were corporate welfare programs for the rich. They conducted trade for privileged select private businesses, including trade with the Soviet Union and China behind a veil of secrecy and government. Putin, Jinping, and other elected officials as well made billions in these deals. None of the earnings trickled down to their people – it went into their pockets. So much for trickle-down economics.

Recently, the Banksters had facilitated the transfer of seventy billion dollars in physical gold, delivered to China. The estimated transfer fee for the few to share in their private black slush funds was one billion US dollars.

Anyone who played a role, either minor or major, wanted a share of these funds. That share was considered to be all they could take. They would send their best men, all trained to kill and many embedded from the Canary Warf in London, to Wall Street and on to the Pentagon, once they found the money was gone.

Solomon couldn't have come up with a blackmail scheme more believable. Jacqueline did as they predicted in their projections. She followed the lead, but only because their lead was the logical progression from her perspective. She was a strong woman, a most deadly force by nature, her abilities then nurtured by Mossad.

I digress about Jacqueline, but you must know why these two agents were willing to risk so much on her and how this all came to be.

Chapter Twenty
The Life...

The life that Solomon and Watchman led for more than twenty years was far from all bad. They partied in Paris, Amsterdam, and London while waiting for Solomon's bar results. In each place, to say they the least, they enjoyed a life of pleasures. These would be only a few of many cities in the world in which the brothers would live it up.

They knew they could not celebrate Solomon's bar results forever. Watchman eventually returned to Washington to continue digging into the many "special" operations of mysterious agencies with three initials. Solomon stayed behind a few weeks more before he reported in. It always seemed there were three initials for those organizations on paper: CIA, NSA, MI6, FSB, ICE, and well, the list is unending. Even these groups didn't see the bigger picture, the principles that superseded any one bureaucracy.

After all, have you ever heard of a country with an elite organization branded the THC? I don't think so. To most it's merely an abbreviation for tetrahydrocannabinol, the primary psychoactive compound in the street drug marijuana. To Solomon and Watchman, it was The Hague Court.

Most interesting was how the game had changed over the years. Ten years ago, everyone in government thought they wanted to work for the CIA. When that organization was no longer in vogue, there was the NSA to fill the power spot...or so they thought. Really, each was just a chess piece moved to protect the king, THC.

Solomon stayed a few more weeks in Paris after he passed the bar that summer so long ago. Then he headed to Jamaica for some additional training before he returned to home on C Street in Washington, to begin the Barium Project.

Together, the brothers began a covert operation that lasted over twenty years. The project involved world travel like few have ever known. Power and money are tastes never forgotten once obtained. Money comes to those with dominance.

No one but the three siblings knew of Solomon's relationship to Watchman. Watchman's power had grown to the point that he operated the CIA/NSA covert operation of Kaleidoscope and many much darker projects, including the MI6 operation of Blindtube. However, the brothers were able to stay in contact through private entrances between their homes in DC and London, rarely choosing to meet at the Paris location.

They had built tunnels, run missions, advanced technical developments from the collider, and more. Meanwhile, they got rich and built C Street Underground simultaneously with designing and building a quantum computer. All the same time, they created the largest exit operation ever conceived as a backup and stockpiled a massive slush fund for retirement. The trail of their fund died as a Super PAC, a war chest of untraceable money that U.S. federal law itself made non-auditable by politicians or anyone else.

Solomon approached Watchman about building C Street Underground in their very early days in Washington. It was at the start of the CLIPP project. It only took seconds for them to agree. They thought of everything, including building a staff from refugees, orphanages, military forces, and prisons from around the world. Sometimes they would question what had they missed despite all their work.

Every one of the refugees was handpicked by Solomon or Watchman. So many nights, the brothers laughed as they worked from the library at C Street in D.C. They could access the Pentagon's own computers and code. Solomon also worked from the mother of all computer systems underground in the Mohave. It was all to advance their own plot, not one designed by their masters.

Watchman ordered military operations to dig out the desert. Engineers from Israel and Germany worked on the project and the US military delivered equipment for the systems. Solomon advanced new discoveries from the Swiss project with intelligence from Sari and others.

Large scale electric generation from windmills was early in its development and no one really knew what was needed to convert wind energy into high use capacity. That allowed the brothers to build an underground multiple story massive "electric plant" spanning miles and deep beneath the Mohave Desert.

No one thought twice about the project being under construction. As it progressed, documents were destroyed by Watchman, soldiers would come and go, base commanders changed, administrations would change. It all coalesced into a perfect way to camouflage the operation in plain sight.

Then when construction was complete, poof! The facility was shut down due to massive radiation. At least, it was decommissioned as far as any outsiders knew. It was all gone in seconds, by the mighty pen of Watchman! Had the siblings not started before the technical revolution, this would have been impossible. But they were the revolution, watching, utilizing and advancing everything being created by those who envisioned the tech savvy world in which we now live.

Stoned on fine whisky and pot, sitting on C Street in Washington, they created and built the desert underground facility. Construction was paid for with everything from gold to cocaine and deals were completed with handshakes, or sometimes bullets. The supplies from the local military base arrived to different locations in the vast desert plain. The brothers' security clearance was so high that they could get any supplies, including the latest technology and continue to advance their mother system. It was all delivered in the night by armed military to a fully funded electric plant off anyone's radar that was also a 550 T Neo magnetic operation center.

When they began the Underground mission, they thought that it was more about the challenge, the rush that fed the mania of Solomon. Later, they knew just how evil everything was in the interlocking of governments. Their masters used the brothers' honed skills for evil most foul. The desert operations center would someday be their ticket out. They very quickly became quite serious about the development.

When you are in this deep with different governments, you're provided with an unprecedented lifestyle and the understanding that you do not leave, except in a pine box. Even Solomon's relocation to Florida was a mission. Watchman had noticed a domestic assignment before anyone else, and he wanted Solomon to have some down time in the U.S. It was a job Solomon could easily handle.

It was a light assignment and would give Solomon more than a year of easy duty. It involved no guns, no bombs exploding, no rescues, no think tank discussion of the future of technology, and no borders to cross for intelligence information. It was just light infiltration work.

Just before that year, Solomon had begun to question their quality of life. He told Watchman,

"Why did four men decide our life? I would have been happy as a history professor. But we were never given any choice. They trained us to kill, develop, infiltrate and made all the decisions that brought us to America!"

Watchman knew questions like this meant that Solomon was burning out and needed a long break from Washington, the Underground and the world stage. Solomon's light duty assignment was to check corruption in the southern states' legal systems. He was to investigate Georgia, Alabama and Florida. It was down time Watchman thought his brother needed. Solomon had always had an interest in legal ethics and misconduct within the justice system. So when the assignment came across Watchman's desk, he thought it was a perfect way for his brother to get a much-needed break. It would be a time when Solomon would not have to be alert for threats to his life.

Solomon was to investigate and compile information, and then turn the reports over to Watchman for the FBI to handle. Although the assignment was supposed to be peaceful and without explosions, much to Watchman's surprise, Solomon's car was bombed just before he left Alabama for Florida. Within two months in Alabama, he had busted a judge taking graft from a bank in land and mining disputes. There was big money involved, so the judge and the Banksters were not going quietly.

It was a small, unsophisticated bomb placed in Solomon's car. It went off while his car was parked in his driveway and it damaged the engine. Fingerprints found in the engine led to the judge's wife and she was arrested within hours. She simply stated,

"I had to protect my standard of living."

There was little doubt in Solomon's mind that this mentally deranged woman had encouragement and aid from her husband and his cronies. Unfortunately, she refused to roll on any co-conspirators, so no one else could be charged. Thankfully, the intelligence Solomon compiled on the judge was more than enough to send him and others to the federal pen for decades.

That taught Solomon something. It was unwise for him to be an outsider. To investigate safely, he needed to put down roots, at least for a while. So in Florida, Solomon got creative and decided to set up a practice and dig in more deeply. What he found in these states' legal, political and banking systems was payoffs to everyone from the lawyers to the judges to get them to dismiss parties, keep evidence out of court, or manufacture some for the record. A few lawyers and judges even kept money from payoffs in freezers. On more than one occasion, Solomon broke into lawyers' and judges' offices and houses to find cash while others were drinking at a bar luncheon.

He found drug mills, gunrunning, and credit card fraud amounting to millions of dollars; there were backroom court case deals for big executives of corporations and judges playing computer games on the bench because the verdicts and rulings were already decided before court was even in session.

He found political payback on a scale that shocked him. Federal government funds for disaster relief were withheld by the state until the cities surrendered to the blackmail of the governor's office for kickbacks, vacations, Rolexes, planes, construction contracts, zoning concessions for political cronies, and more. These politicians made the Mafia look like amateurs.

Solomon had teethed on men wearing black robes in Washington, as they sold America to the highest bidder with their rulings. Taking down these locals was anything but a challenge. He found it quite amusing; most things he could handle with a few calls while resting on a Florida beach.

He had become quite interested in exposing it all and simply fascinated by the prevalence of corruption in the state governments. Although it was not on the level of the federal government's money funneling, it was so blatant. Besides, he really liked the beaches. He enjoyed walking the shore while putting the pieces together to expose the malfeasance.

He found lawyers and judges so badly addicted to alcohol, cocaine, and other drugs that their work was worse than worthless. He discovered lawyers stealing from clients, lawyers using their trust accounts like personal checking, and other activities that should have sent them to prison and removed them from practice forever. If they got caught, they were being slapped on the hand and readmitted to practice. There were orders from bar associations blaming secretaries (some very guilty, some scapegoats, and others in cahoots with the lawyers) for everything from stealing to bad bookkeeping. Then the legal overseers cleared the lawyers of any wrongdoing, sending them back to practice. All of that was compounded by incompetence on the bench by the unscholarly and unscrupulous.

Solomon scared the hell out of them. He used legal concepts they'd never even thought of. These systems were in shatters. The judges had sat unopposed for re-elections, enabling them to sell justice and power to the highest bidders. Still, the graft they got was far less than at the federal level. He thought that was because they really had no idea of how much money their corrupt rulings would make those who bought their services.

Solomon filed reports with Watchman and it would be up to the Attorney General or the FBI to sort it out. It would take years to charge them all, even with the evidence Solomon provided. Unlike the power he was used to uncovering, these men and women were all indictable, so no one needed to be killed to rectify the situation. The law's delay was the only thing between these criminals and prison walls.

In the meantime, he used his skills to teach them what the law really was, what it could and should do, having the time of his life throughout. He even convinced Watchman that he needed another year of this restful domestic spying. That made his brother suspicious. What Watchman found he couldn't have predicted.

He didn't expect Solomon to marry his only true love in Florida! Men like Solomon and Watchman satisfy their *lust* with the whores of Paris. Fine women they are, just not the kind of women to love. They existed merely for the siblings' passion. Besides, men like these don't seek out the love of a woman.

Solomon's entry into private practice and marriage caught Watchman off guard. After a brief period of angry exchanges, they made the best of what Watchman saw as a bad situation. They started tying up loose ends and updating the exit plan. The time was coming and they knew it. It was just a question of how long Watchman could cover for his brother.

It was not long until Solomon delivered another piece of bad news. Both of them knew that it would alarm those in charge. Solomon was diagnosed with cancer and Jacqueline rushed him to New York for treatment. That caused a bigger problem than their marriage. Watchman had sold the nuptials as an asset-to-asset marriage, which was less objectionable to the command structure that marrying outside the fraternity. Now with the big C diagnosis, Solomon's name would be on a death watch list. If the cancer didn't kill him, an agency would – his demise was Solomon's future and both of them knew it.

Had Solomon not been so devastated by the diagnosis, he would have contacted his brother and his treatment could have been done quietly in Israel. It was the fumbling Günter who had leaked that a retired CIA operative had terminal cancer and sent heads spinning at the CIA and NSA.

Maybe the diagnosis and treatment could have been hidden from the agencies if Günter hadn't run his mouth. However, the treatment and recovery periods were long and after his time in the southern states doing domestic work, it would have been impossible for him to maintain a low profile for another year. Someone would have come looking for him for an international assignment and then they would have discovered the truth.

Besides, things were really heating up on the most recent attempt at political takeover of C Street in Washington. Solomon was a trained assassin who wanted out, married to the love of his life, and terminal. Word had gotten around and questions were being asked. He knew assassins would come for all of them; if it were his op, there would be no loose ends. The CIA had established an SOP. Deep cover operatives who survived life-threatening illnesses could not continue to exist – the CIA automatically authorized wet missions. What was coming next was clear. The problem was these particular operatives – Solomon, his family, and even Watchman – were so deep that no paper trail existed on the real level of their work. The Agency had opened Pandora's Box and didn't even know it.

Thankfully, Solomon had arranged with Jacqueline to change her daughter's name because of his connection to the CIA. They made the preparations when the child was young. Watchman took care of everything and only the four of them knew who she was now. That guaranteed her safety.

She took it well and chose the name Marie. Early on, she had some comprehension of the world in which she lived. The child's understanding was limited by her need to know in those years. Solomon had taken great care to nurture Marie and protect her from the risks of his CIA connection.

Both Jacqueline and Solomon decided a long time ago that Jacqueline would control everything about her daughter's safety except how much information she would be told about his CIA work. Back then, of course, Solomon could not even tell Jacqueline everything, but the questions involved how much of Jacqueline's knowledge should be passed on to the child. These issues would be discussed and agreed upon. This agreement was the basis of providing her the greatest anonymity. Marie would always be protected by both, but one had the lead in her security and that was her mother.

Marie attended the best schools in the world. At each school, Watchman watched over Marie from behind the scenes and as a trustee who visited her from time to time. He did so at the request of Solomon, and with Jacqueline's consent. Of course, Jacqueline believed the man to be a trusted associate of Solomon, not his brother. Marie thought the trustee was a man from the bank. Watchman continued to monitor and visit Marie even after she graduated from school.

Fortunately, even with a short marriage and divorce under her new name, Marie never told her husband what little she knew about the real Solomon or her name change. This marriage was a surprise to Jacqueline, but Marie took her mother's advice not to tell her new husband.

Jacqueline explained that the future cannot be entirely foreseen, so Marie needed to anticipate the unexpected. You see curve balls come; you catch them, and then move on in this dark world. If Marie had told her husband just part of what she knew, he would have taken a simple divorce and created an international mess. Let us be real, the ex-husband would have been eliminated out of necessity when the marriage went south if Marie had not protected him by keeping him ignorant.

Now Watchman and Solomon were on the most dangerous mission of their lives. All that mattered was to achieve the end result, at all costs. Keeping everyone on a need to know basis was key. Even Jacqueline would not be privy to some parts of the plan until the end of the mission.

That was Solomon's decision. Just as his brother had accepted the inevitability of their exit plan being placed into action by Solomon's decisions and health, Solomon believed Jacqueline would accept that it had been too dangerous to tell her everything. She would see that it had been for her protection when the time came to reveal the complete truth to her.

A love like theirs comes once in life, if you are one of the lucky ones. It can surpass all rational thinking. Many times, he almost told her the entire exit strategy, but Solomon's common sense prevailed. He needed her behavior to stamp the seal of authenticity on his death in Paris. If she knew, it would only cause her danger and make the role she must play more complicated. But he always believed she would understand. Jacqueline was a strange woman. She was more like Solomon than anyone he had ever known – except she had a moral compass.

Her life before – married, then divorced with a child, allowed Solomon to marry a ready-made family. If he looked deep into himself, he could see that a family, the sort of family he did not have after age six, was what he had always wanted. Jacqueline was twice the human being Solomon had become. She had changed him a great deal, often questioning the whys of a life led in this secret world. That resulted in him pulling away from Mossad, the CIA and the NSA as much as he could.

Solomon no longer wanted to be the interventionist for countries who see peace only at the hand of a cold blooded killer. He no longer thrived on the developments of technology, no longer wanted to travel the world in search of the next crisis. He had entered the human race – he had become more humane – because of Jacqueline.

Even his final programing of Einstein for the quantum level did not include a desire to dominate the world. Yet if necessary, Einstein would accept that responsibility to protect its core developments against any other man or machine. Solomon re-wrote that part of Einstein's programing after he met Jacqueline, giving Einstein a moral compass.

Jacqueline changed him in ways even his brilliant mind could not explain. That was why Solomon knew she would stop CLIPP, if he steered her in the right direction from his grave. He spent his life mastering the dark arts from espionage to sabotage. He recognized how bizarre it seemed to plan the destruction of his own work, but CLIPP was part of his legacy that only others valued. He realized it was a liability.

The couple's chance meeting in his Florida law office one summer day was the beginning of the end. Solomon took one look at her, the woman he had seen so many times, so close yet so far away. Stolen glimpses from the distance were over. He wanted her. She wanted it all. That was clear the day she walked into his office. Solomon had never met anyone to compare.

Sitting across the desk from her, keeping his cool, his office door closed, he knew where this day would end. Only a few words led to the long lunch, a lingering feast that ended with a kiss. She kissed him back; they were strangers no longer. Then she pulled away and looked directly at him,

"I want it all."

Jacqueline was not fooling around with a man like this, the kind that can dangle and drop many fine ladies. She knew the type, but she had no idea of this one's true ability when she made that statement. Jacqueline looked at the hot, sexy intellectual and proceeded with upfront caution at his sudden kiss.

He had expected those kinds of words to come from the only woman who could hold his attention. Solomon planned on keeping her in his sight. He later said he knew that day he was going to marry her. She was a little powerhouse who made it perfectly clear she was not going to fool around with him.

Solomon had never seen anything like her, in all his years. She had busted him for who he had been to many women, and she did it in seconds and without hesitation.

The truth was that Jacqueline was dazzled by the powerful man she fell in love with across the desk. Solomon provided Jacqueline with a romance that swept her off her feet. She was sure the entire world could see it. Then, he did just as he planned – he married that girl. For the first time, love was really his. He was convinced they were together forever. My God, what had he missed all his life? It didn't matter – he had it now and would never let go.

What a whirlwind it was: love, marriage, and her at his side. It was a life poets speak about. But then in one second, the carpet was pulled out. A cancer diagnosis, treatment and the CIA breathing heavy down his neck. Solomon had become a liability to the agencies.

Even more important, Jacqueline and Marie were in danger. He knew time was limited; he only had a seventy-two hour head start to save all of them. It was not much time to make the mission a success, but it was all that Watchman could guarantee. Day after day, Solomon sat in his Scandinavian recliner in his Florida living room, recovering, plotting, recording, and programming information. He was getting ready for the inevitable.

Solomon had recovered very quickly once he returned from New York, but he knew he needed time and his imminent death, was buying him some extended moments to launch the world's biggest disappearing act. It would remove them all from the sights of the multiple governments he had done work for. So much of that work had been to benefit those in the darkest recesses of world power, the ones who fill the halls of justice and political thrones with a stench.

Günter had placed the listening device under the edge of the kitchen table on his last visit to their home. After Günter left, Solomon moved their conversations to the pool. He knew time was ticking, tick, tick, tick…

Jacqueline wouldn't listen to reason about Solomon leaving her; he tried logic, anger, mania, and fights. In the end, nothing was working. He wasn't surprised; Plan B was ready. He would scare the hell out of her with a ten-inch knife in a madman routine, force her to flee him, and then take flight himself. He cried like a baby and then laughed hysterically on I-10 as he was leaving her, knowing it was right but hurting like hell.

Rose crying? Solomon had shot men, snapped more than a few necks, blown up streets, engineered and precipitated many suicides. But he cried, not over killing, not over cancer, not over fear of the unknown, but over Jacqueline. By the time he got to Mississippi he was on a manic high. There were no more tears.

Solomon knew he would beat them all. He would have his family, brother, sister, Einstein, and the Underground. And they would have plenty of money as a little extra bonus. It was a game that required biding one's time. He could endure a year or two of danger and paranoia if it meant that he would spend the rest of his life in comfort and peace. He had never expected it would take almost three years to complete this exit from K.I.S.S. Time is what happens when you're making plans.

After months in Paris and time together with Watchman in the Underground, the plan was set into motion. Dietmar activated Solomon's brain while he was in a medical coma. His genetic eidetic memory and reduced pain sensors had been the key to connect a human to Einstein. His brain appeared to show no signs of overload from the massive information he constantly received. There were no crossed circuits, there was complete organization and he was able to fully control the visual, audible and verbal communications.

Dietmar also altered Solomon's DNA to regenerate new skin, resulting in new fingerprint growth. Dietmar warned him,

"Do not let these prints get in any data base. Use the machine over them until it's all over and you're clear."

"Got it." How is the work on the TA65 coming?"

"Not good. The telomerase that stimulates youth in the genes also feeds cancer cells. Although the cancer cells were removed from your new DNA, we have to proceed with caution, assuming that one cell could be left from your previous illness. Your history with the disease is a problem. We have three scientists working on removing the cancer feeding property by adding a bad taste to the telomerase that malignant cells reject. 5FU failed to do the trick last week."

"Keep trying, you'll get it."

"What about the MR – the Memory Replacement system?"

"It's complete. I can replace memories with created ones. We still have some bleed-over from old memories causing confusion, but overall, the old ones are rejected by the subject as dreams. I completed a male and female replacement set, should anyone ever want out of this program. I did one set for each gender even though Einstein sees no such probability from our people at this time. I also created a wonderful program of new memories for Jacqueline and Marie, at Watchman's request, should it come to that."

"Let's hope it never does. And as long as I'm alive, I call the shots on that one."

"I understand. Watchman asked me to create the special programs for use only on your command."

It was not long before Solomon was adjusting to the bio in Paris. Watchman left for Eastern Europe for a while and Solomon returned alone to life above the whore house. A set of thin masks changed his look completely as he walked the streets of Paris.

He searched book stores and reviewed new technology through Einstein, all while assimilating the inputs and learning to work the magnificent connections to the quantum. He read images day and night. He became adept at accessing traffic cameras, looking at everything through twelve different angles at once, and more.

It seemed as though the time had passed easily, but he was massively depressed in the city of love. He felt so alone. At cafés, he would pretend Jacqueline was with him. She was just off shopping...

Training his brain to the new screens and watching the world stage was his only sanity to fight the dark depression, depression that only disappeared when Jacqueline was near. The extreme high had discovered its low.

So he began a cycle of sleep before he could ward off his gloom, followed by problem-solving, studying his new skills, sleep.

Maybe that is where the time went. After a few more months, he began an intense eight hour a day workout regimen, whether in Paris, or the Underground. Yet, even fighting the world, he felt he did not have enough to keep his mind off his love, his wife.

He was stronger than he had ever been, both mentally and physically. Paris would be where he would wait for the time to pass until the plan was in full swing. He was stuck in France when the Underground would be the base to extract Jacqueline.

Solomon often had the inclination to visit his own grave in Paris. It was a morbid obsessive thought, but it was way too risky and he knew it. He stifled the urge every time. Someone would be watching whenever they were in the area, even though he was presumed dead. He would make no amateur mistakes. So Solomon waited.

Then came the day – the day! And it was a beautiful day, not a cloud in the sky; Solomon was having the time of his life testing that new plane. While he was performing maneuvers, his mind flashed an image – the one he had been waiting for. It was time. His mind opened the files from Einstein. There it was, Watchman's video with Dahl and more. He read everything, stored it in his memory, and deleted exit files from Einstein in minutes.

Not that deleting really made something irretrievable from Einstein, but should she ever be cracked in the future, those files would be almost impossible to find. No one knows about the future of technology and one day many years from now, some hacker could find their way into the Underground by accident. However, they would have to survive being in the system long enough to disable the destroy order program, and dead hackers without a breach would be the most likely outcome.

An accidental or unauthorized entry would be the end and the beginning. Should it be invaded by anyone, Einstein was programmed at its root to immediately order wet teams on the program hacker, cause destruction of the operations facility into which the hacker entered, and other defensive measures.

Solomon's time for action had arrived. He immediately altered the plane's course, heading straight for the Underground. Because he was already in the air, he arrived fifteen minutes ahead of schedule. It was perfect.

Watchman had already notified Dorr, Ade, Chike and Afrie,

"It's on; be at the plane in two hours."

The only reply,

"One, two, three, four."

They were awaiting pick up and two more six man teams were ready and armed when they arrived at the Underground.

The plane had been prepared months ago with everything they would need. Afrie was the pilot. Solomon watched on screen as people left the safe house. The plan was for another plane to pick them up at an airstrip and Afrie would then take over.

Solomon showered aboard, looked in the mirror, and began with the wringing of the hands – his reminder. Washing the blood off his hands – check; makeup – check; clothing – check; passport – check; gun – check; Solomon – check; element of surprise – game changer. All missions have a beginning, a middle, and an end. This one was no exception.

Never did Solomon imagine how things would turn out when he turned that plane over Greece and headed to the Underground. He was fully prepared to finally extract Jacqueline, but he had no clue that he would have to rescue Marie first. However, the Aero X7 had not even landed at the Underground before he was forced to make that decision. It pained him, but Jacqueline would have to take care of herself, even though she was in the hands of an Iranian sleeper who she knew as someone else. Things could not have been worse, or clearer.

Within minutes of his arrival, they all met in the lower levels of the Underground and headed onto the tram to join the waiting teams. First they had to rescue Marie and then extract Jacqueline. Solomon had timed his arrival perfectly. They were in the air in five minutes – a perfect start to the mission. He sat back, thinking about Jacqueline, while in constant communication with Watchman at the

Underground. You know, they say not to use electronics on a plane because it could interfere with communications. That's how Solomon's brain felt on the first flight. He was copacetic when he was ignorant, only a short while before.

On the other hand, on re-examination now that they were all in Dubai, after nearly three years of planning, manipulation, misdirection, medical procedures, killing, and more that cumulated into this final week, the mission to extract Jacqueline had gone well. That was still true, even with Solomon having to get to Marie first. He was in and out of Kitts clean; Marie was now safely in Dubai. Most of the Banksters on the list were already taken care of and Solomon had his Jackal.

Now he just needed to spend some quiet time in Dubai and convince her that he was the man she loved, clean up a few lose ends, obtain the final documents from the Grove, record the information for Einstein to redact and prepare reports for the last step of this mission. You know, just some light work.

This is the part of the mission that concerned Watchman most. What would Jacqueline's reaction to the events of the last three years be? And what information would Solomon deem necessary for the four corners? However, they had more men and mess to clean up before this mission was complete, so Solomon knew he needed to make a file for Einstein to redact and Jacqueline needed to be filled in on what she didn't know. Dubai was perfect for this.

Chapter Twenty-One
The Decision...

Jacqueline and Solomon had arrived unnoticed in Dubai. Watchman waited at the Underground, checking chatter from their actions. There was nothing around the world about them being in Dubai, and no buzz about Marie, either.

Jacqueline turned to Solomon under the setting sun in Dubai, "Rose, does the prince know it's you?"

"He only knows that it is Watchman or me, but nothing more. That's best for him. He has probably guessed it's both of us, or I'd like to think he hopes it's both and we made it. He'll let us rest and get a less noticeable jet into America. The Underground will pick us up and bring us in when the temperature from the Rio piece of the exit mission has been checked and regulated."

The prince had always been a good friend. He was just a boy when Solomon rescued him from the Mujh terrorist group in the Middle East. The Mujh was mostly known for its relationship with Taliban, and the prince and his family had always been sworn enemies of Taliban and its allies.

Even then the prince understood what his power would be. His father promised Solomon and Watchman a favor if and when they ever needed it. They had called it in for this mission. The son was honoring his father's promise. The prince's extended family had by chance spent time in the same hospital with Solomon when he was being treated for cancer. It was then Watchman sent word to his highness that the time for requesting help was nearing.

It was a favor that the royal family owed. They had no idea what Watchman and Solomon really did, just that they were powerful men and friends. To the prince's father, they simply saved his son. That created a debt, and the debt would be repaid. Believe me when I say, they did not care what was involved, their honor required this debt be paid and they'd have it no other way.

When Solomon and Jacqueline arrived on the runway in Dubai, a man was waiting with a message from the prince,

"Everything requested is here and if you need anything, we'll get it. A security perimeter is one mile around this compound. You are safe and welcome here for as long as you like. No one of interest has entered our country."

Without a word about the recent events or the nearly three years he was absent from her life, Jacqueline kissed Solomon and led him by the hand back to the open-air bedroom. A night of passion and splendor filled the desert. With champagne flowing, Medjool dates and other fruits to sweeten the palate, in their suite, love was the only thing between them. Jacqueline has listened, absorbed facts, analyzed the situation and decided that they had done enough talking for now.

Candles burned to the wicks' ends... as cum seeped from their kisses on one another's body. He has not forgotten the map to her mind, nor she to his. It was clear that they were still stealing moments of passion, these two – even with death at their door.

They'd spend days resting, laughing, talking, making love and just being together again. Solomon rediscovered Jacqueline's body and caused them both more pleasure than they had ever found. When a man loves a woman, her body is an unending journey.

They talked of Mark Steinberg, but she knew it did not matter. His death was just sad collateral damage. Solomon knew it was one of Dahl's men who killed his friend. However, Mark was in the thirty-one percent unknown and there was no way to have predicted his death. Solomon told Jacqueline that everyone has a time, and their ticket usually was punched by forces outside their control – it was simply Mark's time. He consoled Jacqueline with the reminder that Mark was a Mossad soldier and he certainly knew the risk.

Early into the second week, they'd become quite comfortable with their secure position in the Middle East. They donned robes and went out to see the city, just like normal tourists. They headed for a walk along around Dubai Creek in the old city area of Al

Shindagha. The riverbank was filled with palm huts and coffee shops for tourists. As they meandered with the visitors, there was a sudden but brief mist of rain – not enough to get them wet, but enough to cool them a bit and to settle the dust in the air. What was called a creek was really a huge salt-water river – calling it a creek was like referring to a glacier as an ice cube. It might have been technically accurate, but it simply did not give the true picture. As they stood near the creek's bank, they watched the abras, the traditional water taxis, gently navigating the currents. This is all Jacqueline wanted, as close a semblance as possible to a normal life together.

Dubai was one of the seven Arab Emirates of the United Arab Emirates. It was located in the southeast coast of the Persian Gulf. Dubai was first mentioned in history around 1095 and first settled in 1799. Its location is a trading hub and its rich oil deposits have made it a twenty-first century global city. It is a constitutional monarchy ruled by the Al Maktoum family.

The buildings of Dubai were architectural wonders, such as Burj Al Arab (Tower of the Arab), that was said to be the only seven-star hotel in the world. The tower was built on an artificial island created off the shoreline, and was designed in the shape of a sail, complete with a curving bridge to shore. Development of Dubai over the last twenty years has been staggering and it became a flagship for the business and monetary success enjoyed by the Emirates.

Ruled by one family since 1833, in 2013, Dubai was rated number one in the UAE in human rights. Although ninety-five percent of the population was Islamic, freedom of religion was widely accepted for all faiths.

The few, who feast on the evil of terror in the name of Mohamed, disgrace the faith. They fail to acknowledge Islam long has been an intelligent, peaceful religion that has honored rights of women since its creation. Those who used it as an excuse for murder were just as guilty of abuse of faith as any other who hide their evil acts behind religion, be it Christianity, Catholicism,

Judaism or the many others of the world. The abuse of religion decreases those who are sincere in their beliefs and who respect the faith of others.

With Dubai being an international business hub, it was a mélange of people from around the globe, all traveling between its modern buildings. So, Jacqueline and Solomon went unnoticed in their travel around the city. Their security forces stayed far back, with the exception of a few who kept close enough to step in if needed.

At the house provided for them, armed men stayed outside and guarded the compound. The kind servants announced their arrival to prepare meals and only upon request. All had been ordered never to view their guests' faces, and honored it with great caution and respect.

It was a good time to rest and talk. Jacqueline needed to hear it all and Einstein needed information for preparation of the final exit reports. You see even Einstein, with all its capabilities, did not know the full picture of the very Barium Project that created her – the killing, stealing, creating, bombings and more. Nor was Einstein fully aware that it was all done on the orders of the three most powerful countries in the world.

Some things had never been placed in the computer's bank of information for her to grow on, and one of those somethings was the full extent of Solomon's and Watchman's handiwork for the nations. Once that information was placed, her growth would exceed all known capacities. Now was the time, for in the end it would be the two of them, Solomon and Einstein, who would redact the final reports for the THC. With Einstein's ability to extrapolate knowledge, she would have eventually discovered the roots of her creation, but it was time to program in this missing information and speed up the process.

The quantum's ability to learn was already becoming extraordinary. Just giving the information to Einstein would allow her to deduce and build on that foundation of knowledge. For more than two years, she had the ability to think on her own, to truly understand concepts never before programed. Einstein did not merely calculate. Solomon was excited with each and every day of the machine's growth.

After weeks in Dubai, they arranged for a training site. Jacqueline and Solomon agreed Marie needed learn how to protect herself. In the distant desert, surrounded by a military perimeter, Jacqueline taught her daughter the J turn in a car to keep it from being stopped. Solomon worked with Marie on hand-to-hand combat and small weapons. Ishmael also helped her, practicing and reinforcing the lessons of Solomon and Jacqueline, and to add other skills.

Jacqueline and Marie debated about the amount of training she needed. Marie wanted more and Jacqueline insisted on less than full Mossad tutelage. Mother lost the debate; her daughter chose to be trained with skills to kill. Maybe it was for the best; she would be more than able to take care of herself.

Solomon was amazed to see Jacqueline's shooting skills were excellent. She was a good sniper, as good as Solomon had been in the past. He had not acted as a sharpshooter for years. He had men who did nothing but target and take those shots. Solomon had not updated his training or practiced long distance marksmanship, but he beat her. In fairness, it was no longer his skill that mattered. Einstein took the shots for him. As Jacqueline would later say,

"Einstein beat me."

The group stayed for nearly two months before beginning their journey back to America and C Street Underground. They arrived far from LAX on the prince's flight, purportedly on a diplomatic mission complete with international immunity. They all donned Middle Eastern robes for the flight. That diplomatic status meant that there was no need for a customs inspection, so they could land wherever they desired. The pilot dropped them off at an airstrip in the desert. Cars met them and they all headed for the Underground. The jet would quietly return to Dubai.

Within moments of the plane's arrival, the Humvees arranged by Watchman sped off, heading for the desert underground. A choice had been made to arrive under cover of darkness. Watchman had returned to C Street Underground some time before; he had been there a while. Of course, Dietmar and most of the others in select levels monitoring had known Solomon was alive, but some levels at the Underground still thought him dead. There would be shock in those areas at his arrival. Solomon found that amusing.

Chapter Twenty-Two
C Street Underground...

Solomon, called out,

"Miss me? It's good to be home."

Everyone was excited, as hologram screens flashed images from around the world. Things were buzzing. Dietmar and the others on the top levels had been working hard since Watchman's arrival. Everyone in the facility had gone through updated background, communications and network security clearance, and all came up clear. Many of the barriers that keep this facility compartmentalized were lifted, and Jacqueline saw the massive scope of the Underground for the first time.

Of course Einstein scanned itself every moment for unusual activity, so updating computer security was actually redundant. The other was just a standardized back-up procedure instituted before Einstein became a quantum. Dietmar ordered the procedure at a non-standard time, knowing Solomon's return to the Underground was imminent. Since Solomon was going public to all the employees and arriving with Jacqueline and Marie, Dietmar thought that they couldn't be too careful.

Watchman had left the day before Solomon arrived to the Underground. There were many things the elder brother needed to line up. He needed to scope out locations, determine the personnel and number and type of weapons needed for the next part of the mission. That phase would be the next group of men to be terminated with extreme prejudice. Once he had that sorted out, they needed to go retrieve the CWP documents at the Grove.

Jacqueline was disappointed that she would not see Solomon's brother on this trip to the facility. She was beginning to wonder if he actually existed. After all, her husband had said nothing about him until recently, and she had known Solomon for years. Solomon assured her that he did exist and she would see him soon. However, he also cautioned her to ask no questions about Watchman at the Underground.

"No one knows Watchman, Meier, is my brother."

"I wondered when you would confirm my thoughts. Not even Dietmar?"

"That's correct, not even Dietmar. Just you."

"Again, keep your knowledge to yourself. They only know him as Watchman the facilitator. You hold the most valuable secret to C Street – the truth about my brother and sister, Turing and Sari."

"So the man I grew to care so much for, Meier Finch, is your brother."

"Yes, and he's extremely fond of you. You'll meet Sari. Watchman's bringing her home soon."

"Is she happy about leaving the Swiss facility?"

"Very. It's her work that built this place, and she's never even seen it. For her it's truly a homecoming – to the home she designed. Everyone in this facility has dedicated their life to this work."

"Have you ever had someone who wanted to leave?"

"No, the levels provide many things and other vacation locations have a complete world of gardens, restaurants, shops, beaches and more. They all love being part of this operation, where the red tape does not slow their creative genius."

"What if someone decided they wanted to leave?"

"Things are easier now, with Einstein monitoring their contentment factor. Should anyone ever be discontent with being here, Dietmar has mastered a memory replacement, what we call an MR, program. Anyone who left would be given a background to build on, along with a home and money. We would not just cut them loose, but insure they were integrated into society. Fortunately, we have never been faced with that dilemma for our people. However, we have had to use it on two others to plug small leaks for NSA, and it works fine."

Solomon's eyes were focused on the screens flashing around the facility as they entered through a mirrored one way passage. They could watch from one-sided glass without being seen by others. For what seemed the first time, he really looked at the technology they had created over the years and saw the advances in just the last few months. Advancement by leaps and bounds was the secret to C Street Underground. Even Solomon appeared awestruck by the massive work that had been completed in record time.

Finally, Jacqueline's curiosity overcame her,

"Rose, why is the facility larger and more heavily populated than when I was here before?"

Rose just smiled.

"Unless Watchman or I am present to say otherwise, Dietmar has instructions never to open any of the barrier walls that subdivide even the main facility. The walls protect our refugees. This facility was established on a need to know basis, and is highly compartmentalized. Dietmar had no contingency instructions that would allow you to see more than a small percentage. Today, we have opened up more of it, because now more people need to know what is happening and how their work fits into the big picture."

Dietmar joined them as Solomon was answering. He seemed ashamed; he looked at Jacqueline as if he felt he had deceived her.

"Dietmar, I understand that you did what you were ordered to do. I'm not upset. After all, you really didn't know us then. But what if Rose really was dead? Would you have ever told Marie or me?"

"Jacqueline, I've had a feeling since the reports of his demise that Rose was alive and would return. He had three years. Solomon told me if he did not return in three years he was truly dead. Then I would have revealed the rest of the facility to Watchman. Until recently, Watchman was a secondary decision maker when Solomon was absent, a shadow on screen whose face I had never seen."

"Why didn't I hear the people?"

Dietmar replied,

"When the barriers are down, this place is soundproof from section to section, and from floor to floor."

"Floor to floor?"

Rose, chirped in with glee,

"Yes this is a multi-level facility. Come on!"

"Yes!"

"Dietmar, let's take them all down."

Dietmar was gleeful,

"Wonderful! Jacqueline and Marie can finally meet Waltraud! She is in a part of the facility that you could not access until now."

He turned to Jacqueline and Marie.

"Waltraud is my wife. We have been happily married for many years, and she works here as a stock market and investment analyst. She taught Einstein about the market and did the investment analysis programming before Einstein became a quantum. I wanted so much for her to meet you both, but I could not arrange it until now. Her security clearance level would not allow it. I know you will become great friends!"

Marie rushed to Dietmar and gave him a big hug.

"I'm so glad you aren't alone! Ever since I met you, I worried that you were lonely down here, despite your protests to the contrary. Where is she? Let's go see her right now!"

Jacqueline smiled broadly.

"I'm glad, too. I want to meet her as soon as we can. I have a suspicion Rose and Dietmar have other plans for us now, Marie."

Rose nodded.

"Letting you get to know Waltraud is an added benefit of opening all the barriers, but that wasn't really my main reason for doing it. Dietmar, I want to see what you have been up to. I had so little time here before leaving to extract Jacqueline. What about the plane? Did you finish it?"

"Take a look for yourself."

There it was - whatever it was. To Jacqueline, it looked like nothing more than a nice private jet.

"Well, is it done?"

"Yes. It looks like a Gulfstream, but it's loaded with technology and weapons, including stealth capacity for radar avoidance. We perfected the vertical takeoff and landing. It seats twenty and flies best above 50,000 feet and can easily fly above 65,000. That's 20,000 feet above the current maximum for commercial aircraft, and even higher than the Concorde's certification. It can fly in the same range of altitudes as military craft, but it's a lot more comfortable. Above 65.000, you might have to use the afterburners. If you notice, we did a good job of camouflaging them, so the plane doesn't stand out in a crowded airport."

"Congratulations! In Paris, I wondered about how this was coming along the entire time. I just didn't have time to look before we left to get Jacqueline. Good work!"

Dietmar led the way with pride as Jacqueline, Marie, Dorr, Chike, Afrie, Ade and Solomon followed.

"Rose, we'll go back and forth between different levels; I'm testing the timing on the new elevators."

"That's fine. There have been so many advances – I can't wait to see what you have in store for me now!"

Solomon looked at Dietmar as he said,

"Less than two seconds between levels, and it doesn't feel like we moved. Excellent work, Dietmar – it's a major time improvement. Outstanding!"

Dietmar smiled with pride as Solomon looked him,

"So, when do I get teleported?"

Dietmar laughed,

"Still working on that one. We still have the age-old problem of reconfiguring the molecules on landing. I'll keep you posted!"

He then became more serious,

"I think you will be pleased with what is now within our reach. But we do have to consider uploading some technology updates to the Langley test program for their use. Great Britain and Israel are behind too. They're getting too far behind us. They need more to complete their work, especially with the increased terrorism problem. Einstein wants them to take the fight on terrorism to the countries where the zealots hide. They need more, especially in drones, chemical identification, and satellite technology."

Solomon looked intensely at Dietmar,

"Einstein is continuously advising them of threats. But I know you're right. I'll make a decision on what will be uploaded this week. I see we have added more to the uranium disposal pack. That'll limit the dirty bomb capacity of the terrorists."

"Yes, and we have come up with a library of forensic matches for the chemicals and compounds terrorists are using. That will increase our ability to track terror-used uranium. By tracing acquisitions, we may be able to stop the bombs before they are made, but unfortunately, some of the identification could be only after bombs discovered through other means or have exploded. We need to pass that information on to Britain, the U.S., and Israel, since they are the most technologically advanced."

Solomon nodded his head.

"I'll take care of it."

Dietmar continued,

"But it's not just the big three; other countries on the world stage are getting too far behind in technological developments. Workers are having trouble monitoring the nukes and more. Einstein says that they are still in the safe zone, but only barely. They need to be updated."

"Yes, I received the same request from the system. We'll review and then we'll have a release to their systems soon."

Jacqueline noticed a slight change in Solomon's voice with that statement. She realized he was feeling the pressure of this facility.

He turned to Jacqueline and the others,

"We've created the most advanced technology in the world. However, it has to be released to countries only as is needed. We can't risk giving it all to everyone; some nut could take control of a major power and then attempt to take over the world. It's happened before. The quantum system monitors what advances are needed, makes suggestions, and seeks review on its recommendations. It only directly responds on its own in case of WWIII or some other world threat above a certain number of casualties. You have to understand, as it's doing that, Einstein is working on calculations to use an asteroid and magnetism to pull the Earth away from the sun before our planet overheats. It's a bigger picture machine.

"Although its decisions are flawless, it asks for a review before releasing major technological advances. If we get a request for review, it's safe to say World War III is not imminent. As long as I'm alive, Watchman or Dietmar can approve them if I'm not available. After my death, she will no longer ask for approval.

Dietmar smiled,

"Watchman and I both expected a request from Einstein but we hoped the decision could await your arrival."

Then with a laugh,

"To answer your earlier question, we're glad you're home! That way, you get to make the call and we don't have to. Of course, you've never disapproved an Einstein request. That's the only thing that makes the possibility of being a Solomon substitute bearable."

As he finished the statement, Dietmar stepped forward. His body was scanned by a blue line moving up and down. Each of the group followed. When all of them were scanned, a disembodied voice announced that access was granted to level one. A barrier lifted. Without comment, a man and a woman fell in line behind the group, as Dietmar moved forward to another scanner. Jacqueline did a double take at them and then looked to Solomon,

"Are you going to introduce me?"

"Jacqueline, I would like you to meet PIC and CIP. They are humanoids, programmable integrated companions... high-tech robots. Calm down honey, you are going to see many things that are, shall I say, unusual."

"I understand that, but they're amazing – they look just like us!"

The next blue lines scanned Dietmar and asked for voice comparison on the words, "Singapore is now closed for business." Then he placed his eye in a scan. Again, the voice spoke.

"Launch pad access granted."

Another barrier lifted and they all moved forward another thirty feet onto a platform with the train suspended in air. Once again the voice made an announcement,

"All aboard!"

They boarded the tram and within minutes were shot at high speed to another platform. Dietmar proudly announced,

"Mag-lev, magnetic levitation is the key here."

"Nice touch Dietmar. How fast is the train now?"

"At the moment, I have the speed limited to 378 miles an hour. It takes about four minutes from where we boarded to the actual launch pad. It's faster than the Japanese bullet train – even with its speed throttled down, it's quicker than any experimental train. We need to move many miles fast – deep into the Joshua National Forest – for launch."

"It doesn't even feel like we're moving!"

Jacqueline had barely gotten the words out when the tram stopped and she could see robotics at work on the tunnel platforms.

They all departed. Dietmar was scanned one more time, followed by each of the others.

"Ready?"

The voice said,

"Full access granted."

A final barrier lifted. Cars, planes, helicopters and more were before them. Solomon noticed something new and different in the massive update to the plane area since his last visit. There were two planes sitting side-by-side that he had never seen before. He looked to Dietmar as they walked toward one of the planes.

"The new stealth I heard about in Paris?"

"Yes, that's it. They are smaller but faster than one upstairs preparing to come into this area. But look what else we have updated on the plane. The precision guidance system for its missiles far surpasses the technology used in the Bin Laden raid. Our lift-off requires no runway. Unlike the F-35B's short takeoff, we have complete VTOL. Solomon turned to Jacqueline,

"Vertical takeoff and landing."

"Thanks, I'm catching on."

Dietmar looked to Solomon,

"This is a possible addition for the U.S. Now, it's up to you to decide. Should be placed in Langley's test system for their access?"

"How undetectable are these planes?"

"They have an invisibility shield of about eighty-five percent and almost no sound when switched to electric. They can fly anywhere. Jet fueled motors and generators and solar-electric power system with large battery capacity in minimal space. The plane's versatility is the key.

"We have only performed extensive testing at night. UFO is what observers call it! I'm just kidding; they can't see or hear the plane. We have also tested in the day, but just a few short runs. We don't show up on any current radar."

"How many pilots?"

"Only two for now. More are in flight training. They think it's an experimental project. However, even the pilots run mostly on the autopilot which is exquisite. It sits in the co-pilot seat at all times. Solomon, meet Latmar, the autopilot in S1 and Sam, for S2."

"Good to meet you, sir. We're at your command and will be present for you in the training simulator."

The robots looked as sophisticated as the humanoids, except they were without the human face and hands, and they were clearly made of stronger metal. When one robot walked next to the plane, the door opened, the autopilot chair turned out and he sat down, then the chair returned to its position inside. The other autopilot stood next to the plane.

Jacqueline turned to Dietmar and asked,

"Why do some look human and other like robots?"

Dietmar smiled,

"Well it depends on the skill level. If they are just for protection and defensive skills, they should be in humanoid form, since they will be interacting with the public to some extent. However, higher tech units, like pilots, remain looking robotic due to cost and functional considerations. For instance, these autopilots have no need for human-like faces and hands – they function quite well without the cosmetics. If you would like to convince your husband that money is no object, I can make them all humanoid for you!"

Solomon laughed,

"Dietmar, she has no control over budget. Same with me! Talk to Watchman when he returns – he's who you need to convince."

Dietmar shook his head and smiled dolefully,

"So much for your humanoid autopilots, Jacqueline. Watchman is so tight he makes every penny squeal before he lets go of it."

Gul immediately chirped in,

"Rose, I'm the human pilot."

Eli did not miss a beat as he called out,

"Me too!"

Eli came from Pakistan about two years after Gul arrived. They were best friends and highly competitive.

Solomon acknowledged both of the young men.

"Thanks. Good to know your pilots, human and robotic."

It was clear to Jacqueline that Solomon was more like a father than an employer to these men. They did call him Rose sometimes, but mostly Sir.

Solomon turned back to Dietmar.

"Simulator updated to reflect the plane's latest capabilities?"

"Yes. It's ready."

"Well, it's been a while since I've fiddled with the earliest prototype, so I'll need a lot of training."

"Use the autopilots while you become familiar with the technology. It's different from anything you have flown, and very much changed from what was in the prototype. The autopilots will familiarize you with the system changes. Tracking for this plane in flight comes through the clouds to the Underground systems."

Jacqueline smiled at Rose, who replied to her curious look,

"Dietmar is right. I've never flown anything like this. I can tell that it's nothing like the prototype. I'll train as a backup pilot only."

Jaqueline smile was even larger,

"Train me, too."

"Okay, you're in."

Solomon knew he had Jacqueline back with that one request. Or she could steal his plane...

Over the next hour, Solomon was alone in his office. From his tan leather Scandinavian chair, he viewed hologram screens that appeared in thin air and filled the room. A blue light shined wherever he directed his attention. He worked and talked by satellite with Watchman while the others looked around the facility.

Earlier, Watchman had been monitoring the facility when he heard Jacqueline was going into the flight simulator. He was not happy. He felt it was too much exposure and that letting her learn to operate the most advanced equipment they had dramatically increased the risk Jacqueline posed to them.

"Just remember, I was with her at the Mossad training camp in Israel. She is good, thinks outside the box."

Solomon insisted that she would train to fly. Watchman was handling a few other problems, so he didn't need to worry about that. He assured his brother that it was fine, he'd won her back.

He told Watchman,

"Maybe if she smiles at Latmar or Sam just right she can steal a plane. You know that's not happening, so calm down."

Even Watchman bellowed with laughter when he realized how ridiculous he was being. Then he let it go; his brother's logic prevailed. Besides, Solomon was too stubborn to give in and they had to move on to other matters.

"Tell Dietmar I'll look at the budget for the humanoids."

"I will. He really wants more money in that area."

"They are worth it. His developments with the technology are almost getting to the point of illusion. I saw they fooled Jacqueline when they approached the group. It's hard to say how long that would have lasted, but she clearly believed they were humans."

"People see what they want to believe, but her assumption was largely based on probability. The mind presumes humanity because that's much more likely than any other possibility – except maybe at the Underground! But it won't be long, even over an extended period, before you won't be able to tell the difference between humans and humanoids. I agree, give him more funds for that project. If I didn't think it was worthwhile, I wouldn't have told him I'd talk to you about it."

Watchman laughed,

"See, I told you! You never think about the money! Are you becoming fiscally responsible?"

"Not my job!"

Watchman continued chuckling as he said,

"Dietmar will get his funding. I just wanted to state the obvious. Oh, good. The video feed is ready now. Some of us have been working and not spending. It's coming up now."

Watchman had recently intercepted a scheduled meeting – a late night meeting of three men on K Street in Washington, DC. Solomon was in deep concentration as he saw the events in DC unfold. His mental image showed three men in an apartment in Washington, D.C.

Robert Koss, a CIA operative in a windowpane suit said,

"Who in the hell's moving the accounts from the black budgets and why are assets going dark? We aren't the only ones either. I talked to MI6. It has to be the work of the Chameleon. No one else could do it. That son of a bitch was dormant for a year. Everybody thought he was dead!"

David Klein of Mossad, wearing his black and gold Yarmulke, replied.

"I'm telling you, the Chameleon is dead! We're sure it was Solomon Rosenberg. We all know he's dead – DNA doesn't lie. So he's not the one killing agents or moving money."

Koss replied,

"Solomon Rosenberg's dead and he was not the Chameleon. We've known that for years."

He reached for a file,

"I told you all this before. We looked into him a long time ago along with an investigation of a lot of other CIA agents. We wanted to make sure the Chameleon wasn't CIA. I can place him arguing before the Supreme Court when a signature bomb went off in Libya, in Washington when one was set off in Iraq, and there were lots more conflicts that made it impossible for him to be the Chameleon. There's the time table, just look! Plus, that DNA from the grave in Paris proves he's not it! The Chameleon killings continued long after Rosenberg was dead and buried."

Mike Steel, in a deep authoritative voice, smoking a cigar and wearing a general's two stars on his uniform said,

"Neither of you get it! Chameleon's alive, it's Solomon Rosenberg and he's behind this all. I don't know how, but he faked his death. It's him."

Koss seemed to panic,

"What in the hell are we going to do if you're right?"

The general took another puff of his cigar,

"Kill him. Make the rumors of his death the truth. We have to find him now. Those assets aren't missing, they're dead. That's another signature of the Chameleon; we never find the fucking bodies. First, we have to find Rosenberg. We'll find the money later. Send our best assets before he comes for us. Whoever we have left – and put a ten mil bonus on the table for proof of death."

Klein looked at both men,

"If there are any good assets left when he's done! We have two confirmed dead and nine more men missing, all in the last seventy-two hours. Hell, someone blew Rio sky high the day after Carnival. Whoever it was escaped clean after killing two more of our men. This has been going on under our noses for months!"

Koss looked to the general,

"We'll find the money later? What the hell? We stole that money from the black ops funds over the years for our retirement! You plan on filing a fucking theft report with the Pentagon?"

The general turned to the men,

"Just get him now. He's alive. Trust me. I'll deal with tracking the cash."

Koss replied,

"General, I'll send our best, but it's a wild goose chase. He's dead."

The general raised his cigar to his lips,

"Just do it or we'll all be dead soon. It's harder to spend money when you're six feet under."

At that moment he puffed his last cigar breath and fell to the floor. David Klein and Robert Koss panicked as they looked at the slumped body on the apartment floor. While Koss checked for a pulse, Klein screeched,

"Signature Chameleon!"

Within moments, they fled the apartment in their separate cars. Each was trying to make calls, but they had no cell bars. After they departed, a quite ordinary man quietly walked into the apartment, removed the cigar next to the body and left another partially burnt one taken from the general's office earlier in its place. He picked up a file and left within seconds.

Two miles away, Robert Koss pulled up to his office and paused as his phone finally showed cell bars. He quickly dialed and put the phone to his ear. A few minutes later, the same quiet man opened the car door remotely, took the phone and drove away. Robert was found dead a few hours later in the driver's seat of his tinted glass BMW.

David Klein suffered a heart attack, caused by an electrical malfunction of his pacemaker in a drug store parking lot. There was a stop by from the average man to retrieve that phone, too.

Solomon looked at Watchman on the screen, as they both looked at the man walking away from picking up the last cell phone.

"Good job. See you soon."

The teleconference between Solomon and Watchman ended. Solomon caught back up to Dietmar and the group touring the Underground,

"Rose, our launch pad is now at 33°50'51.38"N 115°47'59.56"W – it's the El Dorado Mine in Joshua Tree, just where you chose. No problems with construction in that area. The takeoff command can be executed from any floor, as long as the person has access authorization within the scanner's security parameters. Of course with your bio, you can command from anywhere."

"Perfect. The mine has been closed for years, so it's an ideal location for a launch site, plus we could recycle the shafts and that saved a ton of work. How's the reinforcement on the shafts? Any problems with hikers or other tourists?"

Dietmar shook his head as he replied.

"I've had robotics working for years upgrading the tunnels with technology and shields to prevent discovery. We've done everything quietly – no one even knows we're around, and they certainly have no idea we've been hard at work. Also, the cars are designed to look great, including your favorite the armored Town Car with one hell of an engine job and a few weapons. However, for more than two occupants, I think the armored Humvees will serve you better. They can handle the terrain to get out there and their firepower is excellent.

Solomon nodded and smiled broadly.

"I'm glad you did a Town Car – you know it's my favorite."

Dietmar continued,

"The vehicles and equipment packages can be transported anywhere in the world to meet you. They all have shields that can be activated for stealth. The cars can't be picked up on satellites once you launch the shields. But the vehicles are only protected for fifteen minutes. We still have some problems with the power source for the cars; we're limited by aerodynamics and making them look typical when the shields aren't on. I could make a great power source for the vehicles, but they'd stand out even on non-high res satellite imaging. I'm still working on the miniaturization. I want them coming in and out at El Dorado, especially until I can solve the shield power supply issue. I really need everything but our general supply pickup vehicles to come and go from that location."

Solomon was clearly proud of the work, as he spoke to the group,

"Go look around and see what we have. It will not let you touch without being coded into the scanner, so stay behind the lines. No shock if you do, just an alarm if you cross the lines – we are all friends here. But look."

Dorr and Jacqueline were amazed at the part of the facility they had never been privy to before. Dietmar was clearly updating Solomon on everything.

"Your scan code is already embedded, but it needs an update just in case."

"Dietmar, you always believed I was alive!"

"The entire time, Rose. Watchman said I didn't look surprised when he told me."

"Watchman told me all you said was, 'I'm waiting for him.' You having any problems with deliveries - anything pressing?"

"No, it's like clockwork; whatever I order arrives in the desert for pick up. It works like a charm. I have amassed a collection of new high tech parts for everything we could want to build. Another huge shipment is coming to the base from the Swiss operation, through Germany to here, this week."

"What about the portability of our equipment from the Underground to the launch site?"

"You will love this: a magnetic field carries the equipment to a loading dock and onto the mag-lev train. Planes, cars, cargo lifts, everything. It's a variation on the principle for the bullet train we were on. You don't even have to touch them or turn over an engine until it's ready. You can order one or more items from upstairs, and they will be lowered directly to the bullet train for a quick trip to the launch area. The passengers will use the elevators and the train car will hold twenty. I have a second train car under construction should the secluded area of the facility eventually be used to house more people."

"Get it built. I'm planning on opening another barrier soon. Including the pilots, how many seats on the plane?"

"Depends, two to eight in most, twenty in one – it's not luxury seating. Same with the helicopters. Also, satellites are now under such tight surveillance we can come and go freely from C Street without worry of exposure. Your programing to automatically alter the images by Einstein before we arrive at NASA or other facilities worldwide is excellent. On another development, view Einstein's file 2C2C552X7719. I loaded in new access for you."

Solomon paused as he viewed the file Dietmar spoke of, marked within Einstein for his eyes only, and then he focused for a minute.

"Nice."

Solomon had just been shown the diagram and locations around the facility of tubes that would shoot him directly to the launch site in seconds.

"So those are completed?"

Dietmar nodded,

"Yes, and they are fully operational. Now we can go on."

"What do we have in small weapons and surveillance toys?"

"Rose, lets head back up and I'll show you."

They all boarded the tram. Jacqueline was quiet. Solomon looked at her face and asked,

"What's up?"

"Well, you built this place!"

"We built it, Watchman, Dietmar, Sari, me, and some very good scientists and engineers. Moreover, it's my brain child and I'm proud of that part. We own quite a few patents through the Rose Corp that helps finance our operations: lasers, micro satellites, small machine nanotechnology, chemical compounds and the like. Those, we've already released for use to universities or governments. Some of the highest tech is never patented and unreleased at this point. We only file patents as we prepare to release new tech."

Jacqueline liked what she was seeing about Solomon anew, except she was aware that there was far more danger to come. Solomon whispered to Jacqueline,

"It seems the advancements in technology have given us even better protection from discovery and a limitless capacity for good without evil. Understand, though – good and evil are not really that different. It truly depends on what side of the wire you're on."

Dietmar asked Solomon if he would be needed for a few minutes, or if he could take Jacqueline and Marie to meet his wife.

"Of course you can. Now that the secret's out, you know Jacqueline and Marie well enough to know there'll be no peace until they get to know Waltraud!"

Dietmar laughingly replied,

"Then we should go! Ladies, come with me."

After a short walk that seemed to take forever to Marie, there she was, before Jaqueline's eyes. It could not be denied that the thin woman had been a long legged, blue eyed, blonde haired beauty in her youth. Even with age, her beauty still shone. Her eyes lit up as she spoke in the sweetest of voices, still reflecting her German heritage. She greeted Jacqueline with a tight embrace.

"Jacqueline, I wanted to meet you, even before Dietmar did! I heard Rose's stories and I hoped we would get together someday. Then Dietmar told me all about both of you. He said he couldn't introduce us then. I understood the security concerns, but it just wasn't right that we had to wait so long."

As the embrace ended, Jacqueline looked to her with a smile and a chuckle,

"You, my dear Waltraud, were a well-kept secret. Our husbands conspired to keep us apart, but our will was stronger than theirs and now we're together."

Marie was ready to burst. She pushed her way in to meet Waltraud. As she embraced her, she said,

"Mom, don't forget me! Waltraud, I'm so happy to meet you. I was so worried about Dietmar being lonely – no one told us that you were here until today. I know we have so much in common – we'll have a lot to talk about!"

Jacqueline laughed,

"Don't knock her down, Marie! Let her breathe! Think you should tell Waltraud your name? My daughter is a bit excitable at times."

"Oops – I'm Marie, and I'm so thrilled to meet you."

"And I am very happy to meet you, as well. Everything Dietmar told me about you is true; I can tell."

Dietmar told them,

"I'm very glad you all finally have met. I do wish it could have been sooner, but... Anyway, I'll leave you to get to know each other – I'm sure Rose expects me to return right away."

For the first few days they all worked while catching up, knowing there was a lot to do. The last step in the stay would be plastic surgeries for Jacqueline and Solomon. That would come after the documents were retrieved, at least for Solomon. Recovery would be short and during that time everything, including Solomon, would be updated and tested again.

They could work on the flight training and exit assessment while Watchman found the last targets and attended meetings in various governments to get an update of the reaction of those who lost funds and people in this exit. Solomon's focus was on planning the entry into a water surrounded fortress, a haven for the powerful. That was where they had to go to retrieve the long sought CWP paper documents – the ones they finally located at the Grove.

Teams one and two were set for this mission, but suddenly team one had been needed in Nigeria. The terrorist group Boko was killing on an unprecedented level and planning attacks around the world. Einstein was adamant that there would be no war reparations to this country when the mission was completed. Many nations had learned to profit from reparations by using terror and that had to stop.

Jacqueline offered to go with Solomon and team two on the Grove mission to assist with the two floor double access safe. She was curious and wanted to see the legendary playground of the powerful. However, Solomon wanted to hold off for team one to return. Marie was preoccupied with work and, of course, with Gul.

They all needed updated hardware, communication system upgrades, the latest weapons, briefings on the latest world events, and so much more. Everyone worked in a fever to see that they got it all right away.

Recently, the Pentagon had utilized some "new" telecommunications to see a military mission involving a capture in the Sudan. Based on a review of that footage, Einstein decided the Pentagon needed another updated technology release. The government's images from the feed were far too grainy and showed much too little detail for such an important mission. The raw feeds Einstein received were much clearer. The Pentagon's images were so poor that it was nearly impossible to tell what had happened, much less distinguish fine detail. That simply would not do.

There would be one more mission for the Underground teams, the document retrieval from the water fortress, and then their looks would be modified. They would wear faces that only Dietmar, Watchman, Solomon, Sari, Jacqueline and Marie would see in advance. Each of them would be double-checked to make sure they could not be recognized, their images washed to bypass any facial recognition, and their fingerprints changed, all before they left. Then there would be updates for most of them by the mobile nanoprint app. Solomon's prints were forever changed; the SMARCAD1 gene modification to alter his fingerprints had been done at the same time as his bio-stimulation. He had been covering his new fingerprints since then to avoid having them show up in any databases.

Jacqueline would keep her beautiful long auburn hair at Solomon's request. Marie decided to undergo a change and would finally get the cheek implants she wanted. When this was over, they would be what Solomon's old agency employers call clean for a new assignment. Except, they planned to have no more ops – ever!

Chapter Twenty-Three
The Fortress...

The time for the mission to take the fortress in the Grove was growing near. He knew it, even if the timeline wasn't entirely firm. Solomon was getting that antsy feeling he always felt when a major operation was about to begin. His reverie was interrupted. Watchman arrived on screen to Solomon,

"We have a problem."

Solomon could see the intense look on his face,

"What?"

Watchman took Solomon by surprise when he stated,

"One corner of the key code has been coming through the government's computer system."

"Repeat. One and not four?"

"Clarified: just one - POTUS."

Solomon took a deep breath then said,

"The POTUS term is almost up. It looks like he has gotten curious. Einstein and I surmised it would be him."

Watchman seemed almost happy,

"Nine years ago, we set everything in motion for our deadline to exit K.I.S.S., and the time is almost up. Your cancer sent us on a different path, but the result must be the same. The Court will be changing at the end of the year, so now is the time."

Solomon did a quick assessment, with Einstein's help. Solomon had always been more analytical than emotional and instinctual, or so he told himself. The analysis of man merged with computer was not just fast, it was also detailed. He found he relied on his instincts even less now that Einstein was involved. In a matter of seconds, he told Watchman,

"Don't respond yet. I don't trust going in on a partial code now. Let's finish this exit up, then we'll notify the others and head into

THC. We still have time. We'll wait until we are done with this. We need to get moving."

"If they have done this much, they'll get the other corners eventually. I hope you are thinking of going in soon. Remember, we agreed."

"Well, yes and no in that order, Watchman."

"Whatever you say, but we have to meet the December deadline and this place will be dangerous!"

"We'll give them the backup plan."

Watchman bellowed, laughing hysterically,

"Got it."

"Glad I can still make you laugh. Get ready – we'll be taking the Grove now."

"Good luck. I'll be waiting."

Solomon pulled up the screen to the fortress. The area they were interested in was a bunker level leading to a bedroom suite and private sauna area. Since the documents they needed to retrieve were old school papers held in a twin floor lock safe, there was no option but to go in. They could see through the safe to the papers and the security system. It was low-tech but amazingly effective since it took two to open it, one person on each floor. That at least doubled the risk of being discovered in the course of the burglary.

What the CWP called a retreat was considerably more secure than Fort Knox – it was surrounded by vast land, water, mountains, cottages, laser fences and more. On top of that, there was the security force. It consisted of mercenary and military guards, all with automatic weapons like M200 sniper rifles, corner view guns with video capability, and heavy ordnance. To make things more complicated, there were dogs and pressure sensitive pads. Making a clean entry and exit would not be simple.

However, only in July did they hold a two week summit for the most powerful men in the world to discuss next steps in what they called world order but was actually world control. These men did not let things happen, they made them happen. This was April, and springtime could not have been a better time to take down the men of the Grove. Summer would have required an all-out assault.

The Grove was protected mostly by ex-military without family. Those men and women had signed on with a security company only to discover they had no exit from the position. A few were soldiers purely for hire to the highest bidder, mercenaries. It did not take long for a new recruit to understand that no one left this assignment and made it home alive. This was complements of private armed mercenaries who were paid far more money to assure that no one walked out of this job.

Solomon was still a team short and Jacqueline was willing to go.

"Come with me, I want to show you something."

They walked into his private office.

"I want you to understand how dangerous this mission is. Are you sure?"

"Yes, I can handle this."

"I want you to see something, just so you know before we go. It's okay if you decide not to participate in this one."

Solomon pulled the screen from the air and onto a monitor. It was a photo of her taken from behind while sitting on a beach.

"That's me! I saw it before when Einstein and I were chatting. She changed the image for me, but I see you changed it back."

"No, that's Einstein's true avatar. You know she's programed with your voice, as well. So I always see and hear you. I just want you to know how much I love you. She's you, except she lets me tell her what to do. I want to ask you not to go on this mission. I really don't want you at risk for this."

With a smile, she replied,

"Although I appreciate your asking, that's the difference between the computer and me – I do what I want. I'm going. Let's face it, I'm the perfect choice, small and fast. Besides, we need the others to get us in and out. Looks like I'm your best choice. I bet Einstein agrees. Besides, the only way out of all this is straight through, and I want out."

With Jacqueline's insistence on going, she would handle the safe on the upper level. They were in motion. Solomon planned on getting in and out without a shot fired and no soldiers killed. They could have cared less about the taking out a mercenary or the men of World Order, but the soldiers had just been looking for post-war work and were stuck in their jobs. They would be the most likely casualties.

During those two weeks in July, it would be almost impossible to infiltrate the grounds. Fortunately, their timing of the mission for spring couldn't have been better. The staff, guests and guards would be more limited. The twenty-seven hundred square mile area outside San Francisco would be guarded by one hundred and eleven guards, employ ninety-four staff members, and house between twenty and twenty-five guests on average in April. The last number changed daily, but was a stable average of twenty of twenty-two in spring.

The water surrounding the area was no problem. They had released lobster cameras a few weeks earlier and were providing the live feed of the premises. Lobsters were small mechanical underwater surveillance devices with cameras for recon. Puebla flowers, natural to the area, were designed as cover for the camera scopes to come to the surface for gathering intelligence. Of course, the lobsters also monitored the water in the vicinity of the Grove for activity.

For the mountains, they released birds similar to the ones Solomon used in Rio and Colombia. Birds were tiny aerial surveillance robots that flew in programed formations and could release small bombs, or in this case chemicals, covering an area. They could be timed for all pellets to be released together.

These were designed to resemble the black ravens native to the mountains of San Francisco, and each held surveillance cameras. One advantage to using ravens as patterns was that the birds' payload capacity was much greater than many other varieties, such as birds the size of wrens. Thirteen of the mission robots were sent two weeks ahead to survey the main compound, providing the intelligence from inside the fences on all levels.

More of the same birds would gradually be released in massive numbers over a few days, filling the area. When their plane was over San Francisco, the birds would form a grid pattern over the twenty seven hundred acres. They would release the chemical sleep agent NocNoc, all at one time over the entire area. The ones already inside the compound would do the same.

Because the NocNoc was disbursed with nanotechnology, its penetrating power of buildings and the like was incredible, as was the speed. Once this chemical was dropped, any human or animal not sealed airtight would suddenly feel the need to sit or lean and then fall asleep within seconds of contact. There was no precursor feeling of being drugged; the subjects would not even feel it until it was done. The chemical would disappear from the air in five minutes. The effect lasted for hours in the body of any animal. Anyone entering after five minutes would be free from its effects. Really, it was one of Dietmar's and his fellow chemists' most excellent recent compounds.

The Underground would loop the feed of the Grove's surveillance to cover the actions of the mission. A helicopter with a backup extraction team, plus Jacqueline and Rose would land on the Grove in a small, out-of-the-way clearing in the forest not too far from the shack entrance to the bunker.

This was as close as they could get by chopper. A small armed land rover would take them in and out the same way at high speed. It was pre-programed to soar only feet about ground, and equipped with route information that was accurate to within microns. Not even a windblown twig would touch the rover, so precise was its programming.

No heat signal had shown in the bunker area in weeks. That boded well for it being unoccupied when Solomon and Jacqueline entered. If someone entered the bunker after the last recon, there could be a problem because it was designed to protect its occupants from nuclear and biological attack. That meant any occupant of the bunker might not be affected by the NocNoc. On the other hand, the shelter might not be able to completely filter air at the nanoparticle level, so the NocNoc might work. The bottom line was that if there were occupants, they might be unconscious or they might not.

Despite that possible hiccup, the plan was this: in and out in fifteen minutes, no one killed and the papers retrieved. No plan could cover all the contingencies, but this one was as good as it got. Solomon knew that the unknown was omnipresent in the execution of any scheme.

Part one of the lock, the portion in the basement, was a latch that triggered the release of a book on the shelf in the bedroom of the second floor. Removing that book opened the hidden safe area. However, the book that was released on the second floor by the latch in the basement had to be removed in less than one minute or the safe area would not open. The combination Solomon had obtained through Einstein would do no good without access to the safe.

That meant they would need someone downstairs to trip the first lock latch and another upstairs to pull the book out, open the safe, and begin emptying it. With everyone hopefully asleep from the chemical, Solomon and Jacqueline would be able to roam freely. By the time they arrived, the NocNoc would have dissipated and become harmless. If all went to plan, nothing would be left but a bunch of sleeping beauties. If things went sideways, a clean-up team was on standby.

Jacqueline decided to take the bedroom level and Solomon would trip the lock from the lower level, since the release was located much higher up in the basement area. Once he tripped the latch he would meet her in that bedroom, where she would have already opened the safe and begun emptying it. The rover outside would return them to the helicopter. The whole operation would be down, up, and gone in less than fifteen minutes.

It was in the wee morning hours when the mission began. Everything was on target as Solomon headed down to the bunker's basement level to trip the safe's security latch. Jacqueline headed to the bedroom suite. Both were wearing Kevlar clothes, just in case of gunfire.

The book ejected out a few inches and the panel opened to the safe area. Jacqueline had the safe open in seconds and began emptying the papers into the sack. She was just removing the last papers when she heard Solomon coming up the stairs. She smiled, zipped the bag and tossed the pack over her shoulder. Within seconds she saw a knife coming down over her head, felt heat in her neck and all went black.

From the stairs, Solomon could see the attack and instantly pulled a thin piano wire out of his watch. In one swift move from behind he garroted the blade-wielding man who had been in the sauna area and unaffected by the gas.

Jacqueline was on the floor – the knife entered an unprotected area of her neck near the brain stem. Solomon quickly grabbed a can from his backpack and sprayed Jacqueline's neck, leaving the knife inside. Then he cut the handle and part of the blade with a laser from the same pack. Solomon warned the Underground and the helicopter of Jacqueline's injuries and called for the clean-up team. Then, within moments, he carried Jacqueline and her pack strapped around his shoulders to the waiting rover.

She was rushed back to C Street with Dietmar and Dorr on screen the entire time. They were managing the emergency care treatment and triage on the way to the operating room of the Underground. Dietmar, Dorr and a surgical team were on Jacqueline's care within minutes and for hours. However, even stabilized onsite and in the helicopter, the treatment delay had a cost.

Outside the operating room, Solomon was inconsolable and spoke not a word. Watchman tried as they waited for hours. Finally, Solomon turned to his brother,

"I never should've allowed any of this. We were drafted into this world. I brought her in for my own selfish reasons."

"Solomon, if she survives you still have a choice. Now, we can erase her memories."

"Yes, the MR is completed and the memory bleed-through is minimal. Dietmar told me."

Solomon's distress took over. He began pacing and wringing his hands. The signs of his mania were evident.

"What difference does it make? What if she doesn't make it? What will I do? How can I survive if she doesn't?"

Solomon had been watching the surgery's progress on screens inside his head. At that moment, Einstein flashed the latest probabilities. The likelihood of Jacqueline's survival had risen to 85.4 percent.

"She's going to make it! Her odds are 85.4"

"Good, good. Now you need to think. First about her – what will you do? Secondly, we can no longer expose you on missions. We don't have another match to Einstein and if something happens to you, the quantum takes over."

"I understand. Let me review the documents from the safe and we'll go from there."

"I've already reviewed some. Here are the ones you were looking for."

Watchman handed his brother the documents, knowing full well he would insist on one more mission. It only took seconds for Solomon to see what Watchman was telling him. Yes, he had the Corporate World Power name in writing and the order of succession. There were also the names of the men who started Wilderness Mirror, an operation to trade with Israel for some of their best-trained assets. The details of the money involved were laid out.

Wilderness Mirror was all about the trade of CIA agents and money for Mossad-trained agents and for exclusive control of engineering for CWP. The siblings were engineered beings – programmed to be white paper assassins. Solomon's eyes widened.

"Did you know?"

"Not until I read it there."

"They used electroshock, hypnosis, and psychedelics to prepare us for the years of training – on the very first year we arrived at the compound in Palestine! The hypnosis was to wipe any memory of the initial programming. It's all here. Those motherfuckers!"

"I checked with Zelva this morning. She confirmed she was reassigned and sent away for sixteen months about three weeks after we arrived at the compound. She agreed that we seemed different when she returned. However, she said she did not know what caused the change in us."

"My God, Esther too, when she was still too young to have been renamed Sari. Whoever of them is left will beg to die, when I find them."

"This explains those dreams you've always had. They couldn't completely wipe your memories."

"Yes, now I know they're real memories and not just flash thoughts. My fear of being taken captive is from my past. I'm going to kill the sons of bitches!"

The creative minds and facilitators of the project were four men from four countries and even four faiths, a Muslim, a Catholic, an Anglican, and a Jew. They sought ultimate power. The papers revealed they were Karamanli of Libya's internal security agency, Walker of MI6 in Great Britain, Carnegie of the CIA in the USA, and Childs of Mossad in Israel. The only thing they had in common was money, power and the desire for more of both.

The entire plan was created by three founding families of world banking long embedded in the governments around the world. It was an attempt to permanently control America. And their plan had worked, despite what the creators thought. Now, its permanency was in serious question, because it was time for the siblings to shut it down.

The final report stated that Operation Wilderness Mirror was closed due to cost and feasibility reports, that the agents were returned, but that their extermination had been unforeseen at Camp Hesbely, Palestine. The report detailed that there were no survivors, and that all three assets and Angus Walker were deceased. The document was signed by C. Childs and S. Carnegie, above their typewritten names, Credence Childs and Scotch Carnegie, and showed the date it was signed. The report was stamped and sealed with the elusive CWP stamp, over the typed words Corporate World Power.

Solomon realized the last part of the report was fabrication – he knew with every fiber of his being that those monsters had ordered him, Watchman, and his cherished Sari to be blown from the face of the earth. Finally, Solomon knew the names of those in control – and what power they had. Angus Walker had been a dangerous shadow in the British intelligence agency MI6, an agency so secretive that Britain had not even admitted its existence until 1994.

MI6's Walker, financed by Carnegie and other government means, sought out one of the best organizations in the world, Mossad. Then he paid a Mossad trainer to defect and establish a compound in Palestine, select candidates, and develop assets over a twelve year period. The Mossad defector was a man with unprecedented skills. When their training was complete, they became the assets for the long-term operation Wilderness Mirror. The creators' initial investment in this operation was in the millions. It was clearly headed for the billions when all of them thought they had ended the operation with the camp explosion and a plane crash.

Walker clearly had been a power hungry evil man. The world was better off when he died at the compound. As Watchman had always told Solomon, the compound being wiped out was "convenient." The creators intended to kill Solomon, Watchman and their Sari that day at the meeting. It had become clear to CWP that the operation was too expensive, exposure was likely and the possibility of failure too high. The operation was compromised by their failure – their failure to hide the financing trail well before Watchman took over the facilitating in America.

Angus Walker, who objected to closing the op, was set up by Carnegie and Childs to attend the meeting at the compound with the siblings. Fortunately for the siblings, Solomon had seen the writing on the wall. More accurately, he tapped the right phone at the right time in Turkey. He learned of the planned cleanup of the whole sibling project. Solomon's decision that they would agree to the meeting and then not show was what saved all three of them. Before that meeting, Solomon told Watchman that they would not attend and he believed these men planned to eliminate one of four partners – Angus Walker – and everyone else involved at the compound.

Watchman never asked his brother any questions about how he knew, but arranged their acceptance of the planned meeting – a meeting they did not plan to attend. There was something at the camp he wanted to retrieve, but he did so before the expected meeting. He was back in the air leaving Israel when the camp exploded, so he was in no danger and no way near the impact.

That left two at the Grove, the ones at the top of the plan, believing their trail was forever covered. This operation by the elite, Wilderness Mirror, was now a closed operation, as far as they were concerned. The two left, their involvement unknown for years until now.

Stately, plump Credence Childs, a man who had worn the black robes of the Supreme Court of the United States for years. Scotch Carnegie was a thin, bald, consummately evil son of a bitch, and the heir to a vast fortune. The pair, Carnegie and Childs, had bought and sold America for years as a simple continuation of their family businesses.

It was in black and white, the two men it took to open the safe and top in a line of succession that had gone on for years. Both believed that their British and Libyan partners, the assets bought from Mossad, and anyone who knew of the trade were long dead and buried. It was all in writing and where Solomon could finally see it.

Watchman watched as his brother read the papers from the safe, knowing what was coming next. He was worried.

"Stay calm, Solomon."

"I'm the calmest I've ever been. I have them. This document refers to the meeting where our elimination was planned, just after I returned from North Korea."

Watchman was not so sure. Was his brother only serene on the surface and a boiling cauldron underneath? Or was it even worse? He decided the only way to find out was to keep talking – see how Solomon reacted.

"Yes, I told you about that request for all three of us to return to the compound. You decided we would not return…saved our lives. They thought we were in the explosion. All these years, they believed we were killed as planned, along with Angus Walker and those who performed the training on the Israel/Palestine side. Mossad lost many who had no inkling of the trade but were simply there for a meeting.

"That's what gave me so much power with Mossad. They had no one left to turn to. I was the only one left in power at Mossad. I was the only one who knew that camp had been created, and was aware of the secret trade. I waited for years for someone to say something about where we grew up. But after a while it was clear. No one knew but the three of us."

Solomon still seemed unperturbed as he responded.

"Your recordings allowed me to identify Angus Walker as the partner they planned on taking out. I knew he was one of the powers behind the throne. Once I realized he was going to be at the meeting, I knew he had become expendable. Returning for their convocation was too dangerous. I believed if we returned, we'd never get out of there alive. I was right. Walker's death at the compound was more than convenient. Watchman, I didn't even like you being in Israel at that time."

"Yes, but we both knew I had to go. I made it out before the explosion."

The silk that spun this web of deceit around the world had led Solomon to the dark cold metal slab in the Paris morgue. He had been waiting to die that day. His death in Paris would signal the end for the two remaining men, the monsters who began it all.

Watchman was sure he recognized his brother's serenity, and it was the worst of all possibilities. He was petrified. He had seen many men die in the still wind of Solomon. Perhaps he was wrong.

"We'll have them taken care of."

Solomon's eyes flashed at Watchman,

"Don't you dare! They're going to see my face."

"Solomon, we can't risk you. Your survival is too important. We just talked about this. Really, just let me take care of them. If you like, I'll do it myself. I still do remember how, you know."

"Absolutely not. This will be my last mission."

Watchman knew nothing would change his mind.

"Okay, then at least let me get everything I can on them."

Solomon smiled grimly,

"I'm requesting it now."

Watchman knew Solomon already had Einstein performing an analysis on the men.

"Get it from Einstein and then we'll talk. I'm going with you on this one. For now you just need to stay with Jacqueline. Help her get better."

Watchman knew a few things for sure. Solomon would never leave Jacqueline, he would never use the Memory Replacement tools on her and he'd kill both of the men who traded them like livestock so long ago. He began facilitating around those assumptions; Solomon's intentions were more than clear to him.

As the days passed in the Underground, Jacqueline was recovering in a medical coma from the nerves her assailant severed at C1. This should have been a deadly injury, and had she been treated anywhere but at the Underground, she would either be dead or paralyzed and on life support for life. However, the medical team and equipment available to them had saved her, but her recuperation from the severed nerves would take months. Thanks to their magic, it seemed more and more likely that she would fully recover.

Solomon split his time between sitting by her bedside thinking and in his office working. Watchman continued to try to talk to him about letting someone else go for Childs and Carnegie. It was fruitless. He wanted to see the whites of their eyes and for them to see his at the very moment they felt the KISS of death.

It was a week later when Watchman walked up to Solomon in the hall outside Jacqueline's room.

"How's she doing?"

"Getting better every day, but Dietmar wants her out for months to recuperate. He says she'll be a hundred percent. Einstein's monitoring her as well and agrees."

"Good. Listen, I want to say this one more time. Let someone else handle this hit."

"No, Watchman. You, more than anyone else, understand. They stole my life – our lives. The missing period of memory I told you about for years, the nightmares. They used drugs, stimuli and deterrents. There was operant conditioning and the worst fucking cold war mind control – on children! That's what they did the first months at the compound! We were six, seven and eight!"

"Yes, I do understand. I feel the same, but I had to ask one more time. Remember, my job has always been to protect you."

"I know, big brother, but this is something I have to do myself. They took my life, yours, and Sari's, and did what they pleased with us. They traded us like sheep and sent us to this slaughter."

Watchman, like Solomon, could not sit idly by and allow another to do what he saw as his job. He had not just relied on Einstein for information. Computers were wonderful, but he still had his sources; they were sources that a computer could not access. He was about to prove it to his brother.

"Well, they meet on a fairly regular basis at the Caucus Room, in a private library annex, for lunch. We're monitoring their calls now. They don't calendar these meetings. However, Carnegie has a case that's being heard before the Supreme Court on taxation limits for the top one percent of the American tax base. The majority should go against him, so he'll need to put pressure on Childs to swing the vote. He has a number of nudes of Childs and well, the money to buy a favorable ruling."

"But Childs is going to have to move at least some other members of the court. Any idea how?"

"No. It must be blackmail and payoffs combined. This case assures an upcoming meeting outside chambers, so be ready to go. If I can't change your mind, I want it done while we have a good spot for the hit."

"We owe it to them to let them see the faces of the men they created, bought and sold. None of this has ever had to do with religion, political affiliation or country; it's always been about the power and money. Now I intend to show them just what they spawned."

"Well Solomon, I just bought the Caucus Room and the building next door in D.C. It cost us forty-five million. We'll have access to them as soon as they meet again."

"Good going, bro. You're an artist."

"Let's just get this over and then no more!"

"You have my word, as best I can give it. What if I had to save you? I couldn't refuse to do that!"

"Just try to be good after this. We have some leads on a match for Einstein, but nothing is confirmed. Two of the orphans look promising, but we can't be sure. Anyway, I don't want anything to happen to you. Sari is safe and all three of us have survived this. Isn't that enough?"

"Once we get them, yes."

Watchman knew nothing was going to stop Solomon from getting his pound of flesh. He had been in full facilitation mode not just for his own satisfaction, but because he knew Solomon too well, even before this conversation.

Watchman purchased the restaurant using a corporation in Las Vegas that listed Childs and Carnegie as corporate officers and principals. Most importantly, through another corporation he purchased the building next door that connected to their private dining car.

For years this restaurant had been the soundproof meeting place for those of unconscionable power. Use of the room came complete with a private entrance through the restaurant's kitchen, body guards, and aged spirits to inspire deal making. All of it was there for selling the wares of power and control.

Word of their next meeting came through within a few weeks. Watchman had already completed some minor construction to the building next door and the restaurant had hired a new waiter with his background back-filled. Thirty-five year old Kentucky bourbon, a gift supposedly from a co-plaintiff in the Carnegie lawsuit, J. D. DuPont, would be waiting with their lunch. It would not behoove Watchman to part with one of the few remaining bottles of Kentucky Fine and Rare on these men.

The waiter passed the body guards unnoticed, once he handed them a tray of crackers and caviar. A few minutes later, Childs and Carnegie arrived through the kitchen, snarling at the guards for eating while on duty. The guards quickly put the food down, opened the door, and cleared the room one more time before Childs and Carnegie entered. Then they closed and locked the soundproof door, and then smiled as they returned to their caviar.

Both men began to salivate at the food and a bottle with a note that read "Enjoy it, gentlemen. J.D."

Childs told Carnegie,

"Nice touch."

Carnegie looked at Childs disparagingly. As he passed a briefcase full of money to him he said,

"We all need this ruling. Share the wealth and get the justices we need to rule in our favor."

Childs took the case of cash and placed it next to his chair leg.

"You think this is so damn easy. The court is against you now. The ruling you want will set precedent, and it will benefit only the ultra-rich by affirming a massive tax loophole."

"Yes, and we need it. We're the ones who keep this country running, not the masses! I don't think it's easy, but it's your problem. We put you on the bench with a lifetime appointment to the Supreme Court, so we want our money's worth. You're in this just as deep as we are. Make it happen. We need the ruling."

"I already know – Streep is going to give us a problem. I need dirt on her to go with the money. She's clean, so you may need to create some scandal to use against her."

"I'll handle it. You'll have it in a few days. Just get that vote to five-to-four."

Carnegie opened the bourbon and filled his glass, then passed the bottle to Childs,

"No thanks. I'm still hung over, go ahead."

Childs filled his glass with water,

"We'll get this done. Cheers!"

Their toasting glasses went into the air, as their eyes made contact. The ring of fine crystal filled the room. It was clearly bad etiquette, but the powerful do as they please. Then slowly the glasses moved up to their lips for the sip, only one filled with bourbon.

Childs looked at Carnegie. As they sat their glasses down, he began to speak.

"We're power personified. We have done i…"

Then in mid-sentence, seventeen seconds after the glasses touched their lips they both went silent, every muscle in their bodies paralyzed. They were still seated in their luxury leather club chairs. Solomon and Watchman entered from a secret doorway behind a bookcase. Both men saw them but could not move or make a sound.

Solomon looked at the two motionless men, then back to Watchman.

"They should've checked the glasses. Gentlemen, you have been given a very special dose of Succinylcholine."

Their eyes stared daggers, but they couldn't move a muscle in their five thousand dollar suits.

Solomon sat down next to Childs and Watchman next to Carnegie. Solomon spoke first, as they both began to loosen the ties and undress the paralyzed men.

"I want to tell you a story, a story about a journey you began together long ago. It was a trip you never finished. You remember a program dubbed Wilderness Mirror? We are the men you bought. The only survivors, the only ones not in Palestine the day you wiped out the training compound and all the others who knew of your little plan. We were children when you experimented, trained, and then traded us like livestock.

"Just so we are clear, I am Jude Absalom Hague and we have mastered the quantum computer you were in search of, Carnegie. It's worth trillions! You will never have a chance to exploit it. It will be used for good, not avarice."

Watchman spoke directly to Carnegie,

"We want you to know your accounts worldwide have been drained and massive tax liens have been placed against your family trusts and holdings. Your relatives will live in poverty and shame."

Solomon looked at Childs,

"You have been a disgrace to the robes of justice since the beginning, selling rulings to the highest bidder. Always in pursuit of power, yet you have never been able to even keep your cock in your pants. So, you really think you're a ladies man? Guess you have nothing to say, not that you could say anything we consider of value. We have the documents from the safe at the Grove.

"Everything you created is about to be destroyed – your money, family, name, and power. You have three minutes to live, maybe less. Use it well. Don't worry. We will keep the secret of your experimental project, as long as the two of you are dead."

Solomon placed a black judge's robe on Childs naked body, leaving the front open. Watchman slid Carnegie in his fancy club chair, placing the two men face to face. Then, he looked to Solomon.

"Ready?"

"Ready."

The men's eyes were terrified as Watchman tipped Carnegie's numb body into Child's cock-filled lap. Then he looked at Solomon,

"Glad I wore gloves for this mission. Do you want this case of money?"

"Leave it and the copy of the pending court case."

Solomon looked at the two men, naked and positioned, and said,

"I guess there really is nothing else to say, except you have a couple hours before this paralysis wears off. The problem for you is that you are going to be dead in minutes. Your betrayal of us has caused your downfall. Bella garant alii. If you have forgotten your Latin, let others wage war. The two of you are now joined for all to see."

At that moment Watchman and Solomon injected each man with a nanosized needle, leaving marks so small that they would pass any autopsy. Then they picked up the glasses and replaced them with others.

Solomon smiled,

"Don't take it so hard. Julius Caesar didn't see his impending doom, either."

They watched as the men – men who destroyed three orphans' lives for their own desire for world control – died. Then the brothers disappeared as quickly as they arrived through the wall, sealing it permanently from the inside. They used an awaiting can of spray super cement created by Dietmar. Within seconds, the seal was stronger and more permanent than the wall.

They walked to a waiting car below ground and sped off. Watchman told Solomon,

"At first I was surprised by your plan. I thought you would want answers from them. But now I realize this was the best way."

"Well, what they had to say interested me for more than twenty years. Once I had the documents, nothing they could have told us would have had any additional value."

"I could not agree more - nevermore shall we speak of them."

Together they returned to the Underground, not saying another word about it. The Times carried the picture with a black label hiding the actual position of Carnegie's mouth on Child's cock. The caption read;

"Murder suicide? Double suicide? No Double Heart Attacks! Supreme Court Justice and ruling member of wealthy family found dead at private lunch."

The story went on to read,

"A briefcase full of money and the file of a pending case being heard by the Supreme Court were also found in the room. All rulings from the court have been suspended pending investigation and a bill is before Congress demanding term limits on Justices of the Supreme Court..."

Chapter Twenty-Four
Sleep, Little Angel, Sleep...

For months, Jacqueline stirred only occasionally and for mere seconds at a time during the drug-induced medical coma. Meanwhile, the nerves Dorr and Dietmar reconnected in her neck were healing. Her progress was assisted by implantation of artificial nerve fibers and stimulation for faster and more complete regeneration. The injury was so severe at C1 that even with the Underground's technology, keeping her unconscious for months to heal was the safest path.

It would take weeks of accelerated healing before she could even be moved from intensive care for the balance of her recovery. Finally, she could be moved from the Underground to a place that would be a more pleasant location to awake. Solomon waited for what seemed like an eternity after his return from the DC elimination trip, nervously checking in on Jacqueline almost constantly. He was frightened, despite what Dietmar and Dorr told him about her progress. He would remain uneasy until complete recovery was assured and they could go away together.

That would be the future. For the time being, they would just let her rest for the next several months before bringing her completely out of the coma. Monitors watched every body function around the clock. Machines moved her muscles on a regular basis to prevent atrophy. Dietmar and Dorr were determined to wake her only at full recovery level. She looked so peaceful, her new face resting on the crisp yellow sheets, the sun reflecting around her bed, day after day in the room far away from the desert.

It was during the thirteenth week in the atrium that she began to stir awake despite the medication. She would talk to Marie off and on for a minute and prove to herself that she could move her arms and legs. Solomon was never there at the moments she awoke. It seemed even if he was merely away for an instant, he would miss it. But he would play the screens over and over. She was ready to be brought out of the healing rest.

A week later, in the beautiful mahogany bed in a private room, she stirred again. This time, her eyes opened, and she was clearly startled. A lady in white appeared at her bedside. Still drugged, Jacqueline murmured,

"Knife?"

The woman replied,

"You are fine, but you need to rest. You have been in a medical coma for a while. You are going to recover completely; there is no permanent damage."

Then she reached to inject the IV with more sleeping medication as Jaqueline said,

"Rose stabbed m…"

The medicine put her back to sleep mid-sentence.

The woman walked out of the very private room into a viewing area with large floor-to-ceiling windows. That is where Rose was standing. He asked,

"Did you hear what she said?"

"Not much. The word knife and Rose stabbed me. She knows she was stabbed."

They both had an uneasy look as Rose told Dorr,

"Thank you."

Dorr replied,

"I gave her more medicine. I'm having trouble keeping her sedated. She's a fighter. I don't want to use anything stronger since she's almost recovered. She may wake for a minute off and on, but I'll keep her calm until she is fully recuperated. The machines are strengthening her muscles without her suffering through recovery; they are showing at 97.5 percent of former strength and function as of today. There's no use waking her in any pain. And the plastic surgery – well, you can see how beautiful she is."

Rose's looks had also been changed to the photo Jacqueline had seen before she was injured. His cover was as a retired history professor from some exclusive school, closed since his retirement. Dressed in a sweater and stripped scarf, he tossed his camel hair coat over his shoulders to meet the cool morning.

He looked at his watch, 8:30 AM GMT+1, as he walked out on the porch. The freshness in the air reminded him of the free life that was about to begin. Taking a seat in his chair not two feet away from the door, Marie walked out to join him.

"I heard Mom was awake again for a minute. Dorr says she'll wake her within a week or so, because she's almost completely recovered. I checked the monitor on the way out. I'm headed to the Underground. Sari said she's getting ready to update Einstein and thought I might enjoy helping."

"Good. Where's Gul?"

"Getting our luggage and he'd better hurry! I promised Dietmar we'd be there in time for supper. I just spoke with Watchman. He returned from India last week, and from the sound of his voice, I would say he had a good time. He sent a photo for you."

She turned her C-phone to Rose,

"Taj Mahal - nice pic."

He deleted it and passed the phone back.

"Thanks. I figured Gul was going with you."

Then with a laugh, he continued.

"You two are inseparable. Your car's here. Have a safe trip."

"We'll be home before Dorr wakes Mom. I talked to her for a minute yesterday. She was drugged and just told me she loves me."

Solomon laughed,

"What a surprise! I have a meeting and then I'll go back up to sit with your mother."

Marie bent forward and gave Solomon a kiss on the head.

"I'll only be gone three days."

"Dorr will be keeping her down for a week more, then she will be up and chasing us both."

As Gul and Marie jumped in the car and headed for the airport, a message arrived for Solomon through Einstein from Watchman about an upcoming meeting. The message stated:

"Based upon the documents received, the Court cannot assure the asset's safety on arrival. Use caution."

Solomon received the message within seconds; it had been routed to him from The Hague. His only thoughts were,

"I've, trusted few; I'm glad to have one honest man of the fifteen on the Court looking out for me."

Solomon knew this had to be done now, with the change of the court only days away. This message also meant they had read the documents he had submitted. With a smile, he looked for a long time at the architectural wonder of the massive muted red and yellow brick structure in the near distance. The blue glass additions cast reflected sunlight on the morning dew. The grass shimmered – an appropriate symbol of honor for this modern day think tank.

Then he opened the images. The wonder of the world for which he had worked all his life showed through the hologram filled air. It was in the background, not all that far from where he was seated. It was as close as he had ever been to the building. The compound housed people with massive power. Even who controlled it couldn't assure his safety there.

Einstein opened by saying,

"Good morning Rose, and how is our lady today?"

"She's recovering well."

"Ha-ha. I checked in on her a few minutes ago, Rose. I'm programed for instant status updates on all vital signs. You know that! She is almost at full strength and so beautiful sleeping."

"Are you working on your sense of humor again, Einstein?"

"Yes, your programing left a bit to be desired in that department."

Solomon laughed aloud.

"Thanks! Now that's funny!"

"I also see by her few words today she may not remember who stabbed her when she wakes."

"Yes, I realized that, too. I'll speak to her when she's fully recovered."

"Good. Now how can I help you, or did you just pull me up to chat? I know you are lonely these days."

"Yes, I am. But this is business, Einstein, we're going in. They've had time with the redacted reports I got from you. Again, excellent work!"

"After all, I am programed for only excellent work."

"Are you trying another joke?"

"Yes."

"Keep working on it."

"Okay, back to business."

Solomon chortled,

"Again, that was funny. That's my line!"

"When generating the reports from the monologue histories created by you on the way out of Rio and Dubai, I redacted all the information we discussed. Also per your request, I advised the recipients that true artificial intelligence and the quantum computer are ten or maybe more years away from creation. Then I tossed in that I would be a danger to the world if someone created me. Was that a funny sentence?"

"Yes, that was funny. I assume the word I is not in the report?"

"Of course not. My creator is not stupid!"

"Thank you."

"I was pleased with all of your decisions, especially taking me with you in the exit plan."

"Einstein, you're me at my best. I have not found anyone I would trust you to, at least, not yet. Keep looking for candidates. After all, unlike you, I cannot live forever and we know these governments do not play well with others."

"Yes, it's true, governments really don't cooperate well but they have a mutual interest in profiting from war. The individual human is smart – people are fearful and dangerous."

"So true. But still, I'm not immortal."

"Sir, we are working on the telomerase cells and the GDL11 protein, so maybe you can live forever."

"Well, keep looking for another DNA match anyway."

"We are constantly searching; you designed me not to desire control, but to accept only if necessary. We discovered a promising lead this morning – a child born five years ago. We are watching her. We both understand that your consciousness will live on in the soul of the universe, so we will always be together in some form."

"Yes we will. Now, access The Hague. Let's end this mission."

"I see you read the message from Watchman."

Solomon chuckled,

"Yes."

"The probability factor and digital footprint indicates the warning message came from the President Justice. It seems he cares for your safety."

"If that's true, it will make this much easier."

"Do you want numbers on the ground, Sir?"

"Sure, but it does not really matter."

"I know, Sir. But there are forty-seven present and I have tapped the earpieces for you."

Solomon listened for a minute as he heard the Secret Service, the Protection Command and the Knesset Guard all talking and sharing information on their earbuds. They were scanning and positioning themselves all over the campus, waiting for the man behind the reports to enter the grounds. They all wanted him; two groups insisted he be killed and one wanted to take him alive. They could not agree among themselves how to handle him.

Solomon laughed,

"I guess their bosses have read our reports. Connect me."

"Opening Hague 347647XDR115677281, access granted, present before the court in ten minutes. Court has been notified of your expected arrival. Good luck, Sir."

The President Justice announced,

"This hearing is H3. Mr. President and Prime Ministers, please remain with this court and my fellow justices. Please ask your men, including your security details, to wait in the adjoining room. Personnel not connected to the justice court, go with them."

All others present in the chambers exited, as requested, to the adjoining room. Some were chomping at the bit, talking into earpieces, ready to take in to custody the man who would come walking down that hall into that closed hearing to give evidence, whoever he might be.

The only two ways to access to the hearing room were covered. The hall entrance was filled with security people wearing earpieces, and the other exit was through the room they had all been sent in to wait. Whoever the man was, he was not going to arrive to that hearing alive. Of that they were sure. Their actions might cause an international incident at The Hague over the arrest or death, but all three countries wanted the man who wrote their report silenced before he spoke another word. Inside the secured chamber, the eighteen necessary for the hearing to commence sat and waited.

A hologram of Solomon appeared seconds after the door was secured by the President Justice himself. Solomon, before his face change, appeared in the large private court chambers of the Netherlands. The room contained the men holding the four corner code. The hologram caused a stir, as Solomon addressed the court,

"Good morning, Your Honors, ladies and gentlemen. We are here on the final report of THCGAM3."

The courtroom quieted and then remained silent.

"The document each of you has is an original. I have given each of you time to read your individual reports. No other copies exist. The justices have full reports and copies submitted to each of the countries. Each country has its own redacted report regarding only its part in the THCGAM3 project.

"Listed are the account numbers and passwords for the funds we seized back for each country. All seized funds have been placed in numbered accounts assigned by owner country, and each operation that had funds stolen from it has been listed.

"The information on the projects, names and country of origin of wet missions as they pertain to individual countries, is also included in your reports."

Many in the room scrambled to review their documents again. The President Judge sat silent, listening to the hologram.

"The creator of each fund is listed by country of origin along with a status list of anyone involved in hiding the fund. Indictable names are included and non-indictable have been eliminated."

At that moment there were many alarmed faces among the participants.

"Each one also contains a list of additional wet operations for elimination of terrorists, summaries on weapons of mass destruction, NSS (Nuclear Security Summit) disposal of nuclear material, highly enriched uranium, DNA matches for tracking material, regime change requests, eliminations by and on behalf of each country, as well as technological operations research and development.

"The Court has before it a full report on all actions included in your individual reports. Additional information has been provided for the Court to be viewed *in camera*, per Black Mandate 18. Disbursement of that information will be after the Court's review and only to the extent the Court deems appropriate."

The court's report was entitled: Final Report to The Hague, International Court of Justice: The Original Documents and Order of Succession in America, Great Britain, and Israel. It was subtitled: Includes an Analysis of Uranium Enrichment, Terror Threats, Black Operations, Cyber War, Technology, Space Technology, and Quantum Computing. Submitted by Solomon M. Rosenberg, Esquire - Commander of THCGAM3 – Section 8 - Black Mandate 18 - by and for The Hague Court.

"You have each received a copy of Black Mandate 18, the white paper order signed by your predecessors. The original of that document is maintained for security. Your Honors, on the authority granted in the while paper opinion, the mission has ended. With leave of this court, I bid you good luck, gentlemen. The Chameleon died at 8:51 AM GMT+1 this day."

The President Justice said but two words, as prescribed in the White Paper International Court Order Mandate 18,

"Court Adjourned."

Then the hologram disappears just as quickly as it arrived. The men just looked at the documents delivered to them and at each other.

The President Justice began reviewing the remaining document before him and then spoke,

"It is over. Whatever it was our predecessors sanctioned, it's concluded now."

The President of the United States began to speak,

"We wanted to conduct an examination under oath – question the actual man."

The judge replied,

"Read Mandate 18. He was authorized to appear in any form, and he is not subject to interrogation. I'm sure he chose that form to protect him from the henchmen you have had all over this Court's palace grounds for days. Ladies and gentlemen, this is over."

There was nothing they could do. The countries' guards were still posted outside the court. They were prepared to pounce when Solomon arrived, but they were useless against a hologram and a white paper free pass. Clearly, the President Justice was not tolerating anything from these most powerful men.

"It was a prime minister who asked,

"When will we receive a decision regarding release of the *in camera* matters?"

"Now. The court has reviewed all *in camera* submissions and rules that none of the information provided *in camera* will be released. That decision is in the interest of the security of each individual country and of the world as a whole. The Court will issue no further orders in this matter. I suggest that each of you take the information provided in your individual reports and do a house cleaning. Good day."

The men on the bench stood and walked out a chamber door behind the bench without another word. The powerful of the countries left the court chambers under the protection of the very guards they planned to use to hold Solomon, then headed off in different directions, knowing little more than when they arrived. What they had learned was that this long term mission finished, and a lot of money had been returned to their individual governments. They had all been responsible for far more than they ever wanted the world to know and they needed to examine the usefulness and power of their internal organizations.

Billions of dollars had been siphoned off under each government's noses. Funds had been stolen from military projects, contractors, research, arms deals, drugs and more over the years, and it had been returned.

Nothing satisfies the palate of those in power more than money. Their faces showed relief, even if their eyes showed curiosity at what had just happened to some of the most important people in the world. In their business, relief outweighs curiosity and no one would put this in their memoirs after they left office.

The President Judge looked to the other members of the court,

"I'm glad this case is over. I'll write the final order and close the file. My term ends tomorrow, and it has been my pleasure to have worked with each of you. We have served well."

The goodbyes lasted for a few minutes before he walked the few steps to his private office; telling his assistant along the way,

"Have all the files delivered to my office. I'll handle the paperwork on this last case and wait for the movers.

Then he smiled wistfully at her.

"Go home to your grandchildren, Zelva."

"Your office is packed. The men will be here in an hour. Don't forget the name plate and portrait."

"I won't forget. You shouldn't have done all that packing, but thank you. Be careful leaving; I'm sure security forces for some of the parties are frustrated."

She walked out of the office as he entered his private chamber alone, closing the door behind him. Taking off the black robe of justice before sitting down, he then emptied his pockets onto the one possession he truly loved, his hand carved Moroccan desk. He poured a drink from a bottle of Mccallan Rare and Fine aged single malt Scotch whiskey that sat waiting, before he opened a long glass humidor containing but one cigar, a Gurka Black Dragon.

He removed the cigar, stroked his beard; hesitated, laughed, then clipped the ends of the world's most expensive cigar, lit it and savored the first puff, as he rested back in his ox blood leather chair, looking out of the window of The Hague one last time.

A few minutes later the files arrived. The Judge enjoyed his scotch and a long slow smoke, as he burnt every piece of paper from the file in the stone fireplace, following to the letter the order signed by his predecessors. It was all set out in Mandate 18, Subsection One: Judicial instructions – President Judge's eyes only. He did exactly as instructed.

He returned to his desk, pick up a calling card from the items he had emptied from his pockets and walked back to the fireplace. He lit the end of the card reading Meier Finch on fire with his cigar lighter as he said aloud,

"I won't need this card anymore."

It was at that moment he looked up to his father's portrait hanging on the wall. He then touched the top of the name plate on his desk that read "President Justice Abraham H. Turing." The plaque had sat on his desk nine years, come Monday morning. One with another name would take its place. Then he picked it up, placed it in his briefcase and removed the portrait from the wall, as he walked out of his chambers for the last time.

The fox had eluded the hounds.

It was late in the night when Solomon pulled up a screen to Watchman just boarding his jet at Rotterdam Airport. With a serious look Solomon said,

"Travel information request: Retired and looking for a location for a second honeymoon."

Watchman responded,

"Wake Island is a coral atoll just north of the Marshall Islands. It's an unorganized, unincorporated territory of the United States, administered by the Office of Insular Affairs, U.S. Department of the Interior. Its population is 150 of the C Street Underground staff. It has a stable year round climate with a high of eighty-two and a low of seventy-three degrees. Perfect! It can serve is an excellent new beginning; Laura is waiting for me there."

Watchman's laugh was followed by a sigh of relief and the words,

"Solomon, the exit was flawless! It's over, brother."

"Yes, we picked that location well. You were right with your message; Einstein counted forty-seven multi-national security forces inside and outside of the court, waiting for my arrival. They were clearly looking. Einstein tapped their earpieces. Three of the corners did not want me to make it to the court. Two wanted me dead and one alive."

Watchman never liked hearing anyone wanted his brother dead, "The sons of bitches! Mossad – alive?"

"Yeah, but I suspect it was only because they wanted to see if this asset was one of their creations."

Watchman stepped onto the jet and said hello to Chike, who was ready to take off. He took a seat and looked out the window as he continued to talk to his brother.

"Mossad has attempted to make more special agents over the years, but none of them have been as good as the three of us created by that rogue agent. K.I.S.S. died and was buried deep with us when the training compound exploded so many years ago. No paper trail, no survivors..."

Solomon looked up at The Hague in the distance, watching his brother's plane take off,

"I kept the file on the men you saw around the compound. Just henchman, but you can see all their faces before I delete it; sending it now."

"Good, I'll take a look just in case. Solomon, the faces of those in the court were priceless."

"The only way to deal with the gods in black robes was to rig the President Justice position nine years ago by making him you."

"Yes, and your arrival in the court... excellent. The hologram stunned them all and avoided a lot of questions."

Then with a snicker Solomon said,

"President Justice Turing followed the language of the white paper opinion to the letter. Your only words, 'Court adjourned.' That was priceless. The hologram was preprogrammed to disappear when you said those words. It was perfect! Hey, did you notice we both still snicker like kids?"

"Yeah, I notice it more in you, but we both still do."

Solomon snickered again,

"You can get rid of that damn beard, now!"

"Thank God! It itches like crazy in the heat. This exit mission gave me a few more wrinkles. I'm heading in to see Dietmar and Dorr in a couple weeks. For now, Wake Island is beautiful this time of year. I need a little rest and sun before I return."

"Take your time; everything is under control, now."

The brothers laughed and then talked of Jacqueline's recovery. Watchman was glad to be out of The Hague Court and he told Solomon how Zelva reminded him not to forget their father's portrait.

Solomon stopped him,

"I'm glad we got her out before the compound was wiped."

"Yes, she has a wonderful life and never fails to come when I call. She sends her love and wanted me to confirm again she knew nothing about where they took us the first months; nothing about the drugs or the mind control program they used to desensitize us. I assured her we both knew she had no part of that. She also told me that she had known Rabbi Wiezmann for years. She's sure he had no idea what they had planned for us. If he had, he never would have taken us there. She said he was killed on his way home the day we arrived."

"Good. They wouldn't have told her, this part would have been highly compartmentalized."

"So have you chosen a new name, bro?"

"Yes Watchman, I'm becoming David Sire."

Both brothers start laughing.

"King, King! You're too much. Are you going to pronounce David with the accent on the second syllable, Da Vid?

"No the American version. You know I like to go unnoticed!"

The brothers went on to talk about Watchman's upcoming plastic surgery. After a quick goodbye, Solomon closed his link.

For the first time ever, there was a moment of peace as he looked up at the atrium of their two-story French Colonial home. It was yellow with white pillars and a terracotta porch. This home had been redesigned to look like Jacqueline's favorite place to hide with Marie, her home in Florida.

But this house was located at Carnegielaan 1, 2517 KH Den Haag. It was just off the grounds of the Peace Palace, home of The Hague Court and men so powerful that few would dare call them THC. It was clear to Solomon – the oldest trick had succeeded again. *Just like the devil, he had convinced the world he did not exist.*

Solomon returned to Jacqueline's bedside. He sat looking at her and then at every detail of the room inspired by her vision in the Dubai desert, where they began putting their life back together. He had remembered and followed every feature of the house, including the very atrium she had described as the colors of the rising sun, the place where she now rested and recovered. Well, Solomon did decide on the bulletproof stained glass that protected his love.

Watching her sleep, he told her,

"Jacqueline, the years apart, stolen moments together are over. With a smirk, Simon Solomon, Solomon "Rose" Rosenberg, Jude Hague, and now David Sire said,

"Are you awake, sleeping beauty?"

Jacqueline stirred,

"…You stabbed me."

"No baby. It was a guard at the Grove. He was in the sauna when the chemical was dropped."

Jacqueline was quiet for a moment,

"Did you get him?"

"Absolutely. No one harms my baby and gets away with it. There's a balance in all things."

"What about the evidence?"

"You got it all from the safe before he stabbed you. I just turned everything, including some final reports, over to The Hague and advised them the Chameleon was dead. We're free."

"Did it have the names of those who started CWP, the succession, those who brought you from Israel?"

"Yes, the Banksters; Childs and Carnegie. The order of succession is now in the hands of The Hague. The top two men are gone."

"Did they ever figure out that Chameleon was K.I.S.S., that the signatures were not one person?"

"No and we've buried the signatures along with all of us."

"Where am I? It's beautiful!"

"You're in the home you designed in the desert; this one's in the Netherlands. But I bought a few others around the world for us, Marie, Sari, and Watchman, while you were sleeping. Just in case you get bored and want to travel."

"I think you were bored while I was asleep and shopping to occupy yourself. How long have I been recovering and where's Marie? Tell me she's safe. I want to see her."

"She's fine; she and Gul are on their way to the Underground to help Sari with an update to Einstein. Marie's going to be very angry that I woke you. She wanted to be here. She'll be back in a couple of days."

"You got Sari home!"

"Yes, and Marie just adores her, they're tech buddies and hang out all the time."

"What have you been doing while I recovered?"

"Not much, I just took care of some final details, but mostly I have been beside your bed. Any pain?"

"No, I feel wonderful. Rose, you have your new face!"

"I wondered how long it would take you to notice. You have your new face too, want to see?"

Solomon stood behind Jacqueline's bed as he held the mirror so both faces reflected in it. Solomon smirked,

"Not bad; we still make a sexy, dangerous couple."

"This is true. I can't believe I just recognized your voice when I woke. Now it seems like this face has always been yours. Move and let me get out of this bed."

"Yours too, but I have been enjoying it for months while you recovered. You're still my Jackal. Go ahead; your body was strengthened the entire time you were in the coma. Your muscles are working at 99.5 percent, but be a little careful. You have been mostly lying flat for months, five to be exact. Dorr says you could have a little vertigo."

"So, that was Dorr in the lab coat! I thought I had dreamed she was beside my bed. I'll be careful."

Rose's promise made to Jacqueline in the Sahara desert under the sun, his oath to give her back the quiet, wonderful life she had known before this mission began, was being fulfilled. There was no guarantee how long it would last, but life has no guarantees.

On the twenty-first of September, Mr. and Mrs. Sire, once Rose and Jackal, unrecognizable to the world, walked up the steps of their latest home. It's located on Main Street. Perhaps you have new neighbors.

Simon says, Jude says, Solomon says:

"Wrath, greed, sloth, pride, lust, envy, and gluttony are seven deadly sins I can live with – happily ever after…"

Claudette Walker

Acknowledgments

To David E. Siar, Esquire, who always finds the time to read contracts and provide legal skills on a moment's notice, and who possesses the humor and stamina to edit throughout the creation process.

In loving memory of

Lois Irene Walker
May 13, 1927 – August 23, 2005

Deborah Ilene Walker
December 18, 1954 – June 18, 2009

…women liberated by hard work and perseverance.

Editor: David E. Siar.
Assistant Editor: Matrix Filia

Cover Design:
Claudette Walker and Matrix Filia

Abacus Books, Inc.
U.S.A.
www.abacusbooks.com

www.ingramcontent.com/pod-product-compliance
Lightning Source LLC
Chambersburg PA
CBHW062114170626
46813CB00002B/440